THE Surprise PLAY

BOOK THREE
NOLAN
U

Katy ♡ xoxo Archer

KATY ARCHER

THE SURPRISE PLAY
Nolan U Football #3
© Copyright 2025 Katy Archer
www.katyarcher.com

Cover Design © Designed with Grace

ISBN: 978-1-991138-93-4 (Kindle e-book)
ISBN: 978-1-991138-96-5 (paperback)

Archer Street Romance
www.katyarcher.com

CHAPTER 1
ELIZABETH

I fidget with my hands as I head toward the library. I'm telling myself it's because I'm cold and forgot my gloves. Snow that's turned to brown sludge is edging the sidewalk, and the air is clear and crisp. My winter coat is buttoned up to my chin. I could easily put my hands in my pockets to keep them warm, but no... I can't stop fidgeting. Squeezing my unpolished fingernails, I climb the concrete steps and head into the library.

The second I walk through the glass doors, the heat envelops me... but I still keep rubbing my hands together because I'm stupidly nervous.

I shouldn't be.

I've been tutoring students at Nolan U since the second semester of my freshman year. One of my professors shoulder-tapped me and put me onto an academic adviser who was looking for students to add to her tutoring pool.

Apparently, I'm smart enough to help students older than me, and I'm not about to shy away from the money.

I'm here on a partial scholarship, and my parents are really stretched to make up the rest, so if I can help out at all, I will.

The only problem is...

I didn't think I'd have to help a guy like Wily Wilson.

I mean, I don't even know why Ms. Bigsby thinks I'm a good fit. Wily is a senior. *A senior.*

Who's taking the easiest classes he can find. You've totally got this.

It's pointless lying to myself. I'm not nervous because I don't think I can handle the coursework.

With a little sigh, I unbutton my coat and shuffle into the library, staying close to the wall and eyeing the students already in here. I'm surprised how full it is considering school doesn't go back until Monday, but I guess people want to get prepped for their classes the same way I do. Although, some are probably catching up after slacking off between Thanksgiving and Christmas.

My eyes dart from one face to another, quickly working out which students fit into my various categories.

I don't see Wily among them and inch my way a little closer to the main desk. I told him to find me in here at eleven o'clock this morning. I'm early, of course—I have an inability to show up late or even on time. Early *is* on time, isn't it?

Biting my lower lip, I pinch my index finger and beg my roiling stomach to calm the hell down. I shouldn't have looked Wily Wilson up on the school website last night. One glimpse of his beaming face with those perfectly straight teeth, brilliant blue eyes, flawless bone structure, and a head of hair that would make all male models on the planet jealous was all it took to ruin my night.

Athletes.

They're horrible humans, and the fact that this one made my chest flutter with appreciation is really annoying me.

And making me bite my lip and squeeze my fingers and—

Grrr! Stop it!

He's a dumb jock. You've dealt with them before. Be polite and professional, and freaking get paid. That's all you have to do.

I shake out my hands with a huff, then feel the air in my throat catch.

Oh shit!

Taking three quick steps back, I duck around the corner, squeezing my eyes closed and praying they didn't notice me. I grip the edge of the bookshelf and dare to open one eye, peeking across the library and spotting the three girls huddled together at the long table just beyond the main desk. They're whispering and giggling, and now I feel sick.

Dammit. What are they doing here?

I thought they'd stretch out their holiday break and not return until Sunday night. I imagined them heading to Jamaica or some island where they could show off their bikini bodies to drooling men and get themselves a nice little tan.

Resting my forehead against the book spines in front of me, I slowly count to ten, trying and failing to forget that first day of this school year and the moment my world shifted on its axis.

I'd survived freshman year at Nolan U without too many problems.

I was missing my parents like crazy, and living at Nolan U felt like moving to Metropolis after growing up in Fledgling, but I was managing. I loved being anonymous, walking around campus as Miss Invisible. My teachers noticed me, but that's only because my grades impressed them, and I did win one small academic competition, which was mentioned in the school paper. Thankfully, it was on page nine, and hardly anyone read it. They used the worst photo of me ever. I was so stiff and nervous, I couldn't smile. So I just held up the trophy and stared at the lens. Ugh!

Other than that second of semi-fame, I've been able to walk the corridors of my dorm and the sidewalks of this beautiful campus without anyone caring who I am...

Until the first day of sophomore year, when I was heading to my first class feeling upbeat and excited. It took all of half a microsecond for those fizzing feelings to disintegrate when I spotted Jade Buchanan. She was standing with two other girls, all new and fresh-faced and... potentially Team Evil 2.0.

Team Evil, you're no doubt wondering. What is that?

Well, it's a trio compromised of the three most popular girls from my high school—Jade Buchanan, Katrina Marsden, and Carmen Ludlow.

Those girls made my life a living hell. And it was all thanks to Jade and her master scheming.

I honestly stopped breathing when I saw her, my heart thudding in my chest, my skin starting to itch the way it used to.

I thought she was going to Denver University!

What was she doing in Nolan?

The day after high school graduation, I thought I'd never have to see them again. They were a year behind me; I could move on with my life and become a distant memory for them.

But that morning, Jade looked up from her phone, snorted in surprise, then nudged the girl beside her... and I knew in that instant, my life hadn't changed at all.

She'd just rally new minions and persuade them to play her evil little games. And they'd buy into her sales pitch because she's so pretty and fun, and everybody freaking loves her!

My stomach and chest broke out in instant hives, and I couldn't help scratching my belly.

Jade snickered as she picked up her pace and made a move toward me. I took off as fast as my short legs could carry me, and by the time I found my first class, my thighs were itching too.

All I could think was *This can't be happening again! How could life be so unfair?*

Middle school and high school were pure torture for me. Those girls made an art form of taunting and teasing me, dropping snide comments in sweet tones until they could see the tears swimming in my eyes, then acting like they cared and passing me tissues, patting my shoulder, and whispering more acid into my ears before walking away.

My parents kept telling me to keep my chin up and not let those girls drag me down.

"Show them that they have no effect on you and they'll get bored and leave you alone."

How many times had I tried that, only to get knocked

off my feet the next day with another joke at my expense? They didn't leave me alone. When I hid my hurt at their taunting, they just scaled things up a notch.

Like that time Jade poured moldy orange juice all over my hair and the new dress Mom had just made. My parents actually kicked up a fuss over that one and demanded some kind of action from the school. Jade was suspended for three days, and when she returned, she was on a mission: Make Elizabeth Satchwell Cry.

I held out for as long as I could, but it only took two weeks for me to fold. That was the day Katrina pranked me in the hallway, right in front of the hottest guy in school—Peyton Feldman. He was a football player, and I thought he kind of liked me. Truth was, he was just being nice so I'd do his homework for him. I didn't know that at the time Katrina pranked me, though.

I was standing in the hallway, cheeks feeling as red as a fire engine. Peyton had just smiled at me, and my heart had fluttered like butterfly wings. I was waiting for him to hand me his next assignment, give me a little wink, and ask when we could work on it. He flicked his head for me to come over, and I was too busy swooning to notice the slippery yogurt Katrina had flung on the ground. My foot hit that stuff and I let out this weird squawk before landing flat on my back right in front of Peyton. My skirt flipped up, exposing my underwear to everyone in the hallway.

"Holy shit, are those granny panties?" some guy shouted, then pointed at me and laughed like a hyena. Everyone around him started cackling while I scrambled to pull my skirt down.

Jade and Carmen ran over, feigning shock at what

had happened, trying to help me back to my feet, then pretending like I was too heavy to lift. The ground was all slippery, and the laughter intensified. In the end, they asked Peyton to lend them a hand but warned him not to hurt his back. He started laughing and actually groaned and strained like he was trying to lift an elephant off the floor. I'd never felt more humiliated in my entire life. Once I was on my feet and fighting a hot wave of tears, he gave me a friendly slap on the shoulder.

"Chill, Libs. We're just joking."

His teammates were still talking about my underwear and how much fabric it must have taken for my mother to make them.

"She probably has to get her clothes made at home."

"Yeah, like she'd fit in anything at a regular store."

It was harsh. Logically, I knew this. I could buy my clothes at the store like everybody else did. Sure, I might have been a few sizes bigger than what felt like every other girl in the school, but I wasn't so big that I needed specially made clothes.

My mom just liked sewing, and she did such beautiful work. I loved the stuff she made for me. I wore it with pride.

But not after that day.

From that point on, I stuck to boring store-bought clothes and pants with a high waist. Mom was kind of hurt by the move, but I never wanted anyone to see my underwear again.

It wasn't until I went to college that I started using my favorite items in my wardrobe once more.

Glancing at the clothes I chose for today, I skim my hands down the skirt I'm sporting and wince. Oh no. Did

I make a really bad mistake? Mom gave it to me for Christmas, and I should have known better than to wear it today. I didn't think Jade would be back already! College has been this refreshing new start for me, you know?

Last year, I felt like I was finding myself.

But now they're here with me.

And the only difference is the location... and maybe the merciful fact that we don't have any classes together. Although, I still have to pass them every now and then. Thankfully, Nolan U is a big campus, and I'm learning which routes to avoid as I get to know their routines.

This morning, I'm completely thrown.

Surviving high school was so freaking hard. I tried to stay silent and strong, ignoring all of the notes and passing comments, grateful that the girls hadn't resorted to cyberattacks. I have no idea why they never did, until Jade made a snide remark one day that they wouldn't want to ruin their social feeds with my ugly face. Apparently, I wasn't worthy of using up their data. Not when they could harass me in the flesh and get away with it.

After she'd said that, I turned back to my book, the pages blurring as I tried to disappear between the pages. That was my only saving grace. Books. Studying. I thrived on learning. On the promise that if I did well enough, I could get into a good college and be free of Team Evil.

But I didn't go far enough away. I'd been too afraid to move to the other side of the country. My parents were only forty minutes away in Fledgling. This was easier. They needed me. I was their only child.

So, I'm going to survive this year somehow. At least she's not in the same dorm building as me, and at least I can duck around corners if I ever see her or her new friends.

My only priority right now is making it up the stairs without them noticing. Like I'll be able to concentrate at all on a tutoring session if they're on the same floor as me. It's bad enough that I'm meeting with Wily Wilson. I don't need the threat of them just around the corner distracting me.

Inching out from my hiding place, I dart my eyes at them, relieved they all have their heads dipped over their phones. Hightailing it upstairs, I try to keep my clunky steps soft as I creep out of view and make my way up to the second floor.

It's much quieter up here, thank God, and I weave around the first table, heading for one closer to the back. There's a man studying at the table I want, so I move to the one behind him, banging my hip on the chair. With a little wince, I rub my thigh and avoid his glare.

Okay. So not someone who likes to be disturbed.

Dipping my chin, I keep my eyes on the floor, slowing down and carefully avoiding all furniture until I reach the chair I'm aiming for and pull it out.

Plunking into it, I find my phone and text Wily with quivering fingers, letting him know exactly where I am.

Checking the time, I lay my phone down, pull out a pen and paper, plus my laptop... and wait for this inevitably awkward meeting.

CHAPTER 2
WILY

Shit, I'm so fucking late.

If this Elizabeth chick hadn't texted me to tell me what part of the library she was in, I'd still be lying in bed, happily dozing my morning away.

I set my alarm.

I set two!

But I'm still recovering after an epic New Year's Eve bash that kept me up the entire night. I spent yesterday sleeping, so then I was up half the night, and now my body's all out of whack.

I can't believe I'm having to spend part of my winter break studying.

I want to keep celebrating our epic quarterfinal win! I definitely don't want to think about school and how I have an assignment due on Monday. It was actually due weeks ago, but my academic adviser helped organize an extension for me due to football commitments. The professor wasn't very happy about it, but he gave me the winter break to get it done.

The problem is, my tutor quit on me and I haven't been able to find a decent replacement, so my final assignment for that course is still hanging over my head, and if I don't get it in on Monday, then I'll fail the class and not have enough credits to graduate.

Shit!

I've tried to choose the easiest courses I can for this semester in the hopes that I can sail through to the finish line, get my degree, and then go on to be an NFL superstar.

But I can't fucking graduate if I don't pass all my classes. I'm hanging on by a thread, and I fucking hate it.

Accelerating down my street, I pause at the stop sign, too distracted to look properly before punching onto the road and gunning it for the library.

My phone starts ringing and I groan, thinking it's this new tutor about to bitch at me for being late, but then I spot *Butt Face* on the screen. Thank fuck for that.

"Hey, Blakey," I greet her.

"'Sup, big bro. Happy New Year and all that shit."

I snicker. "You're a day late."

"Like I was going to disturb you yesterday. I figured you'd be sleeping all day."

"You figured right."

She snorts. "How hard did you party?"

"Just the usual amount after winning a quarterfinal game and seeing in the new year."

"So a lot, then."

I laugh. "A lot."

She laughs, too, and I glance at my phone screen, noting the time and wincing. I'm so fucking late!

"So, why are you calling, sis?"

"Just checking in."

"You heading back to Chicago today?"

"Yep. Figured I'd get into the swing of things before classes resume on Monday."

"I'm sure you're gonna have a killer semester. You aced everything the first half of your year. You clever little freshman shit."

She lets out a croaky laugh. "I'm no smarter than you."

"And that's a bit of bullshit right there."

"Oh stop. You are not stupid."

"And she just keeps piling on the applesauce." I snicker, hitting my left blinker and turning into the Nolan U campus library parking lot. "I honestly don't care that I'm a dumb fuck, because I'm a great football player. That's my thing. It's all that matters."

"Wily, you—"

"I'm here."

"Where?"

I flick off the engine and gaze up at the building with a sigh. "My first torture session of the new year."

"Physical therapy?" Blake asks.

I laugh. "No. Tutoring session."

"Oh! With... Lemon Face?"

"Her name's not Lemon Face," I grit out.

"Well, whatever it is... good luck, bro!" She chortles and makes me promise to call her afterward and tell her how bad it was. "And don't let me hear that you ended up doing her in the back stacks or something."

I roll my eyes, wishing I hadn't overshared at Christmas.

"I'm not going to do my new tutor."

"You did the last one."

Clenching my jaw, I reach for my phone. "Hanging up now."

"Just go in with an open mind. She's there to help you, remember?"

"Yeah, yeah." I grab my bag, checking that my assignment is in there. "I just hope she'll see things my way and do me a solid, you know?"

"You mean do the assignment for you?"

"Of course that's what I mean."

She laughs. "Just put on some of that Wily charm and I'm sure she'll be putty in your hands."

I grin, scratching my whiskers and hoping my sister's right. This tutor chick didn't seem overly chill and pliable when I spoke to her on the phone, but maybe I'll have more impact in the flesh, you know? Face-to-face is always best.

"Okay, I really gotta go."

"Yeah, me too. Have a great sesh, brother, and text me after, okay?"

"'Kay. Love ya, butt face."

"Love you, too, shithead."

With a grin, I pocket my phone and head into the library, grateful for Blake's call. I was feeling kind of dark about this whole thing, but my little sister's right. I need to find my inner chill and friendly smile. Girls love me, and this one will too. I just have to play my cards right, put on a flirty smile, and work my magic. I'll have her eating out of my hand by the end of the hour, and then I can enjoy the rest of my winter break knowing my assignment is being taken care of.

CHAPTER 3
ELIZABETH

Wily is so late, and I'm getting antsy. If he hadn't texted me a few minutes ago, telling me he was nearly here, I would have bailed on the guy. It's so disrespectful! Like my time's not as important as his?

Typical.

Athletes are all the same—arrogant jocks who think the world should revolve around them. Like sportsmanship is more commendable than brains or creativity. I don't know why we revere them so much. As far as my experience goes, they're nothing special. If anything, they're just a bunch of mean bullies or oblivious jerks.

The guys at my high school weren't cruel in the same way the girls were, but they still knew how to make me feel like a waddling disaster.

I actually heard one of the boys call me that once in our mandatory PE class. Much to my terror, the teacher said that every person playing basketball had to touch the ball at least once. She wanted to see full participation from the entire class, which meant I couldn't just loiter near the sidelines like I usually did.

Forced out of my comfort zone, I shuffled closer to the action so I could get my turn out of the way. Of course I turned over the ball. Of course I lost my team a point, and the groans of annoyance were impossible to miss.

"She's a waddling disaster," one guy muttered darkly, and I'd dipped my chin, begging the minutes to tick by faster.

I mean, walking disaster was bad enough, but *waddling*? That was really driving the stake in a little too far.

As soon as that class ended, I ran ahead of everyone else and got changed as fast as I could. I waddled my ass away from the school gym and walked home in the freezing-cold rain without a jacket or sweater in the hopes of making myself sick, just so I didn't have to face another PE session.

It worked. I came down with a decent cold and had three blissful days off school. It was a nice reprieve, but then I got better and had to go back for more punishment.

Thank God I don't have to do PE in college. I enjoy my morning walks, and that's all the exercise I need, thank you very much.

Picking up my phone, I check the time again and huff, about to text Wily back with a *I'm sorry, but I really have to go.*

But then I sense movement behind me and glance over my shoulder in time to see the blond giant appearing at the top of the stairs. He pauses, glancing around and raising his chin at someone. His smile is so broad and friendly.

Damn, I hate that it's pretty too.

He's a jock. Just a big, mean jock. Don't go forgetting that.

Steeling myself, I iron out my expression when he notices me. His face lights up with an even brighter grin. Didn't realize that was possible, but the guy obviously has way more options on his smile dial than most people do.

My lips curl at the corners, my closed-mouth smile stiff and tight.

He doesn't seem to notice, sauntering around the table and giving the guy who glared at me a fist bump, laughing at something he said before stopping beside me and grinning down. I gaze up from my perch on the chair, craning my neck just to see his face and feeling like a hobbit. I doubt standing up will make much difference either, because this football player is one imposing figure. He must be around six-three, maybe even six-four. And he's broad and muscular, his Nolan U Cougars hoodie straining to get around his big arms.

"Hi." He holds out his hand. "Wily Wilson. Nice to meet ya."

My gaze darts to his big palm and strong fingers before I give his hand a quick shake and murmur, "Hello."

His smile grows, revealing two shallow dimples, as he drops his bag on the floor and takes a seat adjacent to me, leaning in to study my face. His eyes are so bright blue, it's hard not to look at them. "What's your name again?"

"Um... Elizabeth," I mumble, my gaze dropping to the table. I tuck my hands beneath the wood and squeeze my index finger.

He tips his head. "Sorry, what was that?"

Clearing my throat, I force out, "Elizabeth."

And his smile changes again. It goes from full-blown cheese to a soft appreciation, as if he likes the sound of my name.

But that can't be right.

It's Elizabeth—plain, simple, boring.

"Elizabeth," he whispers, like it's a song lyric that makes him feel nostalgic.

Squeezing my eyes shut, I shake my head and quickly clarify, "People always shorten it. My parents call me Bess or Bessie. My grandma calls me Libby. My Aunt Charmaine calls me Lizzy. Kids at school would call me—" I bite my lips together and force my eyes back open. "The point is... my name is Elizabeth Satchwell. And I'd appreciate you calling me that."

"What? Elizabeth? Or Satchwell? Or both?" His eyes sparkle with humor. "Like, do you always want me to say, 'Hello, Elizabeth Satchwell.' 'Thanks so much for that, Elizabeth Satchwell.' 'Wow, Elizabeth Satchwell, you are one amazing tutor.'" I frown at him, and he lets out a short laugh. "What? Are you not an amazing tutor?"

His eyes are glittering sapphires, like he's having the best time in the world teasing me, and I can't decide if I want to slap him across his cheesy face or punch him in the balls.

Neither! You will never do either of those things!

I'm horrified that I even thought that for a second. What is coming over me?

My first line of defense is always to run and hide, and now I'm imagining myself slapping a stranger? This is insane!

I give my head a little shake and scratch my stomach, then curl my arms around my waist to hide the move.

"I'm sorry." Wily lightly chuckles, his eyes still glinting with friendly humor. "What would you like me to call you?"

I shrug and mutter, "I don't know." *None of those things.* I've always felt like my name never suited me. I have no idea why my parents chose it. Mom always laughs that she did it in honor of Queen Elizabeth, but we're not even British! Ugh!

"Okay, well, Tutor Girl, it's nice to meet you." Wily gives me a wink and leans back in his chair, looking completely unaffected by our totally bizarre introduction while I'm sitting here squirming.

This isn't going to work. He's too... irritating. Or unsettling. Or just something unpleasant.

My skin's really starting to itch now.

Dammit! I subtly scratch my stomach again.

"So, want to get started?" He reaches for his bag, unzipping it and pulling out a haphazard pile of papers.

Where's his laptop? Why isn't he more organized?

Rummaging around in the front pouch of his bag, he pulls out a pen and uncaps it with his teeth.

His teeth? Ew!

Not even a pencil case?

Who is this animal?

I would never treat my stationery with such disregard.

That's because you're a stationery nerd. Now say something back!

"Um." I clear my throat and shuffle in my seat again, tugging on my skirt and fidgeting with the top button of my cardigan.

Wily's eyes dart to my fingers, then trail down my body.

I flush, hating his perusal.

What the hell is he doing?

Is he... is he checking me out?

I bristle, then hold my breath as I wait for that standard look of repulsion or disinterest that I usually get from guys like him, but his lips just quirk at the corners, and he looks more curious than anything.

Or maybe he's having to work to hide his laughter.

So, he's one of *those* jocks. Thinks it's funny that not everyone on the planet is ripped and fit like they are.

I squirm, angling my body away from him as annoyance flares inside me. Tapping my space bar, I light up my screen and wish to God my name wasn't on this stupid tutoring list. I wish I didn't need the money!

But you do, so just woman up already and get started.

"So..." I scratch my collarbone. "Maybe we could run through the tutoring you've already had. That'll give me a gauge of where you're at and what kind of support you'll need." I try to keep my tone professional, my emotions in check. I'm good at that, right? I've had years of practice.

"Okay." Wily sniffs, swiping a finger under his nose. "So, you probably know that Coach Jones is a real hard-ass. He's always had the rule that if you slack off in class, you're not worthy to be on the field. He'll bench us in a heartbeat. I mean, the season is basically over—and we're in playoffs now, so he's not about to bench me—but he's still riding me about graduating. And as much as I don't give a shit, my sister made the point that I have spent four years here, so maybe I should at least try to come out with a degree."

"I like your sister already," I quip.

He snickers. "Anyway, last year, I hired a guy, and he did my assignments for me, and that got me through the season. But his workload is getting on top of him this year, so he can't fit me in anymore, and I just need the same—"

"Wait, he what?" I shake my head, only just registering the words. "He did the assignments *for* you?"

"Yeah, I mean..." Wily shrugs. "I've got a really busy schedule with football and everything. It was a good setup for us, you know? We'd meet, I'd show him what needed to be done, then he'd fill in the gaps."

My eyes narrow. "How big were the gaps?"

"Oh, you know." His eyes dart from me to his scrappy pile of papers. He taps his pen on top of them. "It varied."

I'm sure it did. I'm starting to get a pretty clear picture already.

"So, he basically just did your work. You guys cheated."

"No." Wily's eyes bulge, the beat with his pen picking up tempo. "I saw everything before I handed it in. We made sure it sounded like my voice and shit. And he'd go over every assignment with me before I had to present it or whatever, so I was still learning everything I needed to, right? And still had to sit those heinous exams and tests on my own, so I wasn't cheating."

I shake my head, but Wily grins like I'm agreeing with him.

"It was a great setup." He sighs wistfully. "Such a bummer he can't keep going this year, you know? But..." His gaze darts back to my face, his dimpled smile coming into full effect as his voice drops to a flirtatious, husky timbre. "Now I've got you."

I stare at him for a beat, really soaking in what I assume is full-blown Wily Wilson charm.

It's impressive, and I'm sure most girls would flutter their eyelashes, maybe blush a little.

I'm embarrassed to admit that a small part of me is tempted to do just that. My lips are daring me to twitch, my skin threatening to turn the shade of ripe tomatoes.

But thankfully, I manage to balk, this surprised cough shooting out of my mouth as I shake my head. "I'm not going to be doing the assignments for you."

His smile disappears. Then his eyebrows dip together like he's totally confused. "What do you mean?"

Seriously?

"I mean... how are you supposed to learn if *I* do all your work?"

There's this weird pause, the silence between us feeling awkward as he slowly registers what I just said.

And then he laughs.

He laughs like I'm teasing him, swiping his hand through the air. "I'm not here to learn. I'm here to *graduate*. If I could play college ball without taking any classes, I would. I'm only doing this so Coach won't ride me about my grades and Michelle will get off my back."

Michelle?

Oh wait, is he talking about his academic adviser?

My eyebrows rise. "Ms. Bigsby has been on your back?"

"Not literally." He tips his head, his eyebrows quirking like he's now picturing the woman on his back, and ew... I don't even want to know where his brain is going.

My insides heat and I huff, snatching his attention back when I shuffle in my seat and try to figure out what I'm gonna say next.

He glances at me, his smile effortless. "I just want to leave this place with some certificate that tells the world I'm a college graduate. I honestly do not care how I get it."

"Then why bother?" The question pops out before I can stop it.

Seriously? Why am I engaging with this man? We're obviously not a good tutoring fit.

His right shoulder hitches, and he lets out this soft laugh. "I don't really know. I mean, the NFL's gonna draft me, so maybe it doesn't really matter."

Of course it matters! I agree with his sister! He can't waste nearly four years of education and not come out with something to show for it. Education is important. It's meaningful.

I bite my lips together, giving myself a second to think. "So... football is it?"

"Yep. I'm gonna play offensive guard for one of the pro teams, and I'll be set."

"But..." I purse my lips and dare a glance at him. "What if you don't get drafted?"

"I will." He gives me a confident grin—not cocky, just extremely self-assured.

Huh, I wonder what that feels like.

I study his expression, then soften my voice. "Okay... well, what about after football? I mean, don't you want a backup plan? Something you can do once your career is over? A college degree looks good on a résumé."

He lets out a husky laugh. "I'm not gonna need one of those. I'll be rich from playing football. When I retire, I can coach or do commentary. And my parents are already loaded, so..." His bottom lips sticks out like it's no big deal, and any softening I was feeling disintegrates.

"Right." I bulge my eyes. "So, you just want to live off Mommy and Daddy's money, then?"

He snickers, then looks at me like I'm an odd duck. Like I'm crazy for not getting this.

And that's me done. I cannot work with this man.

"Okay, well, um..." I scratch the side of my mouth. "I'm not sure this is going to be a very good setup for you, then, because if you work with me, I'll be making you do your own assignments. I'm happy to support you and help you understand everything, but I won't be doing the work on your behalf."

He frowns again, his pen resuming a fast tap on the table as he studies me with an expression that I'd describe as mildly pissed off and desperately thoughtful. He's trying to figure me out, find the perfect words to win me over, but it won't work.

Thanks to guys like Peyton Feldman, I've learned my lesson. And I won't be used again so this lazy ass can fly through his college courses and come out with a degree while I'm working my butt off on *his* assignment work, not to mention my own.

It's not going to happen.

"I can pay you." His tone is deep, assertive. "I'll give you $100 more an hour on top of whatever you're already getting."

A hundred bucks? Holy crap! Does this guy sleep on a mattress of Benjamin Franklins or something?

Aw, man, that is so tempting, but...

I close my laptop and start packing my things away.

"What? You don't want the money?"

Irritation sizzles through me, but I keep my expression impassive. I'm not about to escalate this growing tension.

With a calm, soft tone, I reply, "I wouldn't be doing either of us any favors. I'm not letting you pass off my work as yours. How does that help you? And besides, it's a form of cheating."

"It's not cheating, and it helps me by giving me a degree." His voice takes on a snappy edge.

My insides bunch, my skin starting to crawl in earnest as I drag my laptop off the table and slip it into my bag.

I should just get up and go. That's the best way to deal with these kinds of people, right?

But for some stupid reason, I look across at him and feel compelled to argue back. "It'd be a degree you haven't earned. It's a waste of your time handing in work that isn't yours. You're not learning anything."

"Well, maybe I'm not smart enough to learn anything!" His voice rises, and the person sitting behind us slaps his book closed with a huff, throwing us a hot glare before stalking away from his table and muttering something about how libraries being a place of peace and quiet is complete horseshit.

I wince over my shoulder and mumble a soft apology that he doesn't hear. Turning back to Wily, who now has his arms crossed and is quietly fuming, I softly murmur, "Everyone is smart enough to learn something. You're just being lazy paying someone else to do your work."

His eyebrows dip into a sharp V, like I've highly offended him.

I swallow, glancing away and scratching my itchy

stomach. "Look, I'm sorry, but if you want that setup, you'll just have to find someone else." I stand from the table, but he snatches my wrist before I can take off.

"But I can't find anyone else." His voice spikes with obvious desperation. "Please. I have an assignment due on Monday, and I've already been given a huge extension. I won't get another one. If I don't get at least a C, I'm gonna fail that course, and then I can't graduate. I'm hanging by a thread here. Just help me out with this one thing; then you can quit, and I'll find someone else to get me through the rest of the semester."

I glance down at his hand still clutching my wrist, then take in his crumpled, pleading expression.

Huh, looks like he really does want a college degree after all.

Guilt swirls inside me, and I end up muttering a soft "Okay, fine."

What? No. It's not fine. Walk away now!

But I don't. I sit my butt back in my chair and point at his pile of papers. "What have you got so far?"

He shuffles through the pages and eventually unearths a crinkled assignment sheet. I give him a baleful stare, and his sheepish smile is... okay, it's mildly cute.

Snapping my gaze away from it, I skim through the instructions. He has to analyze a key character from *Moby Dick* and discuss how the lessons learned through that character's journey can be applied in today's modern society. He also needs to include personal, relatable stories to really show the human connection and that he fully understands what motivated the character to behave the way he did.

Easy. I'm pretty sure I did an assignment just like this

in high school. I can't believe this is something for a college senior, but I guess he's been selecting the easiest courses he can.

"Okay." I bob my head, then look at the rest of the pages he's leaning his forearm on. "So, what have you done so far?"

"Nothing."

I whip my head back, blinking at him. "Nothing?"

He shakes his head, looking completely unabashed by this.

What is wrong with this man?

"It's... it's due in less than a week," I sputter, having internal conniptions at the idea of trying to complete an assignment like this in such a short timeframe. "Have you even read the book?"

His bottom lip pokes out as he shakes his head again. Then he grins at me. "I bet you've read the book, though. An old classic like that is probably on your bookshelf already, amiright?" He winks.

I recoil from that flirtatious smile of his.

He doesn't seem fazed, dialing it up to full beam as he leans toward me. "So, you think you can help me out?"

My lips part—it's impossible not to gape at this guy. He's expecting me to help him work on an assignment for a book he hasn't even read that's due on Monday?

Forget it!

Shaking my head, I stand from my chair. "I can't help you."

"Oh, come on. I'll do anything. Buy you anything. Pay you anything."

"I don't want your money," I hiss in desperation. "I can't help you, okay? I won't. It's not worth the stress."

Hitching my bag, I spin on my heel, crossing my arms and getting away from Wily Wilson as fast as I can.

I don't need some jock completely doing my head in days before my next semester starts. Like I want that kind of aggravation in my life.

He's just going to have to cope on his own.

And yes, I feel a little bad about that, but he seems charming. I'm sure he can talk someone else into doing his work for him. He'll probably find some gullible little freshman, flash his pearly whites at her, and she'll be eating out of his palm by the end of the weekend, handing him a beautifully crafted essay so he can get a degree he doesn't deserve.

Honestly!

I have better things to do with my time.

CHAPTER 4
WILY

I can't believe Miss High and Mighty won't help me out.

What the actual fuck is wrong with her?

She's read *Moby Dick*, I know she fucking has. I could tell by the flicker in her eyes when I called her on it. But she's still not willing to help me.

She could probably write this fucking essay in her sleep, but no, she has to assume that I'm some teachable asshole who's just too lazy to do my own work.

What a bitch!

I huff, feeling kind of bad for thinking that.

I don't like insulting women. Most of them are everything that's good about this world.

But then you get the Elizabeth Satchwells.

You mean, the kind of woman who didn't want to take your money because she genuinely wanted to teach you something?

The kind with integrity?

"Shit," I mutter under my breath, hating my own arguments and wishing I could just stay fucking mad!

This week, I've been nothing but a ball of stress, trying and failing to ignore my assignment and just take the F. I don't know why I can't just settle on that. It would mean I could flunk out of all my courses this semester, and it wouldn't even fucking matter!

But something inside me hates that idea.

I'm a winner!

I don't quit!

And I'm gonna get my fucking degree, even if it is just some meaningless certificate framed on my wall. I'm graduating from Nolan University.

I have no idea why I'm feeling so damn determined about it.

Maybe I just want to prove that Satchwell chick wrong. I'm not a lazy asshole.

Which is why I'm up at the crack of dawn, hunched over my computer and trying to figure out this AI program. We're not supposed to be using it, but how can teachers really tell, right? I mean, we'd be idiots not to take advantage of this technology.

I type in the assignment brief and pick Moby Dick as my character to analyze. The book's named after him, so he must be the main character, right?

The program spits an essay back at me. And I have no idea if it's on the right track. Squinting my eyes at the screen, I read the first few sentences and don't get what they're talking about. I didn't even know there was a whale in this book.

"Fuck." I rub my eyes.

I should get Grady or Tyrell to look over this for me. They're the smartest guys in the house.

But I'm too embarrassed to show them.

Besides, Grady's been off all week. He even skipped the winter dance last night to take Carson's mom to the airport. Teah will be so pissed over that one. Anything where she gets to dress up and look pretty is her jam, and he bailed on her? I haven't had a chance to find out why yet. I was too busy making sure Carson got his girl back.

And by the loved-up looks they were giving each other and the groans coming from his bedroom last night, I'd say they've worked out their shit.

Rubbing my forehead, I glance at the time on my computer and mutter under my breath. I just want to go back to bed and not give a flying fuck about this damn assignment.

But I can't give the professor nothing.

I have to at least try, right?

Leaning forward with a whiny groan, I try to read the next paragraph and nearly slump with relief when my phone buzzes and a text from my old man appears on the screen.

Pops: You awake yet? I'd love a chat.

I call him immediately, smiling at the screen when he answers my video chat.

"Hey. You're up early."

He grins at me. "I'm about to go for a run. I just wanted to check in first, see how you're feeling about the upcoming game."

"Yeah, good." I try not to laugh at him. The guy is more obsessed with football than I am. He's spent his life fueling my passion for it, and he couldn't be prouder if he tried. His son is going to play for the NFL. It's all he's been talking about since my talent started shining in middle school.

I've always been big for my age, and Dad steered me in the direction of football before I could even walk. That's our thing. And his support means the world to me.

Leaning back in my chair, I start up one of my favorite conversations, getting into the nitty-gritty of our play strategy. I'm not really supposed to talk about it outside of the team, but I trust Pops. He'd never betray us. He's passionate about the Nolan U Cougars dominating. Anything that will help me shine for the scouts. The amount of time and money my parents have poured into my football career is impressive. They've made my journey as easy as it possibly could be. And they've always believed in my skill on the field.

Dad even hooked me up with an agent. He knew a guy—a friend from college—and they reconnected over my football career and have become best buds again. They've got my career mapped out, and Dad's there every step of the way, approving and rejecting ideas. I'm pretty sure Austin is supposed to deal with me directly, and he does sometimes, but I'd honestly rather have Dad take care of that shit. It's just easier for Austin to go straight to the one with the strongest opinion. I'm happy to go with the flow on this thing. I love people and everything, but social media is a beast I can't stand. My agent takes care of my image and sponsorships. All I have to do is turn up to stuff, sign the odd shirt, and pose for photos. My parents feed him shots from my football career so far, along with the college's media department, and all that promo shit gets done for me. Which means all I have to think about is the game.

Dad and I talk for nearly an hour before Mom reminds him that he's supposed to be out running and if he doesn't go now, they'll be late for brunch with the Clarks.

"Hello, my darling boy." She tinkles her fingers at me.

I wave back, complimenting her new dress. "Looks gorgeous, Mom."

"Thank you." She winks at me, then blows a kiss before patting Dad's shoulder. "Wrap it up, or we're gonna be late."

"Yes, ma'am." He grins and watches Mom clip away, obviously checking out her ass and loving the view. I wait him out, laughing when he finally turns back to acknowledge me. "What? She's one sexy lady."

"Okay." I wince. No one wants to hear that shit about their mother.

His smile grows a little wider. "You have a good day, son. I'm proud of you."

"Thanks, Dad."

"You're going to do great things on that field on Thursday. I'll be there cheering you on."

Don't I know it.

Since their son joined the Nolan U Cougars, my parents have only missed one game, and that was because Mom was rushed to the hospital with appendicitis. Other than that, they've been in the stands no matter where I'm playing.

And they won't fail me this coming Thursday either.

The semifinals. Holy shit!

Are we actually gonna make the finals this year?

That would be fucking epic!

"I'll catch you later."

"See ya, Pops." I wave him off, dropping my phone on the bed and grinning down at the floor.

Damn, I can't fucking wait!

Gotta get through tomorrow first, man. Hand that assignment in, and then you can breathe again.

"Until my next round of classes start." I snort, shaking my head and getting off the bed, only to be interrupted by an enthusiastic knock that can belong to one person alone.

"Wywee!" Zoey raps on the door again.

"Hey, Cowgirl."

"You wake?"

"I surely am, little missy."

She lets out a squeal and the door punches open, her cute face appearing. She's all dressed up to go outside in a snow bib, mittens, and a beanie. "Wanna pay?"

Oh man, I want to say yes so badly!

I glance at my laptop, the screen saver image of me grinning at the camera next to the legendary Broncos player Peyton Manning morphing into a shot of Blake and me by the Statue of Liberty.

I really should get back to my assignment, but—

"Snowman?" Zoey walks into the room, stopping between my legs and resting her tiny hand on my knee.

I glance down at her, fighting a grin. "You wanna build a snowman?"

"Uh-huh!" She nods enthusiastically, totally missing my movie quote. I don't think she's seen *Frozen* yet. Sienna's kind of strict on the whole screen time thing, and Zander's followed her lead. This kid's allowed like twenty-minute bursts of kiddy games on the iPad, and that's about it.

Which is why she can be fully dressed in her snow gear and ready to play at stupid o'clock in the morning.

"Less go, Wywee!" She tugs on my hand, and how can I possibly say no to that cute little face?

"Zoey?" Zander calls up the stairs. "You're not up there, are you?"

She bulges her eyes at me, then calls out, "No?"

"Zo-ey," Zander growls, and she starts to giggle, crouching into a ball and hiding her head.

My roommate, who now officially lives in the converted garage, is soon standing in my doorway, staring down at his kid with his arms crossed and fighting a grin as he puts on a stern voice. "Zoey Erling-Donohue, you're not supposed to be up here."

"Can't see me," she whispers.

"I *can* see you, and I can tell you that you're breaking the rules. Which means I'm gonna have to take a gem out of your jar."

Her head pops up with a gasp, her mouth turning into a quick pout.

Zander raises his hands, palms up. "You know the drill, kid."

She opens her mouth to protest, then quickly closes it with a cute growl, curling her mitten hands into two little fists and thumping onto her butt. Her face is going bright red as she lets out another growl and shakes her fists in the air.

"She did knock." I go to bat for her.

Zander's eyebrows rise in approval. "Did she?"

I nod and Zoey joins me, her eyes getting all big and hopeful.

"Well, that is an improvement, but you know you shouldn't be up here without asking first. This floor is for the Football Frat guys and other adults, not lil love bugs."

Zoey dips her head, murmuring a soft "I know."

"Hey." Zander crouches down, crooking his finger at her. "C'mere."

She gets to her feet and shuffles across the room, her lips still curled into a sad pout.

Placing his finger under her chin, Zander gently guides her up to face him, and he smiles down at her. "Every choice has a consequence. And you chose wrong this morning, kiddo, which means I have to do something that's gonna help you learn not to do it again."

Her face crunches into an adorable frown.

"But... because you were polite enough to knock, I'm still willing to take you outside to play, okay?"

She nods. "'Kay."

He smiles at her, leaning down to peck her cheek just before she snuggles against him.

And I slap my hands on my knees and stand up. "Well, now I want to play too." Walking for the closet, I fish out my waterproof coat. "Let's go build a snowman, Cowgirl. Yeehaw!"

Zoey giggles and pulls away from Zander, jumping and clapping while I gear up. It takes me a minute to find my beanie, but I'm soon traipsing outside with an excited toddler, my assignment shoved to the back of my brain so I can enjoy a little time with the cutest girl on the planet.

Zander and I walk her down the street to the nearby park so we're not making noise outside the garage. Sienna is enjoying a sleep-in for once, and Zander will do anything not to wake her.

Using the freshly covered field next to the playground —yep, it snowed last night, and Nolan looks magical—we start forming balls that Zoey can use to build her snowman. She runs around us, leaving mini footprints in the snow and directing us with an excited yell: "Bigger, Daddy! Bigger!"

Zander does as he's told, and I laugh, rolling my snowball toward his.

"See if you can find some branches for arms, Zo-Zo. There'll be some under the snow." Zander points to a nearby tree, and I take the chance to form a small ball in my hands and surprise my captain with a missile to his stomach.

He lurches forward with an *oof* before looking up at me. His lips twitch, his eyes silently challenging me— *"You really want to do this?"*

I laugh, already forming another ball.

Zander grins and drops to his knees, scraping at the snow. I get him with a ball to the face, letting out another raucous laugh before he launches one right back at me.

Mr. Snowman is soon forgotten as we pelt each other with snowballs, Zoey getting in on the action and becoming her dad's righthand girl.

It quickly escalates, and I'm forced to take cover behind a tree while Zoey and Zander form their next attack plan.

Sensing their move to the left, I jerk right, slipping

over in the snow and landing with a crunch. My knee pings and I grunt, giving it a quick rub before jumping back to my feet and running to make a fresh snowball while getting pelted in the arm by a beautifully aimed attack from the quarterback.

CHAPTER 5
WILY

Monday morning rolls around, and much to my annoyance, I still haven't finished proofing my assignment.

Proofing it? You haven't even read it!

I print it out anyway. This professor likes to mark paper assignments, so I don't have the chance to make any last-minute changes. Not that I would.

I have no idea what this AI essay really means. Having not read the book and finding the language too waffly for my simpleton brain, I'm basically handing in five pages of applesauce. All I can hope is that the professor skims it and goes *tick, tick, tick* like he usually does.

I just need a C.

One little C.

Gritting my teeth, I do my next set of reps on the leg press, my muscles straining as I push the 700-lb. weights up and hold for a second before bringing them back down again. My thighs are burning, but I keep pushing, knowing this is ultimately good for me.

I'm tired, though.

After a restless night, I've woken up off-kilter and in a foul mood.

But I can't go letting that show, because I'm not a grumpy bastard. I'm the happy guy. The one who never gets bothered by anything, and I'm not losing that reputation over some fucking assignment. The only time I'll ever let my anger really show is on the field... or if some douchebag is treating a woman badly. I've got a thing about it. Anyone willing to beat on a smaller, weaker person deserves to go down with a punch to the face. That's just a fact of life.

Why anyone would want to harm a woman is beyond me. I've always loved them, and my parents raised me to be a gentleman... to treat people with kindness and respect.

I mean, yeah, sure, I've had some one-night stands, and some would argue that isn't respecting women. But I'd counter that it's usually the girls instigating that shit, and I'm simply delivering on their requests. I'm not about to turn down an offer from a pretty lady. And okay, I've thrown out a few offers of my own, but casual hookups seem to be the thing here at Nolan U, and as far as I'm aware, I'm not leaving a trail of broken hearts in my wake.

In fact, last year, a night with Wily Wilson became this bucket list challenge for one sorority. Shit, that was a gooooood semester. You didn't hear me complaining. Sex is a great way to blow off steam. Way more fun than working out at the gym. Although, I enjoy that too.

Setting the leg press back, I give myself a second to

rest before pulling myself up and walking over to the free weights. This new workout has been an easy one to memorize, and I grab the 50-lb. dumbbells and start my bicep curls, checking myself in the mirror and remembering to breathe as I hold my stance.

"Good job today, Carson."

"Thanks, Coach."

I spot my roommate walking into the gym with our head coach. He has a small smile on his face as he wipes the sweat away and goes to the mat behind me. Warmed up after a five-mile run with Coach, he drops down and does thirty quick push-ups before rolling onto his back and starting a quick set of sit-ups.

Coach and Carson have been going out for a run most mornings in the past month, and I've noticed a real change in my roommate. He's found this calm we didn't think he was capable of.

He was working hard to get his girl back, and now that they're reunited, I just hope he can hold it together. She seems to bring out the best in him, so here's hoping.

Flipping back onto his stomach, he does another quick set of push-ups, then catches my eye in the mirror.

"Hey," he puffs and turns onto his back again.

"'Sup." I raise my chin at him, straining to finish the last of my curls before putting the weights back and grabbing my bottle of water.

Chugging back a decent amount, I continue my workout until Coach walks back in, clapping his hands to get our attention, then tapping his watch. "Shower up, boys. Don't want you being late to class."

We all acknowledge him with various grunts and noises, Zander trailing him out first, followed by the rest of the guys working out. I linger, wiping down my face with a towel and catching my reflection in the mirror.

Shit. I know I'm procrastinating right now.

I just really don't want to go to class and hand in my assignment.

But it can't be all bad, right?

If I don't understand it, then it must be good.

Nodding at my reflection, I hold on to that thinking. It's enough to get me showered, dressed, and out of the stadium.

I walk with Tyrell and Carson. We don't say much because both guys are on their phones. Carson keeps snickering and grinning at the screen, which means he's probably texting Nylah, while Tyrell is looking at his screen with this sad frown.

"You good, man?" I lightly punch his shoulder.

"Yeah." He glances at me, shoving his phone away and forcing a smile. "All good. What's your first class today?"

I shrug and he laughs at me, because he's probably got his schedule memorized already.

I haven't even looked at mine. All I know is that I have to hand in this assignment to Professor Pilscher before nine this morning. Shit, I better get moving.

Picking up my pace, I shout a goodbye over my shoulder and head to the Humanities building. I make it to Pilscher's office with ten minutes to spare.

He's just rising from his desk, grabbing his briefcase and looking about ready to leave. "Ah, Mr. Wilson. Thought you might not make it."

"No, sir. I've got the assignment right here."

He glances at his watch, obviously annoyed by my interruption to his schedule, and flicks his fingers at me.

I place the work in his hands, and much to my horror, he takes the time to skim it. My eyes bulge, and I move for the door. "Well, I'll just let you—"

"Stay," he murmurs softly, his eyes still scanning the first page. Then his eyebrows pucker in obvious confusion, and my stomach twists into a knot so tight it hurts.

He glances up at me, and I put on a smile. The move is most definitely not reciprocated.

"What is this?" He waves the pages in the air.

"Um... my assignment."

"Did you even read the book?" he snaps.

"Uh... of course." I force a grin. "I couldn't do it without... reading the book, right?"

His jaw works to the side as he slaps the pages down. "I'm not marking this. I'm insulted that you even think I would."

"Why?" It's hard to keep my irritation in check. "I did the assignment like you asked me to."

"I was looking for a human experience and something that relates directly to *your* life. I made that very clear in my class. You trying to be all clever and choosing Moby Dick proves that you weren't listening."

"What's wrong with choosing Moby Dick? He's the main character. The book is named after him!"

He scoffs and shakes his head with a sigh. "I can tell you used AI for this. There isn't one direct example from your life. It's going to be an automatic fail, Mr. Wilson."

"Come on, sir. I've had a busy season, and—"

"I already gave you an extension!" He points at his desk. "And you managed to hand in all your other assignments without a problem. In fact, they—" His eyes narrow, and he slowly picks my essay back up again, flicking through the pages with an ominous silence that makes my chest feel like it's being squeezed in a vise. His keen gaze lands on me, and I put on another smile until he says, "You didn't do the work for them, did you?"

"Sir, I..." Holding out my hand, I silently ask for the assignment back. I'm not sure what else to do. I can't go admitting I never wrote one fucking essay for him. "Look, it's obvious this assignment isn't up to par. I had a busy vacation, and..." My words dribble off at the dry, very unimpressed expression on Pilscher's face. It steals any confidence from my voice, and I end up whispering, "Please just give me another chance."

"Everyone else managed to get their work in on time, Mr. Wilson, and I'm not making *another* exception for you just because you play football." He grabs his briefcase and steps around his desk. "I'm sorry you were unable to pass my class, but it really comes down to you and the fact that you weren't willing to put in the work." Tipping his chin up, he silently orders me out of his office, and as much as I'd love to stand here fighting for my cause, I can tell it'll be a waste of my breath.

As soon as I'm back outside, I stalk around the building and rest against the concrete wall.

"Shit!"

An automatic fail?

What the fuck am I supposed to do now?

One paper and it's screwing up my chances of graduating.

Not just one paper, dude. If you can't find someone to get you through this semester, then you'll fail them all.

I don't even know why I'm bothering.

Who gives a fuck about graduating anyway!

I thump my hand on the wall behind me and wince at the sting.

"Wily?" A soft voice captures my attention, and I glance to my left, noticing a pretty girl with a sweet smile walking toward me. "Are you okay?"

"Oh, hey, Callie. How are ya?"

"I'm good." Her smile turns into a cringe. "But you don't look very happy."

I let out a snicker, forcing my classic smile and enjoying her response. She blushes, tucking a lock of hair behind her ear and looking up at me.

Her expression is telling me exactly what she wants, and I'm inclined to follow her back to her dorm and just go with it.

We've slept together in the past. She's dated other guys in between, and as she takes my hand with an impish grin, I double-check, "You're not with anyone right now?"

"Nope. Enjoying being single for a while." Her tongue sticks out the side of her mouth. "How about you?"

"You know me, nothing serious for this guy right here."

"Perfect," she purrs, and I can't help a soft laugh. Yep, Callie's gonna make it all better.

Screw that fucking assignment.

Screw college.

All I care about right now is getting it on with this hottie and enjoying some morning delight.

It *was* a delight. We ended up spending most of the day in bed together. We had a great time, and when I kissed her goodbye just before football practice, she gave me a wink and thanked me for a great start to the semester.

Shit, who knows what classes I missed to hang with her, but I didn't fucking care.

Until I woke up the next morning and actually checked my schedule.

Scrubbing my face with a sigh, it's only dawning on me now that I'll have to spend the rest of my week sweet-talking the professors and coming up with decent excuses as to why I missed their first class. I'll need to go online and find the syllabi and which assignments are due when.

Fuck! Should I even bother?

Without Pilscher's grade, aren't I just wasting my time?

This roiling anger bubbles in my chest. Or maybe it's disappointment. I don't fucking know.

I guess I do want to graduate.

I guess I don't want the last three and a half years of my life to be meaningless. I mean, they had purpose—football. But why go through all the angst of working with tutors and scraping through my first couple of years if I'm just gonna pack it in now?

Quitting isn't something that sits right with me.

Fuck it! Graduating *is* part of the plan, and now I can't!

And that fucking sucks.

Thumping downstairs, I stalk into the kitchen, pushing up my sleeves as the smell of frying bacon and scrambled eggs hit me.

Grady is at the stove, cooking up a storm for all of us.

Usually, he'll have music pumping and be humming along, but he's quiet and morose this morning.

"What's up with you?" I mumble, instantly ashamed of my grumpy tone but too pissed off to do anything about it.

"Nothing," he grumbles right back, and we leave it there.

As much as I want to rant with the guy—Grady's a great soundboard, always so calm and easy to talk to—I just don't have it in me this morning, especially if he's in a foul mood too.

I should stick around and make sure he's okay, but I can't.

I just want to get the fuck out of here.

I bypass breakfast, figuring I'll eat later, and head out the door, snatching my various bags and going to the truck. I'll beat everyone to the gym, but maybe that's a good thing. I can get in some extra sets and really burn off this irritation inside me.

I'll need to finish my workout early anyway, especially if I'm gonna check in with all my professors.

Why bother?

The question is still burning in the back of my brain, but for some dumb reason, it's not enough to stop my plans. If Callie hadn't come along to distract me yesterday, I would have gone to all those classes, even though it's a hopeless waste of time.

"Shit!" I bang the steering wheel. "Shit! Shit! Shit!"

And that's when I see her.

Elizabeth Satchwell.

Miss High and Mighty.

She's shuffling down the sidewalk, her shoulders hunched against the cold, carrying a take-out coffee... and all this foul, dark energy inside me seems to rise to the surface at once as I swerve up to the curve, slamming on my brakes and jumping out of the car.

"I failed!" I shout, flicking up my hands as I bark at her. "I fucking failed, and I'm so pissed off with you!"

CHAPTER 6
ELIZABETH

This voice is roaring behind me, and I have no idea who it belongs to or who it's directed at. As soon as the pickup truck screeched to a stop against the curb, I hurried up my pace, not wanting to be anywhere near some kind of argument.

"Hey, I'm talking to you!"

Yikes, that man sounds super annoyed. I'm so glad he's not talking to me.

I walk as fast as my short legs will take me, hoping I don't slip or trip like I usually do. Whoever this guy is yelling at is in for it, and they're obviously scared as well, because they haven't said a word.

"Elizabeth Satchwell!" the man barks.

I suck in a quick breath, realization suddenly dawning.

Oh shit. He's yelling at me.

Run! Run now!

But of course I freeze, my muscles going rigid as I grip my coffee and steal a quick glance over my shoulder.

Wily Wilson?

I start to pivot.

What are you doing?

Don't pivot! Run!

But nope, I'm pivoting. Maybe it's morbid curiosity, I don't really know, but I am turning to face this dragon.

And when I end my spin and take in the giant blond charging toward me, I'm doused with instant regret.

He comes to a stop a few feet away, his eyes flashing wildly. "Remember me?"

"Yes." My voice is so tiny, I'm sure he can't even hear it.

Seriously, why am I not dropping my coffee and making a run for it?

I've never been approached by a hurricane like this before, and for some reason, I can't move.

The bullies I usually put up with are all smarmy smiles and cutting comments.

This is just outright rage... or maybe it's frustration. There is a difference. I think.

Biting my bottom lip, I watch him take another huffing step toward me, then plant his massive feet so he can tower over me with his glacial glare.

"Uh..." I shuffle a few steps back. "Can I help you with something?"

Ugh! Lamest thing to say. Ever.

My eyes dart back to his shoes, and my brain decides to try work out his size. He must be a 12 or 13. Wowzers. I'm in a size 6, which means his feet are twice as big as mine.

"You could have," he snaps, grabbing my attention. My eyes dart back up to his angry face. "I asked. I practically fucking begged. I even offered to pay you, and you just walked away. Fed me to the fucking wolves, and now I'm screwed!" He flicks his arms up and I jolt, each barked syllable feeling like a hit to the face.

"Um. You're... screwed? I don't—"

"I failed my assignment!" He leans down, getting in my face.

I take a nervous step back.

"Shit, I thought you were a genius."

"I'm not a genius," I agree quietly, confused by why he would even think that.

"Now I'm going to flunk that class, which means I won't have enough credits to graduate."

"Wait, wasn't the assignment due yesterday? How do you know your grade already?"

"He skimmed it and then refused to grade it." Wily huffs, resting his hands on his hips and starting to pace. "He told me it's an instant fail."

"Is he even allowed to do that? Why would he refuse?"

"I don't know," Wily grumbles. "Something about choosing Moby Dick for my character analysis."

"Wait, you..." I blink, then have to bite my lips together for a second. "You chose... Moby Dick?"

"Yeah, he's the main character, isn't he? But Professor Pain in my Ass got all shitty, going on about human experience and how it relates to me and my life. I mean, what the actual fuck!"

I wince. *Aw. He thinks Moby Dick's a man.*

This is why you have to read the book.

Wily stops pacing to glare down at me, flicking his hand in my direction. "Why do people keep looking at me like that!"

My lips twitch, and I don't know how to break this to him, so I use the gentlest voice I can. "Moby Dick's the whale. He doesn't really have a character arc in the traditional sense. I mean, I guess you could argue that he's an important character in the book, which he is... But if your professor was looking for a human experience, then..." I cringe. "Moby's like the enemy of the story. The force of nature that affects the other character arcs and—"

"Fuck! Stupid AI bullshit," he grits out, and understanding quickly dawns.

"Oh, yeah. AI's only helpful if you're asking it for the right thing. Did you not notice when you read over—"

"I didn't have time to proof it properly! And I didn't even know what the fuck I was reading, so no! I didn't notice!"

"Okay." I raise my palms, trying to calm him down.

Breaths spurt out his nose, his chest heaving as he mutters something under his breath and glares at me again. "It all comes so easy for you, doesn't it?"

"I—"

"You're smarter than me. Everybody's fucking smarter than me! They don't get what it's like to hear something and not understand it. To read something and not get what the words even mean! You've probably always been a reader, right? You probably have stacks of books in your room that you pore over. Just like Blake." He curses again, then growls and shouts, "Well, not everyone finds it that simple!"

I flinch away from his venom.

This is kind of scary.

I should go.

I should really just turn and go.

But...

Look at his face.

My eyes are transfixed as his expression jumps from anger to desperation to disappointment to pure, clear-cut frustration.

"And it doesn't matter how many tutors I have, okay? Nothing works! That's why I was paying extra to get my assignments done for me!" He slaps the back of his hand against his palm. "That worked. That was getting me through."

I should nod and just agree with him. He's ranting. He doesn't need me to say anything.

So, of course I open my mouth. "But that's not teaching you—"

"Did you not just hear what I fucking said?" He spreads his arms wide. "I *can't* learn, okay?" His expression bunches. "Fuck! I'm never gonna graduate."

His growls and foul language are doing nothing to hide the disappointment in his voice.

Oh my gosh, look at his face.

He honestly believes he can't learn.

No wonder he's been having trouble with his tutors. If he can't get past that belief, he's always going to struggle.

I stand there, drinking in his unrest and feeling this pull inside me.

"You're not stupid, Wily. And you *can* graduate. I'd help you if you were willing to let me."

"You can't help me. You don't get it! I'm not smart enough!"

"You are. I can teach you so that you can take that knowledge and apply it in your life. It's pointless trying to graduate otherwise. And you've been passing so far, which means you must have been picking up something along the way. Your tutors can't take your exams for you, so you must have done okay with those."

He scoffs and shakes his head. "I've barely been scraping by. In fact, I wouldn't be shocked if the teachers have been going easy on me just so I won't get benched."

I ignore that last comment and try to focus on the positive. "But you *are* passing."

"Not anymore," he grumbles, his heated tone fizzling out. "I just wanted to graduate, Brainiac. That's all I wanted."

My eyebrows wrinkle in confusion. I got the impression that he didn't actually care too much. He's getting drafted. He'll be rich. Who needs a degree, right?

But that must have just been bravado.

A wave of sympathy courses through me, and I try to make him feel better. "Look, I'm sorry the professor wouldn't even grade your paper for you, but maybe there's another class you can take over the summer."

He looks up from the icy concrete to glare at me like I've lost my mind.

I swallow and stupidly keep going. "Maybe we could talk to Ms. Bigsby. It's early enough in the semester that we could find one more class for you to take. That'll get you over the credit line, right?"

"You want me to take *more* classes? Are you fucking insane?"

His tone is so cutting, and itchy, scratchy ants start to crawl across my skin. I resist the urge to scratch my stomach.

Just go. Turn and walk away.

But I don't. I keep standing there, staring up at the

big man and quietly asking, "You said the football season was wrapping up, so you'll have more time, right?"

Now he's gaping at me like I've lost every one of my marbles.

"How were your classes yesterday? I mean, you've gotten your syllabi for those ones, and you'll get some more today, so you'll be able to figure out how much you can manage and then—"

"I didn't go to my classes yesterday," he mutters, scuffing the concrete with his big sneaker.

"What? Why?"

"Because I didn't see the point having just failed Pilscher's class!"

I blink, surprised that he's being so scathing about Professor Pilscher. I had him last year, and he was amazing! Sure, he's old-school, but I really liked that about him. He was fair and kind and... he made nineteenth-century literature so much fun.

"That guy is such an asshole," Wily grumbles.

I frown, hating the way he's insulting one of my favorite professors.

Crossing his arms, he shakes his head, looking so angsty that I'm not even sure what to say.

Biting my lip, I try to form the right words and end up with a lame "You really shouldn't be skipping class. That's not going to help your cause, you know?"

"Whatever." He scoffs. "Like you even care anyway."

I open my mouth to protest that of course I care. I'm a very caring person.

Not enough to help the poor guy out when he needed it.

Guilt slices through me, but I defend my actions with

some sound logic. I wasn't about to do his work for him. That wouldn't have helped him at all.

"This is such a fucking waste of time," he mutters, running a hand through his hair and throwing me another hot glare.

"I..." With a soft huff, I give in and say what I think he wants to hear. "I'm sorry I didn't do things the way you wanted, but—"

"Yeah, I'm sure you are." He rolls his eyes. "Just forget it, Elizabeth Satchwell." He flicks his hand up. "Go on and enjoy your damn day. Attend your fucking classes and pass with straight A's."

"Just as long as you attend your classes too," I shoot back.

What? I did not just say that!

Seriously, this guy makes me say things I never normally would.

I bulge my eyes, waiting for the backlash.

He gives me a hard laugh and spits out, "So fucking helpful!" He spreads his arms wide, that scathing look morphing into a pained frown before he spins on his heels and storms back to his truck.

My shoulders slump, my insides starting to tremble as I watch him go.

I've never been yelled at like that before, and it's really unsettling.

My eyes start to burn as I spin and shuffle toward Buckley Hall. I don't want to cry. Like, I *really* don't want to cry. That big oaf is not allowed to make me feel bad for not digging him out of the colossal hole he made for himself.

So why do I feel so bad, then?

I can sense eyes on me, and I glance up and notice a guy with messy blond hair. He has his arm around his gorgeous Black girlfriend. Ugh, she's so pretty... and she's no doubt watching me waddle past and judging me the way every other pretty girl does.

Dipping my head, I avoid her gaze, hoping she's not a gossip queen as well. The last thing I need is rumors flying through Buckley Hall about the waddling hippo who got into a fight with the superstar football player.

CHAPTER 7
WILY

Okay, so I'm kinda feeling bad about the way I yelled at Elizabeth Satchwell.

Shit, she looked so fucking surprised when I started shouting at her, like no one had ever spoken to her that way before.

Fuck.

It didn't stop her from trying to argue back with me, though, did it?

She wants me to take another class, find another way to get the credits I need.

She's out of her fucking mind if she thinks I'm going to take on even more work.

I can't do it.

And now I don't know if there's any point even sticking around. Once we play our final game, should I just move back home and—

"Hey, man." Zander slaps me on the shoulder as he eases past me into the gym.

I blink, not even remembering my walk from the

truck to this point. Bags are clutched in my fists, and I glance back down the hall, shaking my head and feeling like I'm losing my mind.

Zander turns to look at me. "Hey, you good?"

"Uh, yeah." I paste on a smile because that's what he needs to see.

Like I'm gonna let him in on my trials right now. He'll be gutted if I tell him I'm quitting early. He's got grand plans of us graduating together. Sienna's already talking about a special party for all of us seniors... and it's months away.

Tyrell strolls into the gym as I'm dumping my gear and gives me a sleepy, blurry-eyed grunt. The guy does not do mornings. I raise my chin, knowing better than to engage. Apparently, I'm too friendly and chipper in the mornings, but he's not gonna have any issues with me today.

Jumping on the treadmill, I start a gentle jog, warming up my muscles as the gym fills with the regular morning crew. We've been doing this so long now that we can move around each other, instinctively knowing who's gonna be where and who needs spotting. I keep half an eye on Tyrell, knowing he'll be asking for my help in the next ten minutes or so. He likes to get the bench press out of the way first, and as soon as he lies down, I stop the treadmill and wander over to him.

"Ready?" I ask, once his hands are settled on the bar.

He nods and I hover behind him, making sure the bar doesn't land on his chest or neck. The guy likes to push it. We all do. That's part of the challenge, right?

After his first set, he stands up, breathing in through his nose and indicating for me to take my turn.

I pump out eight strong reps before my arms start to collapse. Shaking them out, I stand and notice Carson strolling into the gym.

"'Sup, dickheads." He raises his chin and grins around the room, getting back a plethora of friendly insults.

Zander's "Good morning, fuck nugget" is my favorite.

Carson grins at him, shedding his hoodie and wandering over to the chest press. "Hey, Wiles."

I narrow my eyes at him, wondering why he's saying a second hello to me.

"Hey." I nod, unnerved by the way he's looking at me. "You good?"

"Yeah. I'm... great. Are you okay?"

I frown, my eyes darting to Tyrell before landing back on my scruffy roommate. "Yeah, I'm fine."

Carson nods, obviously not believing me. My eyebrows dip, and he gives me a tight smile before getting on with his reps.

Tyrell and I share a confused frown, but then I shrug, not wanting to dive into it.

Thankfully, Grady shuffles into the gym after doing an obvious run to get here. He's puffing and sweaty, like he pushed it way too hard, and Zander wanders over to check on him.

"Something's up with that guy," Carson murmurs quietly.

I give him a side-eye, still trying to adjust to this new version of Carson. He was the one we always had to keep an eye on. He was the one who something was always up with. But he's found this new calm, and it's bringing out another side of him. Like he's noticing shit he didn't used to.

I don't know if I like it.

I definitely didn't like the way he was trying to see right through me before.

"Are things okay with him and Teah?" Carson turns to glance at me and Tyrell.

We both shrug.

"I wonder if they broke up. Something is definitely riling him, and the fact that he skipped the winter dance..." Carson makes a clicking noise out the side of his mouth. "Nylah mentioned that she saw them arguing at a party a while back."

"Why wouldn't he tell us?" Tyrell's morning voice is deep and croaky.

"Maybe he's hurting too much to talk about it." Carson gives us a thoughtful frown, and I share a weirded-out look with Tyrell.

Yep, this new Carson is going to take some getting used to.

Although, five minutes later, Fleischer struts into the gym, and we get flashes of the old Carson again. His grumpy, sarcastic quips put Fleischer in his place and rile him up pretty badly, but when he starts to ignite a fight, Carson manages to back away, breathing through his nose like it's some kind of managing technique and slipping out of the gym before Fleischer sends him over the edge.

I catch him in the locker room after his shower, and he's back to calm and unaffected.

Well, shit. He really has come a long way.

Staring at his phone, Carson's lips twitch while he

finishes his text, and I know he's messaging Nylah. I'm happy for him.

Walking into the showers, I flick on the water and soap myself down, thinking about all the girls I've been with in college. I remember them all—a stream of pretty faces wafting through my mind. I'm just thinking about my previous day with Callie when Elizabeth Satchwell suddenly pops into my mind.

I frown, lifting my arm and soaping my left pit.

I so don't want to be thinking about her right now, but I can't help it.

Shit, I do feel bad for the way I yelled at her. She didn't even see me coming, and I just pounced like an angry bear.

What a fucking way to start her day. Did I completely ruin it for her?

Fuck, I hope not.

I hope she's one of those chicks who can just brush off an argument and get on with her day. I didn't mean to lose my shit with her. I'm not that kind of guy. I'm Mr. Smiles, always happy. Nothing fazes me.

But this whole "I'm a big, dumb fuck" is really riling me today.

Which is why I force myself to get out of the shower, dry off, and head to class like she fucking told me to.

I have no idea why I do it.

This whole fucking semester is pointless.

But I sit through the introductory lecture on Finances and Accounting, wondering why I chose to take it. Michelle helped me find a bunch of easy classes to finish out my final year, and she assured me I could handle this one.

Yeah, right.

Gazing at my laptop screen, I try to keep up with the professor and follow about half of what she's saying. Shit, I need to find a tutor. There's no way I'll survive the semester without one.

But Michelle is going to be so pissed if I contact her with yet another fail. She was already annoyed with me that none of the other tutors worked out.

Shit, I should try asking for Elizabeth Satchwell's help again. If I haven't permanently put her off me. She's probably going to avoid me at all costs now, the stupid dude who yelled at her in the middle of the street.

Fuck!

Class wraps up and I sit there, still staring at my screen until someone bumps into my arm.

"Oh, sorry." A soft giggle hits me, and I turn to take in the pretty brunette who is smiling down at me.

Damn, she's gorgeous.

Her eyes are big and beautiful, her skin a silky bronze. She's a skinny thing with barely there tits and a slender waist. My eyes skim down her body before popping back up to her face.

She smiles at me, like she appreciates the fact that I'm noticing her.

It's easy to grin back, and I close my laptop, standing tall and dragging my bag with me. I stuff my computer away as we're walking down the stairs, my confidence rebuilding itself as fast as it does on a football field.

This chick is into me.

I know exactly what to do with a girl like this.

"So, finance, huh? You an accounting major or something?" she asks, tucking her long, shiny hair behind her ear.

"Shit, no." I laugh. "I'm just trying to get the credits I need to graduate. This course seems like an easy one to pass."

"I know, right?" She laughs. "That's why I took it too. Figured I'd make my first year at Nolan U a simple one."

"Ah, so you're just a little freshman, then." I grin, my tone playful.

She beams up at me. "And I'm guessing you're a junior?"

"Senior," I correct, kind of hating that I'm taking the same classes as a freshman. Shit, I really am stupid.

"I'm Jade, by the way." She sticks out her hand, and I shake those long fingers, admiring the shape of her face. It's oval—long and pretty, obviously well looked after. She's wearing makeup, and it's clear she likes to take care of herself.

I certainly appreciate it. She's a knockout.

Damn, it'd be nice to have *her* be my tutor, but we'd probably get nothing done. She's too hot, and I wouldn't be able to keep my hands off her... if she was keen.

Which she clearly is.

I drink in her hungry gaze for a second, and my smile grows.

"Wily Wilson," I introduce myself, noticing we're still shaking hands. I rub my thumb over her soft skin before dropping her hand. "It's nice to meet you, Jade."

"You too." She winks and brushes her teeth over her bottom lip—the ultimate seductress move—before turning and walking away, her hips swaying as she leaves me wanting more.

Yep, that chick sure knows what she's doing.

I stay where I am, appreciating the view, until she's around the corner and I'm forced to get back to reality.

Fucking reality.

It's weird for me to feel so dark. I'm not used to these internal rain clouds, but I'm still kind of pissed off that my last semester is going to be total shit. Once football is over, all I've got left is studying and prepping for the Scouting Combine at the end of February. I'm pretty pumped about attending. It's a chance for me to show off my skills to NFL coaches and scouts. I'll get noticed, because... well, they're already noticing me... and then it'll be whoever can win me first, I guess. I want to be fought over. I want to play so well that teams will be busting their guts to get me.

And then I can finally start the life I've been working toward since I was a kid.

Spinning around, I head down the concrete steps and spot a familiar figure walking thirty yards ahead of me. She has a stack of books clutched against her side, and her short legs are moving with purpose. I can tell it's Tutor Girl immediately—that pleated skirt and cardigan? Yeah, no one else her age would be seen wearing that in this place.

She's obviously lost in thought and hasn't noticed me staring at her.

I should call out, grab her attention... apologize for being such a douchebag this morning.

Shit. I actually yelled at her.

I never yell at people, especially not girls.

With a resigned sigh, I pick up my pace and am about to call her name when I'm stopped by two friendly faces.

"Wily Wilson," Ethan greets me like he always does. I give him my usual half hug, then bump Liam's fist with my own.

"How are you guys?" I smile.

"Yeah, good. Season's going well. Missing some of the senior players, you know how it is."

"Baxter, man." Liam shakes his head. "I didn't realize how good he was. Now that he's not playing, we're noticing big-time."

I nod, totally understanding that feeling.

Ethan lightly slaps my arm. "You'll be missed at the end of this year. Shit, man, semifinal playoffs. That's fucking epic."

Grinning, I nod some more and agree with everything they're saying, my eyes darting past them and noticing that Elizabeth Satchwell has disappeared around the corner the same way that Jade chick did.

Looks like I won't be apologizing just yet.

You have her number. Call it.

The phone in my back pocket feels like it's burning, and I start losing focus as Ethan and Liam keep chatting.

Do I actually want to apologize to Tutor Girl?

Maybe I should just leave it. She probably never wants to speak to me again anyway.

"So, what time's your bus leaving?"

I blink, pulled back into focus by the question. "This afternoon. We'll get there a day early. It'll give us a chance to really prep for the game."

"Well, good luck, man." Liam holds out his hand, and I give it a quick shake before slapping Ethan's palm and waving goodbye.

The hockey players saunter off, and I pull out my

phone, tapping my screen with my thumbs and impulsively sending a short text.

Tutor Girl: Sorry for yelling at you.

She doesn't respond. I even stand there waiting, but I get nothing back. Who knows if she's read the text or not. She obviously doesn't own an iPhone, so I can't even tell. Waiting another beat, I stare at my screen, then give up with a huff and head to my next class. Thank God it's the last one of the day; then I can go back home and prep for the one thing I've been put on this planet to do...

Play football.

CHAPTER 8
ELIZABETH

I keep pulling out my phone and looking at Wily's text.

I'm not sure why I haven't responded. I should at least give him a thumbs-up to acknowledge it, right?

But... that seems lame, and I don't know what to say to him.

And if I do respond, will he then reply back? And then I'll get caught in some conversation with a person I don't particularly want to see again.

Biting my lip, I glance at my computer screen. For some bizarre reason, I'm watching the semifinal football game.

Yeah, I know. I don't even like sports, but the whole school is buzzing over this game, and I don't want to be completely clueless when I hear them talking about it in class.

That's what I keep telling myself, anyway.

My eyes dart to Wily. He's standing on the sidelines, waiting for his turn at offense again. His red-and-blue uniform is smeared with mud, and the team looks absolutely exhausted.

"Nolan U is fighting hard for this win," the commentator says.

The camera flashes along the front of the offensive line as they wait for their turn on the field. They all seem oblivious to the fact that they're being filmed, their expressions tense and focused.

"Wily Wilson, the guard to watch. He's having a killer game tonight."

"He sure is, Reggie. He's got a high chance of getting drafted for next season, and any NFL team would be lucky to have him."

I swallow, trying to focus back on the book I'm reading. Flicking the next page, my eyes glide over the text. I've read it before, but it's been a while, and I'm slowly getting back into the story. I remember liking it in high school.

Shuffling on my bed, I curl my legs up, my eyes darting back to the screen as the offensive line run onto the grass and get themselves set up.

I guess it is a big deal that the Cougars have made it this far. They only just made the playoffs last year and were out after the first game. If they win this one, they'll be going to the finals. That's epic.

Trying to get into the school spirit, I watch the play, not fully understanding everything they're doing, although the quarterback just threw a sweet pass that the commentators are going gaga over. Someone down the other end of the field catches it, and the crowd is going nuts as a swarm of players head in that direction.

My eyebrows dip as I closely watch the screen,

wondering if that guy will make it to the end zone. But he gets taken down, and they have to reset.

Geez, football takes forever.

Going back to my book, I try to finish the chapter, but I keep getting distracted between the commentary... and the look on Wily's face when he was yelling at me.

He wasn't mad.

I mean, he *was* mad... but he seemed more desperate than angry. He was frustrated.

"He thinks he's dumb," I whisper, hating that idea.

Wily Wilson is a legend at this school. Now that he's on my radar, I hear his name come up all the time. Everybody loves him. He's popular, funny, kind. I haven't heard a bad word spoken about him.

How can a guy that confident think he's stupid?

"I should have helped him." I pick up my phone again, unlocking the screen and rereading his text.

And I keep doing that all freaking weekend.

The Nolan U Cougars won their semifinal game, so the school was in party mode on Friday night... and Saturday night. The common room at the end of the hall thumped with music. Laughter and cheerfully raised voices kept me awake as I lay in bed staring at the ceiling. I could have gone down and checked it out. Everyone was invited. But just the thought of that sent a cold chill sweeping through me. Parties like that are a minefield, a danger zone. Definitely not the place for me.

I can only imagine what the team got up to. Images of beer and sinfully good-looking people dancing and sharing drunken kisses—and probably more—have been filling my brain all weekend. Heat has been flushing through me followed by spine-shaking shudders. Those kinds of things are so not my scene. But Wily will no doubt have been in the thick of it, celebrating with the best of them.

And what have I been doing?

Hiding out in my room and trying to find the courage to follow through on an idea I just can't let go.

So, come Monday, after my morning walk and coffee, I collect my stuff and head for Professor Pilscher's office. Thankfully he's there, so I don't have a chance to lose my nerve when he replies, "Enter," after my knock.

Easing the door open, I shuffle inside and force a smile. "Good morning, Professor Pilscher."

"Ah, Elizabeth Satchwell. How are you?"

I let out a soft, surprised laugh. I can't believe he remembers my name! I had him for one semester last year. Although, I'm grateful I left an impression, because I'm about to ask a really big favor.

"I'm good, sir." I swallow and shuffle a little closer to his desk.

He looks up, all expectant and curious. "What can I do for you today?"

"Well, um..."

"You're not taking any literature classes this semester, are you?"

"No, I finished up Comparative Literature just before the winter break."

"And I'm sure you did very well." He smiles, and I can't help blushing.

I nod and softly murmur, "A+."

"No surprises there."

I smile at his compliment, brushing it off with a small flick of my hand before playing with my bottom lip.

"So... what is it you need from me, then?"

"Well, sir, um... last semester, you had Wily Wilson in your class."

The man sits back with a sigh, his eyes rolling.

I bite my lips together, nerves rocketing through me as I force myself to continue. "The thing is, he told me that his final assignment is ungradable, and I was—"

"He cheated. He used AI and obviously hadn't read the book. I refuse to grade utter nonsense."

"I understand that, sir. And you shouldn't have to," I agree. "But see, I was supposed to help him with that assignment. I'm his new tutor, and with the Christmas break and everything, I ran out of time to assist him."

Professor Pilscher's eyes narrow. "Do you mean you ran out of time to do the work for him?"

My eyes bulge. "No, sir. I would never do that. I'm not that kind of tutor. I believe strongly that people need to learn and produce their own work. I just didn't have the time I wanted to be able to assist him properly, and he'd left it so late that I just... I hung him out to dry." I wince.

The English professor's expression is deadpan as he threads his fingers together. "That is *his* problem, not yours. He should have been more organized."

"Yes, but he lost his previous tutor and was struggling to find a new one, and I could have helped him, you know? I could have made the time, but I... I didn't. And I'm feeling kind of bad about that."

Clearing his throat, Professor Pilscher taps his hands lightly on his desk. "So, what are you wanting from me?"

"An extension?" My face crumples, my tone going wispy as I ask the impossible.

He shakes his head. "I already gave him one, and he chose to waste it. I'm not repeating that mistake."

"Please, sir. I'll make sure he's organized this time."

He huffs and gives me a stern frown. "Why are you doing this?"

"Because..." My right shoulder rises as I scramble for the right words. "Because he wants to graduate. And he can't do that unless he passes your class."

"And all the courses this semester."

"I can help him with that."

The man's face buckles. "I don't even know why you want to. He doesn't want to be here. He looks so bored in class, it's obvious he's not listening."

"Because he doesn't always understand what he's hearing. It's hard to concentrate when you feel completely lost."

He clenches his jaw, and I hold my breath, studying that ticking muscle on his face. He shuffles forward, resting his forearms on his desk and grumbling, "The NFL will probably draft him anyway."

"That's not the point." I take another step forward and have to wonder why I'm fighting for this football player. I must be out of my mind. "Sir, he deserves to graduate. He's spent four years—"

"Not doing his own work, by the looks of things."

"He'll do this assignment. I promise you." Threading my fingers together, I hold them up by my chin. "Please, just give him a chance."

The professor sighs, mumbling something about irritating jocks.

I press my lips together, squashing my smile.

He's right. Jocks are irritating, yet I'm going to bat for this one.

Why does that feel good?

And why do I want to clap my hands and celebrate when Professor Pilscher finally says, "Fine. You have until the end of the week."

"And the weekend?" I cross my fingers. "Please, let him have until Monday. That's still only five days, and he's gonna need every one of them."

The professor snickers and gives me a hard look. "8 a.m. Friday. It better be on this desk."

I deflate just a little. That timeframe is so tight!

But I'll take what I can get.

With a nod, I say, "It will be, sir. Thanks for... giving him a chance."

"Don't make me regret it." He points at me, then indicates the door behind me.

I bob a curtsy, because I'm weird that way, before spinning out the door with an elated smile.

Why?

Why am I so elated?

I shouldn't be triumphant. I've just sentenced myself to a week of high stress while I try to tutor this giant who doesn't think he's smart enough to get it.

Because you're going to prove to him that he is. And that part will feel amazing.

With a nervous titter, I tuck myself against the corridor wall and pull out my phone.

Bringing up Wily's number, I stare at it, chewing on my lip before pressing the green Call button and instantly wondering why I didn't just text.

What the hell is wrong with me?

Nobody calls people anymore.

But if I hang up now, he'll see a missed call from me, and then I'll have to bumble my way through a text message explanation and—

"Hello?" His deep voice fills my ear, and an involuntary shiver runs through me. It's not one of those creepy shudders, though. It's warm and feels almost... nice.

What the hell is happening to me?

I should not be doing this.

Hang up!

Or freaking say something!

I open my mouth to respond... and nothing comes out.

CHAPTER 9
WILY

"Hello?" I say again, wondering if I'm getting a butt dial, then tipping my head as I try to picture Elizabeth Satchwell's butt.

The two times I've seen her, she's been wearing skirts or a long sweater that covers her ass, but I bet she's got a classy bubble butt. That girl's got some curves on her. I checked her out in the library—as I do every girl I ever meet. Okay, probably sleazy, but I can't help myself. I love women. They're beautiful, and if I were a praying man, I'd thank God every day for putting them on this planet.

From what I can tell, Tutor Girl has some luscious tits under that cardigan of hers. I bet she's an E, maybe even an F or a G. Holy shit. Have I dated a girl with tits that big before?

Why the fuck are you thinking about her tits?

Snapping my eyes shut, I rub my forehead and try one last time before hanging up. "Hello?"

"Uh... hi. It's, um... it's Elizabeth... Satchwell."

I grin, finding her awkwardness kinda cute. "Hey, Satch. How's it going?"

"It's Elizab—never mind." She sighs, and I can't help a soft snicker.

Why's she calling me?

Is she finally responding to my lame-ass apology?

I pick up the soft fabric ball from the stack beside me and launch it over the sofa when Zoey yells at me from behind the beanbag. "Ting! Ting! Wywee!"

I have no idea what she thinks these balls represent, but she wanted to play Cowboys and Cowgirls and obviously figured that the ol' west was all about throwing balls at each other and shouting random words like "Pip! Pip!" "Bop! Bop!" and "Ting! Ting!"

It's fucking hilarious.

"Foo! Foo!" New syllables are shouted back at me, and another ball lands near the couch and rolls past my leg.

"So, I—" Satch starts to say, then abruptly stops. "What was that? Are you busy?"

"Ahhh, yep. I'm currently in the middle of a very important game of Cowboys and Cowgirls."

"What?"

"I'm playing Cowboys and Cowgirls with Zoey."

"Who's Zoey?"

"Well..." I roll around the couch, throwing another ball while Zoey squeals and sends a sparkly pink pom-pom my way. When did she add that to her arsenal? "I like to call her my goddaughter, even though she's technically not."

"O-kay."

"She's one of my teammate's daughters."

There's a pause as I crawl on my hands and knees around the armchair to better position myself.

"Your teammate has a daughter?"

"Yep. Zander Donohue. The quarterback. You know him?"

"No."

"Okay, well, he's a daddy, and we live in the same place..." I wait until Zoey appears, then let out a roar and grab her around the middle. Peals of laughter fill the room as I swing her around before plunking onto the floor with her in my lap. "I get to play with this little cowgirl when I'm home."

"Shouldn't you be in class right now?"

I frown, pulling the phone away from my face so I can check the time. "Oh shit."

"Oh sit!" Zoey yells, raising her arms in the air while I press a finger to my lips and try to get her to shut up.

"Don't say that, Zo-Zo," I whisper, then wince. "So, yeah... I'm supposed to be in class right now. I didn't realize it was so late. Coach gave us the day off after our epic win."

"Yeah, I saw—I mean... I heard that you guys won. Congratulations."

"Thanks." I grin, tickling Zoey's tummy and figuring I've already missed half the class, so there's no point rushing to get there.

"Well, are you, um... free later on today? I don't want to encroach on any of your class time, and I have a class starting in about thirty minutes, but I'm available later this afternoon." She sucks in a quick breath like she's nervous or something. "Will you be... free?"

My lips twitch before growing into a surprised smile. "Are you asking me out?"

I was seriously not expecting that. I thought she'd hate me after the way I yelled at her.

"No!" she gasps and then splutters, "I'm not... I don't date... I mean, why would I be asking you out?"

O-kay, so she's not flirting with me, then. Weird. Most girls do. I'm not being arrogant; it's just a fact.

"Wily?" Her voice pitches, and she sounds near panicked now. "Why would you ask me if I'm asking *you* out?"

My shoulder hitches when I finally respond to her. "You wanted to know when I was free. I just assumed—"

"For a tutoring session! I want to know if you're free for *tutoring*."

I can't help a gruff laugh. "I thought you didn't want to tutor me."

Zoey starts playing with the ties of my hoodie, pulling the string all the way down on one side. I throw her a baleful look, and she giggles, pulling on the other side until it's scrunched tight around the back of my neck.

"Well, I... I guess I felt kind of bad about bailing on you, so I went and spoke to Professor Pilscher, and he's agreed to let you resubmit your assignment. You have until Friday, and if I'm going to help you, then we really need to get started as soon as possible."

It takes me a second to register what she's saying.

She did what?

"Pay, pay, pay!" Zoey starts jumping on my lap, and I quickly still her, staring at the wall and kind of reeling.

"You went and saw Pilscher? For me?"

"Well, yeah. I mean... I can tell how much you want to

graduate, and I really think you're capable of doing it. So, if you're willing to work with me, I can help you write that *Moby Dick* essay."

"Are you serious?" My words are a breathy whisper now. I can't believe this.

"Yes. I mean, I'm not going to do the assignment for you, but I can help you plan out the essay, and we'll write it together. I'll make sure the work is mostly your thoughts and ideas. I can just help you with some of the wording. I promised the professor it will be *your* work. But I'll walk you through it, you know? I reread the book over the weekend to refresh my memory and—"

"Wait, you reread the book?"

She hesitates before responding with a confused "Yeah?" like it's the most obvious thing she would have spent her weekend doing.

I shake my head, still trying to wrap my brain around this while also keeping Zoey still on my knee. She's bouncing like a basketball, giggling and trying to get my attention back. But it's not going to happen, because I have to know...

"Why?" I rasp.

Satch sighs. "I don't know, to be honest. I guess I just couldn't get that look on your face out of my head. You weren't angry with me the other day, you were frustrated that you might not be able to graduate. And I want to help you do that. But only if you're willing to put in the work."

Holy shit.

I don't know if anyone has ever seen me that way before.

"Zoey! Where are you, kiddo?" Sienna's voice wafts down the hallway.

Zoey jumps up, running around the couch with a fabric ball in each hand shouting, "Ting, ting, Mommy!" as she throws her "weapons."

"Bop! Bop!" Sienna laughs back, batting them away before grabbing Zoey around the waist and hoisting her up. "Time to get ready for playgroup."

Zoey gasps. "Dayton?"

"That's right."

The little girl claps her hands, then waves goodbye to me, blowing me kisses. I catch one, then blow another back, and her giggles disappear down the hallway.

"So, Wily, are you... willing to put in the work?" Satch asks, tone all serious.

I swallow, running a hand through my hair.

How can I say no?

She spent her weekend reading a boring-ass book for me. She went and saw a grumpy-ass professor for me.

I can't reject that kind of effort.

So, as much I really don't want to work on another fucking essay about white whales and whatever other shit went down, I find myself saying, "Yeah. I'll do it."

"Okay, then." Her voice brightens. "What time are you free to meet?"

"Since I don't have practice this afternoon, I guess I'll have to say today."

"Cool. And do you want to meet in the library or...? We just need a space that's distraction-free, so wherever that is for you."

Distraction-free. I brush a finger across my bottom lip. "My room will work. It'll be quiet, and no one will be walking past the table trying to talk to me. It should be distraction-free, unless Zoey's on the loose and doesn't mind breaking the rules." I laugh.

"Your... room?" she squeaks. "Uh... okay. So, you're not in a dorm, I'm guessing."

"No, I'm at Football Frat."

"Football what?"

"You haven't heard of...?" *Seriously? Has she been living under a rock?*

"Foobawl!" Zoey shouts as she runs down the hallway, pulling on her winter coat. "Foooobawl."

"Sorry," Sienna murmurs, chasing her into the living area. "Have you seen her beanie?"

I look around, helping Sienna out, who is obviously running late. Lifting up the beanbag, we unearth Zoey's hat and mittens.

"Thank you." Sienna smiles, racing after Zoey, who runs into the dining room still shouting, "Fooooobawl!"

"Who was that?"

"That was Zoey's mother, Sienna. She lives at Football Frat too. Although, they're in the detached garage, so it's like they half live here. Kinda." I tip my head and grin.

"Okay, then." Satch lets out a nervous chuckle.

Satch. Yeah, I like that for her.

Satch, the tutor girl.

Satch, the one who's gonna save my ass.

CHAPTER 10
ELIZABETH

To say that I'm nervous is the understatement of the decade.

I'm about to walk into a den of lions.

I mean, jocks.

That's gotta be worse than lions, right?

Why the hell did I agree to this? I was second-guessing myself the entire way in the Uber. I should have just walked, to be honest; it's not that far, and I do love to get out in the fresh air, even when it's cold. The sting of winter on my face is always so invigorating.

If I'd known it was so close, I wouldn't have caught an Uber so soon. Now I'm stupidly early.

Closing the car door, I wave goodbye to the driver and hover on the sidewalk.

Do I go in now?

Or maybe I should walk the block a couple of times first.

Or maybe—

"Satch! You made it!" I glance up and spot Wily

waving at me from a window on the second floor. He has a towel draped around his neck. His smile is wide, his blond hair wet and mussed. "I thought we were meeting at four?"

"Oh, yeah, I..." I point to my wrist, then shake my head. "I didn't realize Football Frat was so close to campus."

"Right on its doorstep." He grins and flicks his hand at me. "Come on up."

I point toward the front door. "So, you just want me to..."

"Yeah, let yourself in." His head disappears back inside, and I release a shaky breath.

"You can do this," I murmur under my breath, my legs practically shaking as I walk up the front steps and imagine what awaits me inside.

I bet a bunch of super-cool, super-hot football players are lounging around in there, all relaxed and completely unaware of how intimidating they all are. I'm gonna be the injured gazelle struggling to keep up with the herd, and every head in this pride of footballers will snap my way as soon as I walk through the front door. Then they'll all be thinking about how fast they can devour me.

Would you stop, please? They're not going to eat you.

And Wily's nice. You don't have anything to worry about.

The thought calms me a little, but I'm still not convinced and lose the courage to "let myself in." Instead, I knock once and nearly flinch when the door opens immediately and a tall Black man gazes down at me.

I take a quick step back and blink up at him.

"Can I help you?" His voice is deep and rumbly.

Oh shit, this is terrifying.

Tugging on the edges of my skirt, I swallow and try to smile up at him. "I'm looking for Wily Wilson?" My voice comes out as a soft squeak, and I hate that I'm not more confident.

But this one looks mean.

His face is so serious and he's *really tall*, and I can see his huge biceps and pecs. The fitted T-shirt he's wearing hides nothing, and—

"Hey, Ty, is that my tutor girl?" Wily calls down the stairs.

"Uh, yeah, I think so," the man replies over his shoulder, looking me over. "A shorty with cute brown hair and big hazel eyes?"

"That's the one. Send her up."

I blink. No one has ever referred to me that way before.

Cute?

I'm not cute.

People never call me that.

I flush, not sure where to look as he steps aside to let me pass.

Keeping my eyes to the floor, I try not to breathe as I shuffle through the front door and make a beeline for the stairs.

"Second door on your right," Ty's voice rumbles behind me as I trip on the first step. "You okay?"

"Yep, I'm good. Thank you." My cheeks flame and I pick up my pace, scrambling up the stairs and only tripping again on the second-to-top one.

Holy crap! I must look like such a moron!

But when I glance back down, Ty isn't standing there watching me, frowning at me or laughing. He's just gone.

I blink, unused to this kind of behavior.

What is this strange place?

I figured I'd be swamped with curious gazes and sneering looks, snide comments and intimidating glares, but... the house seems quiet, calm almost.

A door opens across the hall from me, and I turn with a gasp, blinking when a guy with dirty blond hair strolls out of the bathroom, a towel slung over his shoulder. He's shirtless and looks like the embodiment of Adonis. I can see every curve and ridge of his torso. He's just skin and muscle, and the towel wrapped around his waist is hanging so low I can see the top of that triangle thing that leads down to his—

Oh my gosh, would you look away already!

But I can't.

I've never seen anything like him before!

He jerks to a stop, giving me a curious frown, his eyes narrowing like he recognizes me or something. And then he starts walking right toward me.

Why? Why is he approaching?

I tense.

Does he know me? What's he about to say? What's he about to do!

I scramble to speak before he can tease or touch me.

"Wily's room?" I squeak.

His lips twitch when he stops, eyeing me up one more time before pointing over my shoulder.

Whipping around, I spot the two doors and immediately notice a big sign on the left one.

King Wily. Ruler of the northern realm. Curtsy upon entry.

"King Wily?" I whisper under my breath.

A soft snicker makes me flinch, the guy mumbling, "He was playing princesses with Zoey yesterday. You don't have to curtsy."

"Oh, o-okay. Thank you." I try to smile, my palms sweating as I grip my laptop bag and inch toward the door.

It's kind of cute that Wily plays with that little girl. That should help me relax. He's great with kids. That's the sign of a good, safe, nonthreatening person, right?

At least it should be.

I tentatively approach the door. Reading the sign one more time, my smile grows as I remind myself that mean, horrible jocks don't play princesses with their not-technically goddaughters.

Raising my hand, I go to knock, but the door opens and a plume of delicious-smelling deodorant hits my nostrils before my eyes take in what can only be described as... *gloriousness.*

Another shirtless man assaults my senses, but this one is bigger, broader, more mouthwatering somehow.

Wily is standing in his doorway in nothing but a pair of sweats. His chest is sculpted porcelain beauty. I can see the definition of his muscly torso, branching out into two solid arms that are all power. Glimpsing the crop of hair under his armpit, I then can't stop myself from tracking down the rest of his body to that sexy triangle that disappears into his low-lying waistband.

Seriously, another one?

This day is gonna kill me.

Pull yourself together, girl! They're just bodies.

Yeah, but this one is way hotter than the last guy, and he was Adonis!

I don't even know who to compare Wily to. Hercules, maybe? Thor? He is blond. Grow those locks down to his shoulders and yep, he's Thor.

"Come in." He walks into the room, and I'm introduced to his back muscles, which are just as impressive as the front ones. He's so long and broad and—

Stop looking!

I turn away, taking in his room while he talks to me.

It's a bit of a mess, clothes strewn all over the place, shoes haphazardly dumped on the floor. Empty water bottles litter the area around his trash can, and there's a damp towel bunched at the end of his king-sized bed. Which is unmade.

I sniff the air again, the dissipating deodorant making way for the underlying man smell. It's ripe and real, wafting up my nostrils when I get too close to his stinky laundry hamper.

Okay, then.

Biting my lips together, I pick my way through the chaos and come to an awkward stop by his desk, which is covered in books, papers, protein bar wrappers, and empty Gatorade bottles. I'm guessing he doesn't use it very often. Glancing over my shoulder, I spot the large TV and PlayStation console, noticing the cacophony of remotes and wires.

Oh boy.

Looking back at his desk, I move forward and collect the trash, clearing off the space.

Yeah, this desk is a poor, forgotten feature in this room. I can't imagine it gets a lot of lovin'.

Time to change that.

With a determined nod, I pull out his desk chair only to find his laptop sitting on it.

"Sorry about the mess." Wily clears the rest of the desk and helps me set up for our first official study session.

By the time I take a seat, my frazzled nerves are starting to settle as I get my head in the right space and figure out the best way to help this Nordic god smiling down at me.

It helps that he's now wearing a shirt.

I can do this.

My heart may be racing every time my eyes skim any part of his body, but I'm a sensible woman. I can handle my attraction because I am not interested, nor will I *ever* be interested, in falling for some jock.

Even if he does look like Thor and smell like pure addiction.

CHAPTER 11
WILY

Tucking a lock of wet hair behind my ear, I walk over to the door, steeling myself for what's to come. I fucking hate studying, and that look on Satch's face is so unreadable. It's obvious the mess in my room is too much for her, but I don't even notice it.

I've always been a bit of a slob, but our housekeeper came three times a week back home, so it wasn't too much of a problem. She kept things under control. But I don't have one of those here, so my room gets a little out of hand sometimes.

All the time.

About once every six weeks or so, it all gets too much for Grady, and he yells at me until we can find the floor and then makes me vacuum and dust this entire space. I hate it, but I kind of need him to keep me in check, so I try not to let my anger show.

I'm good at keeping my emotions even—most of the time. I'm not a naturally angry guy. Not much bothers me, which is why my yell-fest at Satch was so surprising. I should probably apologize again.

Grabbing the door handle, I go to swing my door shut. "Hey, about the other day—"

"Can you leave your door open, please?" Her voice is soft, and I glance across the room, surprised by the comment.

"Excuse me?"

"The door. I'd prefer you to leave it open." She bites her lip, her round face flushing pink before she dips her chin and starts squeezing her index finger.

"O...kay." I can't help a confused frown. I thought she wanted a distraction-free study session.

Oh wait. Oh shit. Does she think I'm gonna make some kind of move on her?

"You don't have to worry." I walk away from the door. "I know this is a study session. I'm not gonna jump your bones or anything. Even though you did try to ask me out."

She looks up with a gasp, and I wink at her when her cheeks flush an even darker red. "I did not try to—"

"I'm only teasing," I cut her off before she gets all flustered on me.

I take a seat with an easy grin, my eyes drifting down her body. She's wearing a pleated skirt again. It looks homemade, and I wonder where she gets her clothes from. Maybe she's really into sewing. Or maybe she shops at some kind of 1950s memorabilia store, because that shirt and cardigan combo looks like something my grandmother used to wear.

She squirms in her seat, tugging on her clothes, and

it's only then that I realize I must be making her uncomfortable.

I try for a smile, hoping to put her at ease, but her eyebrows dip into a soft frown and she clears her throat, pulling out a copy of *Moby Dick* along with her laptop and some handwritten notes.

Oh shit. Here we go.

Be grateful, dude. You might be able to graduate after all. Play this nice and don't fuck it up.

"So, uh..." I clear my throat. "Thanks for helping me with this."

"That's okay." Her voice is soft and sweet as she arranges her stuff.

I watch her fingers move as she opens her pencil case and carefully pulls out a pen, placing the cap on the end of it. She brushes her palm over a fresh sheet of paper before glancing at me, then picks up her notes.

Clearing my throat, I try to explain. "I only took this class because I thought it'd be easy, but it's kicked my ass... just like everything else has."

"You're smart enough to pass this class," she murmurs, reading over her notes.

I snicker and shake my head. "No, but—"

"Yes." She turns to give me a firm look. "Everybody can learn, Wily. You included. We just need to discover the way that you learn best."

I blink at her, wanting to argue some more, but she starts talking before I can.

"Now, you're obviously a physical person because you're very good at sports, so I'm guessing the best way for you to learn is through hands-on things, which is why you probably excel in classes like PE, metalwork, shop, things like that."

"Yeah." I nod.

"And reading a book is challenging for you? I'm guessing you prefer graphic novels or movies, stuff where there's more action and less words?"

I nod again, my chair squeaking when I shift on it.

"So, a book like *Moby Dick* is a really hard task, and you shouldn't be beating yourself up over not being able to manage it easily." Her lips twitch. "Although, I get the sense that you didn't try to manage any of it at all."

My laugh is husky and self-deprecating.

"But if you want to graduate, you're just gonna have to get over it and work with me." Digging into her bag, she pulls out a plastic fidget toy. "You take this." She places it in my palm, and my fingers immediately start flicking the switches on the cube, my thumb spinning the dial before I flip it over and see what else is on this thing.

While I'm messing around, she goes on to tell me all about *Moby Dick*.

Holding the book in her hands, she thumbs through the pages and describes the basic storyline. But she doesn't use any of the language from the book—I can tell because she's throwing out modern-day words that actually make sense to me, and by the time she's done, I think I actually fucking understand the story.

"What?" I whisper when she gets to the end. "They all died?"

"Except for Ishmael."

"But wait..." I shake my head. "That jackass Ahab destroyed everything over a whale?"

"Mm-hmm." She smiles at me, her head bobbing.

"So, based on that..." Her eyes sparkle with enthusiasm. "Which character do you think we should study?"

"It's got be the Ahab guy. Holy fuck. I mean, he was obsessed. He was treating that whale like some ex-lover who burned him and took everything he had."

Her lips twitch like she's pleased with what I just said. "Well, Moby took his leg, so he was pretty pissed off about it."

I run a hand through my hair. It's dry now, so it flops right back over my forehead as I lean forward in my chair, tapping the fidget toy on the edge of my desk.

"What can you tell me about him as a person?" Satch asks me. "What kind of man was he?"

"I think he was seriously fucked in the head," I answer quickly. "I mean, from what you've said, he let that whale dominate his life. What started out as simple revenge turned into a destructive nightmare."

"Do you think he was a good captain?"

"Hell no." I shake my head, thinking of our team captains and how they'd never lead us down some treacherous path like that. Coach Jones would kill their asses if they let personal vendettas get in the way of the game.

"So, then... what lessons can we learn from what he went through? Is there anything or anyone in your life that you can think of who might have destroyed something good because of anger or revenge? What can you take from the story that we could apply to society today? I mean, whale hunting is a big no-no, right? But are there any examples you can think of where people have taken payback a little too far? And how do we stop that from happening again?"

I blink at her, my brain scrambling to come up with something good. Because I want to be good for this girl. I don't even know why, but every time I've answered her, she gives me this barely there smile or her lips twitch, like she likes what I'm saying. I want to see that look again. It's driving me to think and come up with answers that are good enough.

"Sorry." She winces. "That's a lot of questions. Let's take it one at a time." Angling her pad, she writes down the first question, then gives me an expectant look. "What can we learn from Captain Ahab?"

I blow out a breath. "That trying to kill white sperm whales is a really bad idea."

She giggles and taps her pen on my knee. "Professor Pilscher is looking for relatable human experience, so try and think about something in your life that you can apply it to. Like..." Her lips twitch again. "Like football. That's your passion, right?"

"Yeah." I sit up a little straight, that one word giving me a small confidence boost. I can talk football all damn day.

"Okay, so let's pretend that another player did something bad—like an illegal play—and you were injured because of it."

"Don't even say that," I mumble.

She giggles again. It's a cute sound. "We're just pretending. Now, how would you feel?"

"If I couldn't play anymore?"

"Yeah."

"Like my life is over."

Her eyebrows wrinkle. My answer obviously makes her sad or maybe confuses her, but she doesn't say anything, just nods and keeps going. "And if a particular person was responsible for... destroying your life that way, what would you want to do about it?"

I raise my eyebrows at her. "What would I *want* to do, or what *should* I do?"

"Exactly," she whispers, her eyes lighting with a bright smile. "You've got the makings of a great essay here, Wily. We're going to pretend that Ahab is an injured football player, and we're going to imagine how he could have messed up his life by being obsessed with revenge against the person who hurt him. And then we're going to compare it to how a successful person can overcome their grief and ultimately triumph. It'd be great if we could find some real-life examples from your history—either from your own experiences with football or maybe a player you've looked up to and admired."

I sit back, my lips parting as I stare at her.

"Sound good?"

"Sounds... doable."

And there goes her smile, stretching full and wide across her round face, and making me feel like a million fucking bucks.

CHAPTER 12
ELIZABETH

I'm really proud of Wily.

By the time our tutoring session wrapped up, he looked like he actually *wanted* to work on the essay with me. The fidget toy I gave him seemed to help, and I'm glad I'd spent some time researching strategies for supporting reluctant learners.

Fidget toys popped up a few times, and I figured it was worth a shot. I'm so relieved, because I do think it helped him focus. His hands were busy the whole session, yet his brain was engaged with me and what I was trying to draw out of him.

I'm so stoked that the answers he came up with were actually his own. He's seriously not stupid. He just needs to be asked the right questions.

And it led to some great discussions. I ended up staying way longer than I meant to, and time disappeared as Ahab was set aside so Wily could explain the rules of football to me. There are a *lot*, and I struggled to follow all of them. It's a complex game for someone who hasn't grown up watching it, but he was patient, answering all my questions and obviously happy that I seemed interested. He drew me pictures and diagrams, enthusiasm bubbling out of him. I'm not sure he was even aware of how much brighter his tone was, how much faster his words came as he explained the game to me.

His joy.

His passion.

It was a pleasure to watch, and my brain is already ticking over with ways I can use football to make this essay as easy for him as possible.

Just before I left, we set up another tutoring session for this afternoon.

And here I am, sitting in the library feeling all proud of Wily Wilson again.

We're tucked away in a back corner where no one can see us, and Wily is telling me in a whisper-soft voice why he thinks Captain Ahab behaved the way he did. Seriously, the guy is going way deeper than I thought he would, and I'm typing down his words, desperately trying to keep up with him.

This essay is going to need a lot of editing, and we'll have to ditch some of this stuff, but I'm loving this brain dump. Wily has got some great ideas here, and I'll definitely be able to help him shape them.

I have half a mind to ask Professor Pilscher if Wily can present his essay orally. He's so much stronger that way, but I've already asked the man for this big favor, and I don't want to push it. The professor is old-school, and although other teachers are open to creative ways of assessment, I highly doubt Pilscher will be.

"Okay." I save the document so far and check my

notes for the next question I think he should answer. It'd be great if we could tie in that football story he told me, about how he got tripped up in his first flag football game when he was five years old. He spent the rest of the time trying to get the kid back and ended up with two penalties and missing out on several scoring opportunities. Afterward, his coach told him off for focusing on the wrong thing.

It kind of backs up the whole point, doesn't it? We can deal with slights against us in a healthy, positive way, or we can make it worse for everyone and get all pissed off and vengeful. If Wily had just left it and gotten over himself, he could have potentially helped win the game for his team. Instead, they lost, and that kid who tripped him got a double-win.

Sure, that seems unfair sometimes, but my parents always taught me that de-escalating conflict by shaking off the other person's bad behavior is always the safest bet. Which is what I do.

Although, I'm not about to go into *my* history with this man beside me. Let's just focus on him and the lessons he had to learn growing up.

"Okay, so, with this flag football story..." My words trail off as I skim my handwritten notes. And then my stomach lets out this totally humiliating growl.

Slapping my hand over it, I bulge my eyes and pray that Wily didn't notice.

A soft snicker pops out of his mouth, and I curl my shoulders.

Shit! This is so embarrassing!

"I guess it is getting kind of late. Have you had dinner yet?"

I shake my head. I'd been nervous-snacking up to about ten minutes before I was due to meet him, and since arriving at the library, time has flown. He's so easy to talk to that it took us about forty minutes to even start working on his essay. All he did was ask me how my day was, and I made one little comment about my linguistics class, which led into a story about one of his freshman professors, which made me laugh. He's too easy to listen to, and I swear I was trying to get on with the essay the whole time, but he kept on saying things that I couldn't *not* respond to, and yeah... we started late, and now it's late and he's probably hungry too.

He came straight from practice, slurping on a protein shake, but now he's looking at his phone and saying, "Let's go get something to eat. Bring your stuff. We can work at the diner."

"You sure?" My face scrunches with uncertainty.

"Yeah, absolutely. It's on me. A little thank-you for helping me out."

"You don't have to do that. You already pay me for these sessions. I can just—"

"Satch." He gives me a kind smile, his blue gaze mesmerizing. "Let me buy you dinner."

I can feel my face flushing again and give him an edgy smile.

"Come on. I know this great place." He pops out of his seat, helping me to gather up my stuff and talking about Eat Your Faves. I've heard of it but never eaten there before. I think it's quite popular with Nolan U students, which is why I've avoided it. I force myself to shuffle after Wily, giving him a polite smile when he steps aside to let me go first down the stairs.

Clunking down to the bottom, I keep my chin tucked in and nearly bang into a table, but he snatches my arm and quickly pulls me to the left. I narrowly avoid scraping my hip on the corner and bite my bottom lip before murmuring a soft "Thank you."

"No problem." His voice is cheerful, but I quickly check his face to make sure he's not laughing at me.

He's not.

I frown, still trying to figure this jock out.

Saying hi to a few people we pass, he waves and lifts his chin as we head for the exit. We pass through the sliding doors together and pop out into the cold night air. It's crisp and beautiful. I shove my hands into my pockets and move into step behind him, but he pauses and waits for me, obviously wanting to walk side by side.

Oh man, I'm so not used to this. I don't know what to do with it!

Can't I just follow him? Tuck in behind his building of a body and disappear into his shadow?

Stepping into the parking lot, I wonder which car is his and then am not surprised at all when we stop beside an expensive-looking truck. That's right. He pulled up beside me that morning, and I'm only just remembering.

He said his family was loaded, and I can't help wondering if this truck was a birthday present or something. It's all shiny and looks pretty new. The lock beeps, and he moves to the passenger door and opens it for me.

What? He's opening my door?

I give him an uncertain frown as I shuffle up beside him and wonder how the hell I'm supposed to get into this thing. It's huge! The tires come up to my waist, and I'd have to go on tiptoes to look through the windows.

This is ridiculous. Why do people even need trucks this big?

"Here you go." Wily places his hands on my hips, giving me a little boost.

My breath catches, heat coursing through me as he lifts me like it's no big deal.

He's acting like opening doors and helping short girls into his truck is the most natural thing in the world.

Scrambling into a sitting position and straightening out my skirt, I stare at the dashboard and dare not look at his face while he closes the door.

He must have been raised by a gentleman or had a mother who insisted that he behave like one.

My dad's the nicest guy in the world, but he's not a "hold the door" man. Mom likes to open her own doors.

Me... I've never had the chance to think about it.

I have no idea what kind of woman I am.

As Wily wanders around the front of his truck, glancing toward me with a friendly grin, I hug my bag to my chest and wonder if maybe I do know.

But he's just your tutoring student. He's not opening the door because he's trying to win you over or anything. He's just a gentleman.

I bob my head, reminding myself of that fact when he starts the engine and music blasts through the speakers. I flinch, then laugh when he starts apologizing.

"That's okay. I love The Barenaked Ladies."

"Me too!" He blinks. "Shit, I can't believe you know them."

"Oh yeah. They're amazing." I tap my finger to the beat, then turn to frown at him. "Why wouldn't I know them?"

"I don't know, you just seem—" He pauses, shaking his head.

My insides pinch, but I find myself asking anyway. "I just seem what?"

He smiles. "I haven't been able to figure out what kind of music you're into."

He's not saying something, and now I'm wondering what I did to give him the impression that I wouldn't enjoy a funny, interesting, alternative pop band with intelligent lyrics and entertaining beats.

What kind of music does he think I'm into?

Ugh—maybe I don't want to know the answer to that question.

I hug my laptop a little tighter and murmur, "I'll listen to pretty much anything. I love all music and appreciate all the different genres."

"That's cool." He smiles, and I have to look away because this is awkward.

I don't think he believes me.

And I guess, why would he?

I don't look like the kind of girl who can rap Eminem's "Lose Yourself" word for word, then quickly punch out a show tune followed by the legendary rock anthem "Smells Like Teen Spirit." He'll never know how much I love Nickelback or Beyoncé or Etta James or the Jackson Five. He'll never see my Beach Boys playlist or my Disney Channel Favorites. And he'll never know that my favorite song to belt out in the shower is "Dream a Little Dream of Me" or that I love driving and singing along to country pop like Thomas Rhett and Chase Rice or punk rock by Good Charlotte, Green Day, Marianas Trench, and Busted.

I'm eclectic, okay?

Although my favorite genre, if I really had to pick one, would be music from the '50s and '60s. My parents own a retro diner, and I grew up around that music. They even have an old-school jukebox that they've lovingly maintained, and I know every track on that thing.

But that doesn't mean I'm stuck back in time.

Glancing down at my pleated tartan skirt and thick black stockings, I wonder if people think I am, though.

Shoot. I should have worn something different tonight.

I own one pair of jeans. It's probably worth pulling them out again. I could pair them with—

"Do you like milkshakes?"

"Huh?"

"I know, stupid question. Everybody likes milkshakes. I'm a chocolate guy, and I'm guessing you're a..." He glances at me, his lips curling into a smile. "I'm gonna go strawberry."

My lips twitch, and I hate to correct him, but... my nose wrinkles. "I hate strawberry."

"Damn, I thought I was on the money with that one."

I can't help a grin.

He glances at me, his eyebrow arching. "So, you gonna make me keep guessing?"

"Oh, um, salted caramel is probably my top pick."

"Nice."

"Followed closely by plain ol' vanilla."

"Hey, it's a classic. Nothing wrong with that."

His smile is broad and beautiful, and I catch its full beam as we drive through the well-lit intersection. This strange feeling bubbles in my stomach, and I work to ignore it.

"So, why are we talking about milkshakes?"

"Because we're going to the best diner in town for milkshakes. They're thick and creamy and all things good."

"Are you allowed them, Mr. Football Player?"

"You bet I am." He raises his eyebrows. "Or at least that's what I'm gonna keep telling myself. With the number of calories I burn in training, I can get away with a milkshake or two." His wink is adorable, and I force my gaze away from it.

He makes my cheeks hot.

I don't like it.

Or maybe I kinda do.

My stomach bubbles again, and I try to squash the feeling by talking about Captain Ahab and the types of food his crew probably ate on the *Pequot*.

"Ugh. I hate to think." Wily shakes his head. "Let me just enjoy the fact that we get to eat delicious diner food." He laughs. "Unless you think I should be mentioning his diet in my essay."

"No, you don't... He doesn't... That's probably not relevant."

"Oh good. Because I don't think my brain can handle too much more."

I let out a nervous titter and try to remind him, "You're capable of more than you think."

He doesn't respond, and we're left with BNL tunes. I resist the urge to sing along with "Odds Are"—one of my favorites—and stare out the window until he's pulling into a diner parking lot that makes me think of home.

It's not as retro as our family diner, but the booths and the smells that hit me the second I walk through the door make me pine for Fledgling.

I miss my family so much sometimes.

Thank God they're only forty-five minutes away.

Still. It's not like I'm having dinner with them every night, and sometimes I get hit with the biggest wave of homesickness.

"Table for two." Wily holds up his fingers. "And can we get a booth? We're studying and need to spread out a little."

"Absolutely." The girl smiles at him, her eyes big and flirty.

I glance up at Wily's face, not surprised by the way he's checking her out as she leads us to a booth.

Ugh. Jocks. So freaking typical.

Although Wily has been breaking a lot of my stereotypes, it's a good reminder.

He's still a hot-blooded male who's into sexy woman. And he can probably get any one he wants.

This weird bubbling sensation inside me can just get lost, thank you very much. Wily is a college student who is paying me to tutor him. Nothing more.

Shaking off my winter coat, I then shuffle into the booth and get my laptop set up before I've even looked at a menu. I need to keep this professional, right?

"Here, at least figure out what you're gonna eat first." Wily holds a menu out for me, and I force myself to take it. I give it a quick skim and settle on potato skins and chicken tenders with ranch dressing. Yum!

I wonder if they'll be as good as my dad's. He's perfected chicken tenders. The herbs he adds to the crumb are perfect! And the special dipping sauce he makes... mmmmm! My mouth's watering just thinking about it.

And there goes my stomach again.

I scrunch over on myself while Wily laughs and gets the waitress's attention.

"Hey." He smiles up at her. "Alexis."

"Hi." She beams back, dipping her hip, her high ponytail swinging.

And I may as well be invisible.

I should be grateful. Invisible is better than the laughingstock.

Dipping my chin, I mumble out my order when she asks me for it, and then Wily finishes for me...

"She'll also take a salted caramel milkshake, please, and I'll grab a chocolate." He winks, and the waitress blushes as she scribbles down that last note and practically skips away from the table.

"Do you know her?" I ask as we watch her prance away.

Though I'm probably looking at her quite differently to the way he is.

"Nope." He turns back to face me. "I think she's new."

"But you called her by name."

"I read her name tag." He winks at me. "People are always nicer to you if you take the time to show a little interest in them."

I raise my eyebrows, fighting a grin. "I'm pretty sure she'd like you even if you didn't say her name."

He shrugs and gives me a tired smile. "A lot of girls do."

Wow... how can someone say that and not look like

an arrogant putz? But he's just stating it like it's a fact of life he has no control over.

I tip my head, my eyes narrowing as I study him, but then he puts on a grin like he's pulling a mask over his face, and I can't help myself.

"You flirt with a lot of girls."

"They flirt with me." He shrugs. "And I'm a friendly guy."

My eyes continue to narrow, and he lets out a short laugh.

"I'm serious on the friendly thing. I like to be nice to everybody. If some people interpret that as flirting, that's really not—"

"No, no, no." I shake my head. "What you were doing with that girl just then... that was intentional flirting."

He opens his mouth with exaggerated offense. "I was being nice."

"And checking her out." I laugh the words, then quickly pull myself together. "And winking and eyeing her up like you were imagining what she looked like under that uniform of hers."

Holy crap, what am I saying?

I'm never this bold with people, calling them out on their shit. Why do I think I can do it with Wily?

His lips part a little farther, his mock expression changing to genuine surprise. It's like I've caught him red-handed, and I can't tell if he's impressed or annoyed by that.

I shrink down in my seat, pressing my back against the booth.

After a painful beat, he seems to make a decision and

turns my cheeks crimson by admitting, "I do that with all girls."

My face scrunches. One: to try and hide the fact that if he did that with me, I would want to crawl into a hole and die. And two: to try and hide the fact that he probably didn't do that with me, and that makes me feel even worse for some weird reason.

Oh yeah, and then my face starts buckling with disgust because "Ew. That is so creepy."

"What?" He shrugs. "I'm not going to act on it. I only ever hook up with girls who want to be with me."

"Still. I don't think your friends would appreciate it if they knew you were mentally undressing their girlfriends."

His eyes bulge like I just slapped him or something. "I would never do that."

"You just said you do it with all girls."

"Okay, fine." He raises his hands. "I don't do it with *all* girls."

I keep watching him until the tips of his ears turn bright pink, and I have to snort derisively. "You're gross."

Dipping his head, he squeezes the back of his neck and softly admits, "Girls are beautiful, okay? I like looking at them. But I'd never disrespect them or hurt them or do anything to make them feel less than." Looking back up, he holds me still with his intense blue gaze. "You get me?"

I bite my bottom lip and nod, telling myself I should just drop this. But then my mouth opens of its own accord. *Again.*

"It's lucky they can't read your mind. Because by the sounds of it, all you're doing is turning them from a human being with a soul to just a body you can drool over."

He closes his eyes, obviously disgusted by my interpretation. "That is not accurate at all. I didn't mean to say it like that, okay?"

"More like you didn't mean to *admit it*."

What are you doing? Shut up, you're gonna piss him off!

He lets out a soft huff and rests his forearms on the table, leaning toward me, his face flickering with irritation. "I respect women, okay?"

"Uh-huh." I cross my arms, surprised by how I'm not just letting this go. He's getting annoyed with me. I should seriously drop this!

It's really not my concern.

"Look..." He sighs, shaking his head while the tips of his ears glow red again. "I don't know how to say this without sounding like a complete asshole, but I think women's bodies are beautiful, and I have this habit of wondering what they look like under their clothing."

I can't help making a face. "Well, can I suggest it's a habit you try to break? Because it's gross, and if you ever get a girlfriend or a wife, they won't appreciate it."

Leaning back with a sigh, he eyes me up, tapping his fingers on the booth between us and finally nodding. "That's fair, and I've never thought about it that way. It's just a quick thing I do."

"It's an ick thing you do, and you need to stop," I mutter, my insides flaring.

I never talk to people like this. Seriously. It's the most confrontational I've ever been. Ever! I have no idea what's come over me, and I'm so relieved when he gives me an abashed look and then swallows.

"You know, Satch." He wags his finger at me. "You're good for me."

I flush, my shoulders twitching. "What do you mean?"

"I need someone in my life who's gonna call me on shit like this."

"R-really?"

"Yeah. I mean, my sister, Blake, usually does, but we haven't lived in the same town since I left for college. And I've had no one here to check me, you know? Most of the people I hang with are guys who are just like me or girls who want to get with me. But you..." He grabs a fork out of the holder and starts wagging it at me. "You're—"

"Here we go." The waitress appears, her chipper voice cutting off whatever he was about to say.

It's a good thing, because my heart had lodged itself in my throat and I was about ten seconds away from choking on it.

Placing our food down, Alexis gives Wily another flirtatious smile. He grins back, his eyes starting to trail downward until he shakes his head, his gaze snapping to mine.

I smile at him, both surprised and impressed. He gives me a little wink, thanking the waitress and not looking at her when she wanders away.

"Wow. How much is this killing you right now?"

Staring down at his steak and potatoes, he picks up his knife and looks up with a triumphant grin. "It didn't hurt as bad as I thought it would."

I laugh, not sure I believe him.

Grabbing his chocolate milkshake, he raises it in the air. "Cheers, Tutor Girl. Looks like you've got more than just *Moby Dick* to teach me."

With a hot blush, I lift my glass. "Cheers." We clink, then sip, and for reasons I can't fathom, I find myself smiling at this jock who I should seriously not like at all.

But there's something strangely charming about him.

Annoyingly charming?

Or just plain charming?

Dammit.

No wonder everybody loves him.

CHAPTER 13
WILY

I can't believe Satch called me out like that.

She dropped it once we started eating, but it kept humming in the back of my mind while we talked about the one concert she'd been to for her sixteenth birthday —Taylor Swift. Why am I not surprised that she's a Swiftie? Her mom took her, and the animated way she told me about it showed how much that night meant to her.

I then told her about the various concerts and sporting events I'd been to since I was old enough to attend, and she sat there trying not to gape at me. But of course I'm gonna go to the Super Bowl every year, and Blake needs a bodyguard when she goes to see all of those bands she loves so much, right?

And all the while I was talking and she was trying to hide her surprise... I couldn't stop thinking about what she'd said before the food arrived.

The whole "turning girls from humans with souls to just bodies" thing made me feel like total shit.

I don't do that.

Or maybe I do a little, and fuck... I am a total creeper.

When the waitress eventually comes back to collect our plates, I make sure I look her in the eye when I say thanks and force my gaze back to the pages in front of me when she walks away.

Even with all that effort, I still feel like a world-class dick.

Shit, Satch is so right. If my buddies knew that I'd checked out their girls—albeit very briefly—they'd pluck my eyeballs out. I can't go hurting my team this way. I need to stop this shit.

But damn, it's gonna be hard.

This campus is filled with hot chicks, and so many of them intentionally cross my path. It's hard not to notice them.

Your girlfriend or wife won't appreciate it.

Satch is right.

Not that I'm interested in having a girlfriend right now, but one day I want a wife and family. Will I still be checking out other women when I have one waiting at home for me?

Hell no.

Which means I've got to start practicing now.

Blake always calls me a man slut, and we both think it's funny.

But the way Satch spoke to me before makes me kind of hate the fact that I am. She looked at me like it was something to be ashamed of, and my peacock feathers have taken a serious hit. That's what Blake always tells me I have.

"Strutting around campus with your peacock feathers in full bloom, you cocky shit." She would shake her head at me and laugh.

Spinning the blue fidget toy around, I glance up and watch Satch finish typing the sentence I just gave her. It obviously wasn't a very good one, because she's reworking it a little. I'm losing concentration. It's hard to think when I've got her look of disgust in my head.

"Do you think I'm an asshole?"

"What?" Her head jolts up, and she blinks at me in surprise.

I'm kind of surprised too. I don't know why I even care what this woman thinks of me. She's my tutor. It's not like I'm trying to get it on with her or anything, but for some reason, the idea of her thinking less of me is driving me nuts. I scratch the side of my mouth and stare back at her.

Her surprise starts to fade, her lips pursing as she takes in my expression. "Are you referring to our earlier conversation? About the mental undressing thing?"

I nod and clench my jaw.

"Wily..." Her lips twitch. "I may not like that you do that, but I don't think you're an asshole." Her tone is soft and reassuring. "You have so many great qualities. Just because you do one thing I don't like doesn't mean I'm going to write you off."

The sweet look on her face makes me smile, and soon her lips are spreading wide as well. I'm about to get hit with one of her full beamers when her expression falters and she dips her chin, hunching over and staring at her laptop screen.

"You okay?"

"Yep." She accentuates the *P*, and the tension radiating off her is palpable.

"You sure?" My eyebrows dip together. I can feel it.

She darts a look at me, then past my shoulder before she nods, slapping her laptop closed and shoving it into her bag.

What the hell?

"Where are you going? Are we done for the night?"

"Just need the bathroom," she squeaks, her cheeks flushing bright red before she bolts out of the booth and does this awkward little jog past the counter.

I watch her go and wonder if she's got her period or something. I know some girls get some horrible shit going on. Blake's told me all about it. There was a girl in her class last year that got the worst periods. I didn't want to know all the details, but I got them anyway.

It's called flooding, and it can be quite horrific by the sounds of things.

Shit, I'm so glad I'm not a woman.

I tap my fingers together, waiting for Satch to come back. She'll probably want to leave right away, especially if her skirt has gotten caught in the crossfire, so to speak.

Pulling out my phone, I jump up from the booth and wander over to the counter to pay. I'm kind of bummed out that our session is over already. I really want to get this essay done. It's due tomorrow, and we've still got to finish the third paragraph and do the conclusion.

Ugh. I hate conclusions.

And then we've got all the editing and final proofing to go. Satch mentioned shuffling some stuff around and then maybe cutting a few bits here and there.

I know, right? Cutting! I'm usually stressed about trying to get to the minimum word count, and now she's talking about how we have *too much* to work with.

What the actual fuck?

It makes me want to belt out a triumphant laugh.

This Captain Ahab guy has given me so much to work with, and Satch keeps asking me the best questions. She makes me look at things from a different perspective, and the answers just pop into my head.

Unbelievable.

"Hey, Wily."

I spin and spot a girl behind me. She looks really familiar, but it takes me a second to remember her name.

"Jade." She points at herself.

"I remember," I assure her, and I can't tell if she believes me or not. "You're in my finance class. Nice to see you again."

"You too." She brushes her fingers through her silky hair, and I check out those shiny locks, then force my gaze not to wander down the rest of her body.

From memory, she's slight with petite curves that she obviously tries to accentuate as much as she can.

"So..." She looks around, her glossy lips rising into a hopeful smirk. "You here alone?"

"No, I've just been working with my tutor." I point to the booth Satch and I were sitting in before my eyes dart toward the bathroom sign.

I wonder if I should go check on her.

But she probably wants her privacy if she's dealing with... whatever it is she's dealing with.

My eyebrows pinch together, but Jade distracts me

with a hand on my arm. "What's your tutor helping you with?"

"Just a novel analysis essay. *Moby Dick*," I murmur.

She hisses. "I hated that book in school."

I'm about to agree with her, but for some reason, I tip my head and say, "It's not so bad. That Captain Ahab's an interesting dude."

What the fuck did I just say?

Are these words seriously coming out of my mouth?

Jade titters, her right shoulder hitching. "If you say so." She brushes her teeth across her lower lip, and it's hard not to notice how full and pink her mouth is.

I bet it tastes delicious.

Her lips curl into a sultry smile and I blink, forcing my eyes away. There I go again, turning her into nothing but a body.

Looking into her eyes, I go for a friendly smile but find her outright hunger kind of unnerving.

Seriously?

What is happening to me?

I should be asking if she needs a ride home with the expectation that she'll invite me in and we can get a little busy. Or maybe we'll just make out in my truck, and then we can go our separate ways with a sweet little buzz.

But...

Satch.

I glance back at the table, then look over my shoulder again. She's taking ages. I hope she's okay.

"So, once you're done with tutoring, do you want to hang out?" Jade gazes up at me, all sweet and hopeful.

I smile down at her, loving the sound of that, but—

My phone buzzes in my hand, and I glance at the screen.

Tutor Girl: Not feeling too great. I'm just gonna walk home. We can finish the assignment tomorrow morning. Do you think Coach will let you skip one gym workout so we can finish it up in time?

Walk home?

In the dark?

At this time of night?

Fuck that!

"I gotta go." I glance down at Jade and wince when her eyebrows start to pucker. "Sorry." I lift my phone. "My friend needs me."

This seems to appease her, and she nods. "Maybe another time."

"Yeah." I move away from her, this weird urgency firing through me.

Why didn't Satch ask me for a ride?

Snatching up my stuff as fast as I can, I bolt out the diner door, checking the road and spotting her in the distance.

"Satch! Wait up!" I shout before racing to my truck. "I'll give you a ride!"

She kind of jerks on the sidewalk, slowing her steps, then shakes her head and picks up her pace.

Shit.

What the fuck is up with her?

I thought we were having a good time together, and now she's bailing?

Because she's not feeling well, you douche. Show a little sympathy.

Jumping into my truck, I rev the engine and squeal out of the small parking lot, rushing to catch her before she has to walk another step.

CHAPTER 14
ELIZABETH

Wily said to wait up, but I can't.

The second Jade Buchanan walked into the diner, my blood ran cold. I was surprised she wasn't with her usual posse. Maybe they were meeting up with her soon. I couldn't risk it. The thought of her seeing me was too much.

The thought of her seeing me with Wily Wilson was something I seriously could not bear. Who knows how she'd use that against me?

She probably would have strutted up to our booth and made sure Wily knew every humiliating thing that had happened to me in high school, all the while making sure she came off like the glowing humanitarian who befriended me despite all my faults.

So, I did the only thing I could—I bolted for the bathroom.

In retrospect, I should have gone out the front door. It's not like I can fit through the bathroom windows and make my escape that way. Instead, I was forced to lock myself in the end stall, bunching my fingers into little fists while my stomach pitched and surged. My skin itched, my pulse raced, and I chewed on my bottom lip until it hurt.

"Breathe," I reminded myself. "Just breathe."

Closing my eyes, I sucked in a few shallow breaths, then managed to deepen them until my heart had slowed to a less erratic beat.

All I had to do then was find the courage to walk back into the diner.

I started praying that Jade had popped in for a take-out order.

As I snuck out of the bathroom, I went into snail mode—head tucked down as I inched across the floor, making zero eye contact with anyone. My plan had been to rush to the booth, quickly tell Wily I wasn't feeling well, then run out the door before Jade spotted me.

But then I noticed her talking to Wily.

Not talking... flirting.

And he was into it, smiling down at her with his beautiful blue eyes and broad grin.

Shit, he was probably mentally undressing her and thinking about where they were going to hook up.

It was a punch to the face, the stomach, the chest.

And it shouldn't have been.

Of course Wily is going to flirt with gorgeous girls like Jade. He doesn't care that she's a heartless mean girl. She has a body to die for with perky breasts and a skinny waist. Her clothes are always so cool and chic, and she walks with a confidence I can only dream of.

They're the perfect pair, really, and I didn't want to go messing up their night.

Although, they really aren't a perfect pair, because she's a soulless bitch and he's a nice guy. Well, mostly.

The point is, he could do so much better than her.

And I should really warn him, but who am I to tell him who he should or shouldn't sleep with? If he's after hot, mindless sex, then Jade is probably an excellent choice.

So even though it made bile surge up my throat, I slunk out of that diner unnoticed and texted Wily that I was heading home.

I never expected him to follow me, and now, as his truck pulls up beside me on the sidewalk, I'm not sure what to do.

Why isn't he still flirting with Jade?

Why is he here?

Is it the essay? Maybe Coach won't let him take the morning off training.

Even so, I'm still surprised he's bailing on a hookup with the super-hot Jade Buchanan. He must *really* want to graduate.

Huh. Go figure.

I force myself to stop walking as the passenger door swings open and he leans across the seat to talk to me.

"Are you okay?" His voice is all urgent concern, and it takes me a second of confusion before I remember that I'd texted him I wasn't feeling well.

"Oh, yeah. I just..." I pat my stomach.

"Lady problems?" He winces.

My face flushes and I shake my head before realizing that lady problems would have been an excellent excuse. Damn my honesty!

With a soft sigh, I'm forced to admit, "I just... figured

our tutoring session was over, and I didn't want to disturb what you had going on with J—that girl." I swallow and look down, straightening a pleat in my skirt.

A sudden laugh bursts out of him. "Yeah, that chick is one hot ticket, but this assignment won't write itself. We've got twelve hours left before it's due, and I'm sure Coach will let me skip a session for this, but... I felt like we were on a roll. If you're up for it, I'd love to get it done tonight." He keeps smiling at me. "I'm glad you're okay and not really sick."

My eyebrows shoot up and I totally miss that last sentiment, because I'm too busy balking. "You're putting an assignment above a 'hot ticket'?"

He grins, clearly as surprised as I am. His eyebrows rise as he tips his head, his gaze twinkling. "I guess I am." With a flick of his fingers, he beckons me into his truck. "Come on, let's go find a quiet space to get this shit done."

"I..." Looking up at his outstretched hand, I tentatively shuffle toward this monster vehicle of his. It's impossible to say no to the hopeful look on his face. He really wants to get this essay wrapped up, and I really want to help him.

Placing my bag in the footwell, I try to get into his stupidly big truck without taking his hand, but of course I lose my balance, and his strong fingers are curling around my arm in an instant. Hauling me up, he doesn't seem to mind when I lurch forward against him, my boobs squishing into his arm before I can right myself.

Oh my gosh! This is humiliating!

Quickly jerking back into the seat, I pinch my index finger and keep my eyes straight ahead, only remembering my seat belt when he pulls away from the curb.

My hands are shaking as I try to clip it in, and in the end, he has to help me, his solid hand making the snap an easy one.

"Thank you," I whisper.

"No problem." He smiles, and I study his profile for a second. "So, where are we going? Back to the library? Or maybe your dorm?"

"M-my dorm?"

"Yeah, I figure that'll be more private. Unless you have a roommate. If that's the case, we could just go back to Football Frat again."

"I don't have a roommate." I shake my head and suddenly wish I'd kept my mouth shut.

"Perfect." His voice rises with enthusiasm. "Which dorm are you in?"

Oh shit, what have I done?

Is he seriously about to enter my room?

I should bail and say I prefer Football Frat, but when I open my mouth, "Buckley Hall" pops out.

What the hell is wrong with me?

"Oh nice. I bet the renovations on that are good."

"Yeah, I have my own bathroom." I can't help smiling. "I moved into Buckley Hall at the beginning of last year, but then that fire happened, and I got relegated to the overflow housing. It was so noisy and crowded, and I was sharing a room with three other girls. I found it kind of overwhelming."

"Oh yeah?"

"I guess I'm a bit of an introvert." I point to myself. "I'm an only child, and I'm used to my own space. To go from a single room to sharing a bunk bed was kind of shocking. But the girls were nice enough. They were all friends and just kind of left me to my own devices."

"What?" Wily frowns. "They didn't include you?"

"Oh, it's okay. I didn't want to be included."

His eyebrows pucker. "Still. You'd think they would have taken you under their wing."

I flick my hand through the air and shake my head. "Really, it was fine. And the school worked really hard to get Buckley Hall fixed up ASAP, so I was back in there just after spring break and was able to make it my own. Luckily, I was assigned a room there again this year, so I set it all back up the way I had it."

"Cool." He pulls into the small parking lot just in front of the building.

"You can park in one of those three spots." I point ahead of us, and he picks the one closest to the building.

Turning off the engine, he spins to face me, obviously concerned about something. "You don't get lonely?"

I shrug and look away from him, pulling on my coat sleeve until it covers my hand. "I... no. I like my own company."

"But not all the time, right? I mean, you have friends and stuff, don't you? People to hang out with? Support you?"

My stomach squirms, and I scratch the itch that's quickly forming. "My parents are very supportive," I softly murmur while opening the door.

"Wait." Wily touches my arm before I can leap down and risk an ankle breakage.

I do as I'm told, watching him run around the truck and forgetting how to breathe as he reaches in and helps me down.

His hands are tucked under my no doubt sweaty armpits. Thank God for my thick winter coat.

"Uh... thank you." I take a step back from him and bump into the open truck door. Letting out a self-deprecating laugh, I point at myself. "I'm a shorty. Always have been."

"Your legs still reach the ground." Wily winks at me, his smile playful and adorable.

My stomach stops squirming and starts to bubble again.

I ignore the sensation, darting away from his truck and wrestling the key card out of my bag while he locks up.

Oh man, I hope my room is tidy. I usually leave it just so before I walk out the door each morning, but occasionally I'll be running later than I'm comfortable with. What was it like this morning? I seriously can't remember.

Panic surges through me like an army of ants, my skin starting to itch as Wily holds the door for me and I slip into Buckley Hall, praying for whatever angels are available to do a quick sweep of my room.

Oh please, like he's gonna care! You've seen his room, remember? It's a bomb site.

Chewing on my lip, I wrestle to contain my laughter as we wait for the elevator.

Yet again, logic wins.

I just wish it'd let my emotions join the party sometimes. They're always off scurrying around with worries and doubts while logic is just lying back with a smarmy smirk and shaking his head at my riotous insides.

Why can't those two just get along?

I'd give anything to be as cool and unaffected as Wily always seems to be.

Looking up at the tower beside me, I tune into his voice as he steps aside to let me walk into the elevator first, then starts telling me about his first year in a Nolan U dorm and how he jumped at the chance to become part of Football Frat.

CHAPTER 15
WILY

"So, yeah, when a space opened up, I snatched it. I took the place of the previous senior, and then the other guys joined us over the rest of that year. Then Tyrell moved in at the beginning of our junior year. It's been a good crew."

"Do you all get along?" Satch is fidgeting with the buttons of her coat while we ride the elevator up to the third floor.

"Yeah. I mean, there's the odd moment. Carson's got a bit of a temper on him, but he's getting better. And Grady gets pissed off with how messy everyone is sometimes." I laugh, picturing Grady's irritation.

"Hanging up towels—it's not a new concept, people! And get your shit off the coffee table. It's not a trash receptacle!"

Who the fuck says *receptacle* anyway?

Grady does.

I snicker to myself, glancing down at Satch, who's gnawing on her lip.

Is she nervous or something?

Oh shit, maybe she doesn't want me going to her room. Will we have to leave the door open again?

Shoving my hands into my pockets, I swivel to check on her. She's so short, her head barely reaches my shoulder as she fidgets beside me. "You're cool with this, right? Studying in your room?"

"Uh..." She glances up, notices that I'm looking down at her, and quickly darts her eyes back to the floor. "Yeah, of course."

And she's lying. Just like she lied about not feeling well because she didn't want to get in the way of me talking to that chick.

I shake my head but offer up a simple solution. "We can go to the library instead, if you want."

"No, it's fine, really. We'll get fewer interruptions here."

"You won't have your dorm buddies popping in?" My lips twitch as I wait for her to look up at me again.

But she doesn't play fair, her eyes staying glued to the floor. I join her, noticing the marked difference between her tiny black shoes and my big sneakers. Shit. It's like I've got clown feet compared to hers.

Her head shakes as she mumbles a soft "No."

And there goes that surge of concern again.

"You do... have friends, right?"

"Uh-huh." She answers too fast, nodding as she focuses her gaze on the elevator doors.

I shift, trying to get into her line of sight. "Satch, are you—"

"Here we are." The doors pop open, and she flashes me a quick smile before darting past me and into the hallway.

I follow after her, wondering what the story is with this girl.

She's sweet. A great tutor. Kind of shy and unsure of herself, but why would that make her friendless?

Everybody needs somebody, right?

I hate the idea of her wandering campus with absolutely no one to hang out with.

I couldn't cope with that kind of shit. People make life worth living. I have to be around them. If anything, being by myself drives me insane. I get antsy when I'm alone. Which is why I make sure I can be friends with everybody.

Satch seems the exact opposite, and I don't get how she could possibly be happy living this solo life. It must be so quiet and boring.

"This is my room," she murmurs, unlocking the door and glancing at me with an edgy, closed-mouth smile.

Why is she so nervous?

I'm not about to jump her.

Seriously. What kind of man does she think I am?

The kind that mentally undresses women.

Shit, why the fuck did I admit that to her?

"Um... come in." Satch beckons me with her hand, and I step into her room, eyeing it up with a quickly growing smile.

Wow.

It's so neat.

Grady would love it.

Her bed is made, the cover pulled tight and crisp. Bet she does those special corner things my mom loves. She always insists that our housekeepers know how to make a bed properly.

"Imagine this is a luxury resort. I want the beds made the way you would if you worked there. And if you could fold the toilet paper into a little triangle, I'd love that too."

I remember one housekeeper asked if she wanted a swan towel on the end of the bed each day as well, and Mom gave her a confused frown, totally missing the sarcastic quip and asking, "Why would I want a swan towel?"

Wincing behind my mother's back, I made a face that had the housekeeper smiling, and then I winked at her before walking out of the room.

Our various housekeepers have been pretty accommodating over the years. Mom is always so warm and friendly, and she pays them really well, so the staff we've had have mostly been loyal and hardworking.

Satch places her bag down, and I bet it's in the same spot it always goes. I grin and scan the movie posters on her wall. They're all framed and are retro images from the '50s and '60s, I think.

Singin' in the Rain, The Sound of Music, and Bye Bye Birdie.

I've heard of the first two, but I have no idea what that last one is.

Letting my bag slide off my shoulder, I dump it on her bed before pointing to the door behind me. "Open or shut?"

"Oh, uh..." She eyes the door, then the hallway beyond like she's actually having to think about this.

Seriously?

"You can... shut it." She spins away, pulling out her laptop and setting it up on her neat little desk.

It's got hardly any clutter on it. Just a mug of pens and highlighters and a few books stacked in a neat pile.

Closing the blinds, she then reaches behind her desk and pulls out a stool. "Sorry, I don't have two chairs."

She indicates for me to take her plush office chair and goes to take a seat on the stool.

"No way," I quickly tell her, grabbing her arm and making her stand back up again. "I'm taking the stool."

She blinks, like the idea of taking her own chair hadn't even occurred to her.

"This is your room," I remind her, then start to smile. "You get to sit in your own chair."

"But you're my guest. You should have the nice chair."

I make a "Pshh" sound and shake my head before shrugging my jacket off and dumping it beside my bag.

Satch watches me for a second, then slowly unbuttons her winter coat. She wrestles it off, then hangs it on the hook behind the door before pulling her cardigan straight and shuffling toward the desk.

Eyeing me one more time, she inches toward the stool, and I quickly sit on it before she can even think about being some kind of martyr for me.

Does she have any idea how much she's helping me?

Like I'm gonna make her take the fucking stool.

"Sit down," I softly coax her, adding in a smile while I open her laptop and get us back on track.

With a resigned little sigh, she takes a seat and starts reading what we were working on before she bolted to the bathroom.

I'm still confused by her behavior. And the fact that she tried to sneak off because I was flirting with some chick. And now I'm wondering why she's giving me the impression that she has no friends.

Why wouldn't someone want to hang with her? She's smart, kind, thoughtful.

Sure, she doesn't dress in the usual way... My eyes skim down her body, and I swear everything she's wearing looks homemade.

Obviously sensing my perusal, she glances at me, and my eyes quickly jump to her laptop screen. "So... Ahab."

"Yeah. You've just finished giving me your third point paragraph, and now we have to find a quote or example from the book to back up your thoughts on the fact that Ahab's relentless determination, which society would normally think of as a strength, is actually his weakness." Her bright gaze lands on me, all hopeful and expectant. "Can you think of a situation in the book which proves that?"

I scramble to come up with a good one, because I want her to give me that proud smile. The one that says, *"Yes! You're getting this!"*

"Well..." I scratch the side of my face. "There's the fact that he ignored the crew's warnings."

"Yeah." Satch nods. "But you've kind of used that as an example in paragraph two. It'd be great to think of something else."

I can tell there's an answer she's looking for, and damn, I want to deliver like a fucking boss. But my brain's gone blank, like it always fucking does. I hate that I can't come up with simple answers the way everyone else can.

"Um..." I blink and, in the end, have to shrug, because shit, I haven't even read the book, and I can't remember all of the stuff she read me from SparkNotes.

Shit!

I slump, tapping my knuckles on her desk before snatching a pen out of her mug and playing with the cap. I pop it on and off, hoping it'll help restart my brain.

Satch's lips twitch, and she changes screens. "Let's have a look at the text."

Bringing up the book, we read the page together. Then she starts hinting at a particular section until I finally come up with "Oh wait! In the final part, he's completely reckless, and it ends up sinking the ship... and it kills him and basically all his crew."

And why the fuck I didn't come up with that immediately is so fucking embarrassing.

It's the most obvious answer, and my stupid brain had tucked it out of sight like it was worthless.

"Excellent." Satch grins at me. "I like that you used the word *reckless*, because it describes his actions perfectly." She leans closer to the screen while my chest puffs with just a touch of pride.

Seriously. I came up with one little word, and she's making me feel like a fucking genius.

"Okay, so let's put that in your own words, then use an actual line from the book. We can tie that back into your flag football example if you like, unless you have another one we can use to really drive your point home about reckless behavior and how it can affect everyone around you in a negative way."

She makes me work for it, scouring the text and finding a line I can use. The smile she gives me punches right through my fucking chest. She's so happy with me. Proud of me, even, and I'm not sure I deserve it.

But damn, it makes me feel good.

I then run through a football example, which she helps me word in a way that makes sense, and before I know it...

"All we've got left is the conclusion." She looks excited, and I start worrying that I'll have no idea how to wrap this shit up, but she talks me through it, typing down my words and refining them. She doesn't just change them; she pauses and questions me until I come up with something better.

I've never had a tutor go to this much effort before. It's fucking amazing!

By the time we're done, it's one-thirty in the morning, and Satch is fighting a yawn.

"I'll print this out and proof it in the morning," she says. "I want to come at it with fresh eyes, and I really need some sleep first."

"Okay, cool." I stand, hitching my jeans. "I'll swing by here in the morning, and we can make any last-minute changes before handing it in."

"Sounds good to me." She stands up, her arm brushing against mine as she maneuvers the chair back into place.

My finger ducks out, skimming over the back of her hand, and for some reason, I do it again, holding my fingers over her soft skin. My thumb ever so gently curls around her wrist and...

What am I doing?

She goes still, staring up at me with these vulnerable eyes that are so big and, I don't know... endearing? I think that's a word.

I don't know why I'm touching her, so I let go, unable to ignore her surprised expression. "Thanks for everything, Satch." My voice comes out all soft and husky. "You're a lifesaver."

Her cheeks tinge a pretty pink, and she dips her head. "It's no problem. You've done really well. You deserve a good grade for this."

"Only because of you."

She shakes her head. "You've worked really hard, and I'll make sure Professor Pilscher knows it."

With a grateful nod, I grab my stuff and head out the door, pausing one last time to look at her. The soft light from her desk illuminates the side of her round cheek, and in that glow she looks... I don't know, really pretty. I smile at her. "Good night, Satch."

She bites her bottom lip but can't stop her grin. "Good night, Wily."

CHAPTER 16
ELIZABETH

As much as I wanted to sleep like the dead, I ended up having a restless night. I couldn't get Wily out of my brain. His scent seemed to permeate my room—this manly deodorant smell mixed with male sweat or something? That should be totally gross, but as I was getting dressed this morning, I kept sniffing the air like I was searching for that smell again.

Seriously. What is wrong with me?

Grabbing my only pair of jeans, I put them on and check my reflection in the mirror. My lips pull into an unhappy frown the way they always do. I wish I could wear these like other girls at school, but my legs are so solid, and all my bulgy bits seem to get highlighted to the extreme when I wear pants like this. So, just like I always do, I end up taking them off and going for a dress instead.

My mom made me this one last year to help with the colder winter months. It's made with material that has merino wool in it, so it's super warm. Not that I feel the cold too much, but I love how soft the fabric is. And I like the way it swishes around my ankles when I walk.

It's probably not the height of fashion, but I don't care. I'm pretty sure even if I *tried* to be chic or cool, I wouldn't be able to pull it off. My brain just doesn't think that way.

And so I settle for comfort.

Throwing a scarf around my neck, I pull on my winter coat, pack my bag, and head for Java Jeans. I know Wily said he'd meet me here this morning, but he's working out right now, and I figure I can sneak in my daily walk and a quick caffeine injection before I have to see him.

My lips twitch as I picture his face, his blue eyes so bright and happy every time I compliment him. He obviously has no faith in his academic ability, and I'm still not sure he gets how much of this assignment he's done himself. I've just been asking him questions—he's the one coming up with the answers. That's all him, and he *should* feel proud of himself.

I check my room one last time before closing the door, my lips growing into a broader smile as I picture him hunched over my little stool. His body is so tall and broad and muscular, and he looked comical squished up against my desk last night.

So sweet of him to let me use my own chair, though.

He does seem to have some real gentlemanly qualities.

Barring the mental undressing thing, which I really don't want to think about.

Hurrying outside, I murmur a soft thank-you to the girl who held the door for me, then set a quick pace to the coffee shop. I like to get my thirty minutes in each day, so I take the longer route there, avoiding all the hot spots where Team Evil 2.0 likes to hang. Although it's probably early enough that I'm in the clear.

I'm a little out of breath by the time I get to Java Jeans's front door, so I take a second to suck in a few mouthfuls of air before reaching for the handle.

"Oh." I step back and let a couple walk through the door, then end up holding it for the girl behind them and the other guy behind them.

I'm now fifth in line and scanning the board for my order. I don't know why. I always get the same thing anyway.

"Hey, Elizabeth," a friendly voice chirps behind me.

I flinch and spin, pasting on a smile when I spot a girl from my Rhetorical Theory class. "Oh, hi, Megan. How are you?"

"Yeah, great. Just grabbing a cup of joe before I have to face Professor Lynch. Have you ever had her?"

"Lynch," I murmur, shaking my head. "I don't think so."

"You'd definitely know if you had." She laughs. "That woman gives new meaning to the word *battle-axe*."

"Yikes." I let out a soft laugh, my stomach starting to itch. I ignore the sensation, curling my fingers and begging myself not to scratch that spot just above my belly button.

"How about you? What are you up to today?"

"Oh... um..." I blink and try to think of something cool to say, but seriously? Like that's ever going to be possible. "Just getting my morning coffee too."

"Nice. Do you want to sit together? We can moan about evil professors until we have to go to class." Her smile is so bright and expectant, and I'm not lying when I say a part of me is tempted, but...

"I'm sorry, I can't. I have some homework I need to do while I'm here."

"Oh, no problem. I get that." She grins, then indicates for me to move forward.

I spin and notice the space in the line, quickly filling it while flushing hot with embarrassment.

My turn's next and I quickly order, my hand shaking just a little as I pay through my phone. "Thank you," I mumble to the server and shift to the counter where my order will appear in a minute or two.

I pretend to be doing something on my phone while secretly watching Megan. She's so warm and friendly, easily coaxing a smile out of the teenager behind the counter. They have a little laugh together while she pays, and I stand here wondering how people do it.

Megan walks over to me with another warm smile. She doesn't seem upset that I rejected her invitation, but I'm feeling awful about it. Should I have said yes? Was I too rude?

Why didn't you say yes? It's not going to take you that long to proof Wily's essay.

A shudder rumbles in my stomach, and I shift awkwardly on my feet.

No wonder I don't have any friends. I can't even respond to the people who are nice to me.

That's because nice doesn't always equal nice!

It's true. I've learned that the hard way. Sometimes nice equals a false sense of security that leads you into a lion's den (aka Natasha Lowinksi's birthday party), and you end up getting pranked by Jade and Carmen, who you didn't know were going to be there.

Upon reflection, I now know that Natasha must have been in on it too. It's pretty humiliating coming out of the bathroom to find every single person at the party has disappeared...

I walked around the house, calling their names and didn't know what to do. In the end, I sat in the middle of the empty lounge and started crying.

That was when Mrs. Lowinski came back and found me. She told me everyone had gone to the playground for the outdoor games, and she'd only just noticed I was missing. She apologized with a laugh and dragged me to the park, where everyone proceeded to laugh at me for being the last to arrive and I got picked as "it" for their game of tag.

Of course, I couldn't catch anybody and ended up out of breath and red-faced while they all scampered out of my reach, goading me to catch them.

Mrs. Lowinksi eventually wrapped up the game, but not until I'd fallen over and scraped my knee. After that, it was time to walk back to the house for cake and presents. I thought that part wouldn't be so bad, until Natasha opened the gift my mom had specially made her. It was a tote bag made from material with ballerinas dancing on it. It'd taken me hours to hand-stitch Natasha's name in with beads. Mrs. Lowinski thought it was stunning, but the other girls all snickered behind their hands. My face was flaming as Natasha gave me a weak smile and said, "Thanks," before shoving it aside to focus on the jewelry and makeup she'd been given by the others. Jewelry and makeup my parents could never afford, and I knew nothing about. I wasn't into that kind of thing. To me, getting a personalized tote bag to put books in was the coolest idea ever. I thought Natasha would love it.

Instead, it was soon trampled on the floor with the other wrapping paper, and I wouldn't be surprised if it was thrown out after I left.

I managed to hold it together until my dad finally came to pick me up. As soon as we pulled away from Natasha's house, I burst into tears and promised myself I'd never go to another birthday party again.

Taking a seat at a table near the back of Java Jeans, I try to push the memory from my mind. That happened when I was ten. You'd think I'd be over it by now, but it wasn't just that one part. It was all the other instances when people at school had shown me kindness only to burn me later.

It's seriously not worth getting too close to people. They only let you down and turn out to be something that they're not.

Megan is probably a sweetheart. But she seems like the type who is friendly to everybody. I'm nothing special to her, and she'll probably forget about me by the time she's finished her coffee.

She remembered your name. She initiated contact.

Everybody always initiates contact. But what they do after that... that's the part I can't trust.

Pulling out Wily's essay, I stare at his name on the page and realize I've been trusting him this week, haven't I?

Only because I'm tutoring him. That's different.

But you've been doing more than tutoring. You've been

hanging out. You ate dinner together last night, and you weren't scared to challenge him. And you didn't sit there freaking out that he was about to turn on you.

I have no idea why I don't worry more when I'm around him. If he walked in right now, I wouldn't say I was too busy.

Because you're holding his assignment!

But that's not it. And I know it. And it's confusing me.

Scratching my frown lines, I then grab a pencil and start reading over the essay. Picking pieces off my blueberry muffin, I nibble and read until a familiar voice has me jumping out of my skin.

"Morning, Satch!" Wily booms, despite the fact that he's standing right next to my table.

I swallow down my gasp and crane my neck to look up at him. He's so tall. Such a presence. His eyes so blue and vibrant, his smile so broad and playful.

I can sense every eye within a ten-foot radius is on us, and it makes my cheeks flame.

"Uh... good morning," I reply softly. "What are you doing here?"

"Well, I came to buy you a coffee before coming to collect ya, but you're already here." Pulling out a chair, he takes a seat beside me, raising his chin to acknowledge the table next to us.

"Wi-ly!" someone shouts from across the café, and my tablemate glances across, laughing and giving the finger to a tall guy with sandy brown hair. He cracks up laughing and gives the finger back before taking his girlfriend's hand and walking out of the store.

Once everyone has said their hellos to the popular footballer, he finally turns his attention back to me.

"Do you want another one?" He points at my coffee cup and empty plate.

"Um..." I glance at the leftover crumbs and shake my head. "No, I'm good."

"It's on me." His smile is so persuasive, his eyes so keen that I end up folding and ordering an orange juice. "Excellent choice."

He walks away from the table, greeting more people with his loud, friendly voice. I can't help watching him. He's like a celebrity in this place. It's insane.

Squirming in my seat, I try to focus on his essay until I hear his voice wafting back to me.

"My tutor. She's helping me out with an assignment. Fucking lifesaver, man. I'd be lost without her."

My head jolts up, and I spot three pairs of eyes on me.

Swallowing, I quickly glance back down at the paper, hunching over the table and begging them to look away.

I hate the sensation of everyone watching me.

Bad things always follow that kind of behavior.

Holding my breath, I stare at the black words printed on these white pages until they start to blur. I don't even know what I'm reading anymore.

And then Wily's back, plunking down in the chair beside me, his knee resting against my chair. "Here you go."

"Thanks," I whisper, eyeing the orange juice and suddenly having flashbacks to Jade's cruel trick in the cafeteria.

Why the hell did I order orange juice?

Feeling obliged to take it, I carefully pick up the glass and take a sip, then wipe my mouth and try not to grimace when I swallow. The smell of moldy orange juice soaking into my hair is still ripe in my memory. Even after all this time, I can still feel that flush of humiliation, that pain of disappointment as I watched that gross orange liquid soak into the new clothes Mom had made me.

"So, how's it looking?" Wily taps the pages, distracting me from my nightmare.

I jump all over it, shifting in my seat and looking up at him. "Yeah, it's reading well."

"Any changes required?"

"Just a few grammatical errors at this stage. I'm wondering if it'd strengthen your essay to elaborate the second paragraph here." I swivel the sheet so he can read over the lines I'm indicating. "But that's up to you. We're probably not talking huge shifts in your grade over it."

"If it'll get me a pass, then I'm happy with it as it is."

"This work will definitely get you a pass." My lips twitch. "You've done a great job, and if you fail, I'll be having words with Professor Pilscher myself."

"Oh, will you now?" Wily's eyes start to dance, and that tingling sensation I only ever feel around him bubbles in my belly.

I swallow and look away from him.

I'm sure my cheeks are glowing right now, and I don't want him to notice.

"Well, should we get this over with, then?" Wily points at the paper, then finishes his bagel in one mouthful.

My eyes bulge as his cheeks puff out and he gives me an impish grin.

"That was half a bagel." I try not to laugh. "You just put half a bagel in your mouth."

He shrugs, crumbs flying off his lips as he talks with his mouth full. "I'm like a pelican."

Fighting my laughter is impossible now, and the sound pops out of me before I can stop it.

He grins around his food, his eyes sparkling, his gaze like a magnetic field I can't get out of.

He's so...

"Wily Wilson." A girl walks up, wrapping her arm around his shoulders and kissing his cheek. "How are you?"

"Yeah, I'm great." His voice perks up, matching his grin as he wipes the last few crumbs off his short whiskers and they start up a friendly chat.

She doesn't even notice me, and that's totally fine. I quietly pack away my stuff, even managing to take my plate and glasses up to the counter before Wily catches up to me.

"Sorry about that. I've been friends with Piper since we were little kids. She and I went to elementary school together."

"Cool." I bob my head, then can't help smiling when he opens the door for me.

"Yeah, we lost touch because her parents sent her to an all-girls academy. She was a bit of a troublemaker back then, and they thought it'd straighten her out." He laughs. "Anyway, she ended up at Nolan U, and she always says hi whenever we pass each other."

"She doing better now?" I pull my bag on, making sure both shoulder straps are secure.

"Yeah, scored herself a levelheaded girlfriend who keeps her on track, apparently. I've met her a couple of times. She seems nice."

I smile up at him. "You really are friends with everyone, aren't you?"

He shrugs. "Always have been."

"I bet you were smiling at like four weeks or something crazy."

"What?" He laughs. "What do you mean?"

"Well, most babies start smiling around six weeks. That's the average age, but then you get those babies who start smiling early, and I guarantee you were one of them."

"I doubt my mom will even remember, but I'll have to ask her next time I see her." His gaze lands on me, and I can't hold it this time. My cheeks are heating up again. "When did you start to smile?"

My nose wrinkles as I pretend to think about it. I already know because my mother kept a meticulous diary of my life, and I can see the page in my head as if I'm holding it.

Libby smiled today! My sweet girl. She's six weeks and five days old, and she looked up at me with those big, trusting eyes and I finally managed to coax a smile out of her. It was the most beautiful thing I've ever seen.

My insides go all warm and mushy. My parents are older. I'm their miracle baby, and they've always made a point of celebrating each and every moment. I've sometimes found it suffocating, but since moving away from them, I've learned to appreciate what it's like to have two people in your corner. They love me more than anyone ever could, and I can't take that for granted.

Heading to the library, I listen to Wily's workout story from the morning. He's so good at spinning a yarn, and we're walking into the library before I know it.

Thankfully, the line for the printer is short and we don't have to wait long before his essay is coming out of the machine. I sniff the air, loving that smell of paper that's been freshly printed on.

Gathering the pages, I staple them together and steal a quick whiff.

Wily snickers. "What are you doing?"

Oh my gosh, he just saw me do that!

I must be fire-engine red right now, and I've got no place to hide!

All I can do is admit with a sheepish grin, "There's nothing like the smell of a new assignment you're about to hand in."

He looks at me like I'm weird, and I wait for the teasing barb, but he doesn't say anything. Instead, he takes the pages from my hand and gives them a deep sniff.

"Still warm," he murmurs.

"I know." I can't help a grin.

Ugh. I probably look like the biggest dork right now.

Taking one more sniff, he nods and murmurs, "I get it."

My insides twirl and jump, and I beg myself to calm down. I'm not getting giddy over this man. I won't let myself do it.

"Shall we go?" Heading for the door before he can reply, I lead the way to Professor Pilscher's office... and notice that the closer we get, the slower Wily's steps become.

It really should be a case of me jogging to keep up with his long strides, but he's actually walking behind me now.

Turning to face him, I gaze up at his tight expression, and before I can stop myself, I take his hand and give it a squeeze. "You can be proud of what you've done here."

He swallows and nods, squeezing my hand back. "Thank you."

"Come on." I grin. "Let's go show Pilscher how smart you are."

CHAPTER 17
WILY

She doesn't know what she's talking about, but I let Satch lead me into the Humanities building anyway. I don't know why I'm suddenly so nervous. It's just an assignment. I've handed in plenty before, and if anything, this is potentially one of my better ones.

But that's the thing.

It's *my* words this time. Not somebody else's that I've just proofed.

These are my ideas.

And sure, Satch held my hand every step of the way, and I should have confidence in that, but Pilscher hates me and he's going to be grading this assignment with that in mind. I'm the dumb shit who doesn't deserve to pass. I'm good for football, and that's it.

I've been reminded of that my whole life.

So why should the fact that I have an amazing tutor change anything?

Dude, it changes everything! She's gonna help you graduate, man. Stop acting like a douche and be grateful.

Gritting my teeth, I check myself and rap on the professor's door.

"Enter."

I hold the door so Satch can walk in first, and I can instantly tell she's a star pupil because the guy smiles at her like she's a welcome sight.

"Well, good morning, Miss Satchwell. How are you today?"

"Very good, sir." She shifts to point at me. "Thought I'd accompany Wily so I can tell you how hard he worked on this assignment."

Pilscher's smile disappears. "Did he now?" Holding out his hand, he flicks his fingers, and I pass over my work, my chest tightening uncomfortably.

Seriously. Why do I even give a shit?

How can I feel more on edge now than I do when I'm facing down a Mac truck on the field? Some of the guys I go up against are even bigger than I am, and yet I never feel an ounce of fear.

But this office with its book-lined walls and stuffy furniture is giving me fucking heart palpitations.

The pages sound loud in the quiet space as Pilscher flicks through what I've done.

"Hmmm," he eventually murmurs, then looks at Satch over the top of his glasses. "How much did you actually do?"

"Well, I typed it," she answers. "But they are all Wily's words. I refused to put in anything that he didn't come up with himself."

Pilscher's eyes narrow and then he looks at me, his frown skeptical.

"It's true," I back her up. "She was a hard-ass, sir.

Wouldn't let me get away with slacking off. Made me really think about the book, you know?"

"Uh-huh." He slaps the pages against his leg and eyes me up like I'm a bug he wants to squash with his shiny black shoe. "And what can you tell me about *Moby Dick*? Give me one main takeaway."

"Uh..." My brain immediately starts to fritz out, the pressure quickly turning off the lights in each section.

Oh fuck.

Fuck, fuck, fuck!

Satch clears her throat, and my gaze darts her way.

She gives me a hopeful smile and mouths one little word.

"Reckless," I punch out, relief soaring through me as I cling to that one idea. "Captain Ahab was reckless. His determination drove him to forget about common sense. He put his need for revenge above everything else, and it made him kind of crazy. If he hadn't let his emotions control him that way, then maybe he wouldn't have sunk his ship and lost most of his crew."

The words sail out of me with minimal effort, and my surprise is mirrored on Pilscher's face as he takes me in and then looks at Satch.

"Did you tell him to say that?"

"No, sir." She's grinning like I've just won first prize at the county fair. "That was all him."

"Hmmm." There goes that sound again, although this time it's lighter, maybe not so critical. "Well, I look forward to grading this, then."

His eyes dart back to mine, and then he shoots a glance at Satch before nodding, his lips flirting with a grin.

I'm not sure if I'm supposed to say anything else, and to be honest, I'm still kind of reeling that I managed to just spurt all of that Ahab shit and not get laughed at for sounding ridiculous.

But holy shit.

I just came up with that myself, and I fucking knew what I was talking about!

"That'll be all for now. I'll be in touch with your grade soon." Pilscher raises his chin toward the door, and I practically leap toward it.

I can't get out of this space fast enough and nearly forget to thank him until Satch nudges my arm and bulges her eyes at me.

"Oh!" I spin back and paste on a smile. "Thanks for the second chance, sir."

Pilscher gives me a steady look, then nods and murmurs, "Thank her."

And that's exactly what I fucking do.

The second we're down the steps of the Humanities building, I spin to face Satch, grabbing her face and planting a firm kiss on her lips.

She goes stiff beneath my touch, so I pull back just as quickly and smile at her like it's no big deal. "Thank you. Seriously, Satch, you are a fucking legend." Picking her up, I spin her around and laugh the words, "Thank you!"

She gasps against my shoulder, her body going all rigid again.

Shit, I probably shouldn't have just picked her up, but I kind of don't want to put her down just yet.

I need her to know how grateful I am, and what better way to do that than hug the girl.

"You're the best, Satch!"

She lets out an awkward laugh and I stop spinning, leaning my head back so I can look at her face.

Her cheeks have gone bright red, and the smile she's giving me is super cute.

"It's, um…" She clears her throat, patting my shoulder. "It's my pleasure. Working with you was fun."

"Yeah. It was, right?"

I shouldn't sound so surprised. She's an amazing teacher, so of course she was gonna make it interesting.

She pats my shoulder again, and I should really put her down now. Her feet are dangling off the ground, and she might be getting uncomfortable squished against me like this, but…

I like the feel of her in my arms.

She's got soft curves, and her awesome tits are pressed against my chest.

I kind of wish she'd put her legs around my waist so I can run my hands up her thighs and—

Dude, no! She's your tutor! Don't go ruining it. Just control yourself!

Getting back to business, I ask her one last question before putting her down. Maybe if she's in my arms, she'll be less inclined to say no. "Think you can help me study for my upcoming finance test?"

She smiles. "If you want me to."

And I can't help smiling back. She really does have a pretty mouth. And I like the way her eyes kind of glow with this look like she's the privileged one for getting to work with *me*.

Man, does she have that the wrong way round!

I'm about to tell her that when a derisive snort pops out of a girl sauntering past us.

"He's supposed to do his weight training at the gym, hippo. You might want to suggest he put you down before he strains something."

The beauty narrows her eyes at Satch before giving me a *"you're welcome"* kind of smirk and...

What the actual fuck did she just say?

"Put me down, please," Satch whispers, her cheeks even redder than they were before. She starts to wriggle against my hold on her. "Now. Put me down." She's fucking desperate, and I lower her to the ground, still reeling over what I just heard.

For a second, I was trying to convince myself that I must have heard it wrong, because no one would talk to Satch like that. I mean, why would they? She's completely harmless.

But as I watch my tutor straighten her clothes and wrap her arms around her waist, I realize that I wasn't just hallucinating.

That bitch actually said it.

She fucking called Satch a hippo.

And I don't know if I've ever seen red this bright before. Anger flares through me—an open blue flame—and I turn with a growl, shouting after that walking mouth turd. "You better stay the fuck away from her!"

Satch gasps, her eyes bulging as she covers her mouth, shaking her head at me.

I'm too pissed off to stop myself and am actually fucking glad when that bitch turns to face me.

"Excuse me?" Her haughty tone makes my skin crawl. "I was doing you a favor. When you're dealing with weights like that, you should really have a spotter and be working within the safety of a gym." She obviously thinks what she's saying is fucking hilarious as she raises her hands. "If you want to risk injuring yourself before a big game, well, I guess that's on you."

This is unbelievable. She's still going?

Can she not hear the trash coming out of her mouth?

Satch sure can. Her expression is pinched and wounded as she pulls her jacket sleeves over her hands and turns to walk away.

Nope. Not happening.

Snatching her wrist, I stop her before she can take another step and pull her back against my side. Swinging my arm around her shoulders, I give the bitch a pointed look and loudly tell anyone who's wise enough to listen, "You're talking to the smartest person I know, so watch your fucking mouth!"

"Oh, please." The girl rolls her eyes, giving Satch a derogatory stink eye that makes me wonder if they know each other. "I know plenty of girls who are just as smart and a damn sight prettier too."

My tutor squirms against me, and I have to tighten my hold to keep her beside me.

I am so fucking livid right now, I want to close the space between me and this chick and—

This is one of those cases where it should be okay to hit a girl.

I'll never do it, but for the first time in my life, I want to. This chick needs shutting up, and if she doesn't stop looking at Satch like that, I'm gonna lose my shit!

Moving Satch behind my back, I stand up taller and bark at the woman. "You better keep walking, lady. And if I hear you talking to my friend that way again, there's gonna be a world of trouble coming after you."

"Oooo," she mocks me. "Are you threatening a woman?"

"You're not a woman," I scoff. "You're a fucking viper. Keep that tongue inside your mouth and stay the hell away from us!"

She blinks like she can't believe I just said that, and I grab Satch's hand and pull her in the opposite direction before I do something stupid.

I'm beyond pissed that someone would talk to my tutor that way.

But the thing that's riling me more than anything is the expression on Satch's face. She's obviously heard it all before, and that makes me want to break something.

CHAPTER 18
ELIZABETH

"Who was that bitch?" Wily spits.

I flinch and he huffs, lowering his voice immediately.

"Who was she, Satch?" He pulls me to a stop once we're around the corner, his eyes rich with concern as his voice drops to a controlled, husky growl. "Do you know her?"

Opening my mouth to respond, I swear I try to say something, but nothing is coming out!

I can't believe he just did that. The way he spoke to her. The way he stood up for *me*.

I... I...

Oh shit, she's gonna tell Jade, and she'll be so pissed!

"Satch?" Wily's still holding my hand, his thumb now rubbing circles over my palm. It tickles a little, but I don't want him to stop, because...

He told her to shut up and leave me alone. He shouted it at her.

No one ever does that.

They usually laugh and give embarrassed little head-shakes. Sometimes they'll softly murmur, "Come on. Don't say that." But Wily full-on threatened Jade's friend. I don't know what her name is, but she's the blonde member of Team Evil 2.0.

He called her names! He told her to watch her mouth.

Worrying my lip, I start to panic that he'll get in trouble for doing that. What if she reports him for verbal abuse or for threatening her? What if the people standing around heard him say that stuff and *they* report him?

What if she's now meeting up with Jade and planning a revenge mission against me—the hippo girl she's been trying to keep in her place ever since elementary school?

"Hey, stop doing that." Wily brushes his thumb over my bottom lip. "You're gonna make yourself bleed."

I give it one more nibble before pressing my lips together so he can't see them anymore.

"Satch." He wiggles my hand. "Tell me who that evil little viper was." The way he spits out the last couple of words is a clear indication that he's getting agitated again, and I really don't want him heading off to class too angry to hear anything.

So, I force out a breath and try to play it off the way I usually do. "Don't worry about it. Honestly. It's not a big deal."

"Are you kidding me?" He bends down so he can get in my face. Tipping my chin up, he looks me right in the eye. "Satch, it's a big deal. People shouldn't be talking to you that way."

"Well, it's..." My shoulder hitches. "People hassle each other sometimes."

His eyes pop even wider, his mouth opening in clear vexation. "That was not playful hassling, that was outright verbal abuse!" His expression is so exaggerated it's almost comical, but I can't find it in me to laugh because I'm still burning with humiliation.

I dip my head and swallow, figuring I'd rather melt into the concrete than have to admit all the nasty words I've had thrown at me over the years.

"Who else has spoken to you like that before? Has she?" He points behind himself and I peer around his body, sudden terror seizing me.

Is she there? Did she come back?

But the coast is clear.

It's just us. Hiding around the corner of the building. I'm safe here. With him.

I sag with relief, but that only makes Wily's eyebrows flicker, his expression deepening with concern.

Crap. I need to tell him something, right?

But...

I don't want to!

It's so humiliating.

I don't want him to know all the things that were done to me. Why should I give him reasons to see me the way they do?

Lowering my chin, I bite my lips together again and wait out the silence. It's awkward and horrible, and Wily will get impatient soon. But that's good, right? Maybe he'll huff and walk away, and we can just forget this whole thing.

"You know her, don't you?" he finally mutters. "She's definitely spoken shit to you before, and you just let her."

"What?" I look up, not sure how to feel about that. "I... you don't... I..." I huff and finally manage, "People are entitled to their opinions."

"That wasn't an opinion," he hisses. "It was bullshit!"

"Well, isn't it better to just ignore it, then? I mean, how else am I supposed to respond?"

He tips my chin again, his eyes bright with intensity. "You look at her, and you tell her to *shut the fuck up*."

My eyes bulge, my skin starting to burn like I've just been dancing naked in a sandstorm.

"I... I can't..." Shaking my head, I take a step away from him. "I can't say that to someone."

"Well, you should." He gives me an emphatic look like *I'm* the crazy one for not immediately jumping all over this. "Besides, she's not a someone. She's a viper! A full-blown, foulmouthed bitch. And she deserves to be put in her place."

"It'd just make it worse." I grip my bag straps. "It's better to stay quiet and walk away."

"I'm guessing that's what you've been doing for the last however many months, right?" He huffs, his expression dangerous. "How long has this been going on?"

I don't respond. No way! He will lose it if I tell him everything.

I glance up in time to see his eyes narrow like he's trying to study me and read my mind, scan back through my history and watch all those ugly, demeaning situations play out in full color.

That can never happen.

I squirm and shuffle a few more steps away from him.

He closes the gap in one smooth stride. "It was last year, too, wasn't it? Has she been tormenting you ever since you got to Nolan U?"

I close my eyes and shake my head but wonder if it's just easier to let him believe that.

"She's not in your dorm, is she?"

I shake my head, relieved that part *is* true.

"Satch?"

"I don't want to talk about it." My voice is so quiet, I sound like a timid little mouse.

Running a hand through his hair, Wily huffs and looks back over his shoulder, like he wants to chase down the viper and let her have it again. "Shit, I can't believe you've had to put up with that. Where the fuck does she get off anyway? Calling you a hippo and talking about your weight like that. What the hell does that stick figure know?"

Oh gawd, I don't want to talk about my weight!

"I have to go," I quickly mumble, trying to dart around him.

"No, no, no, I'm sorry," he rushes out. "I'm trying to make you feel better, not scare you off."

"You're not scaring me. I just..." Gripping the sides of my dress, I give them a nervous tug and glance up with a curious frown. "Why are you trying to make me feel better?"

His eyebrows pucker, his head tipping to the side. "Because... someone was mean to you. I didn't like it, and I'm sure you didn't either."

"I... I..." My shoulders hitch, and I've probably just given away the fact that I'm so used to this now. I never like it, obviously, but maybe I'm getting better at shrugging it off? "I don't know," I end in a whisper.

"Satch..." Wily rests his hand on my arm. "You know it's not okay for her to talk to you like that, right?"

I nod.

"And you can't let her get away with it. So, if that ever

happens again and I'm not there, you've got to promise me you'll stand up for yourself."

My face bunches as reluctance storms through me with a resounding *No way!*

Irritation flashes across Wily's expression, but his voice comes out soft. "Ignoring them is one strategy, I guess. Walking away works, I'm not saying it doesn't, but damn... I want you to show that bitch that she has no right to treat you that way. I want you to stand tall—"

I snicker at the absurdity of that statement.

He stops and takes a second to laugh with me before correcting himself. "Okay, fine. I want you to stand as tall as your body will let you, and I want you to tell that girl to shut. The fuck. Up." He bends down to catch my eye again. "Can you do that for me, Satch?"

"No." I shake my head and cringe. "Even if I wanted to, I couldn't."

He gives me a skeptical frown, his left eye twitching. "Yes, you could. Come on. Say it to *me.*"

"What?" I bulge my eyes at him. "No way."

"Satch. Come on. Tell me to shut the fuck up."

"No."

"Say it."

"No."

"Say it!" He points at me.

"I can't!"

"Yes, you can. Now do it."

Clamping my lips together, I shake my head until I feel like it's gonna come right off my neck.

Gently taking my face between his large hands, he stills me and starts chanting, "Do it. Do it. Do it, do it, do it, do it, do it—"

"Okay, stop." I raise my hand to shut him up.

He lets go of my face and stands tall, crossing his arms and giving me an emphatic look. "No. The words are *shut the fuck up*."

I flush hot, my insides writhing as I look around to make sure we're alone before glancing up with a pained frown and whispering, "Shut the fuck up."

"Sorry, what was that?" He touches the side of his ear and makes a show of straining to hear me.

I fight a grin, biting my lips together yet again before finally saying, "Shut the fuck up?"

"Is that a question? Or are you telling me what I need to do?"

I wince.

"Come on, say it with some balls, Satch."

"I don't have balls."

"Girl, you can have the biggest cojones in the world if you want to. Now show me some power!" He beats his chest like a gorilla. "I want volume. I want you to shout that shit!"

I flinch and give the person walking toward us a polite, awkward smile.

He eyes Wily like he's a crazy person before spinning on his heel and heading back the way he came.

Wily's oblivious, going on about decibels before taking my shoulders and giving them a squeeze. "Say it with some conviction."

My teeth sink into my bottom lip. He brushes his thumb over the spot again before pointing at the ground. "We're not leaving this spot until you do."

"Wily, I've got class."

"Then you better get on with it, because *we're not*

leaving this spot until you do."

It's impossible to argue with the guy, especially when he dips his hip and pretends to flick a lock of hair over his shoulder.

"What are you doing?" I grip my bag straps with a confused frown.

He struts away from me like a catwalk model, then spins and strikes a girlish pose. To say he looks hilarious is an understatement.

"I'm giving you motivation by pretending to be that bitchy little viper." Putting his hand on his hip, he checks his nails like a sorority girl from *Legally Blonde* or something, then gives me a scathing look. "Got something to say to me?" His girly voice is too funny, and I can't help bursting out in laughter.

"Say it, Satch. I want you to say it."

I cover my mouth to try and control my giggles and finally manage, "Shut the fuck up?"

"That's another question," he singsongs in his high, girly voice. "Now what did you just say to me, hippo girl?"

My laughter vanishes. I feel like he's just slapped me across the face. Hearing that word out of his mouth hurts. But it also pisses me off. I know he's just playing, but *grrrr*! Now he knows what they used to call me, and I hate that so much!

Jade has poisoned those girls against me, telling them all the things she used to taunt me with, and they've bought into it, picked up where Carmen and Katrina left off.

I'd rather die than have her poison Wily too. I can't have another Peyton Feldman situation on my hands. I honestly don't think my heart could take it.

Wily's been different.

He hasn't been the standard jock I was expecting.

He's been sweet and funny, and he's never looked at me like I'm less than.

If anything, he treats my smarts like a crown jewel and looks at me like I'm special.

And now he knows that I'm just some stupid hippo girl who—

He doesn't think that. He got super pissed that someone would even dare say that to you.

A soft growl builds in my throat.

"What was that, hippo—"

"Shut the fuck up!" I shout, the words popping out so loud and fast that I end up surprising myself.

Wily blinks. And I blink right back.

And then he lets out a loud whoop.

"Yes!" He punches his arms in the air and closes the space between us.

Before I know it, he's lifted me off my feet again... and I'm hugging him back in celebration.

Why I'm celebrating, I'm really not sure, but man... that felt so good!

I just told Pretend Viper to shut the fuck up!

"That's my girl!" Wily laughs as he puts me back on my feet and gives me a playful wink. "My little potty mouth. I'm lovin' it!"

Wrapping his arm around my shoulders again, he pulls me against his side, and we wander off to class. I swear I'm walking on air right now. What's concrete? It doesn't exist in this place. Only white, fluffy, euphoric clouds are under my feet right now.

No one has ever made me feel like this before. Like I matter, and not just because I'm related to them.

I matter.

Glancing up, I watch Wily as we walk side by side. He's saying hi to people, grinning and greeting them like it's second nature.

And I'm the invisible girl beside him.

But... not to him.

For just a moment there, I was the center of his world, and he wasn't gonna quit on me until I'd said those four words and made myself feel like I actually had the power.

Even if it was for just a second... I'll take it.

CHAPTER 19
WILY

I haven't seen Satch since we parted ways this morning. And I can't stop thinking about her. All day she's been playing in my mind. That flushed, humiliated look on her face when that bitch was talking to her like that.

Shit, I was so pissed! How dare that girl speak to her that way.

What the fuck was her problem?

Satch is a sweetheart. She wouldn't hurt a fly, and she definitely didn't deserve to be made to feel like a hippo.

But then I got her to smile.

Thank fuck for that.

I was desperate to make her feel better before I left her... and I think I did.

She did a pretty decent yell after a shit ton of coaxing, and that surprised smile on her face after those words came out of her was golden.

Shit, I can't believe that twig made her feel like a whale.

"Hippo," I snarl under my breath, still riled that someone dared to insult my lifesaver.

And she's not even that big.

All that bullshit about me straining a muscle?

Satch isn't heavy!

Sure, she's not as skinny as that stick figure is, but she definitely wasn't weighing me down.

If anything, she was really nice to hold. I like her soft edges. She felt good in my arms, kind of squishy, not all skin and bone like most of the chicks I get with. It was fun wrapping my arms around her and lifting her off her feet. I liked the sound of her giggle in my ear. I loved the look on her face when she finally told me to shut the fuck up.

Turning off the shower, I stand there for a second, watching water slide down the tiles while images from my morning start over on repeat. From the second I saw her nibbling on that muffin in the coffee shop to that moment she walked away from me, shuffling along the very edge of the sidewalk so she didn't bump into anybody.

"How many times has she been bullied?" I ask the wall, hot anger firing through me once more.

I don't have time for shitheads who make other people feel inferior. I may be a dumb prick, but I've never been an asshole, and I can't tolerate the fucking filth that came out of that girl's mouth this morning.

Damn, Satch was just gonna take it like she believed that shit.

Can't go letting that stand.

A banging on the door snaps me out of my stupor. "Dinner, dude!" Tyrell shouts. "Hurry it up."

I jump out of the shower and quickly towel myself off. Practice was a light one this afternoon, so I decided to miss the locker room rush and clean up back here. Zoey specially asked if I could eat dinner with the family tonight, so I'm making an effort. I think all the guys are. She's one persuasive toddler.

It doesn't take me long to get myself dried and dressed, and I'm soon padding down the stairs and catching the two-year-old torpedo who launches herself at me the second I step into the dining room.

"Wywee!"

"Hey, Cowgirl!" I catch her, tossing her int the air with a laugh and loving her squeals.

"Not so high." Sienna winces, covering her eyes.

Zander laughs, wrapping his arms around her and kissing her forehead. "She's okay, Sparks. Wily will always catch her."

"Yes, I will." I pull Zoey close and raspberry her neck.

Giggles fill the room as Tyrell and Grady file into it.

"Okay, that's enough, you two." Sienna flicks her fingers, beckoning me to put Zoey in her highchair. I do as I'm told, strapping the little wriggler in before taking a seat at the other end of the table.

"Where Carton? Nyah?"

"Carson and Nylah are out tonight, baby." Sienna takes Zoey's hand and gives it a little kiss.

"Date night," Zander fills in.

"They've got some making up to do, I guess." I grin at my friends, stoked that Carson finally got his shit together and didn't lose the best thing that's ever happened to him.

"Me want day." Zoey touches her chest. "Zoey day nigh'."

Sienna grins, smoothing her hand over Zoey's curls before glancing at Zander.

His smile is all mush as he leans around his girlfriend and tells their daughter, "I'll take you out, Lil' Bug. Just you and me. We can go on a daddy-daughter date."

She perks up, grabbing her plastic spoon and announcing, "And me want day Kai too."

"What?" Zander frowns.

"Zoey day Kai," she explains like this is so freaking obvious.

She's become pretty good friends with a few kids in Nolan, and her top favorites are Kai and Dayton. Sienna and Kai's mom are around the same age, and they've been hanging out quite a bit, plus Kai's dad would bring him around when he was working on the garage renovations.

Sienna starts to grin, sharing a wink across the table with me.

I take the pasta bake from Tyrell and scoop some onto my plate while Zander shakes his head and pops Zoey's balloon with gusto. "No way, kid. You're not going out with some boy until you're at least twenty-five."

"No, Daddy!" Zoey laughs.

"Yes, little girl."

She shakes her head, still laughing like he's crazy. "Zoey day Kai."

Sienna snorts, then slaps a hand over her mouth and starts giggling as well.

Zander shoots her a side-eye and mutters, "Thanks for the support, Sparks. Now our daughter's gonna be running around town with some boy who is two years older than her."

This only makes her laugh harder, and soon I'm snickering, too, though when Zander's eyes shoot across the table to meet mine, I give him a solemn nod.

There's no way in hell some guy is touching our Zoey.

Whoever is brave enough to eventually date that girl... yeah, I feel sorry for him already.

There's not one man in this house who wouldn't give everything to keep her safe. And even when we all move out and end up wherever we do, that policy will still stand. I'll fly as many miles as I have to for my little cowgirl. And everybody at this table knows it.

"So, boys, how was practice?" Sienna asks once we've all dished out our meals.

Zander launches into a detailed rundown, and I chime in with a few comments, in between pulling faces at Zoey and making her giggle.

Tyrell starts talking strategy with me for the upcoming game, and Grady...

He doesn't say a damn thing.

I scrape my plate, sharing a look with Zander before stuffing the last of the garlic bread into my mouth. He gives me a subtle headshake, and we both eye our morose friend.

He doesn't seem to notice, which is so out of character for the guy. He's sharp as a tack most of the time, but ever since the winter dance, he's been off.

My guess is that something has gone down with Teah. Have they broken up?

I kind of want to ask, but when Tyrell tried last week,

he got a quiet, icy pushback. "None of your fucking business."

Tyrell and I were both so shocked by his grumpy-ass response that neither of us said anything as he stalked out of the kitchen.

So, yeah. Grady and his girl are over. That's gotta be it.

I just don't get why he's not telling us about it. When things were going great with Teah, you couldn't shut the guy up. He was so in love with that girl, it's all he could talk about.

And now they're just over?

I really want to know what went down between them, but Grady's obviously still not ready to talk.

Shit. Do we have to give him space?

Can't we just pin him to the floor and force him to tell us?

I hate secrets. I'm an open book around these guys. They're my family. We live together. We share shit. It's what makes us tight.

Can't believe Grady's icing us out. It's so not helping him.

I have one more silent conversation with Zander, asking him if space is really what our buddy needs.

He bulges his eyes at me, and I sit back with a small frown before putting on a bright smile for Zoey, who's starting to look worried.

With a soft snicker, I touch the side of my mouth and point at Zoey. "You've got a little something on your face, kiddo."

Sienna turns to look at her daughter, then bursts out laughing.

A little something?

Zoey is covered.

That girl has pasta sauce from her chin to her ears. Her cheeks are rosy with it, and the curls around her face have an orange tinge.

Zoey giggles and that sets Zander off, and soon we're all laughing at our little girl. Even Grady cracks a smile before rising from the table and clearing his plate.

I watch him go, wondering if I should follow him, corner him in the kitchen, and try to get *something* out of him.

But my phone rings before I can.

Pulling it from my pocket, I check the screen and murmur, "Better take this," before standing up and putting on my brightest voice. "Hey, Pops. How's it hanging?"

Dad laughs the way he always does, like I'm his pride and joy. "Hey, son. Have I caught you at a good time?"

"Yeah, just finished dinner." I wander into the living room and perch my butt against the back of the couch, gazing out the window at the street traffic.

There isn't much, just a man walking his golden retriever under the streetlights. I watch them amble past as Dad tells me about his plans for the big game ahead.

"The final, Wily. Your mom and I are so proud. We've invited your grandparents, and Uncle Tomas and Aunt June will be there too. The neighbors talked me into giving them four tickets, and they'll be bringing their kids along, plus your cousins from Arizona are coming over for it. That leaves two spare seats. Is there anyone else you want me to invite?"

Satch pops into my head immediately, but I shut that thought down before it can fully form.

I doubt she'd want to come anyway.

And why would I even want her there? She's my tutor, not...

Your friend?

Why not. You like hanging out with her.

The thought spins through my brain as I try to answer my father. "You've saved a seat for Sienna?"

"Yep. Just one, right?"

"Yeah, she's leaving Zoey with Zander's sister for the weekend. His parents already have tickets, and I'm pretty sure Nylah's gonna be sitting with her family."

"Okay, well, if you think of anyone else, let me know; otherwise, I'll have no problem giving these away at work. Hank and George have both been breathing down my neck ever since you made the finals."

I force out a laugh, trying to ignore the pressure that's making my neck muscles ping tight.

"We're so excited for this game, son. You're going to play great, the way you always do, and secure your spot in the NFL."

"Dad, it doesn't work like that."

"Oh, come on. Your performance this season has been stellar. Any pro team will be lucky to have you. Austin says it's a guarantee. We just want to see you get drafted with the best."

I nod, wondering where I'll end up later this year. Which team is gonna secure me? Where will I be living? Who will I be playing for?

"...and after the Scouting Combine, there's only a couple of months to wait until we'll finally know. And rest assured, your mother and I will be throwing the biggest draft party the state of Colorado has ever seen."

A gruff laugh pops out of me. "Don't get too ahead of yourself, Pops."

"I'm not. You've been preparing for this your whole life. Your teddy bear used to be a football."

I roll my eyes, picturing Blake's face scrunching in disgust. She is so over that story.

"We knew from the second you wrapped your baby arms around that thing that you were destined for the game. And you've proved us right over and over again, son. We're so proud of you."

"Thanks, Dad."

I tuck my hand under my armpit, staring out at the lamplit street and the house beyond. It's lit up on both floors, and I can picture the students inside. I can't remember all their names, but I know the guy on the second floor is a total study nerd. He'll no doubt be hunched over his laptop stressing about how to perfect whatever assignment he's working on. I can't see his desk from here, but I know he'll be sitting at it.

For some reason, Satch pops into my head again, and I wonder where she's sitting right now. She's probably studying too. Catching up after giving me so much of her time. Damn, I didn't even think about that until now.

Shit, I hope she didn't fall too far behind. She spent *hours* helping me get that essay right. I can't wait to get my grade back. Probably the first time I've ever felt that way, but come on, I'm getting graded on work I'm actually proud of. It's such a different feeling to everything else I've handed in.

Please, God, let it be a good grade. I have no idea why

I'm so desperate for something decent. I guess I just want to be rewarded for genuine effort.

"So, you keep working hard, and I will be cheering you on from the stands." Dad wraps up the call with his usual spiel about being my biggest supporter.

I thank him once again and am almost relieved to say goodbye.

Not sure why.

I usually don't mind his little pregame pep talks. I'll get at least two more before I run onto the field, and they usually amp me up.

But not tonight, obviously.

Why?

Is it the Grady thing that's getting to me?

Or—

My phone buzzes and I glance down, expecting a GIF from my sister or a text from my mother, adding to Dad's praise-filled phone call.

But it's neither.

And I'm probably smiling way too big right now, because all I'm being offered is a chance to study.

Tutor Girl: I'm free to help you prepare for your finance assessment next week. But why don't you get your big game out of the way first? Ping me when you get back to Nolan. Good luck!

I reply with a thumbs-up and a smiley emoji, telling her I'll be in touch soon.

Part of me wants to keep the conversation going,

check to see how she's doing. But I doubt she wants to rehash her embarrassment from this morning, so I leave it at that, climbing back up the stairs, kind of mystified by why I'm looking forward to a study session as much as I'm looking forward to the game.

CHAPTER 20
ELIZABETH

So it turns out that trying to tutor a student while the Nolan U Cougars are competing in the finals is impossible.

Not only for the student who can't concentrate but for me as well.

In the end, I just give up, and we huddle in front of his laptop and watch the game together. I've never really been one for watching football, but this is the second game I've checked in on, and I'm actually nervous as I watch our team compete for the title.

This is huge.

The Cougars have only made it to the finals a few times in the past, and the team hasn't been for a good five years at least, apparently.

So this is their chance for glory, and they are giving their all to claim it.

Holding my breath, I watch the offense set for their next play and wince at the crunch of pads and helmets as the ball is shot back to Zander Donohue.

"Come on, Zan-Man," the guy beside me whispers.

It feels weird sitting this close to him. I'm usually in the adjacent seat and coaching him through technical writing, which the poor guy really struggles with. He knows what he wants to say but is hard-pressed to word things in clear, precise ways. That's what I'm here for.

But when he couldn't stop checking his phone and I finally coaxed the truth out of him, I knew his assignment was the last thing we'd be able to focus on.

"Shall we just watch it? We can catch up on this work another time."

"Yes!" He whooped and tapped his laptop, bringing up the game on his screen, then handing me an earbud.

I was so surprised by his silent invitation, and instinct told me to decline and leave him to it.

But then the thought of seeing Wily stopped me.

So I moved my seat, and now my arm is lightly brushing against the freshman beside me while we cheer the Cougars on from the second floor of the library.

Wily pushes a guy, blocking him from running after the wide receiver when he punches through a gap and starts sprinting for the end of the field.

"Carson McAvoy with a great burst of speed," the commentator says. "But can he get clear to receive the— oh," he hisses. "Taken down with a crunch. Boy, the Cougars are taking a beating tonight."

I wince, biting my bottom lip as I watch Wily run over to help Carson back to his feet. The wide receiver hobbles for a minute, then finds his footing, slowly jogging to the sideline.

Man, I don't know how they do it.

Their bodies get punished on that field, yet they keep getting up and fighting.

They're warriors, in a way.

Men who just won't quit.

You've got to admire that about them.

Although I've always avoided athletes like the plague, especially football players who have a tough arrogance that rubs me the wrong way... I have to admit that seeing what they do on that field maybe helps me understand them a little better.

They bleed and break for the glory of their team.

Maybe they deserve just a touch of that cocky pride they always wear.

My insides rumble and squirm as I think back to some of those high school football players who made me want to shrink between the cracks in the pavement.

But spending time with Wily has made me realize that not all athletes are the same. And not all athletes are hardwired to pick on the uncoordinated fat girl who can't catch a ball.

The guy beside me hisses, and I tune back in to what the commentators are saying.

"It's not looking good for the Cougars. The gap is only getting wider, and they've only got one quarter left. Can they make this last fifteen minutes count?"

I cross my fingers under the table and start praying they do.

But my silent pleading goes unheeded.

The Cougars give it everything, fighting with a desperation that's palpable... but in the end, they can't close the gap and end up losing by five points.

"No," my student whimpers, burying his face in his hands and... is he crying?

Okay, awkward.

What am I supposed to do now?

"Uh..." I lightly pat his shoulder. "Are you okay?"

"I thought this was our year." He sniffs, looking up at me with glassy eyes. "I really thought this was our year."

"I'm sorry." I wince.

He sighs, his shoulders finally hitching before he slaps his computer closed and holds his hand out for the bud in my ear.

"Oh." I hand it back and smile. "Thanks for letting me watch with you."

"Yeah." He sighs again, packing up his things and slumping away from the table, already texting someone else and completely missing my goodbye.

I stay where I am until he's out of sight, wondering how Wily's feeling right now.

Poor guy.

He lives and breathes football and probably had his heart set on winning.

He must be so gutted.

I wish I could text him and find out, but that's not my place. It's not like we're friends or anything.

He was friendly to you the other day.

He stood up for you against Viper Girl.

My lips twitch as I relive his antics as a catwalk model. He was so sweet. Those tingles spread through me again, and I don't bother fighting them. For just a second, I let them bubble and grow until my mind is consumed with the good-looking blond. His smile, those blue eyes, his big, powerful body lifting me off the ground.

No one's ever lifted me like that before.

Well, not as an adult.

My dad stopped picking me up when I was like eight or nine.

My feet haven't left the ground in over a decade.

But they did the other morning.

They dangled in the air because two strong arms held me tight against a solid chest and—

My phone starts ringing.

I jolt, whacking my elbow on the table as I come out of my reverie.

"Ouch." I give it a rub while wrestling the device out from the front pocket of my bag.

Only just catching the call in time, I whisper a quick "Hey, Mom. I'm just in the library. Can I call you back in a sec?"

"Yes, of course, sweetheart. Talk to you soon."

She hangs up, and I hurry to gather my things. Rushing down the steps, I slip on the second to last one, catching myself against the railing and forcing a tight smile at the woman who saw me.

"You okay?" she asks.

I nod and rush past her, my cheeks burning as I bolt out the glass doors and into the cold air outside. It feels good against my skin, and I suck in a deep, crisp breath before calling Mom back.

"Hey," I greet her. "How's it going?"

"I'm good. I was just missing my girl and thought I'd check in."

I smile. Missing me. We spoke yesterday... although that was about the diner and the fact that Dad has to hire a new cook because Ralph is finally retiring. It's about time—the man is like seventy-nine or something—but he's been an institution at our family diner since my parents opened it twenty-eight years ago.

They're going to miss Ralph so much, and all I can hope is that his replacement is a perfect fit. I'm not sure my dad will cope if the kitchen's not running smoothly.

"I'm doing well." I give my standard response.

"Yeah? Still acing all your classes?"

"I'm trying."

Mom laughs. "Of course you're acing them. You've always been the smartest girl in the room."

I cringe. I should be smiling. Being the smartest is awesome and a great compliment.

But for once, it'd be cool to be the prettiest girl in the room... or the most popular.

That is never going to happen. Let it go!

Logically, I know being smart is better than both those things, but—

"What else have you been up to?" Mom asks. "Please tell me it's not all study, study, study."

"No," I lie.

"So, you're getting out there? What social events have you gone to?"

Aw, crap. Why does she always have to ask for specifics?

"Well, I watched a football game today."

"Really? Did you know what was happening?" She laughs.

I grin and admit without thinking, "Someone explained the rules to me, so I was able to follow along."

"Oh, that's wonderful. So, did you go to a sports bar with them to watch it? Who is this football tutor of yours?" She laughs again, and all I can do is wince.

I'm so not ready to tell her about Wily. She'll go ahead and ask a million questions about him, and who knows what will come out of my mouth.

No, it's better just to play it safe.

Scuffing the sidewalk, I tell her, "I watched in the library."

"By yourself?" Mom sounds so disappointed. It's nice to be able to tell her that I was watching with my tutoring student. "Oh, well, that's something. Nice that you were doing something a little social."

Hardly. We barely talked during the game.

But I'm not about to admit that.

I open my mouth, hoping to bring the conversation back around to her and Dad, but she beats me to it.

"And how about dorm life? Is everyone being nice to you?"

My insides scrunch into a tight ball as thoughts of Viper Girl's nastiness pepper me. She's not in my dorm, but her face flashes through my mind, because I know Mom's really checking to make sure that I'm not being bullied again.

Mom can never know that Jade is now attending Nolan U, and that she's recruited new minions for her Hate on Hippo Girl cause. It'll eat her alive, and I'm not going to put that on her. She'll only stress about what might be happening to me and then tell Dad, which will make him worry, and they have enough on their plate right now.

My silence is protecting them, and I can handle those girls... as long as I avoid their normal routes and stay invisible.

"Bessie? People are being nice to you, right?"

"Yeah," I assure her. "People in my dorm are lovely."

At least I think they are. I don't actually hang with any of them, but no one pays me much attention, and that can only be a good thing.

Mom lets out a lyrical sigh. "Well, that's wonderful to hear. I'm just so keen for you to make a good friend. You know, I've heard that the friends you make in college can last you a lifetime."

I let out an awkward laugh, not sure how to respond.

"You are trying, aren't you, sweetheart?"

My throat swells, and it's an effort to force out a cheerful "Of course." I want to tell her that I had dinner with a friend the other night, but did I really?

It was a tutoring session that involved food!

And other conversation.

My insides tingle as I think about the animated look on Wily's face as he told me how epic going to the Super Bowl was.

"Because I just don't want you to hide yourself away and let... things from the past stop you." Mom grabs my attention with her quiet words, and I start munching on my lower lip. "Those girls from high school made you feel like it wasn't safe to put yourself out there, and it's not fair for your college experience to be hampered by them. I don't want you to feel like you have to hide in the shadows anymore. You're free of them now, and it's your right to experience all college has to offer."

With burning eyes, I stare in front of me and try to keep this lie going. I feel kind of bad when she makes statements like that and I don't correct her.

Part of me wants to wail, "But Jade is here! I have to protect myself, Mom. I have to!"

But instead, I force a smile into my voice. "I know, Mom. And you don't have to worry. I'm having a good year."

"Are you sure?" Her doubt always makes me feel bad for some reason.

Like she doesn't believe I can have fun unless I'm going to parties and hanging out with a bunch of rowdy people.

She doesn't get that fun for me is snuggling up with a movie musical and singing along with the actors… or drinking my coffee every morning at Java Jeans and watching the world pass me by… or disappearing into the pages of a good book and getting so absorbed that it actually feels real.

I love those things.

That ball in my stomach bounces around, an energy I don't understand making it vibrate. Rubbing the itchy spot above my belly button, I try to ignore these weird sensations inside me.

I'm happy with my own company.

I don't need friends!

Wily flashes through my mind. His sweet smile. The way he held me, made me laugh.

It felt so freaking good to have an ally. To have him shout at that mean girl on my behalf.

But…

I'm happy on my own.

I keep trying to sell myself on that line for some reason. Tonight… it's not holding as much power.

Pausing at the edge of the curb, I check the street for traffic before shuffling across the road and noticing a group of girls giggling together as they walk ahead of me, all talking at once.

They sound so happy.

So connected.

I've never had that.

I can't imagine I ever will.

And something about that thought makes that ball in my stomach shrivel. It's replaced with a heavy, aching feeling that I know all too well.

I keep trying to deny it, but as I walk home talking to my mother, reality hits like a power punch...

I'm lonely.

And I don't know how to make any friends.

CHAPTER 21
WILY

We've had a night to sleep off our loss.

To say we all shuffled off to bed highly deflated was an understatement. Even I couldn't rally the will to be positive.

I, Mr. Glass Half Full, went to bed utterly devastated.

I don't know how the team slept.

I tossed and turned, woke up groggy and depressed.

Shuffling out to the bus with cameras clicking in our faces was an effort, but no harder than having to sit through those interviews after the game. It fucking sucked. We've all been coached on what to say and what to avoid, and the interviewers seem to love me because I know how to put on a smile, make a joke, even when I'm feeling like shit.

And I did—I performed the way I was supposed to, pretended like the loss was manageable.

But shit... I was gutted.

The bus ride to the airport was solemn, subdued.

The plane ride back to Nolan wasn't much better.

And now we're back in Colorado, heading to campus with only quiet murmurs happening around us. Grady's got his headphones on and is staring out the window, Tyrell's having a quiet chat with Zander, and Carson's on his phone, texting... it's gotta be Nylah. His lips keep twitching like he's fighting a grin.

I frown and look away from him, gazing out the window at the familiar highway. How many times have we traveled this road back and forth to away games?

And that was my last one.

Shit.

My last game as a Nolan U Cougar.

No wonder I'm feeling so empty.

Playing college ball has been the highlight of my life so far. I've loved every minute of it... and now it's over.

"Okay, gentlemen." Coach Jones stands up, clapping his hands to get our attention. "Phones and tech away please, guys. I want your full attention."

He waits out the shuffling as everyone gets themselves organized, and we're soon all staring at him with morose curiosity.

"That was a tough game yesterday."

A ripple of disgruntled murmurs spreads through the bus.

"But you can hold your heads up high. When we get back to school, you can walk onto campus as proud men because you fought hard. You gave it your all. Every player who walked off the field yesterday had nothing left in the tank, and that's all I can ask of you." Coach smiles, his white teeth flashing. "You are an excellent team. You're a team who made it to the finals. The finals!" He starts clapping, then lets out a whoop. "The finals, gentlemen! You are an excellent team!"

The other coaches start cheering, and soon that enthusiasm travels down the bus until a deafening crescendo of celebration takes over.

He lets us go for it, blowing off whatever steam we've been bottling up before finally bringing us back down.

"That's the energy I want to see, because this isn't over. We may have finished our season, but we've still got practices to attend. We have to prep our men who are hoping to go pro. They've got the Combine coming up. It's still weeks away, but we want them in peak condition, don't we?"

Another round of cheers goes up as those nearby slap me on the shoulder. I look at Zander, who's also getting jostled, and we share a grin.

"And we want to keep developing our younger players, getting them ready for next season while those of you who are ready to lead prep yourself for that shift too. So..." He claps his hands again. "This isn't over. This is a fresh beginning to our next season and the journey beyond college ball. This is an exciting time for us, and we're gonna walk off this bus and show every student at Nolan U that we are proud of what we've achieved this year. You with me?"

And here we go again, laughing and cheering as we head back to campus.

We are pumped and fired up by the time we finally pull onto the school grounds, and the reception that awaits us is exactly what we needed.

The band and cheerleaders are out in force, along with a large gathering of students and faculty.

They cheer us off the bus, and I feel like a celebrity as I high-five those I pass and get hugged and kissed by numerous girls.

I greet them all with smiles and thanks, enjoying the hyped-up atmosphere.

For a second, I find myself scanning the crowd for Satch, but I don't see her, and it's impossible to ignore my disappointment.

Holy shit. Am I looking forward to my tutoring session tomorrow?

I can't help a soft laugh as I dole out another high five and realize how excited I am about hanging out in the library to study.

Never thought I'd think something like that. Not in a million years.

CHAPTER 22
ELIZABETH

I'm meeting Wily in thirty minutes, and I'm already getting ready. It only takes fifteen minutes to walk to the library, but I want to be there on time and... for some reason... I want to look good.

Why?

Why can't I just throw something on like I normally would?

Why was I unhappy with my original skirt and sweater combo?

Why is my favorite cardigan suddenly not good enough?

I frown in the mirror, taking in my reflection and the olive-green dress I chose. It has a pretty blue swirl through it. I love this fabric. Mom and I picked it out together last time we went shopping, but—

My shoulders slump and I unzip my skirt at the side before reaching for the dress I wore yesterday. It's navy blue with an orange ribbon at the back. I do like this one. And I feel comfortable in it.

Tugging on the fabric, I get it sitting as best as I can, then select my favorite winter coat. I hardly ever wear this one, because it's white and I have an inability to keep my clothes clean, but I take a risk anyway, sliding it on before adding a touch more lip balm to my mouth.

I don't really wear makeup.

Mom has never been into it, and I've never really had anyone show me how. I could watch YouTube clips, but what if I screw it up?

I seriously don't need to give people any more reasons to hassle me.

Clearing my throat, I turn away from my reflection before I'm tempted to change again. My fingers shake as I spray two squirts of perfume on. Aunt Shayla gave it to me for my birthday last year, and I've only worn it one other time.

Why are you wearing it now? It's a tutoring session, not a date!

I huff, annoyed with myself for losing my head but not having time to wash the scent off. I'm now running later than I want to be, so I finish tying my boots as fast as I can, then head out the door, double-checking first that I have everything I need.

Wily hasn't told me much about this finance test he's doing, so I'll have to figure out my teaching plan when I get there and I see what he's specifically studying for. I'm sure I can throw something together. I grew up watching Dad do his books for the diner, and I've got a pretty good head for numbers. Whatever class Wily's taking is bound to be one of the easier ones, and I should be able to pick it up fast enough.

Anything I don't know, I'll just research and teach

myself before the session after this one. I'll do everything in my power to get him prepped for his test.

Buttoning up my coat in the elevator, I try to calm the insanity in my stomach. Seriously? What is wrong with me?

I have no idea why my body is reacting this way.

It's a *tutoring* session. That's it.

Just because Wily stood up for me the other day and I haven't seen him since is no reason to get all tingly and lose my head.

But he stood up for you!

He was sweet and funny, and you like him!

My eyes bulge as the thought dawns on me.

No. No, I can't do that.

I can't go liking the guy.

The last time I had a crush on a football player, he used me to do his homework for him, then laughed at the size of my underwear.

I'm not having any kind of mushy feelings toward Wily Wilson.

He just happens to be a nice person who just happens to be a football player.

That's it.

That is so not it.

He also happens to be a super-hot, super-strong, gorgeous man who literally swept me off my feet, and a sweet older brother who takes his sister to concerts, and a fan of one of my favorite bands, and can strut like a catwalk model in order to make me laugh, and pretends to be King Wily for a two-year-old princess, and—

Stop it! Stop finding reasons to fall for this guy.

Too late! You like him. You really like him.

I ignore the taunting voice in my head and barrel outside without paying proper attention.

A mistake I'm about to pay a very high price for.

"Hey, hippo," a sultry voice says, and I jolt to a stop.

Oh shit. No! Not now. Please not now!

I scan the three girls in front of me. All skinny. All beautiful. All mean.

Jade's hair is in a high ponytail, her green eyes two laser beams ready to cut me in half. Viper Girl's to her right, glaring at me like I'm a slug she's just found in her salad. And then there's Kelsey Cartman, her clawlike nails digging into her designer jacket as she looks me up and down and lets out a derisive snicker.

The only reason I know her name is because I was asked to tutor her, and after one painful session, she refused to work with me again, telling Ms. Bigsby lies about how I'd called her stupid and unteachable. Thankfully, Ms. Bigsby was smart enough to know that was bullshit, but it was still humiliating having to sit in her office and be accused of this stuff by Kelsey. Her crocodile tears made real tears fall out of my eyes as I begged Ms. Bigsby to believe me.

I don't know what I would have done if she hadn't.

I have no idea who Kelsey is working with now, and part of me wonders if it was all just a setup to discredit me. Maybe Kelsey never needed tutoring at all, but Jade convinced her to put her name forward just so she could ruin my rep and cost me my tutoring job.

I wouldn't put it past my lifelong tormentor to pull something that low.

Swallowing the hot surge of bile burning the back of

my throat, I shuffle to the side, ready to move around them, but they quickly jump in front of me.

"We need to talk," Jade spits.

"No thank you," I whisper, trying to dart around her again.

No such luck. Kelsey pushes me back.

I wobble on my feet but don't fall over. Gripping my bag strap, I stare at the ground and start to count. It's something that will distract my mind and stop me from spiraling into full panic mode.

One. Two...

I wish it would stop my heart from racing. It's pounding so hard and fast I feel dizzy.

Three—

"Shut up and listen," Viper Girl snaps at me.

"Wily Wilson," Jade continues. "I don't know what you think you're doing hanging out with him, but that is not an option for you, okay? He's off-limits, and this is your one warning to stay away from him."

The tingles I've been fighting all morning fizzle away, replaced with a heavy disappointment.

He's waiting for me right now.

Am I just supposed to not go?

Leave him hanging?

Glancing up, I look between the girls and feel my insides rebel against that thought. I'm not about to let the guy down. He's counting on me.

"I'm his tutor," I murmur. "He needs help with school."

"I'm his tutor." Kelsey puts on a voice, openly mocking me before cackling. "We all know what a shit tutor you are."

Jade ignores her friend and glares at me. "He can find another tutor."

"I'm pretty sure he wants to work with me." I suck in a breath, bracing myself for their reaction.

"You better watch yourself, Fatty Satchwell." Jade steps forward and I flinch, backing away from her. "You're playing with things that don't belong to you."

"Last I checked, they don't belong to you either."

What are you doing? Are you fighting back?

Stay safe, you idiot! Just shut up and run away!

"What did you just say to me?" Jade's eyes narrow even farther as the other two girls step in line with her. They're like dragons, about to breathe hellfire all over my short, round self.

I bite my lips together and look back to the safety of the ground.

That's when Cackles starts to sniff the air and laugh like a hyena again. "Are you wearing perfume?" Her mockery is hot tar, coating me with a burning sensation that makes my cheeks flame. "Oh shit! Are you on your way to see him right now?"

I shake my head, desperate for them not to smell my lie.

"You better not be." Jade grabs the lapel of my coat, fisting it and dragging me toward her. "Now you listen close. I'm not sure when you're seeing him again, but you cancel it."

I try to shake her off me, but she holds on a little tighter, her breath hitting the side of my face.

"Did you hear me? I want you to stay away from him."

My eyes start to burn, my throat swelling to the point of pain.

"You guys okay over there?" someone calls from the door of Buckley Hall.

"Yes. Just catching up with an old friend." Kelsey puts on a smile and waves to the curious bystander while Jade starts smoothing down my jacket, then wraps her arms around me.

"It's so good to see you!" she says way too loudly, her voice irritatingly sweet and sticky.

I try to wriggle out of her embrace, but the other girls jump in on this group hug and don't let me go until whoever was checking on us has disappeared.

As soon as she's gone, I'm released, and they wipe off their clothing like it's now germ-infested.

"We're really saying this for your own good." Jade looks over her outfit, checking for marks and blemishes before flashing her green gaze at me. "Wily Wilson is out of your league."

"We just don't want to see you get hurt." Kelsey's sweet voice is like metal scraping on metal. It makes my spine twitch, which only adds to my already itching skin.

"It's really important that you know your place." Viper Girl's pointed tone does not match the saccharine look on her face. "That's all we're trying to say."

"You see, Wily and I..." Jade smooths a hand down her ponytail. "We have a connection. The two of us... it just makes sense, you know? And I don't think you tutoring him is the best idea."

I can't help a soft scoff. "Are you worried I'm competition?"

Their howling laughter makes me wish I'd just kept my mouth shut.

"No." Viper Girl's laughing so hard she can barely talk.

Anger simmers. It does sometimes, although I know better than to let it show.

Except... Wily did the other day.

Maybe it's okay to let yourself be a little pissed off. It feels better than fear, doesn't it?

I frown, curling my fingers into fists and blurting, "You worried I'm going to tell him about all the horrible things you've done to me over the years? You worried I might tell him the truth and put him off you for good?"

Jade gasps, her hand firing out and cracking me across the face.

I bite back my whimper, knowing that crying in front of her will only make it worse.

"Jade," Viper Girl softly whispers, darting her eyes to her irate friend before looking to Kelsey.

All three of them seem surprised by Jade's outburst. Jade included.

Her voice shakes as she straightens my jacket collar and pastes on a smile. "I don't know what you're talking about."

I give her a confused frown. "You just slapped me." I brush trembling fingertips over the burning sting on my cheek. I'm kind of reeling. She's never gotten physical before. Her weapons are her words.

The thought of her treatment of me escalating into physical torment makes my eyes start to water.

"Don't be so emotional." She crosses her arms, her nostrils flaring. "I just had to get your attention somehow. You really need to understand this, Libs, and I don't think you're getting it."

"Oh, I get it." My voice is so soft and shaky I'm not sure they can hear me. "You're worried I'll tell Wily the truth."

"Like he's going to believe you," Kelsey sneers.

Jade steps forward, stamping her heeled boot right next to my foot, her seething anger making me shrink back. "If you even *try* to say something to him, you'll regret it, you understand me? *Stay away* from Wily Wilson." Her eyes flash, and I shuffle back out of slapping range. Tucking my chin down, I cross my arms around myself and pray they'll let me walk past.

They do, and I pick up my pace as soon as I'm clear of them.

"Stay away, hippo!" Viper Girl calls after me.

I hunch my shoulders and mumble, "Shut the fuck up," before scampering to the library.

I'm not even sure I want to go anymore.

My face hurts.

My skin is no doubt red if the sting is anything to go by.

Rubbing my tender cheek, I contemplate bailing and heading back to my room. But what if they're still standing there, waiting to pounce on me again?

It's so unlike Jade to slap me that way. Her assaults are always verbal or prank-like, something that can be laughed off.

I really must haven't gotten to her.

She's probably not used to me arguing back. I usually just stand there and take it. And she must have told her new posse that, because they were dishing it out like I'm a zero threat.

Because you are.

Aw, man. How much has she told them? Probably everything. I can just picture them huddled together in her dorm room, laughing their heads off while Jade regales them with stories about all the cruel pranks Team Evil played on me in high school.

I never once stood up for myself then. Touching my cheek again, I remind myself *why* I quietly take it.

But...

It did feel a little bit good arguing back.

I got under Jade's skin for once.

Me.

Insignificant, unimportant me.

Walking through the library doors, I grip my bag straps and head to the stairs. It's always so quiet and peaceful in here. It's one of my favorite places to hang out.

It's why I tend to hold my tutoring sessions here. It's usually a haven.

Climbing the stairs, I pause at the top and scan the tables and shelves around me. They're littered with various students working on assignments or having whispered conversations.

Wily's no doubt waiting for me around the corner.

Should I go?

I'm late now, thanks to Team Evil 2.0.

Their warnings flicker through me again, and I hesitate.

Maybe I shouldn't go.

What if they catch me with Wily?

What if they find out that I've broken their rules?

I hate to think what their retribution will look like.

But...

Creeping forward, I work my way down the aisle of books and peek my head around the corner.

There he is.

All tall and beautiful, sitting in his chair... waiting for me.

He's got headphones on, his head bopping along to whatever music he's listening to, and I can't help watching him for a second.

My lips twitch, then grow into a smile when he mouths the words, then plays a little air guitar.

He's adorable.

And funny.

And I really want to tutor him right now.

But I probably shouldn't.

Sadness sweeps through me as I rub my cheek again and go to turn away.

"Satch!" Wily calls, his voice booming across the quiet space.

I wince, hunching my shoulders as the woman at the table nearby gives him a marked frown and hisses, "Shhh!"

"Sorry." Wily's voice is still way too loud as he pulls his headphones off and waves me over.

Crap. What am I supposed to do now?

His head tips, his eyebrows puckering in obvious confusion when I still haven't made a move. He waves me over once more, and I can't just bail on him now. He's seen me!

Sucking in a nervous breath, I squeeze my index finger and head toward him, bumping my hip on the table closest to me before slowing to a snail-like crawl and eventually stopping beside him.

CHAPTER 23
WILY

I gaze up at Satch, wondering what her problem is. Why was she hiding in the aisle? She'd obviously seen me and looked like she was about to bail.

Did I do something wrong?

She seems so nervous and uncertain right now. She won't look at me, and her face—

Wait a second.

What the fuck?

A low growl rumbles in my throat as I lightly take her wrist and ask, "What happened to your face?"

She bulges her eyes at me, wriggling her wrist out of my grasp and shaking her head. "What... what do you mean?"

"Your face." I reach up to gently brush my thumb over the red stain on her cheek.

She flinches away from me, darting a look over her shoulder before pulling out her chair and not taking a seat.

"Satch." I place my finger under her chin, forcing her to look at me again.

When she's standing beside me and I'm sitting like this, we're basically eye level.

I study the blemish, anger rising through me like a firestorm. "Did that bitch come near you again? Did she do this to you?"

"No." She eases away from me, unbuttoning her coat and shrugging it off her shoulders.

Her hands are shaking as she hangs it over the back of her chair, clearly avoiding eye contact.

I stare at the unblemished side of her face while she takes her sweet time getting organized.

"Satch," I try again, my voice gruff and ragged.

"It's nothing." She bends down to focus on her bag. The zipper sounds loud in the quiet space between us, and I grit my jaw as she takes forever placing her laptop down along with paper and her pencil case.

Finally taking a seat, she glances at me and admits, "I tripped on my way here and whacked my face. It's embarrassing, and I didn't want to tell you."

My insides settle, although I still hate the thought of her falling over and hurting herself.

"Are you okay?" My tone drops to a soft whisper, and I reach for her face again. "What happened?"

She doesn't fight me so easily this time and lets me look. "I was running late, and I slipped and smacked my face on my doorframe."

Brushing my thumb over the red mark, I can picture it all so clearly and hate that I wasn't there to catch her. "Can I get you an ice pack or something?"

"No, it's fine." She brushes my hand away and gives

me a tentative smile. "Really. I'm okay. I'm a bit of a klutz, so this isn't new for me." She lets out a self-deprecating laugh, but it's too tight.

Is she too flustered for a simple whoopsie, or does it hurt more than she's letting on?

What actually happened?

I don't know what to believe, especially when her eyes dart back to the tabletop.

Shit. She's probably embarrassed, and I'm making a big deal out of this. Forcing her to tell me was a dick move.

Annoyed at myself, I give her arm a light, playful tap. "Hey, don't worry about it. We all fall on our asses at some point. And I embarrass myself on the regular."

Her laughter is soft and breathy. "I highly doubt that."

"Oh no, I definitely do."

She glances up and I wink at her, hoping she's starting to feel better.

I don't know why I'm so compelled to see her smile turn genuine. Maybe it's because she's a good, kind-hearted person, and I don't like seeing her hurt.

"I've got a bunch of stories I could tell you." I lean back in my seat, looking at the ceiling as I pick the most embarrassing one I can think of. "Like last summer, my sister, Blake, and I were playing hide-and-seek with our little cousins, and I had the best spot. It was under the decking of our beach house, and she had been searching for ages. I was crammed into that space quietly laughing because I could hear how annoyed she was getting, not being able to find me..." I tut and shake my head. "And then I had to go and stand on a fucking crab. The thing pinched my toe, and

I thought I was being eaten by The Meg. I freaked out and started screaming, running out from under the deck and completely beaning myself on the cross beam."

"Oh no." She gasps.

"I had a lump on my forehead the size of Everest, and Dad had to crawl under the deck to pull me out of there." I give her a cringing smile. "Not my proudest moment. Blake's never gonna let me forget it. And that little butt face made sure all my teammates knew about it as well. She sent pics to Zander and Grady and..." I shake my head.

"That's awful." Satch's face is all sympathy, her eyebrows wrinkling.

"Yeah, if you saw the size of the crab I was freaking out about, you'd understand why everyone laughed themselves silly." I wink and grin at her, stoked when her lips curve into a twitching smile.

I wait a beat and watch it slowly grow, her face flushing a pretty pink.

Leaning forward, I catch her eye, and she finally looks right at me, her smile growing even brighter.

"So... I figure that's enough embarrassment for one day. Should we get started?"

She nods, reaching across me to pull my wayward stack of papers toward her and...

Damn, she smells good.

I lightly sniff the air and have to resist the urge to bury my nose in her neck and get a good whiff.

Did she smell this good last time we were together?

I can't remember.

Whatever she's sprayed on... holy shit. She mustn't

have been wearing it last time, because I don't think I would have been able to concentrate.

Leaning back in my seat, I give her a minute to look through my haphazard notes and try to focus on math and numbers and anything that isn't Satch smelling like a fucking goddess.

What the hell is wrong with me?

She's my tutor.

My friend.

That's it.

Glancing at her, I can't help quickly checking her out. She's wearing this blue dress that looks good on her. I like the scooping neckline; I can see that line where her boobs are touching and—

Don't check her out, man!

Forcing my eyes back to her face, I notice the way her lips move as she tries to decipher my shitty handwriting.

"My professor talks really fast," I try to explain. "I can't keep up sometimes."

"That's okay." Her tone is sweet, her smile kind when she looks at me and says, "Why don't you tell me in your own words what this test is going to be about?"

I open my mouth to respond, and that familiar infection seems to spread right through me again, blank spaces filling up my mind as that pressure takes over.

"Hey." She pats my wrist. "Breathe in, then breathe out." She smiles when I do it. "And again... Good. That's good. Now, let your mind relax... and grab something to fidget with."

"Oh, yeah." Rummaging in my bag, I pull out the fidget toy she gave me and focus on the blue plastic as I roll it between my thumb and forefinger and try to think.

"Breathe," she reminds me.

I suck in another breath, then exhale and tip my head back. "Okay. Finances. I think the test is gonna be about… investment, maybe? They were talking about growth funds and how we can use them to build personal finances for retirement or something." I cringe and look at her. "Does that sound like a thing? Are growth funds a thing?"

She grins, her smile wide and beautiful as she looks through my paperwork. "Growth funds are definitely a thing. Good job. Why don't we go over what you've learned so far this term. You tell me what you can remember, and I'll compare it to these papers here and we can fill in any gaps."

Shuffling in my seat, I do my best to recall what I can.

In all honesty, I'm surprised by how much I remember. I don't necessarily understand it all, but there are a lot of words swimming around in my brain, and they seem to pop out in an order that makes sense.

As usual, Satch stops me when I lose my way, asking me questions to get me back on track and jotting down notes as we go.

I like her handwriting. It looks like a font, all neat and evenly spaced. It's not scribble like mine. I can actually see each letter of each word like I'm reading a print book. Holy fuck, how does she do that?

"Okay, so my guess is that this test is going to give you a few scenarios about a particular financial situation, and then you'll be asked to consider the best course of action."

I nod, a spike of worry cutting through my abdomen.

Shit. I hate being put on the spot like that. Test situations always suck.

"It's nothing to worry about." She rests her hand over mine. "I know tests are scary, but you can do this, and there's no need to rush. There'll be plenty of time for you to take a breath and have a think before you have to start doing any kind of calculations or writing, okay?"

I nod, not really believing her but not wanting her to feel bad. She is trying to help me, after all.

She pauses, watching me for a second and obviously thinking something through.

"You know what... let's try this."

"Try what?" I ask as she stands up and points to her chair. "What are you doing?"

"You sit there."

My face buckles with confusion, but I do as I'm told, shifting into her seat and wondering what the hell she's up to.

"Now, I want you to pretend that I've just moved to the US, and I have my first job here. My English is good, but it's not my first language. And I don't really know how the money systems work in Colorado or across the United States."

I squeeze my fidget toy. "O-kay."

"I want you to teach me what I need to do in order to help me grow the finances I already have and what I should be doing with the money I'm now earning. I'm not a full citizen yet, I'm on a permanent resident visa, so I won't have access to government benefits. I'll need to start by using the stock market for long-term investments, so... how do I do that?"

My throat restricts, making it hard to swallow. "You..." I point at myself. "You want me to teach you?"

"Yes." She smiles.

I like the shape her mouth makes when she does that. She's got pretty teeth.

Can people have pretty teeth?

I don't know, but hers are pretty.

Or maybe it's those plump lips I'm digging.

"The best way to learn something is to apply it," Satch tells me. "An even better way to learn something is to teach it to someone else. And that's what I want you to do. So, you pretend that I don't know anything about investing and explain what a growth fund is to me and how I can make it work for my future."

My mouth goes dry as I shake my head. "I can't do that."

She lets out a soft laugh and places her hand over mine again. Her short fingers look so small against my gorilla hand.

"Yes, you can." Now it's her turn to reach out and tip my chin.

I reluctantly look her in the eye the way she wants me to.

"You're smarter than you think, Wily Wilson. Now teach me." Her hopeful expression is so... how the fuck do I say no to it?

Everything in me is screaming *Don't do this! You're gonna suck and make a fool of yourself!*

But if I tell her that and bail like I want to, she'll be really disappointed. And I will do anything not to be the guy to make her frown.

So, against my better judgment, I shift in my seat,

pulling a blank sheet of paper toward me and trying to figure out where to start.

Okay.

Investments.

Growth funds.

She's pretending to know nothing.

For me. She's playing clueless so I can come across like the smart one.

I dart my eyes to hers and she gives me an encouraging nod, and this sensation kind of blooms in my chest. I don't know what it is or what it means, but it makes me want to ace this task just so I can see her smile.

And ace it I fucking will!

She wants me to play pretend. I'm the king of pretend.

Clearing my throat, I gather up my pages, tapping them into a neat pile and becoming the investment adviser she wants me to be. "So, Miss Crapadopolis..."

A laughing snort bursts out of her, and she slaps a hand over her eyes as I continue this charade.

"I hear you're new to the country, and you're seeking some financial advice."

It takes her a second to get her giggling under control, but finally she looks up and gives me an impish grin. "Yes. That would be... uh... very helpful." She's putting on an accent that I can't identify.

In fact, I don't think anyone could.

It's some combination of European that is probably a blend of French, Spanish, and Italian.

I'm not sure, but it's fucking hilarious, and I can't help a short laugh of my own while I click on my pen and get to work.

I walk her through basic investments, explaining the

stock market as best I can. She asks me questions that push for more details and I'm pretty sure I deliver... if the grin on her face is anything to go by.

Score for Wily! Smile number one. How many more of those can I get?

She keeps playing clueless and refuses to drop that accent, forcing me to continue. I've soon launched into various types of ways to invest in the stock market, and by the end of my thirty-minute spiel, she's nodding and telling me she'd like to invest ten thousand dollars in an index fund, and which one should she go for?

My lips twitch with a grin as I then run her through various types of index funds, and in the end, she's leaning toward the S&P 500.

"An excellent choice, Miss Crapadopolis."

She giggles. "Thank you, Mr. Money. You explained that beautifully. You must be a very smart man."

I smile but can't nod in agreement. She'll get it one day. I'm not as clever as she thinks I am.

But you did just teach her something about the stock market.

And shit, am I blushing right now?

Clearing my throat, I focus back on the paper I was scribbling all over. My messy digits and letters are hard to read, and I want to cover them up with my arm, but Satch pulls the page away from me before I can.

"That was so good, Wily. Seriously. You did such a great job." Her praise soaks into me, and I lap it up like a thirsty dog. "You were clear and easy to understand. You answered all of my questions without waffling. You definitely know more than you think you do."

"Yeah, well, I was surprised how much came out of

me just then. My brain didn't even freeze up once." I shake my head, kind of in awe as I only just realize that. "Wow. That was... I mean, you're incredible."

"Me?" She laughs and brushes off the compliment. "I'm nothing special."

"No, you are. That's the thing. I've worked with so many tutors, and none of them have made me get stuff the way you do." I keep staring at her, enjoying the soft pink of her rounded cheeks. "Do you have a major yet? Like, do you know what you're hoping to do after college?"

She shrugs. "I'm not exactly sure yet. Maybe something to do with literature?"

"Become a teacher." I lightly grip her arm. "You have to. You're so good at it. Seriously amazing."

"I'm not amazing," she mumbles.

"Yeah, you are." My hand shifts from her arm to her face, coaxing her to look up at me.

Those big eyes of her finally find mine, and I drink in her soulful gaze.

There's something in that look that...

Oh shit, she's...

Does she like me?

I've seen that look enough times to know it.

Girls crush on me. I'm not being arrogant, they just do. I've been hit on more times than I can count, and I know this look.

But I also don't.

Because she seems to see me in a way that no one else can.

She thinks I'm smart, capable of more than just football, and...

223

I brush my thumb over the curve of her cheek, my eyes darting back to those plump lips again. They look so fucking kissable, and I really shouldn't.

I can't go getting distracted by my tutor this way.

But how can I not kiss those beautiful lips?

She's staring at me like I'm something special... like maybe she wants me to kiss her.

So before I can talk myself out of it, I lean a little closer.

Her breath catches for just a second before my lips press against hers.

CHAPTER 24
ELIZABETH

What is Wily doing?

Oh my gosh, he's kissing me. He's actually kissing me!

And this isn't some mindless peck on the lips after handing in an assignment. He's put some thought into this. He stared at me for a breath-stealing moment, then glanced at my mouth and made a choice...

To kiss me!

Wily Wilson is kissing me because he wants to.

Holy shit.

What do I do with this?

Uh... maybe you should kiss him back.

How?!

I've never kissed a guy before. I have no idea what I'm doing, and it's taking everything in me not to freak out.

Just breathe.

His lips are covering my mouth. How am I supposed to breathe?

I can't do this.

Yes, you can. Don't you dare move, Elizabeth Satchwell!

Wily's hand shifts on my face, trailing around to the back of my neck while his tongue darts out, brushing along my lower lip.

Oh shit! What was that?

Do I open my mouth?

Yes! Just like they do in the movies!

At least try it.

My lips are trembling as I tentatively part them to see what it feels like.

Tipping his head, Wily changes the angle, his tongue gliding across the tip of mine.

Oh my gosh, that feels so freaking good!

Am I doing it right?

I don't know if I'm doing this right.

Do I...?

My brain starts to sizzle, panic taking me out as my heart rate accelerates to this heady rhythm that makes me dizzy.

I can't do this.

I don't even understand why he's kissing me.

And then for some wretched reason, Jade's face pops into my head, her green eyes flashing.

If she saw us right now, she'd kill me!

Screw her! She's not the boss of you.

Just enjoy this kiss and—

I can't!

How can I enjoy this kiss when it shouldn't be happening?

Wily Wilson does not like me that way.

He shouldn't.

I'm not his type.

I'm not—

Ripping my mouth away from his, I give him one gasping, gaping look before bolting from my chair and darting around the closest stacks.

"Satch?"

Ignoring his confusion, I run into the back corner of the library.

It's seriously the stupidest thing I could have done.

One, I left all my stuff behind, and two... I've cornered myself.

How the hell am I supposed to escape from here?

CHAPTER 25
WILY

"Satch?" I call her name again, leaving all our stuff on the table in order to find her.

Why the hell did she take off?

Did I do something wrong?

I thought she wanted me to kiss her, but maybe she didn't.

Although, she did kiss me back. I mean, for a second there, I thought she was into it—until she suddenly freaked out and took off.

I don't know what the hell's going on, but I know that I can't walk away. Like hell I'm leaving things this way.

"Satch?" I keep my voice low as I head down the first aisle of books, then pause to see if I can hear her.

I think there's a quiet shuffling to my right, so I turn that way and soon find her cowering in the corner.

What the shit?

Her back is pressed against the wall, her cheeks pale, her eyes huge.

"Satch," I whisper, raising my hands. "It's okay."

"I..." She swallows and grimaces, her pained frown making my chest tight.

"I'm not gonna hurt you."

"I know." She nods, looking at the ceiling and crossing her arms. The move squishes her boobs together, and it's hard not to notice.

I force my eyes away from the luscious sight and run a hand through my hair. "Look, I'm... I'm sorry. I thought you wanted to kiss me, and so I made a move and—"

"It's okay. We don't have to talk about it." She rushes out the words. "We should just pack up and go. I'm gonna—"

"Satch." I step to my left, stopping her from bolting away from me again. "I want to talk about it. I think we should. I don't want there being some kind of crazy weirdness between us."

She winces, shuffling just a little more to her left.

I move with her, then lean my arm against the wall behind her and gaze down with what I hope is an expectant look. I'm not trying to pressure or intimidate her, but she can't just leave like this.

She stares up at me with her big, vulnerable eyes, and I give her a soft smile, brushing her hair back from her face and whispering, "It's okay."

She eyes me for a second more, then lets out a shuddering breath and rasps, "I've never kissed anyone before, and I don't know what I'm doing." She huffs. "You've kissed me twice in the last week, and it's freaking me out because I don't understand why you would even want to."

What? Why would she say that?

"And it's even worse because now I'm worried that maybe I kind of like you, and not just because of the kisses, but because tutoring you has been the best time ever. And is that lame? That's totally lame, right? Because who lives for a tutoring session?" Her voice pitches, but she rushes on before I can stop her. "But I mean, it's like a compliment, too, because it's only *your* tutoring sessions that I live for, so it's not completely lame and... and..." She winces. "And now I don't even know what I'm trying to say anymore." She blurts the end of her explanation in a squeaking voice that is just plain adorable.

Well, shit. She freaked out because she thought she didn't know what she was doing. I can't wait to tell her she's got nothing to worry about. And I also can't wait to tell her that kissing her was a no-brainer.

You get how luscious your lips are, right?

Yep, I'm totally gonna use that line.

But I don't get a chance before she's talking again.

"When I first met you..." A shaky breath tumbles out of her. "I thought you were gonna be just another big, dumb jock who used me for my brain and didn't give a crap about me. I mean, I was expecting this to be a frustrating experience with someone who didn't really care. But..." She starts squeezing her index finger, her voice getting soft and muffled as she dips her chin and talks to the floor. "You're really not like that at all. You're funny and interesting and sweet, and you do care about stuff." Her gaze flicks back up, landing on me with this bright intensity I can't look away from. "You care about graduating, and you care about your team and your friends. You're not just some self-centered, pretty-boy, brainless jock."

I snicker and shake my head. "I'm not exactly the smartest guy in the room, Satch."

"But you *are* smart." She grabs my wrist, staring up at me, her eyes so big and beautiful that I can't do anything but drink them in. "You're so many wonderful things, Wily. You're so full of life and this contagious energy. No wonder you have so many friends. You're so incredibly popular, and I'm probably the last person you'd ever like back, but... you..." She bites her bottom lip. "You just kissed me. And you seemed to want to, so... for just a fleeting second, I thought maybe the impossible might be possible. And it totally freaks me out." Her voice drops away to a barely there whisper.

I have to strain to catch what she said while I watch her teeth scrape over her bottom lip before sinking into it again.

"Hey, stop that." I gently coax her lip free, then brush my thumb over the red spot she left behind. Gazing down at her, I try to process everything she just spilled. I'm sure she didn't mean to let it all out like that. Panic obviously took over, and she unleashed all this stuff she's been hiding away.

And thank fuck she did, because... whoa.

I wonder how long she's been feeling this way.

Does she really think I'm all those things?

I cup the side of her face, drinking in that open expression of hers, and holy shit, she really does.

And for some reason, it means... so much.

She's not some girl trying to sweet-talk me into kissing her so she can say she got with Wily Wilson, the star football player.

She doesn't know how rich my family is. She may have guessed, but it probably doesn't even come close, so she can't be after me for my money, right?

That look in her eyes... she seems completely genuine in what she's saying.

And that... that's why...

"I wanted to kiss you." My voice comes out husky and raw. I end up smiling because I'm sounding like a sap here, but I can't seem to help myself. "I really wanted to kiss you." Lightly caressing her lip with my thumb, I gaze down at her and give her this cringing smile. It's my sorry-not-sorry face, and I really need to stop that, because I should be remorseful for what I did.

Rubbing a hand over my mouth, I let out a soft sigh and try again. "Satch, I'm sorry that I stole your first kiss. I didn't even ask, I just took it because I couldn't stop myself and... well, that was wrong. I shouldn't have done it."

"No, that's okay." She rests her hand lightly on my chest, tracing the outline of the Cougar logo on my sweater. "If I'm honest, I wanted you to kiss me. But being the complete novice that I am, it probably didn't register in my conscious mind until after it was happening, and..." She winces. "I'm not sure I'm very good at it."

"You are." I grin, giving her a reassuring smile. "You were really good, and those lips of yours are... mmmm." I wink. "And you smell so good."

"I do?" She blinks, then touches her mouth. "They are?"

"You do. And they are, Satch. They definitely are." I brush my nose against hers and sense her lips quivering with a smile. "Think it'll be okay if I kiss you again?" I whisper.

"Um..." She breathes out a soft breath that tickles my chin. "I... I mean, if you want to."

Leaning back, I look down at her, my eyebrow arching. "Do *you* want to?"

Her mouth trembles open as she squeaks. "I think so?"

I move away from her, leaning back a little farther and rising to my full height. "I want you to be sure."

She gives me a weak smile, and I can't go pushing it. Shit, I've never seen her so vulnerable, and it doesn't matter that I want to press my mouth to hers and drink her like she's my favorite brand of beer.

This isn't about me right now.

"Hey, you know what?"

"What?" she breathes.

"I want to take you out on a date."

And then she stills. In fact, I think she just stops breathing. Her eyes go even bigger than they were before, and did she just whisper, "A date?"

She's so quiet, I can't really hear her.

I give her a second to repeat herself, but I think she's going into some form of shock, because she's still gaping at me like I'm crazy.

It makes me laugh as I gather her short little fingers in mine. "Yeah, a date, Satch. It's this thing where two people who like each other spend time together doing something fun."

She nods, then gives me a skeptical frown. "Me? You want to go out with me?"

"Why do you look so surprised?" I try not to laugh. "We hang out when we're tutoring. All I'm asking is that we hang out when you're *not* tutoring me. Come on, it'll be fun."

Biting her lips together, she still looks kind of uncertain, so I give her hand a little shake. "You're not like any girl I've ever gone out with before." She dips her head and I tip it back up with my finger, encouraging her to look up at me again. "And I'm really digging that."

Her lips quiver, flirting with a smile that I am desperate to see.

"Come on, Satch. Let me take you out. For dinner. Okay?"

"Are you sure you want to do that?" Her nose wrinkles, her skeptical frown injuring me.

"Okay, either you're trying to let me down easy or—"

"No," she quickly cuts me off, her cheeks flaring bright pink. "I want to go. I just want to make sure that you actually want to go and you're not just being nice to me."

"Satch." I lightly laugh out her name, taking both her hands in mine. "I wouldn't ask if I didn't want to. Just like I wouldn't have kissed you back there if I hadn't wanted to."

"Oh." She lets out a shy little laugh that makes my chest ping.

I can't help leaning toward her, whispering against her lips, "I kinda like you, too, and I'm really sure I want to take you on this date. All you've got to do is say yes."

I can sense her lips curling into a smile just before she gives me a chaste peck on the lips and proceeds to make my fucking day.

CHAPTER 26
ELIZABETH

I can't believe I said yes.

What was I thinking?

The word just slipped out, and the delighted smile on Wily's face was impossible to deny. I couldn't turn around and change my mind.

So here I am, twenty-four hours later, in a right panic while I try to figure out what to wear.

He'll be here in fifteen minutes, and I'm still standing in my underwear, staring at my open closet and feeling at an absolute loss.

I should bail.

Don't you dare!

But what if Jade finds out?

I close my eyes, cursing myself for thinking about her.

She's not my boss, and she can't tell me what to do.

I can go out with Wily if I want to!

Fear rips through me, one quick swipe that makes me clutch my belly and give my soft flesh a squeeze.

You're going.

I nod, trying to swallow the boulder in my throat, and inch a little closer to my closet.

All of my clothes are hanging up neatly or folded in the cubed shelving beside it. All I have to do is reach forward and take something out.

But what?

Biting into my lip, I start to jiggle on my feet, the urge to pee suddenly swamping me. This always happens when I'm nervous.

Running to the bathroom, I relieve myself before wrestling my underwear back on. I went for those super-tight pants that hold everything in. They're like a modern-day corset, coming up to just below my bra line. Mom bought them for me for Cousin Leo's wedding. I got lots of compliments from family on my dress that night, so it's worth wearing them tonight, right?

It doesn't matter how uncomfortable they are.

Wriggling around, I snap the fabric into place along the top of my thighs, then rush back into my room when I hear a text come through.

Wily: Wear something warm. It's cold out tonight.

I blink, frowning as I reply.

Where are we going?

. . .

I chew on my lip while I wait... and wait... and finally get a response.

Wily: It's a surprise. See you in ten.

Checking my watch, I'm actually relieved he's going to be a few minutes late because I am *still not dressed!*

"Warm," I murmur to myself, walking back to the closet and pulling out my one pair of baggy woolen pants. They come in at the waist, which works well for me tonight with this straitjacket underwear I've got on.

Pulling them up my legs, I brush down the fabric, checking my reflection and feeling pretty good about the choice. All I need now is a warm shirt and a sweater.

I throw on a plain, long-sleeved black thermal and then add my cable-knit sweater, tucking in the front part like I saw this pretty girl do once.

Tipping my head, I study the look, untuck it, then study it again.

I think I change my mind about... three hundred and thirteen times before Wily knocks on my door.

Expelling a soft gasp, I spin away from my reflection, my sweater haphazardly tucked into the front of my waistband and probably looking ridiculous. But I can't leave Wily standing in the hallway.

With trembling hands, I turn the bolt and slowly open the door.

And there he is.

All tall and beautiful, in his jeans and winter coat, his

broad body taking up the doorway as he grins down at me.

"Bought you flowers." He holds out a colorful bouquet—cheerful reds, yellows, and oranges.

"Gerberas." I smile, taking it from him and shaking my head in wonder. "You bought me flowers."

"Of course I did." He eases past me while I continue to stand there staring at this unexpected gift.

His body bumps against mine and he steadies me with his hand, gazing around my room before looking back at me. "This is a date, right?"

"Y-yeah. I just..." I let out a nervous, choking laugh and admit, "No one's ever bought me flowers before."

"Really?" Wily's head jolts back like I'm outright lying. "Never?"

I shake my head, wondering why he's so surprised.

"What about prom? You didn't get a corsage or something?"

My cheeks flare pink and I shake my head, biting my lips together. I'd rather die than admit that I went to prom my junior year with my cousin Leo, and it was a disaster. He ditched me by the punchbowl and ended up dancing with a bunch of other girls, then got caught in the stairwell full-on making out with my stats teacher. He was already in college, and I'm pretty sure Miss Hemsworth got the lecture of a lifetime from our school principal, but she didn't get fired.

I ended up hovering near the food table and nibbling on treats, tapping my foot to the beat and begging time to freaking hurry up.

Needless to say, I skipped senior prom.

It would have been a million times worse with the

likes of Jade, Katrina, and Carmen there. I just couldn't put myself through it.

My parents and I spent the evening with the karaoke machine I got for my birthday that year. We had a blast.

"Well, that's a sin right there. Pretty girls deserve pretty flowers."

I tense, eyeing him with confusion.

"What?"

"Are you mocking me?" I murmur.

He frowns, obviously trying to figure out what I mean. "N-o. Why do you think I'm mocking you?"

My cheeks flush and I shake my head, softly mumbling, "I'm not a pretty girl."

Oh shit? Did I just say that out loud?

I wince, hoping he didn't hear me and keeping my eyes trained on the bouquet.

"What did you say?"

"Nothing." I shoot him a smile, then glance back down, not moving until he's standing right beside me and tipping my chin up.

He looks me over like he's studying a piece of artwork. I swallow, trying not to be unnerved by his perusal. Brushing his thumb across my cheek, he leans down and lightly sniffs my face.

"What are you doing?" I tremble.

"Just wondering if you're wearing that perfume again. I seriously love that stuff."

A soft giggle shakes out of me, and I lean away to look at his face. "You... want me to put it on?"

"Hell yeah." He winks and takes the flowers out of my hands. "You got a glass or something I can put these in?"

"Oh, um... in the bathroom. You can use my toothbrush mug."

"Sounds good. You get your smell on while I sort these out."

Disappearing into my bathroom, I watch him go, still shaking my head at how bizarre this all is.

The hottest man I have ever met just gave me flowers, called me pretty, and is about to take me on a date.

Is this even real?

A small part of me is just waiting for that moment where reality kicks me in the face. Like it did for Josie Grossie in *Never Been Kissed*, when she thought her ultimate crush was picking her up for prom, and instead he egged her in the face.

That's never happened to me, but I was always paranoid that it would.

And now I'm putting myself in the perfect position to be pranked and humiliated.

Not by Wily. He wouldn't do that to you.

Squirting on my perfume, I replace the bottle and try to believe myself as I turn around and watch Wily walk back in with my flowers.

He puts them next to my bed, then takes a big sniff of the air. "Mmmm, yes, baby. That smells fantastic!"

Demolishing the space between us in two easy strides, he wraps his arms around me, lifts me off my feet, and buries his nose in my neck.

"Shit, I could snort you like a line of cocaine."

"Uh... please don't?" I give his shoulders a light, uncertain squeeze and try to ignore the tingles racing through me as Wily laughs and places me back on my feet.

His eyes are sparkling with amusement as he holds out his palm. "Shall we go, my lady? Your carriage awaits."

I'm about to place my hand in his when his words register and I pause in midair. "Please tell me you didn't get a carriage."

He barks out a loud laugh. "Your Ram 1500 awaits."

It's impossible not to giggle. It's even harder not to place my hand in his and let him pull me out the door.

Oh my gosh.

I'm going on a date with Wily Wilson!

His arm snakes around my back, tucking around the side of my waist as he walks me to the elevator. We're nearly there when I remember my winter coat, and we have to race back to grab it. He also asks if I have a beanie and gloves.

Seriously, where is he taking me?

He won't say a peep, fighting a grin as he helps me put my jacket on, then pulls the beanie down to cover my ears.

"You'll find out soon enough." Taking my hand, he leads me back down the hallway again and this time we make it to the bottom floor.

As soon as we step outside, Wily wraps his arm around my shoulders again, gathering me close to his side. I'm forced to put my arm around his waist to keep my balance, but I don't mind so much.

He feels good.

I notice a few surprised gazes when we walk to his car, my body flaring as I try to avoid eye contact.

Wily, on the other hand, seems oblivious. He's

currently telling me about football practice this after-noon and how he's enjoying the lighter sessions.

He's walking beside me, acting like this is the most normal thing in the world.

He really has no idea, does he?

Tonight, he's making the impossible possible, and I'm still struggling to believe it.

CHAPTER 27
WILY

Satch is a twitchy little thing, but there's something endearing about her uncertainty. It's funny, when we're in a tutoring session, she's in her element, confident and sure of herself as she teaches me things like she was born to do it.

Right now, she's a deer in headlights, nervously following me into the football stadium like I'm leading her to a public execution.

Seriously.

I let out a soft laugh, hitching the big bag on my shoulder while running my hand down her back. "Relax."

"Are we allowed to be here?" she whispers, her eyes darting around the low-lit tunnel.

"Probably not." I shrug.

She gasps and gapes up at me. "I don't want to get you in trouble."

"You won't." I propel her forward. "I paid the heads groundskeeper and security guards to stay quiet. Bodie lent me a key, and as long as we don't mess up the field, we're all good."

"What are we even doing here?" She crosses her arms like she's cold, and I tuck her under my arm.

"It's date night, Satch. I'm taking you to my sacred ground."

She glances up, and I catch the edge of her smile in the dim lighting.

Grinning down at her, I give her shoulder a squeeze and turn her right. We walk down the tunnel, my insides thrumming like they always do. It doesn't matter if it's practice or a game, my stomach starts to buzz every time I walk this tunnel.

Popping out onto the moonlit field, I grin up at the empty stands and let out a whoop.

My shout bounces off the opposite wall and echoes back to us.

Satch leans against my side, still tense as a board of wood.

"Seriously, you need to relax." I rub her arm. "We're not gonna get in trouble." Taking her hand, I pull her onto the field and walk her right into the center.

I then spread my arms wide and do a slow spin. "Welcome to my holy place."

She laughs, watching me turn before looking around us. "It's impressive. I didn't realize it was so big. It must be really intimidating when the stands are full of people."

"I love it." I inhale a breath of cold night air. "When the crowds are roaring for your team, it's the best feeling in the world."

"I can imagine," she murmurs, and I watch her lips curl into a soft smile.

It's a full moon tonight, so she's drenched in this ethereal glow that makes her look like the angel she is.

I brush my knuckle around the curve of her cheek and love the way she glances back at me, all shy smiles and sweet innocence.

How can anyone possibly be mean to her?

How can no guy have ever taken her out before?

That's insane.

And it irritates me. I probably shouldn't be annoyed. Lucky me. I got to be her first kiss, the first man to buy her flowers. Shit, I'm her first ever date.

That's a huge privilege, and I should be celebrating that fact.

But I'm annoyed that no one's seen her before.

How could they not notice how smart and kind she is?

How pretty her sweet face is?

How hot those plump lips are?

Damn, I want to kiss them again.

But I can't go launching myself at her.

She deserves a decent date... a little fun. She deserves to get to know me in a new way.

"This is cool." She smiles at me. "I love that you're showing me this. Thank you."

"Thanks for being willing to see it." I slip the duffel bag off my back and crouch down, unearthing a picnic blanket and the pillows I stuffed in there. The food I bought and prepared earlier is in a bunch of different plastic containers, and I pull them out, placing them on the blanket along with a few camping lanterns Grady let me borrow.

Carson told me I was insane to take some chick out in the middle of winter for a picnic.

"You'll freeze your balls off, and your dick won't work properly."

"I'm not going there to have sex with her," I muttered, and he stopped and stared at me like I'd just said I was a unicorn. "What?"

"Seriously? Don't you always have sex with your dates?"

"No." I frown at him.

"Please, you're like the Joey Tribbiani of Football Frat."

"I am not." I started getting pissed off for reasons I couldn't even understand. "Like you can talk. You used to sleep with every vagina that walked past you."

"That is bullshit, and you know it." He pointed at me, his face contorting with a snarl. "I'm not saying I didn't sleep around, but you are definitely worse than me, and you can't tell me you're not prepping this picnic while thinking about her tits in the moonlight."

A low, harsh growl reverberated in my throat. "Talk about her tits again. I dare you."

He raised his eyebrows at me, letting out this surprised chuckle before shaking his head. And I just had to stand there scowling at him because dammit, he was right.

I had totally thought about what her large, luscious tits would look like in the moonlight.

But I wasn't going to act on it.

I never acted on it unless they wanted me to. I just happened to go out with a lot of girls who were frisky and free with their lovin'.

Satch isn't like that, though.

She's not about to strip naked on this field and spread her legs for me. I'll be lucky if I get a kiss.

Please let me get at least a kiss.

I swallow, surprised by just how much I've been thinking about the feel of her tongue lightly brushing against mine before she freaked and bolted away from the table.

Focusing back on my setup, I switch on the camping lanterns, lining them up around the edge of the blanket. I'm trying not to check out Satch as she wanders around me, still staring up at the stands and marveling at the size of the stadium.

I don't want a one-and-done with this girl.

I'm not even asking her out to get her into bed and... okay, dammit, Carson was right to be surprised.

This date *is* different.

There is zero expectation of sex because Satch is for sure a virgin, and I'm not gonna pressure her into anything. She also doesn't seem the type who's desperate to lose it. She doesn't need the status of giving it up to a star football player like that chick I let talk me into it two years ago. We dated for a couple of months after that, but then she ended up falling for a guy in her economics class. He was super smart and made her laugh all the time.

I was her introduction into the physical stuff, but he was the guy who stole her heart.

I've never been a heart stealer.

I seem to be the guy girls like to have light, flirty fun with. I'm the guy you screw at a party and swoon about with your girlfriends.

I'm not the one you take home to meet Ma and Pa unless you're trying to get them off your back. Yes, I've done that for a girl once too. It was all for pretend, just so they'd stop trying to set her up with this lawyer at her dad's firm.

It worked, and we had some very hot, wild sex at her parents' beach house before the rest of her family arrived and we played the role of loved-up college kids.

But once the long weekend was over, we got back to Nolan and went our separate ways, only reuniting every few weeks when she needed to prove she was still in a relationship. That ended last year when she met Mr. Right and our game of pretend came to an abrupt end.

My eyebrows dip as I pull out the thermos of hot chocolate and glance over my shoulder. Satch is staring up at the moon with this sweet smile on her face, and for reasons I once again can't fathom, the thought of this being a one-off thing is sitting really ugly in my chest.

Which is why I will not be sleeping with her tonight.

Because I already know I want another date.

I want a chance to make her giggle again, the way I did yesterday.

I want to hear her voice as she tells me about her life.

I want to *know* about her life.

And I want her to get a bigger peek into mine.

Pulling out my football with a grin, I spin it in my palm before standing up and getting her attention. "Heads ups, Satch."

I lightly flick the ball, spiraling it toward her, and she yelps and jumps away from it like I've just thrown a live grenade.

CHAPTER 28
ELIZABETH

Aw, crap. Why did I do that?

I am such a loser!

Humiliation burns me as I watch the ball dribble across the grass.

Wily's laughter is a soft chuckle as he jogs past me to collect it. Scooping the ball into his large hand, he rests it against his side and smiles at me. "It's not gonna bite you, Satch."

"Sorry." I wince, glancing behind me at the gorgeous picnic setup. My gosh, he's gone to so much effort for this, and I really don't want to ruin his plans, but... "I'm not good at PE or anything to do with balls."

He snickers and dips his chin.

And I register what I just said.

My eyes bulge in horror.

Oh shit! Could I be any more embarrassing?

The urge to bolt overwhelms me and I turn, spying the tunnel we came in through and wondering if I can find my way back to the parking lot. My phone's in my coat pocket—I could order an Uber and head back to my room, where I can bury myself under the covers and pray for a swift end to my humiliation.

But before I can take a step, Wily jumps in front of me, holding up the football. "You can catch this, you know."

I shake my head.

He snorts. "Just like I'm not capable of writing an essay, right?"

She tips her head and gives me a pained frown. "You are capable of writing an essay."

"And you're capable of catching this ball. You just need to not be afraid of it." Taking my hands, he cups them around the ball. "Like this." He adjusts my fingers and then pushes the ball against my chest. "So, it's gonna come at you, and you grab it and pull it in like that. Try it."

He pulls my hands and the ball away from my body and then pushes them back, and I kind of hug it to my chest.

"That's it." He grins. "Okay, now fire it my way."

He's standing like a foot away from me, so I just hold the ball out for him to take.

His laughter is that soft chuckle again as he takes it and shuffles back a few more paces. "Ready?"

"No." I hold my hands up, and he gives me a look that makes me change my answer. "Yes?"

"That's my girl. Okay, here we go."

His girl. The words flush through me like a warm breeze, my lips twitching as the tingles inside me swirl from my belly to my chest.

"Eye on the ball." He waggles it in the air, and I do as I'm told. "You're not afraid of it, okay?"

I nod.

"Say it."

I whine in my throat, but he repeats himself until I'm forced to mutter, "I'm not afraid of the ball."

"Now shout it!"

"I'm not afraid of the ball!" I bellow, flinching when the sound echoes back to me, before letting out a surprised laugh.

"Good girl." He grins before gently passing it my way.

I watch the football, tensing, then pluck it out of the air and pull it to my chest.

"Nice." He applauds.

And I go still, glancing down at the ball in my hands before suddenly bursting out with a loud laugh. "I caught it!"

"You did." He gives me two thumbs-up.

"But I... I got it!" I hold the ball up, completely shocked by this miracle... until I fumble the ball in my hand and it lands with a small bounce by my feet.

Quickly scooping it back up, I remind myself to never over-celebrate.

"Okay, now pass it back." He flicks his fingers at me.

"Um. O...kay." Biting my lip, I throw it up and cringe as the ball goes wildly out of reach.

Wily stumbles after it and only just manages to get his fingers to it.

"Sorry."

"Don't apologize for keeping me on my toes, baby." He winks at me, and now the word *baby* is buzzing through my system like a sweet kiss.

I've never been called that before. I read it all the time in books and see it in movies, and I've always thought I wouldn't like such a childish nickname.

But the way it came out of his mouth just now...

I think I've found my new favorite word.

"You ready?" He holds the ball up like a star quarterback, and I raise my hands, preparing for his easy pass.

It sails through the air, not too fast, and I manage to get my hands to it, only to fumble it to the ground.

But he won't let me give up. "That's all right. Try again. We'll get this."

And so I keep going.

I drop it ten more times... but I also manage to catch it eight.

Eight times!

And not once does he make me feel bad for any fumbles or missed throws.

A couple of times, I managed to aim and pass the ball right to him, and the praise pouring out of his mouth made me feel like I'd just completed a game-winning touchdown.

Seriously.

I have never met a jock like Wily Wilson before.

And it's taking maximum effort to convince myself that this isn't just a dream.

CHAPTER 29
WILY

Satch is hilariously stoked and excited at being able to catch a ball less than half the time I threw it at her.

It was pretty funny watching the sweet concentration on her face.

She obviously likes to get things right.

Man, her apologetic wincing every time she dropped the ball made me wonder who taught her how to catch in the first place.

As I gather the ball to my chest, I walk forward and have to ask, "You play catch with your dad much?"

She laughs and shakes her head. "No. He was always too busy working in the diner. When we did have time off, we'd be doing other stuff, like watching movies or playing board games. Things like that. We're more of an indoorsy bunch." She looks me up and down. "Unlike you, I'm guessing."

"Yeah." I take her hand, leading her over to the picnic blanket.

The air is cold tonight, and the tip of her nose is going

red. I can feel the chill of her fingers through her gloves and figure it's hot chocolate time.

"My dad had me in the backyard throwing a ball before I could walk." I unscrew the cap of the thermos while she takes a seat on the pillow opposite mine.

"Really? That seems young."

I shrug. "The guy has always been passionate about football."

"Did he play in college?"

"He tried." I wince. "Think it always bugged him that he didn't make the cut. He's a decent athlete, but he's not fast enough to keep up, and he's not big enough to block well."

"Thanks." She takes the mug of hot cocoa and curls her gloved hands around it. "Smells good."

I smile, not wanting to admit that Sienna was the one who made it for me.

Satch blows on the steaming liquid before taking a tentative sip. "Your dad must have been stoked when you came along. Were you big as a kid too?"

"Yeah, I've always been big for my age." I swallow down the hot brew and end up burning my tongue. Gritting my teeth, I hide my discomfort and set my drink aside, pulling out the PB&J sandwiches I did actually make myself. I'm just about to open the container when a sudden thought hits me, and I groan. "Shit, you're not allergic to peanuts, are you?"

"Nope. I'm not allergic to anything." She grins as I take the lid off and hold one out for her. "Oooo. Nice. Did you make these?"

"Yes, ma'am. These are a Wily special."

"Impressive," she murmurs, wiggling her eyebrows and taking a bite.

"Not the classy dinner you might have been expecting, but I—"

"I love this," she interrupts me. "This is better than a restaurant or diner or anywhere else you could take me." Her eyes start to glow in the lantern light. "You're showing me a piece of your soul... and it's beautiful."

Shit, I think I'm blushing. "I wasn't sure you'd be into empty plastic chairs and a field of grass. But I just wanted to show you my reason."

"Well, I'm glad you did." She looks around us, then up at the night sky. "Do you think it's going to snow tonight?"

"I'm not sure." I hold my palm up, ready to catch flakes, but nothing's falling. "We can leave if you—"

"No, I want to stay." She smiles. "Of course I want to stay. I feel like we're the only two people on Earth right now, and I love that."

She flashes me those white teeth again, and I can't help staring at her mouth and the beautiful shape it makes when she smiles.

Her nose wrinkles at my perusal and she dips her chin, taking another bite of her sandwich before bobbing her head like a pigeon and looking anywhere but at me.

We eat our sandwiches in silence, me devouring three to her one.

She finishes off her cocoa and I offer her a refill, which she accepts. It breaks the quiet between us, and I'm soon talking about the Scouting Combine and how vitally important it is.

She seems really interested as I explain the ins and

outs of the week I've been preparing for and how it's going to help me get drafted.

She asks me more questions, pulling details out of me, and soon I'm walking to the center line of the field and showing her my various positions and the lines I run on the regular.

"There are always variations." I walk back to the picnic blanket. "Each game is different, but you get the idea."

"Absolutely. There's actually way more strategy to football than I realized. You showed me that when you taught me the basic game structure, and I've only watched two games so—"

"Only two?" I gape at her. "In your whole life?"

She nods and softly admits, "They were both yours."

That makes me still and I gaze down at her, all tucked up on the picnic blanket, her winter coat wrapped around her bent legs.

Taking a seat beside her, I run my hand down her arm and try to find the words to tell her how much that means to me.

But nothing comes out.

Instead, I reach for the chocolate chip cookies Zoey, Sienna, and I made this afternoon. Okay, fine, I didn't really make them, but I did steal a few dark chocolate chips and gave them heaps of encouragement as *they* were making them.

Opening the container, I offer Satch one and admit without thinking, "You're the first girl I've ever bought here."

She pauses before taking a treat, her lips slowly rising into a closed-mouth smile. "Are you serious?"

"I am." I nod, shaking my head like even I can't believe it.

I don't know why I wanted to bring Satch here, but as soon as I asked her out on that date, this place popped into my head... and I couldn't let it go.

I wanted to picnic with this girl in my favorite spot. And no other woman has ever made me want to do that.

Holy shit.

Stealing a cookie, I shove it into my mouth and hook my elbow around my bent knee.

"Mmm. These are good. Yours too?" she asks, but my mouth's too full to answer her. "Coyote's Cookies." She grins, taking another bite.

"Coyote?" I ask, crumbs flying out of my mouth.

She giggles and brushes them off my short whiskers. "Yeah, Coyote. No one ever calls you that?"

She looks confused by why they wouldn't... and I'm totally mystified. "Why would they call me Coyote?"

Tipping her head, I watch her eyebrows flicker as she stares at me like it's totally obvious. "Wile E." She raises her eyebrows. "You know... Wile E. Coyote."

"Who?"

Her mouth pops open, her eyes going huge. "You've never heard of Wile E. Coyote?"

"Was he like... some cowboy or something?"

"No." She laughs, touching my arm as she tips her head back. "I thought everyone knew who he was."

"Fill me in, Satch. I'm feeling like a moron here."

"No, no, of course you're not. If anything, it shows that you are completely cool and modern, and I am stuck in the '50s when that cartoon first came out."

"Oh, he's a cartoon." I nod, still having zero idea what she's talking about.

"Yeah, my parents had a Looney Tunes DVD when I was little, and we'd watch it sometimes. It was a bunch of cartoon characters, and I loved Wile E. Coyote and the Road Runner the most." She starts to laugh like she's rewatching an episode in her mind, and I'm making a mental note to YouTube this guy. "He's this funny-looking coyote who is always out to get the Road Runner, who's this super-fast bird that eludes him at every turn. He thinks of these really inventive ways to try and catch him, and he fails every time. It's really funny." She giggles some more, then looks at me with an impish grin. "I'll have to show you sometime."

"Wily Coyote." I lean back, resting my hand just behind her. "I like it."

She grins, resting her head against my shoulder for a second, like she's not even thinking about what she's doing. "Can I call you Coyote?"

"Baby, you can call me whatever you want."

She sits back and looks at me, her button nose wrinkling. "I'll only ever call you good stuff."

"I don't know." I click my tongue. "This Wily Coyote guy doesn't exactly sound like a winner."

My dry comment makes her snort with laughter, and I'm loving that sound even more than I did yesterday.

She tumbles against me, her cheek squishing into my shoulder, and I let out a loud coyote cry that bounces and echoes back to us.

This makes her laugh even harder, so I do it again and she soon joins me, the football stadium rich with our howling.

"I'm liking Coyote," I murmur, brushing my lips against her forehead.

Damn, she smells so good.

I'm having the best time tonight.

I've never been on a date like this before, and I must be insane because this is so much fun. Maybe I've just never met a girl who I thought would appreciate it.

Until now.

"Wanna dance?" I softly ask, the idea hitting me out of the blue. But dancing's romantic, right? Chicks love that kind of thing.

Her head pops off my shoulder, and she gives me a nervous wince. "I'm not much of a dancer."

"I'm sure you're better than you think you are."

I stand and hold my hand out to her. I have to wriggle my fingers and bat my eyelashes before she gives in with a soft laugh and lets me pull her to her feet.

Stepping off the blanket, I guide her into the center of the field and turn, giving her a dramatic bow that makes her laugh before pulling her against me.

She reaches up, resting her hand on my shoulder, and I hold on to her other one as if we're about to waltz, but I don't know how to do that shit, so we just kind of sway back and forth in the cold night air.

And then she starts to hum.

I don't know what the tune is, but it sounds old-timey... jazz-ish. And it makes me smile. This girl can hold a tune, that's obvious, and I lean my cheek on the top of her head, wrapping my arm more tightly around her and pulling our arms in to tuck them close.

Shit, this is romantic.

And I'm not even trying to make it that way.

It's just happening because Satch makes me want to—

Oh yes! Is that snow?

I glance up, a smile lighting my face as the first flake flutters past me.

It's snowing.

It's fucking snowing, and if that's not movie-made romance, I don't know what the hell is.

Satch's head pops away from me, and she looks up with an excited gasp. "So pretty. I love it when it snows all gently like this." Her nose wrinkles as a few white flakes land on her skin, then quickly disintegrate. She laughs and softly sings, "Snowflakes that stay on my nose and eyelashes."

I recognize that tune, but I don't know what it's from.

She grins and whispers, "*The Sound of Music.* 'My Favorite Things.'"

"Okay," I whisper, because talking at full volume right now just feels wrong. "Sing it to me."

With a shy smile and a little more coaxing, she softly starts singing the song, and we sway under the snowflakes, hidden away in this perfect stadium bubble.

As the song comes to an end, I gaze down at her pretty face and have to ask, "You ready to let me kiss you yet, Satch?"

Brushing her teeth over her bottom lip, she stares up at me like I'm the only thing that matters right now.

Then she rises to her tiptoes and presses her lips to mine.

CHAPTER 30
ELIZABETH

The second I kiss him, those tingles that have been firing through me all evening spark and ignite, setting this delicious flame of pleasure racing through me. His lips, not so foreign this time, are warm and inviting. I smile against them, then get hit with that giddy kick the second the tip of his tongue peeks.

Threading my arms around the back of his neck, I rise a little higher on my toes and act on instinct, parting my lips and meeting him halfway.

This time, when our tongues glide against each other, I don't freak out.

This time, I welcome the intrusion.

Because it's not an intrusion. It's an introduction. A meeting of tongues, if you will.

And I really like it.

Wily's hands trail down to my waist, his arms snaking around me as he leans down to deepen the kiss.

I let it happen because it feels like the most natural thing in the world.

No, it's better than natural.

It's wondrous.

Intoxicating.

Mind-blowing.

Snowflakes softly fall around us, icy fingertips touching my exposed skin, but I barely notice them, too wrapped up in this warm oasis of a kiss.

I love how big his hands are.

I love the way they're gripping my waist.

His lips are soft and delicious.

His tongue tastes like peanut butter and cocoa.

Wily starts to pull away, and for a second, I worry that this kiss is about to be over, but he's just changing angles, tipping his head and reconnecting our mouths in this perfect dance.

I'm dreaming.

That has to be it, right?

But it's not!

Pinch me now, it's not a dream!

Bending his legs, Wily lets out this delectable groan, his grip around my waist tightening as he stands tall and brings me with him. Our mouths are that much closer as he lines up our heads.

Part of me wants to wrap my legs around his waist, but I'm too nervous to do it. I'm not even sure I can, so I just dangle, kissing him like I need his tongue in order to take my next breath.

He eventually puts me back down, but he doesn't break away from the kiss. We start to sway, making out and dancing in the snow for I don't know how long.

But the dream just keeps going until Wily's watch starts beeping.

With a disappointed groan, he pulls away from me, brushing the tip of his nose against mine and giving me the kind of smile that could melt my heart in a second.

In fact, I'm pretty sure my chest is filled with defrosting ice cream right now.

"We gotta go," he whispers. "I promised to lock up the place by ten."

"Okay." I swallow, not wanting to release him.

He's not moving either, so we just stand there gazing at each other until his alarm starts going again.

Forcing myself away from him, I step back on shaking limbs and fumble my way through our snow-covered picnic cleanup.

Shoving everything into his bag, I scoop up his football and hug it to my snowy coat. He grins at me, brushing snowflakes out of my hair before wrapping his arm around my shoulders and walking us out of the stadium.

This giddy giggle is sitting in my belly, all bouncy and pert, wanting to burst out of me any chance it can get.

I fight to keep it clamped down, but it's pretty hard when I think about what I was just doing on that field.

Yep, I was making out with a tall, hot, funny, gorgeous man who danced with me in the snow and then kissed me like he meant it.

I keep waiting to come to, for reality to hit, and I'll open my eyes and realize I'm tucked up in bed and my imagination has been toying with me. But as Wily locks the gate behind us, then opens his truck door and helps me into the passenger seat, I realize this dream is still going.

As soon as the doors are closed, Wily gets the heat

pumping, and we sit in the stadium parking lot for a minute not saying anything. I don't know why he's not starting the engine and driving me back to Buckley Hall.

Throwing him an awkward side-eye, I silently ask him, but he just runs his fingers lightly over the top of the wheel.

Finally, while my brain is scrambling for something to say, he whispers, "I just had the best time. I'm not ready for it to end."

"I loved it too." I smile at him.

He nods, his lips twitching.

"We can stay here if you want. Talk or... whatever." I end in the softest whisper, my stomach jittering with excitement at the thought of kissing him again.

I want his hand to curl around the back of my neck, or maybe thread through my hair. I want his lips to sink against mine as his thumb brushes a soft line across my cheek.

"I want to invite you back to my place, but..."

I blink, the cold crash of reality starting to pinch me awake.

He just said *but*.

Here we go.

I can't go back to his place, because he's embarrassed at the idea of dating me.

"I'm worried if I do that...," he continues.

Everyone will see us together, and then he'll need to explain why he's asked me out. People won't get it, and—

"I'll want to take you up to my room and..."

Wait. What?

My body flushes with a mixture of pleasure and trepidation as he leaves the sentence hanging. Letting me fill in the gaps with wondrous, terrifying ideas of what we could get up to in his room.

Turning in my seat to face him, I ignore the belt clip digging into my hip and blink at him. "You'd... want to take me up to your room?"

"Yeah." He clears his throat, his gaze a little playful and a whole lot hungry. "And I wouldn't want to be studying."

I swallow, breathing shallow as my heart rate ratchets up a notch. "Do you... um... do you take m-many girls up to your room?"

I'm trying to ask casually, but honestly, the way I'm stumbling over my words makes me sound like a nervous idiot.

His laughter is soft and husky. Scratching his short whiskers, he keeps his eyes trained out the window and nods. "Yeah."

"But you don't want to take me," I whisper. "I understand."

"No, no. What?" He jerks around to face me, cupping the side of my face and looking kind of desperate. "I *really* want to take you. That's what I'm saying."

I swallow again, not really sure how else to respond.

"But if I do that, I'm gonna want you on my bed. I'm gonna want to..." His eyes float over my body, lingering on my chest before skimming down to my legs.

My heart does this weird kick.

"I need you to be different," he whispers.

"Why?"

"Because you're... special." He shrugs, his lips

twitching into a soft smile before the tip of his tongue darts out the side of his mouth. "You're also a virgin."

Heat pours into my cheeks like two hot irons have been pushed into either side of my face.

"Is it that obvious?" I try to make it light, but my joke falls flat, my nervous giggle only compounding the awkward silence that follows. "I'm really not that special, Wily. I'm just an inexperienced girl who—"

"No, you are." He runs his hand down my arm and threads our fingers together. "You're special, and I..." He sighs. "God, this makes me sound like such an asshole, but I usually only date girls who want to keep things super casual. You know? We go out for a drink and get busy, then go our separate ways. Or maybe we'll enjoy a few hookups, but there's never any sense of getting close or getting to know each other."

I start nibbling on my bottom lip.

"But I want to get to know you, Satch. You're not one-and-done. I want a second date."

The trilling inside me whips into a frenzy. "Are you saying that if we sleep together, you won't get one?"

"No." He snickers, then shrugs. "Maybe. I don't..." He clears his throat. "This is all... new for me too."

I give him a skeptical frown. "I get the impression that you date a lot of girls."

"No, I mean... making PB&J sandwiches and taking you to my sacred ground... I don't do that. And I have no idea what compelled me to treat you differently from everyone else, but I've just had to, you know? Which means I can't go putting my hands all over you the way my body is screaming at me to."

I wrap my arms around myself, putting on a brave

smile and going into protective mode. The thought of his hands all over me, exploring every intimate part of my body, is equal parts fascinating and terrifying, enticing and mortifying.

He skims his thumb over my bottom lip, then lightly traces the shape of my mouth before running his fingers down my chin and caressing the side of my neck.

I close my eyes, reveling in his delicate touch.

"I want you to be ready. You have to want it as much as I do," he whispers, his jacket rustling as he leans toward me and brushes his lips across my cheek.

I still can't believe he *actually* wants it.

I mean, I'm me. Little ol' insignificant me.

He could have any girl on campus, but he's stressing about being careful with me so that he can get a second date?

This is seriously unreal.

His lips are feather soft as they work their way up to my ear, lightly teasing my lobe before he whispers, "I want to get this right with you, Satch."

I nod, unable to talk past the pulsing lump in my throat.

As his mouth trails back along my cheek, I turn my head, capturing his lips before they get too far away.

He moans, leaning into it and gently gripping the back of my neck.

A delicious shiver runs through me, and I open my mouth, confident in my search for his tongue.

It meets mine, the tip caressing me in a slow, smooth dance.

Gripping his jacket, I keep him in place when he goes

to pull away, letting the windows steam up around us as we make out in the warmth of his car.

Another moan rumbles in his throat, his hand meandering down my back, traveling over the curve of my hips before gently squeezing my butt.

It's a scintillating surprise, and I want him to do it again, but he pulls back and won't let me chase his lips when I try to.

Holding me steady with a grin, he licks his bottom lip and shakes his head. "I never saw you coming."

My expression scrunches with uncertainty. "Is that a good thing?"

He answers me with a stunning smile before starting the engine and taking me home.

He walks me to my door, then to my disappointment behaves like the perfect gentleman and refuses to come in, even after I invite him.

His voice takes on a raw, rasping quality, like the word *no* is causing him discomfort, but he says it three times, so I really know he's not coming in.

I end up laughing, holding on to my door and the frame while I say a soft goodbye. "Thanks for the perfect date."

He grins. "You gonna be up for another one?"

"Yes. A thousand times yes."

"Excellent." He nods. "Let me come up with something good, and I'll let you know."

"Anything." I brush my hand down his chest. "Just being with you is perfect. You don't have to do anything special for me."

Gathering up my fingers, he kisses my knuckles and

makes me feel like Princess Satch before giving me a wink and walking away.

"Good night, Coyote," I call after him.

He spins with a smile that will be permanently burned in my brain. Blowing me a kiss, he bows with a flourish. "Until we meet again, milady."

Closing my door with a giddy laugh, I lean my head back against it and stare up at the ceiling, completely delirious.

That was... the best.

I know I have no other dates to compare it to, but come on!

That was living out a fairy tale.

He's so sweet and funny, and he made me PB&J sandwiches and cookies and...

Sighing like some lovestruck teen, I do a dreamy twirl, reliving every second of our date until I'm flopped on my bed and dreaming about the way his tongue felt against mine.

His kisses.

Oh my gosh, his kisses!

And he wanted more.

He didn't want to take me back to his place because he thought he couldn't control himself around me.

That's nuts.

Like... he wants my body.

Running my hands over my breasts, I give them a gentle squeeze, a nervous titter bursting out of me at how tingly they feel. Seriously, as much as the idea of going all the way with a guy scares me... the prospect of going all the way with Wily is tantalizing.

Do I want that with him?

Yes! Hell yes!

Sucking in a shaky breath, I hold it, wading through a plethora of emotions from panicked anxiety to outright lust.

I'm not sure when or if it will ever happen with Wily, but at least I know this much—I do want it.

I just have to find the courage to let it happen.

CHAPTER 31
WILY

So, my spank bank is usually filled by porn videos or reliving a particularly spicy encounter. But when I got home from my date with Satch, it was absolutely necessary to lock my bedroom door and have myself a session.

And the only thing on my mind was Satch's luscious body. I couldn't help mentally peeling off her clothes and picturing what was underneath. My fantasies of her cries of pleasure as I made her come had me pumping my dick like a piston.

I'm still thinking about those curves of hers as I stand on the football field, trying to concentrate on practice. All I can do is picture us standing in the center, dancing to her sweet tunes, then what it would have been like to lay her down on that picnic blanket and...

Oh shit, I want to make her come.

I want her to experience every good thing sex has to offer.

But I didn't take that chance.

It's too soon for her. I know it is.

She's only had one decent make-out session.

And holy fuck, it was hot!

Her tongue is crazy fine, and I couldn't pull away from her.

I thought about it a bunch of times as we were standing in that snow, her feet no doubt starting to freeze the way mine were.

But I just couldn't do it.

Every time I went to pull away, my body cried out in protest, so I stayed put, held her a little tighter, enjoyed the feel of her sexy tits squished against my chest.

Oh fuck, I want to see those beauties. I want to hold them. Kiss them. Claim them as my own.

But I can't go doing that shit just yet.

She's not ready.

The selfish part of me hopes she comes around fast, but I will not be pressuring her.

I've never made a girl feel like she has to give in and sleep with me. At least I hope I never have. Usually, it's them jumping all over me. And Satch was into those kisses, I could tell. But if I'd taken it further, how would she have reacted? It's got to be different with her because she's special.

Shit, I didn't even see it at first.

But all those hours we spent together working on that assignment and studying... she must have just been chipping away at me, burrowing deep until I'm the guy who wants to take her out for picnics and dance with her in the snow.

My lips twitch. It was like a rom-com last night, and I loved every second of it.

"Heads up!" I hear a shout just before I get hit in the

arm by a flying football. "Shit, Wily! Where are you today?"

"Sorry!" I raise my arm in apology to Grady and collect the ball off the field.

He shakes his head at me and jogs over. "Are you good, man?"

"Yeah, just... distracted."

His eyebrows wrinkle. "What's the matter?"

"Nothing." I shake my head.

Just thinking about a girl.

Like I can admit that to him. A month or so ago, probably. He was still living in Loved-Up Land then. But I can't go talking about the immense crush I have on my tutor. I don't want to make him feel bad.

Squeezing his shoulder, I give him another silent apology before throwing the football up. "I'm good, Flash. I swear."

He gives me a skeptical frown, catching the ball and flicking it between his hands. "Scouting Combine's gonna be here before you know it."

The look in his dark brown eyes is hard to read, but I can't help wondering if he's really not looking forward to it. Not because he doesn't want us to do great, but because he's gonna miss his friends next year.

He and Zander are tight, and Grady's still got one more year before he graduates.

Football Frat is gonna be so different, and I bet Grady's worried about who'll be coming in to replace Zander, Tyrell, and me.

He looks away and mutters, "Just want to make sure you're focused and prepared."

"I will be." I nod, slapping his back before he takes off

for his area of the field. I have no idea why he even threw the ball at me in the first place.

Probably because he could see you weren't focused.

Shit, that's so Grady. He's always keeping an eye out for us, doing little things to get us back on track.

I watch him run to Carson and have a quick chat before breaking into their next exercise.

"Let's go!" The offensive coach blows his whistle, and I spin back toward Tyrell and the other linemen, catching up with the drill they're doing.

Crouching down, I let out a soft hiss, my knee catching for a second before I shake it out and reset.

I've got to get my head back into this thing and stop thinking about a curvy brunette who felt so fucking good in my arms.

I never knew I'd be into a girl like her, but she's taking me out faster than I can counter... and I'm happy to let that happen.

At least I think I am.

Worry about how this shift in the relationship might change our tutoring sessions, and my ability to graduate, starts eating away at me, the thought coming out of the fucking blue and killing the happy buzz that's been keeping me going all day.

Fuck.

By the time practice is over, I've set up camp in the "maybe this is a bad idea" zone. I hate that zone, but I've got to be logical about this, right?

A whole lot of sweat and exertion is starting to clear the romantic fog I've been living in all day. My aching body is reminding me why I'm really here and what my ultimate goal is.

Standing in the shower, I rinse off the winter dirt and scrub my body clean.

Shit. Maybe we shouldn't be aiming for a second date.

And I definitely shouldn't be sleeping with her.

Now's my chance to gently shift things into the friend zone, right? Because who am I kidding?

I'm not gonna be able to sit beside her and concentrate on anything she's saying if my horny body is raging for another taste of her.

And that's not the only thing I should be considering here.

In April I'll be drafted, and as soon as graduation's over, I'll be off. Satch still has two more years at Nolan after that. Will we just break up? Or do we try some long-distance thing? Am I even capable of that?

Disappointment scorches me as I soap under my pits, then rinse the shampoo out of my hair.

Fuck. I'm gonna have to friend-zone this situation.

I really don't want to, but it's the right thing to do.

No more dates and making out.

I just need to stay focused on passing my classes this semester, graduating, and then following my football dreams.

By the time I'm done washing, I'm in a foul mood and miss half the chatter in the locker room. I towel off as fast as I can and get dressed, needing to get out of here. I need some space and quiet so I can figure out how to tell Satch that I can't take things further.

Fuck!

This sucks.

Snatching my phone, I spot an email notification and

sit down to clear it only to read the message and then jump back up with a loud whoop.

"Holy shit." Carson flinches, shoving my shoulder for scaring him.

I laugh and shove him back. "Sorry, man, but I've got to celebrate."

"Why?" He frowns at me.

"I just got an A-. A fucking A-!" I holler.

The guys around me stop what they're doing to snicker and grin at my ridiculous happy dance.

"Did you hear that? An A-! And it's all my own work! I did that shit! Me!"

"Good job." Zander laughs, lightly punching my arm while Grady gives me a proud smile and Tyrell applauds me.

"Glad the new tutor's working out, man."

I nod, my chest near bursting as I text Satch without thinking.

She gets back to me before I've finished packing up my stuff.

Satch: That's amazing! I'm so proud of you! Do you want to come over and we can look through his comments? The paper should be up on the student portal.

I stare at her words, my doubts from the shower niggling at me, but like hell I'm not going over there.

It's for tutoring, right?

It's all good.

I bolt out of the locker room, not even saying goodbye

to my buddies. It's unlike me, but I'm on a mission. I have to see Pilscher's comments, and I have to thank Satch in person.

She made this happen for me.

Her.

The girl with the beautiful eyes and the gorgeous face.

The girl who danced with me in the snow and—

Fuck. I'm getting all mushy again.

Shit. I don't know how I'm supposed to navigate this, but as I punch out of the parking lot, I'm driving faster than I normally would, and it's all because of her.

CHAPTER 32
ELIZABETH

I've already got my computer set up with the student portal page by the time Wily gets to me. I am so excited, my insides are buzzing. And it's not just because I get to see him again. It's because he got an A-, and I am so proud of him.

A grade like that for Wily is huge, and I want him to know that we need to celebrate the shit out it.

I giggle at myself, giddy and bubbling as I wait for him.

The second he knocks on my door, I swing it open and jump up to my tiptoes, wrapping my arms around his neck.

"I'm so proud of you!" I squeal, hoping I'm not deafening him, but come on! He got an A-!

Wrapping his arms around me, he plucks me off my feet and carries me into the room, closing the door behind us.

I giggle, leaning back when my toes touch the ground again and reaching up to hold his face. Gazing up at those beautiful blue eyes, I say it one more time because I am bursting. "I am seriously soooo proud of you. You did it, Coyote."

My grin must be beaming. I feel like I'm sparkling right now, and it's all because of him.

He smiles back at me, and for a second, I wonder if he's gonna kiss me, but then he swallows and lets me go, taking a step back.

"Should we look at the essay?" His voice is deep and lacking the gentle warmth I basked in last night.

He's still happy to see me... to be here.

But something's off.

I worry my lip and nod, those giddy bubbles popping in record time. Shuffling to my laptop, I wake up the screen again and nudge it toward him.

"You'll need to enter your username and password."

He leans past me, his bulky body so big... so touchable.

I resist the urge, curling my fingers into my sweater sleeves and trying not to sniff his freshly washed hair or the deodorant he must have sprayed on after practice.

Why does he have to smell so good... and be so big and beautiful and right here?

"Okay." He pulls the stool around from the side of my desk and takes a seat, glancing up at me with an expectant look. "You gonna sit?"

"Yeah." I plunk into my chair and focus on the screen in front of him, too afraid to look at his face.

He's not saying anything. He's not touching me.

And all those familiar fears start rising to the surface again.

He was just being nice to me until he passed. Now

that he got a good grade from Pilscher, he doesn't need me anymore. He was just using me to pass that paper, and he'll—

Stop it. He's still got the rest of the semester to get through.

And Wily's not like that. He's kind, remember?

I steal a quick side glance at his profile. His eyebrows are scrunched together, his jaw clenched tight as I pull up his paper for us to go through.

It must kill Professor Pilscher, but school policy is that every assignment and grade has to be uploaded to the student portal, which means that his *"I only mark paper"* stance must be a pain in the ass to deal with when it comes to grading. He probably gets an assistant to scan the papers into the portal.

I squint at the screen, enlarging it so we can read his comments in the margins.

"Oh, that's good," I murmur, pointing at his praise for paragraph one.

Wily nods, then points at the screen when I scan down to paragraph two. "What does he mean there?"

I explain the comment, telling Wily I understand the criticism and where he could have improved.

He nods, all serious, and my insides continue to deflate.

What happened to the sweet smiles from last night? Why isn't he touching me, looking at me like he wants to kiss me?

Forcing my eyes back to the screen, I scan down a little farther until we get to the final comments.

"You really did well," I murmur as I finish reading them.

Staring down at my hands, I pinch the top of my index finger and fight the sudden rush of tears.

What are you doing?

Don't you dare cry!

Not until after her leaves!

"Satch," Wily whispers, and I tense, refusing to look at him. "I'm so grateful for all your help."

"Yeah, that's okay." I nod, swallowing the thickening in my throat as I wait for the *last night was a mistake* speech.

"I should give you a bonus for being such a great tutor."

"No." I shake my head and force out a dry laugh. "You don't have to do that."

He goes quiet beside me, and after a few painful beats, I have to look over and check on him. This is killing me!

The second I turn, I wish I hadn't.

He's staring at me with this expression I can't decipher. He looks almost pained, and I don't know what that means.

Crap. He needs to leave. I can't do this.

Clearing my throat, I lean to the other side of my chair and force a brave smile. "Well, I guess you've got places to be. Unless you need my help with your upcoming test." I can't help a sigh as I look back down in my lap and mumble, "Or another assignment."

He doesn't say anything, and I wince.

Yeah. This is it.

Here comes the speech.

He'll be nice about it. I'm sure he will. And he'll probably have some really valid reason for not wanting date number two. Is it because I'm a virgin? Am I too innocent for him?

That seemed to be an issue last night.

Maybe he doesn't want to be with someone he can't sleep with right away.

And if that's the case, then I don't want him anyway. He might be hot, and the things he said to me last night were spine-tingling and all, but if he's only in it for sex, then this isn't something I want to pursue.

Even though the thought of it ending is killing me.

And even though the idea that I won't ever get to sleep with him is surprisingly crushing.

Seriously, what is wrong with me?

I look up again, drinking in his face, those flickering eyebrows, that ticking in his jaw.

Should I give him an easy out?

He's too nice to want to hurt me.

Closing my eyes, I softly whisper, "It's okay, Wily. You don't have to say anything. Just go. I know I'm not the kind of person you usually go out with, and I get it. You've had some time to reflect, and you've realized that—"

His large hand covers my fidgeting digits.

I glance up again, and now he's the one drinking me in.

"I need you to help me graduate," he rasps.

"I know." I give him a tight smile. "And I will."

He shakes his head. "How?"

I tip my head in confusion. "Well... just how we have been. Unless you need me to adapt my style to suit your needs better or—"

"No, I mean, how am I supposed to concentrate on anything when you smell so good and you're so kind and you make me feel so... and you're sitting here looking so..." His lips start to curl up at the corners. "All I can think about is kissing you, and I don't know how I'm gonna be able to learn anything or concentrate on anything else but you."

I go still, my lips parting as surprise whips through me like a tornado.

I don't even have time to react before he's cupping the back of my head and pulling me close.

Our lips crash together in a hot, hungry kiss, and I grab his hoodie, curling my fingers into it as his tongue lashes against mine.

He groans as we deepen the kiss even more, his hand running up my leg and gripping my hip. He nudges me forward and I follow his lead, climbing into his lap and nearly toppling over on that little stool.

I yelp, grabbing his shoulder as we tip sideways.

He laughs, pulling us both to our feet. I gaze up at him, all out of breath and lost for words. He's staring back at me, his face flickering once more with doubt before he shakes his head and lunges for my lips again.

I can't resist him, reaching up and fisting the back of his hair as I dive into this heated kiss.

This one's different from last night.

It's not the slow, soft touch as he taught me how to kiss. It doesn't match the dancing snowflakes that glided down around us.

This kiss is hot and frenetic, and... I'm loving it!

Letting out a whimper, I reach up even higher on my toes, trying to get as close to him as I can. He's so tall and I'm too short and—

He scoops his arm around my waist again, plucking me off the floor and spinning to sit on the edge of my bed.

I stand between his legs, our mouths aligned more easily, and change the angle of the kiss.

He feels so good!

Like, *so* good!

My heart is thrumming, my body pulsing with a hot new beat I've never felt before. Areas of my body that I've never really noticed are singing, waking up from a life-long slumber and asking to join the party.

My nipples are buzzing.

In between my legs feels funny—this weighted kind of yearning that's new and tantalizing.

I whimper again, gripping the back of his hair as his hands curve around my waist, then sail over my butt, giving my cheeks a squeeze.

Gasping into his mouth, I try to swipe my tongue along his again, but he pulls back, checking my face. "Is that okay?"

I nod.

"Are you sure?"

I nod again, frantically. "I like it," I manage to whisper, then give him a nervous frown. "As long as you like it."

"Satch." He laughs my name, his mouth rising into a stunning smile. "I like it." And then his mouth is on mine again, his hands squeezing my ass while his tongue demolishes me with heady swipes and licks that are addictive.

His hands keep exploring, moving from my butt cheeks to my hips, then up my back. He pulls me closer, squishing our bodies together, and when his hands glide back down, his thumbs skimming the sides of my breasts, my knees start to buckle.

He catches me, hauling me back up and pulling me against him.

Resting his chin on my shoulder, he holds me tight, catching his breath, and all I can do is wrap my arms around him and hold on as well.

Inching my body forward until I'm flush against him, my eyes bulge as I feel the hard shaft pressing into my abdomen.

Holy shit, is that...?

I swallow, this wondrous smile forming before I can stop it.

Part of me wants to pull back and have a look at it, but I'm too nervous.

He's hard.

For me.

Our kissing gave him an erection, and... and what do I do now?

"Satch," he whispers, and for a second, I tense, waiting for him to tell me that kissing me is great and all, but he can't do this. "How?"

I lean back, needing to see his face and understand what he's trying to say.

"How am I supposed to resist you?" he clarifies, looking sweetly worried.

It's impossible not to smile as I cup his face. "I'm not sure how I'm supposed to resist you either."

This doesn't make him feel better.

If anything, he looks more worried. "You're the best tutor I've ever had. I don't want to lose you."

"Why would you lose me?"

"Because I need to be able to study around you—"

"Wily." I cup his face with both hands now, forcing him to look me in the eye. It's a lot easier when he's sitting and I can stand in front him. We're finally eye to eye, and I tell it to him straight. "You're not some horny animal who can't control himself."

He winces like maybe that's not true.

I laugh and shake my head. "Okay, fine. *I'm* not some horny animal who can't control herself. We'll just set boundaries and then enjoy the rewards."

"What do you mean?"

"Like..." I tip my head as I come up with a quick strategy. "Okay, how about this? No kissing before or during a study session."

He nods.

"No touching. We sit adjacent to each other, not right beside each other, and then once the study session is over, we can make out as much as we like."

His lips twitch, and he skims his finger up my arm. "So, you mean, if I work hard, you'll reward me?" Curving his hand around, he brushes his knuckles lightly down the curve of my breast.

I shiver and let out a soft laugh. "Or you'll reward me for being such a good tutor."

"You are a good tutor." His hand curves around my waist and he pulls me close, murmuring against my lips, "You're the best tutor I've ever had."

"And you're my favorite student," I whisper back before claiming his tongue once more.

CHAPTER 33
WILY

"So, you've got the hots for another tutor," Blake teases me.

I roll my eyes, suddenly wishing I hadn't called to check in on her. I hadn't heard from her in over a week and figured I should be a good big brother.

And now *I'm* the one getting grilled.

How did "What's up with you?" turn into me telling her I took Satch out on a date?

"Wait. This isn't Lemon Face, is it?" Blake's voice pitches. "You're banging Lemon Face?"

Anger flares through me hot and fast, and I hold up my fingers, counting off my comebacks as I list them off. "One, she's not a lemon face—that was just a really bad photo. She's got a stunning smile that lights up an entire room when she lets it show."

"Lights up an entire room?" Blake mocks me. "Oh, shithead, what has happened to you?"

I ignore her teasing in order to clarify, "And two, I'm not banging her."

She snorts. "Yeah, right."

"I'm not!" I bark at my phone, slowing down at the stop sign and growling as I check the intersection. As if I would *bang* sweet Satch. I've never had a problem with that terminology until now, and hearing it out of my sister's mouth is pissing me off.

"Wait, are you serious? You're not sleeping with her?"

"No!"

"But you said you took her out on a date."

"Shit, you really do think I'm a full-blown manwhore."

"Okay, let me rephrase," Blake comes back, annoyingly calm. "When was the last time you took a girl out and didn't end up in bed with her?"

I open my mouth to respond... and I've got nothing.

"Mm-hmm."

"Shut up," I mutter. "She's different."

"Obviously."

"I mean it, Blakey. She's really different."

My sister can sense the shift in my tone, and the teasing lilt drops from her voice. "What makes her so special?"

"I don't know." I shrug, a smile tugging at my lips. "She's sweet and funny and smart. She listens when I talk, you know? Like, she really listens. There's no ulterior motive—she just seems genuinely interested in what I have to say. And she doesn't look at me like I'm some dumb jock who's only good at football and sex."

"Wow," Blake murmurs. "Is this freaking you out?"

"No." I tap my finger on the wheel as I wait for a father and his son to cross the road, then pause again for the chick with bouncing tits to dart across behind them.

She waves a thank-you at me, and I lift my chin in acknowledgment before easing over those zebra lines.

"It's got to be freaking you out a little bit."

"It's not."

"It is," she singsongs.

"It's—" I huff. "Okay, fine, it is. I don't know what to do with this. I haven't had a serious girlfriend since high school."

"Whoa. One date and she's your girlfriend already?"

"I don't know." My voice pitches. "But she's something, and—"

"Don't tell Mom and Dad you have a girlfriend. They'll lose their shit and go off about how you can't get distracted *this close to getting drafted*." Blake puts on a voice that sounds nothing like either of our parents.

"Exactly." I nod. "And they're right. I should be throwing all my time and attention into the game, but all I can think about is my next tutoring session or when I'll get to see her again. She's taking up serious headspace that I can't afford to lose, but when I went to tell her that the other night, I just couldn't do it, and we ended up making out."

"Making out." Blake snickers at me like I'm some blushing grade-schooler.

"I mean, what am I supposed to do here? I really like her. Like *like* her. She's not some one-and-done. I want to keep hanging out with her, but what if things get all serious? How am I supposed to leave her and—"

"Okay, dude. Take a breath." Blake's voice is sharp down the line. "You're getting way ahead of yourself here. One date and you're scrawling her initials all over your brain? Just chill. For all you know, she'll be totally sick of you by the time you graduate, and it won't even be a thing."

The thought's a punch to the ball sack, and I grunt in response.

"I'm just saying to slow the hell down and take it one date at a time."

"But should I keep hanging out with her or cut ties now to avoid heartache later?" I groan, hating the idea of cutting ties. I love hanging out with Satch. That's where I'm headed right now. I don't want to face the rest of the year trying to avoid her. That would suck.

My sister goes quiet for a beat, and I hold my breath, waiting for one of her usually wise responses.

She's a pain in the ass, but she's got some smarts on her, and she's often the first person I go to for life advice.

But instead of giving me any, she tuts and says, "Look, I don't know, man."

"Come on, butt face," I whine. "Help a brother out here."

"Okay, fine." I can see her eyes rolling as she lets out an exaggerated groan. "Look, Mom and Dad would probably say yes, end this before it really starts, focus on the grand prize you've been working toward, but..." She huffs. "Screw that, you know? I say live in the moment. Enjoy her company, see where it leads. Hang out, make out, have sex, don't have sex. Just go with the flow and see what unfolds."

My lips twitch, loving the idea of doing just that. So much of my life has been this big push for football. It's like I've been on a one-way train without getting off at any of the stops.

Maybe Satch is my stop before the big leagues.

Maybe she's just what I need to get me to graduation, and then...

Who knows?

Maybe she'll be over me by then.

Maybe we'll just naturally part ways.

Or maybe she'll be my long-distance girl, and we'll figure out a way to make it work.

I mull that over while Blake starts telling me she's gotta go.

"Wait, wait, wait." I pull into a parking spot outside the library. "I called to check on you, and we've spent the whole time talking about me."

"But isn't everything always about you?" she says sweetly.

"Hardy-har-har." I deadpan. "Come on. What's up with you at the moment? How's college life treating my little freshman sister?"

She clears her throat. "It's fine. It's study and classes and work and—"

"Parties?" I groan. "You're not getting drunk every weekend, are you?"

"No." She laughs. "Please. You know me. I'm the good girl, remember? I'm Mommy and Daddy's little angel."

"Yeah, right," I tease, although that's kind of accurate. She's been that way since the day she was born. Always doing the right thing, being the smartest girl in the room, and getting all the accolades.

"But I really gots to go, bro."

"Okay, but just one last thing..."

"What?"

"Are you happy?" I don't know what compels me to ask that, but I need to know that my lil' sis is doing okay.

She takes too long to answer, and I start to worry until she lets out a laugh. "Of course I am. I'm always happy."

And then she's gone.

Without even a goodbye, that cheeky little shit hangs up on me.

I gape at my phone for a second before texting her.

Me: Did you just hang up on me?

She replies a beat later with a laughing emoji and then the middle finger, then a quick text.

Butt Face: I told you I had to go. It's not my fault you talk too much.

Me: You're such a pain in the ass.

Butt Face: Love you too, shithead. Now leave me alone so I can get on with my day, loser.

I laugh and send back a string of GIFs before grabbing my bag and shouldering my door open.

Seriously. That girl.

She drives me crazy, but I love her like no one else.

Closing the door with my hip, I stare up at the library, fisting the bag in my hand and reminding myself to just go with the flow and stop trying to talk myself out of hanging with Satch.

So what if she's living rent-free in my mind right now?

That's not going to stop my football career, right?

There's nothing wrong with having a friend who just happens to be a girl who I just happen to love making out with.

My blood stirs as I think about her wedged between my legs, her sweet tongue in my mouth and her lush body squished against mine.

Shit, that was hot.

I wanted to explore every one of those curves, and the fact that I have to wait before I'm allowed to do it makes it that much more tantalizing.

Taking the stairs two at a time, I weave my way through the stacks and around the corner.

Satch is waiting for me, hunched over her laptop and a notepad, reading, then scribbling, then playing with her bottom lip before typing something.

She must be working on one of her own assignments, and I feel bad for a second that she's going to have to stop and help me with my shit.

Resting my shoulder against the end of the book-shelf, I watch her for a minute, drinking her in. My lips rise into a smile as I trace the line of her cheek and neck with my eyes. I let my gaze linger on her chin, remembering the taste of it when I nipped it between my lips.

And now I'm moving down her body, over the swell of her boobs and whatever else is hiding behind those loose skirts and dresses she wears. I want to explore every inch of her.

When she's ready, Casanova! Calm the fuck down and walk over there, you idiot.

Jolting upright, I cut my sexy daydream short and quietly approach her.

Resting my hands on either side of the table around her, I lean down and whisper a soft greeting before nibbling the side of her neck.

She giggles and pulls away from me, turning her head to give me a reprimanding look. It makes me think of a sexy schoolteacher.

"Not until we're done." She holds up her finger between our noses. "Now, sit down, mister."

"Seriously?" I plunk into my chair with an exaggerated huff. "Not even a hello kiss?"

"We're doing this for your benefit." She's shaking her head as she nudges her chair away from me, rearranging the setup so I can't even reach her anymore.

"You're mean." I pull my lips into a fake pout, and she fights a grin, her cheeks tinging pink.

"Get out your stuff. The sooner we get through your work, the sooner I can taste you again."

Her sexy little comment has me sitting at attention like a well-trained dog.

And I do my very best to concentrate as we go through some finance problems she found online.

"This is probably what you're going to be facing on your test."

I work through them, focusing on the page in front of me and not how good she smells. I calculate that shit as fast as my brain can manage, and thank fuck it only takes forty-five minutes for me to pass the mini test she gives me.

Sitting beside her, my knee bobbing in agitation as she checks the last answer, I rest my chin in my hand and just let myself stare.

Her button nose wrinkles, her light brown eyebrows dipping as she looks over the last question. Her nose is cute. And I love the way her plump lips move as she whispers the calculations to herself and then nods, ticking my page with a smile before looking up at me.

"It's official. You're a finance wizard, and you're totally going to pass this test."

She's talking shit, but if it means I get to kiss her in a second, then I'll just let her go with it.

I reach for her face, but she sits back and gives me a pointed look. "You need to believe me, Coyote."

Pausing, I take in her serious expression, my hands flopping onto the table.

"Tell me you're going to pass this finance test."

I open my mouth to do as I'm told, then stare at the pages sitting between us. "I'm gonna... I'm gonna try. Test situations tend to kill my brain, but I'll—"

Pinching my chin between her fingers, she moves in close, her eyes burning bright with conviction. "You are capable of passing this test. And before that timer starts and you open that test booklet, I want you to say that to yourself. And I want you to believe it, because it's true. So... say it. *I am capable of passing this test.*"

I suck in a breath and go for a joke. "You are capable of passing this test."

"No." She shakes my chin. "Wily Wilson, you say it. Just like you made me shout out that stuff outside the Humanities building."

"You want me to shout it?" I look around and give her a dubious frown.

"Stop trying to get out of this." She grins, leaning forward in her chair until she's stretched across the table in front of me. "I want you to say it."

I gaze at her, studying those pretty eyes, so determined. So convinced.

Shit, what if she's right?

Am I capable of doing as well as she thinks I can?

"I can pass this test," I whisper, then clear my throat and say it with a little more conviction. "I can do this."

"Yeah, you can." She giggles. "Because you just passed the test I gave you, and it's going to be no harder than that one. So you, my beautiful coyote, are going to nail this thing, and I can't wait to celebrate with you."

I grin, running my hands down her arms. "Think maybe passing this mock test is worth a celebration?"

"Most definitely." She giggles again, checking the tables around us to make sure no one's looking before reaching for me.

The second her mouth hits mine, I reach around her body, pulling her out of her chair and between my legs again.

Her laughter is sweet, but I cut the sound off with my tongue, running my hands up her body and threading my fingers into her hair.

Fuck, she smells good.

She tastes even better.

And this body is something else.

"Come on," I whisper against her lips before jumping out of my seat and grabbing her hand.

Abandoning our stuff at the table, I pull her into the

back corner of the library, hiding in the shadows of the very far aisle and pressing her back against the wall.

She lets out a soft whimper when I lean down and kiss her, her worries about our stuff getting stolen forgotten when I slide my tongue back into her mouth. She folds against the wall, turning to putty as we lose ourselves in these heady kisses.

Making out with her is the best. I can't stop my hands from exploring her body, skimming her shape and rounding over her breasts.

After the first pass, I pause, pulling back so I can see her face.

Her eyes are bright with yearning, and she nods.

"It's okay?" I double-check.

"Yeah." She reaches for my hand, placing it back over her right boob. "I like it."

Squeezing her soft tit, I feel a burst of desire fire through me before leaning back down to kiss her again.

She likes it.

And oh fuck... I like it too.

CHAPTER 34
ELIZABETH

So, it's safe to say that Wily Wilson is about as addictive as sugar.

Actually, maybe he's even more addictive than sugar, because kissing him is even better than eating a chocolate bar.

His tongue is candy all on its own.

And his hands.

Oh my gosh, his hands.

I love the way they roam, tease, and touch.

He hasn't done anything more than feel me up yet, wriggling his fingers under my shirt, his thumb skimming across my bra. It's hot, heady stuff, and I've nearly asked him to take it off so I can feel his hands on that sensitive part of my skin, but I chicken out every time.

It's been a few weeks now, and we're still tutoring most days, then rewarding ourselves with a make-out session.

We've been out on a bunch more dates. The last one was my treat because he passed his finance test with a

74%. He couldn't believe it, and I had the pleasure of saying "I told you so" multiple times in between proud kisses and affirmations.

I love hanging out with him so much I can hardly stand it. Being with him is easy and fun. I forget where I am half the time, which is why I'm trying to be really careful about where we go.

I can't afford to be spotted by Jade, Kelsey, or Viper Girl when I'm with Wily, so each time he suggests we go to a diner or any of those public places, I talk him out of it. I don't know if he's noticed me doing it, but so far, we've stuck to the quiet sections of the library or one of our rooms for tutoring. And as for dates, the dark movie theater was perfect, and an obscure Turkish restaurant that's miles away from campus has worked out great.

Oh, and we've gone back to the football field, which I'm pretty sure is my favorite.

It didn't snow the last time, but we still danced under the stars, and that was perfect too.

"Are you even listening to me?" Mom asks, and I quickly blink, looking away from my dorm room window to let out a sheepish laugh.

Holding the phone a little closer to my mouth, I say, "Sorry, Mom. My mind wandered there for a second. What did you ask?"

"I wanted to know if I should invite all of your cousins around for your birthday dinner or if you just want to stick with a smaller group."

"Oh, I don't mind. It is Valentine's Day, so I don't want to ruin anyone's evening by having to come to my birthday."

"Stop that right now, young lady. They would be

honored to attend your birthday dinner. We're all so excited you'll be coming home for the weekend."

I nod, glad she can't see me cringing. I usually live for those weekends I go home to hang out with family, but for the first time ever... I want to stay in Nolan.

"Is there... anyone you'd like me to invite from school? You could bring a friend back with you if you wanted to, sweetie."

I bite my lip, wondering what she'd say if I mentioned that I'd like to bring back a gorgeous, hulking football player.

Nope. Can't go doing that.

Wily won't want to spend his weekend in Fledgling. That would be so boring for him.

And how would I even introduce him to everyone?

"Hi, this is Wily, my tutoring student and the guy I like to make out with. But please don't tell anyone, because I can't have Jade's parents finding out and then telling her about it, so you know, zip it everybody!"

I cringe. Ugh. Yeah. I so can't go there.

Wily and I will just have to spend Valentine's Day apart.

And that's probably a good thing, right? Because I need to get used to living without him. After he graduates, he's going to be off who knows where playing football, and I just have to enjoy this for what it is.

A glitch in the matrix.

A dream that I'll eventually wake up from.

My phone starts beeping with an incoming call and I check my screen, my insides jumping with delight when the name *Coyote* pops up.

"Hey, Mom, I have to go."

"Okay, sweetie. We'll see you next weekend, then. I love you."

"Love you too," I sing, quickly hanging up before I lose Wily's call. "Hi."

Oh my gosh, I sound like a tween, my voice all soft and wispy.

"Hey, beautiful. How's it going?"

"Good. How was practice?"

"Light and easy. Coach wanted to get home early. Carson told me he's got a special date night with the missus. I think it's their wedding anniversary or something. Anyway, worked in our favor. Practice wrapped up about twenty minutes ago."

"Wow. That's awesome."

"So, what are you doing?"

I swing back and forth in my chair, nibbling the end of my pen as I gaze out the window and picture him standing in his room. Is he shirtless? Is his hair wet from a shower?

My lady parts start to tingle, my body thrumming with this new energy I'm already addicted to.

"I was just talking to my mom," I tell him. "And then I was thinking I'd proof my assignment, then... I don't know, read a book or watch a movie or..."

"Come hang out with me?"

I grin. "Really? You're free tonight?"

"I'm free to hang out with you. I just need to wait for Carson to get back with my truck, and then I'll come and... Wait." He sucks in a quick breath.

"What?"

"Nylah lives in your building."

"She does?"

"Yeah. She's on the second floor, I think. Run down and see if she's there. You can catch a ride."

"What?"

"I loaned Carson my truck to go and get her, so see if you can catch a ride."

I sit forward in my seat, nerves thrashing me as I entertain the idea of going downstairs to look for a perfect stranger and ask for a ride. "Like... right now?"

"Yes. Go, go, go, girl. I'll see ya soon."

"Uh... I'm not sure I can." I cringe, hating the idea of letting him down, but I've never met Nylah Jones before. I've heard all about her, but every time I've gone to Football Frat, she either hasn't been there or I haven't seen her because I like to hang out in Wily's room.

I've had a short chat with Sienna, who seems nice, and I've stacked blocks with Zoey, who is just plain adorable, but...

Nylah Jones?

Yeah, I don't know her.

"Baby." Wily's reprimand is soft. "Yes, you can. I'll text Carson now and tell him not to leave without you."

"But I don't know Nylah."

"You've seen her at Football Frat before."

"No, I haven't. I don't even know what she looks like."

"You know what Carson looks like, so just run downstairs and find him. He'll be in my truck, and I know you know that beast. You're running out of excuses, Satch. You can do this. I'll let Carson know."

And with that, he hangs up, and I'm left gripping the sides of my chair and trying to find the courage to go and ask this girl I don't even know for a ride.

Plus her boyfriend, who is just a little bit scary.

Wily swears he's a good guy, but Carson hardly ever smiles, and the few encounters I've had with him have been borderline terrifying.

No, they haven't. Stop being so dramatic and get up!

Biting my lip, I really sink my teeth in, my body starting to quiver as I sit here staring at my door.

They'll leave without you, and then Wily will be upset. You'll miss out on time with him because you're being a scaredy cat.

"Shit," I mutter, forcing myself up and grabbing my coat before I can change my mind.

Cramming things into the pockets, I bolt out my door and rush to the elevator.

Crap, I may have missed my chance already. I took too long being indecisive, and now they've probably already left, and I'll be standing on that curb feeling bummed out because I didn't—

"Hold the door!" I call, jumping into the elevator and giving the girl in front of me a polite smile.

She shifts to the very edge of the space and keeps her eyes trained on her phone.

The ride down is painful, and I spend the short time straightening my jacket and trying to remember how to breathe.

Ding!

The doors pop open and I dash out, seeing Wily's truck through the glass doors and bolting for the exit.

A slender woman with a long black ponytail is walking toward Wily's truck. She got a slight limp, but it's not that noticeable. Not when her skintight jeans are showing off her perfect shape so beautifully. I can't help admiring her size 6 butt as she waves at her boyfriend.

I hurry it up before I lose my nerve.

"Hey!" I call out as I hit the stairs, running down them... and, in my haste, miscalculating the last step. You know, the one I've been stepping off for months now. The one I've walked down a thousand times before.

Yeah, that one.

It gets the better of me and I tumble onto the cold concrete, my bare hands slapping onto the rough surface at the same time my knee lands with a crunch.

Humiliation rushes through me at about the same speed as the pain, but I'm pretty sure it hurts worse.

I am such a moron!

Letting out a soft whimper, laughter from my past echoes through me as I stay on my hands and knees and keep my head tucked down. Cold moisture is soaking into my sweatpants and crap. Am I seriously wearing sweatpants?

What was I thinking?

I should have taken the time to change.

This is the worst idea ever!

I hate being rushed, and I should have just said no. I could have waited for Wily to come get me later. Or I could have freaking walked over by myself!

It would have given me time to shower and put nice clothes on, but no, I had to run out the door in my slouchy sweats, looking like a total slob and now falling on my ass for the world to see.

"Are you okay?" a voice calls, and I glance up in time to see the pretty Black girl limping back toward me.

It's Nylah. It has to be. She was waving at Carson before, and...

Oh shit, this is so humiliating!

I struggle to my feet, not wanting her to have to help me. Wouldn't want to strain one of her perfectly slim muscles, right?

Brushing off my stinging hands, I nod when she approaches and mumble, "I'm fine."

"You didn't hurt yourself?" She touches my arm, giving it a little rub. Her eyes are so full of genuine concern, and I stare at her, waiting for the laughter to break through.

People can only hold their worried frowns for so long.

But nope.

She's still not laughing.

I swallow and rasp, "I'm fine, really."

Smoothing my hands down my coat, I ignore the burn and wish the pavement had cracked and swallowed me up when I notice Carson sauntering toward us.

Oh shit, oh shit, oh shit!

"You okay?" he calls, and I nod, not wanting to look at him.

"I might just go back inside." I point over my shoulder. "I don't want to hold you guys up, so... you go."

"And show up at the house without you?" Carson snickers, gliding his hand around Nylah's waist and kissing her forehead in greeting before looking at me with his hard, piercing gaze. "Doubt it, lady."

"W-what?" I dig my hands into my coat pockets, hoping to warm them up. Maybe they'll hurt less that way.

"What Carson is so eloquently trying to say"—Nylah pats his stomach—"is that Wily will be really disappointed if we show up without you. I'm guessing he knows you're coming?"

"Yep." Carson nods. "He just texted me and said I had to bring you back to the house. So..." He tips his head toward Wily's truck. "Let's go."

"Are you... are you sure? I don't want to encroach."

Carson snickers and shares a quick look with Nylah before glancing back at me. "You have to come with me, kid. Wily will have my ass if I show up without you." His eyes start to twinkle. "And I know you know what pissed off looks like on that guy. It's not pretty."

I frown, confused by the statement.

How does he know that I know anything?

How much has Wily told him about me? About us?

My insides flush with even more embarrassment as I shuffle after them, reluctantly climbing into the back seat of the truck.

Carson gives me a hand up, and I can't help a soft hiss when the fabric of my sweats digs into my knee.

"You good?" he asks.

"Yes," I whisper, pulling my coat around my legs and not wanting to look at him.

He studies me for a second, I can feel it, then closes my door and walks around to the front.

Nylah's already buckled up and ready to go.

She glances over her shoulder, grinning at me as I reach for my seat belt.

I give her a closed-mouth smile, hoping she's not about to start up some conversation I don't want to participate in.

My knee hurts. And I'm still burning with humiliation.

I just need a second to balance myself.

Music blasts through the truck the second Carson starts the engine, and I flinch while Nylah laughs.

"You're gonna go deaf." She reaches for the volume, then skips the song.

"Hey," Carson complains. "That was my jam, kitty."

"Sorry." She laughs but doesn't bother skipping back to replay the song. Instead, she starts bopping along to the next track and singing.

Carson shakes his head. "You are so not sorry."

She laughs some more and winks at him. "You're right. I'm so not sorry." Then she belts out the words to the bridge before launching into the chorus.

She has a beautiful voice.

I would sing along with her—I love this song—but my knee hurts and...

Shifting my coat aside, I steal a glimpse at my sweats. Yep, they're ripped. And yep, that's blood.

Oh my gosh!

Now I have to spend the evening with bloody sweatpants on, and that's so gross.

Seriously. I can't believe I fell over in front of these two super-cool people who are driving me to my super-gorgeous boyfriend's house.

Wait, boyfriend?

Is that what he is now?

Before, you weren't sure what he was.

Biting my bottom lip, I gaze out the window, my insides coiling as I wonder if he even wants to be my boyfriend or whether we're best to not label it when he'll be leaving permanently after graduation.

Glancing back to the front, I watch Carson and Nylah as he takes her hand, threading their fingers together and kissing the inside of her wrist while she sings. He then gives her this sweet, loved-up smile, and...

Oh man, I'd love Wily to want to be mine.

Because I'm his.

There's no doubt about it.

Why else would I rush out the door in nothing but my ugly sweatpants?

Why else would I let these two talk me into turning up at his place with blood on my clothes and an embarrassing story about tumbling down my front steps?

Only a girl in love can be that stupid, right?

CHAPTER 35
WILY

I'm pacing like an eager puppy, darting from my window to my bed. I don't know what the fuck is wrong with me, but Carson is taking forever to get back with my girl.

Yeah, that's right. I said it.

My girl.

Because like fuck I want anyone else having her.

Spending time with Satch since the semester began has become addictive. I didn't realize it when we were studying together, but it just grew like that plant in the corner of Mom's kitchen, which I didn't even realize was getting bigger, but then all of a sudden, I started to notice it. I started to smell it and watch it bloom, and the colors took over the space until it's the first thing I see every time I walk back into that familiar space.

That is what Satch has become for me, and I fucking can't wait to see her.

Walking back to my window, I check the street and feel like a kid waiting for his birthday guests to arrive, especially when I notice my truck rounding the corner and I let out a whoop.

Flinging my door open, I run downstairs, jumping around the basket of laundry that needs to go up to Carson's room and practically tripping over the front mat.

Slow the fuck down, dude.

Sucking in a quick breath, I open the door and try to play it cool, but that goes out the window the second Carson pulls into the driveway and I bound down the front steps like a golden retriever.

Yanking open the back door, I beam at Satch, who gives me a shy smile, her cheeks flaring red as she tucks a lock of loose hair behind her ear.

"You good?" I hold out my hand to help her out, and she shuffles to the door, wincing when she swivels to face me. "What happened?" My joy gets sliced in half by instant concern. "Are you hurt?"

She shakes her head, but Nylah rounds the car and smiles up at me. "She fell coming out of Buckley Hall. Those stairs are slippery in the winter."

She winks at Satch, who gives her a barely there smile.

"Did someone push you?" My voice is deep and rough.

Satch glances up to bulge her eyes at my question while Nylah lets out a confused laugh.

"No. No one pushed her. Why would they do that?"

Satch shakes her head, and I press my lips together, even though I kind of want to rant about the bitch who called her hippo. It happened weeks ago, but I'm still riled about it.

Satch hasn't said it, but I know she keeps an eye out

for her whenever we're on campus together. She's super warm and friendly when we're hidden away somewhere private, but if we ever spot each other in open public, she won't come within reach.

I've asked her about it, but she just said she doesn't want the world gossiping about us.

"You're a popular guy."

"So?" I queried her, not getting the secrecy at all.

"I just... don't like people talking about me."

I guess that's fair enough, so I've tried to play it cool and keep our relationship on the down-low around school. It's an effort, but I keep PDA to a minimum... unless we're behind closed doors. When we're at Football Frat, I can be myself, which is why I have no hesitations about wrapping my arm around her and helping her out of the truck.

I spot the blood as soon as her coat shifts out of the way and softly hiss. "Ouch."

"I'm okay," she mumbles, hobbling beside me up to the house.

"You're bleeding."

"She's what?" Carson spins around in surprise, glancing down at her leg when I point to it. "Why didn't you say anything?"

Satch quickly covers her damaged sweats with her winter coat while Carson looks right at me.

"I didn't know, man."

"That's okay." I give him a closed-mouth smile, although I'm still kind of pissed that he didn't check on her more carefully.

How did she fall?

It must have been bad if she's bleeding.

Has she got any other injuries?

I want to pepper her like a detective but sense she's not gonna say a damn thing with Carson and Nylah watching, so I wrap my arm around her waist and help her up the front steps.

It's awkward with our height difference, but I refuse to let her go until she's gripping the inside railing and walking up to my room. Even then, I keep my hand on her lower back and gently support her.

"Can we get you anything?" Nylah calls up after us.

"No, I'm good," Satch throws back over her shoulder.

I frown at my girlfriend's back, wishing she wasn't being so stoic about all this. It's okay to bleed and ask for help.

Guiding her into my room, I help her out of her coat, smiling when I notice she's wearing the hoodie I left in her room the other night.

Good. I wanted her to claim that thing. I hope she's been sleeping in it. I love it when girls do that kinda shit. I love that she's keeping me with her this way.

"You wanna sit?" I point to the end of my bed.

"No, I'm good." She crosses her arms, curling in on herself as she hobbles a step away from me.

"Satch. Sit." I say it softly, but this isn't up for debate. "Let me look at your knee."

With a reluctant huff, she shuffles to my bed and takes a seat. I crouch down in front of her, checking out the ripped fabric.

"You're gonna need to take these off so I can get a better look."

"What?" She flushes.

"I promise I'll be a perfect gentleman." I wink at her,

grabbing the throw blanket off the side of my bed. "Wrap this around yourself. I'll be back in a sec." Walking to the door, I pause in the frame and glance back at her. "I'll get the first aid supplies, and you..." I point at her with a grin. "You take those pants off."

She flushes again, but this time she's fighting a grin.

Good. I need her to relax and trust me.

I just want to look after her, and I'll tell her that as soon as I get back to my room.

But first things first.

Trotting back downstairs, I hunt out the first aid kit in the top of the pantry and field a bunch of questions from Carson, Nylah, and Tyrell, who are all in the kitchen.

"You sure she's okay?" Nylah asks.

"Yeah, she's just got a banged-up knee."

"Her hands might be sore too." Nylah grabs a carrot stick off the board, grinning at Tyrell when he tells her to stop stealing his dinner.

"Yeah, she landed pretty hard," Carson murmurs, flicking through the car magazine that arrived for him in the mail today.

"Poor thing." Nylah shakes her head. "I turned in time for the aftermath, but she was just on her hands and knees, face bright red. She must have been so embarrassed."

"Yeah, she embarrasses easily." I wince, pulling snacks out of the pantry and loading up.

Walking past the fridge, I wrestle a couple of drinks out of the door, then grab an ice pack from the freezer as well.

"Catch you guys later."

"You're not gonna come down and socialize once she's

patched up?" Nylah's tone is teasing, and I spin back to watch that smirk on her face grow a little bigger.

I grin back at her, shaking my head and announcing to the room. "I'm keeping her all to myself tonight, guys."

"Ooooo." Nylah laughs. "Someone's gettin' lucky."

Carson pops up from his seat, reaching her in two quick strides and lightly smacking that cheeky ass of hers. "I hope you're talking about me, kitten."

She gives him a baleful look and then tips her head, tapping her chin. "The question we need to ask ourselves is... has Carson done enough to get some lovin' tonight?"

Carson lets out a low growl, pulling her against him and nibbling her neck.

She starts to giggle while Tyrell gags and complains. "I'm making food here, people." Holding up his knife, he points it at them in warning. "If you start doing it in here, there will be a formal protest, you feel me? I ain't playin'. No sex in shared spaces. That's a house rule!"

I snort when Carson amps it up and Nylah starts moaning like she's having an orgasm.

"Get out of the kitchen!" Tyrell yells as I laugh and take the stairs two at a time.

Satch is waiting for me on the bed, her bloody sweats folded neatly on the floor and my throw wrapped around her.

"Is everything okay down there?" She looks past me with a nervous wince.

"Yeah." I flick the door shut with my foot. "Carson and Nylah are just ragging on Tyrell while he's trying to cook. The guy always gets stressed in the kitchen. But Grady, who usually loves to cook, has been kind of off lately, so we're having to step up."

"What's wrong with Grady?" Satch shifts on the bed while I unload my armful of supplies, handing her the ice pack. "What's this for?"

"Nylah said you hurt your hands." I take her fingers, studying her palms and lightly brushing my fingers over the red hue on her skin before grabbing a T-shirt off my floor and wrapping it around the ice pack. "Here, hold this for me, will ya?"

I gently press her palms on either side of the ice pack and turn my attention to her knee, softly telling her what I know about Grady.

"I think he broke up with his longtime girlfriend, and he's taking it pretty hard. I've never seen him go through a hard time before, but from what I can tell... he obviously likes to work through stuff on his own. He hasn't really let any of us in, and I'm not sure how hard to push him."

"He'll come to you when he's ready." Satch smiles down at me. "Some of us prefer a little privacy when we're hurting."

I pause for a second to gaze up at her face before skimming my knuckles down her cheek... then shifting the throw blanket off her leg.

CHAPTER 36
ELIZABETH

My breath catches as my aching knee is exposed to the air.

Taking off my sweats without hurting that graze was impossible, and in the end, I just had to wrestle them off and grit my teeth through the discomfort.

As soon as that gray fabric was puddled at my feet, I winced at my boring beige underwear and quickly wrapped the blanket around me.

I then folded my sweats and started the painful wait, listening to noises downstairs. The rising and falling of voices. The laughter.

For a second, I couldn't help wondering if they were laughing about me. The hippo who fell over and cracked the pavement.

Closing my eyes, I try not to relive Katrina's taunts. She used to love blaming every crack in the sidewalk on me.

She'd follow me home from school sometimes and ask, "Did you fall over there? Oh, and there too. Oh wow, look at the size of that one! That's definitely a hippo crack."

Before I could spiral too far back in my memory, Wily walked through the door, his arms piled high with goodies and first aid supplies.

And now he's carefully checking out my knee, and I'm melting on the end of his bed.

"Is it still sore?" he gently asks, his tone soft and husky.

"A little," I admit, my breath catching when he starts to dab the outer edge with antiseptic. "But I'll be okay."

He smiles up at me, glancing away from my knee for a second. "It's okay to hurt, baby."

This soft, self-deprecating laugh pops out of me, but I quickly suck the sound back in. "I just don't want to make a big deal of it. All this fuss for just a little graze."

He smiles, lightly blowing on my damaged skin and sending my insides into a frenzy. His fingers skim down my leg, and I can't breathe. Seriously. I can't breathe.

Letting me go, he rustles through the kit, pulling out a large Band-Aid and testing the size on my knee before peeling the backing off and delicately applying it to my skin.

His fingers feel so good. His touch is so delicate, yet I can feel it through every fiber of my being.

He's never touched my legs before. Not without fabric in the way, and his hand resting on my thigh like this... his thumb caressing me while he softly kisses the spot around that bandage...

My insides quiver.

"I like looking after you," he murmurs, trailing his lips

to the top of my knee and kissing a spot there too. "I want to make you feel better, Satch."

"You do," I quickly tell him. "I just have to look at you and life gets a little brighter."

His eyes land on mine then, sparkling with appreciation.

Setting the ice pack aside, I skim my fingers down his face, my heart rate accelerating as my mind flies to places I've been dreaming about. Images of naked bodies. Wily lying on top of me, giving me something I've never experienced before.

The pads of his fingers are still resting on my thigh, and I never want him to stop. I want those fingers to keep traveling, exploring, touching. My skin is sizzling for it, begging him to make me feel this good all over.

I wish I could say that to him, but I don't know how to find the words.

All I can do is lean forward and kiss him.

He meets me halfway, his soft mouth melting against mine like it always does.

I love kissing him.

I love his hands on my body.

I want more.

I've been wanting more ever since our first date, but I don't know how to ask.

How do I say that I want to feel his body moving over mine with no clothes in the way?

Every time he touches me, he goes a little further, and I'm internally crying out for more, but then he'll pull away, not wanting to push it.

But maybe I want him to push it this time.

Running my hands down to his neck, I deepen the

kiss, then splay my hands over his shoulders before holding my breath and tugging on his shirt.

It's a bold move I've never tried before, but I can't back out now. He knows exactly what I'm silently asking.

Pinging away from me, he checks my face, his eyes lighting with excitement as I tug at his shirt again. Helping me out, he pulls it over his head, flinging it on the floor. I stare at his perfect body, reaching out for those pecs... mesmerized by his defined ridges.

He's so beautiful. A shaky breath rushes between my lips as I trail my fingers over his body.

He rises up to his knees, giving me better access while he runs his hands lightly up my thighs. They disappear beneath the throw wrapped around me, and I shiver when they reach my upper thigh, skimming the edge of my panty line.

"Is this okay?" he rasps.

I nod and quickly check, "Is this okay? Does this feel good?" Turning my hand, I run my knuckles down his six-pack, then start traveling back up to his puckered nipples.

"You feel good, baby," he breathes against my neck before running the tip of his tongue up to my ear and sucking the lobe into his mouth.

A puff of air spurts out of me, followed by a moan that I can't control.

He feels so good.

More, more! my body starts begging, and I move before I can change my mind.

Unzipping the hoodie, I push it off my shoulders, then grip the bottom of my shirt and start to lift it.

Catching Wily's eye, I give him a nervous wince,

nearly changing my mind. But the look of pure yearning I see flashing across his face is too sweet to deny.

So I close my eyes and go for it, pulling off my shirt and setting it down beside me.

My heart is thundering so hard, I won't be surprised if he can see the beats pulsing just beneath my skin.

I have no idea if Wily likes what he sees. My eyes are still closed because I'm pretty sure I put on my plainest, comfiest bra after my shower today, and he's probably seen way prettier ones than this.

"Shit, I love your tits."

My eyes pop open in surprise. "What did you just say?"

He dips his head with a soft laugh. "I didn't mean to say that out loud, but it's true." He points at my chest. "They are gorgeous."

I gasp and cover them with my hands, crossing my arms over my body. "R-really?"

He nods. "They're big and beautiful, and I really want to touch 'em." He looks hungry, and I glance down at my chest, wondering what the big deal is. They're just breasts. They're cumbersome and annoying. They bounce and get in the way and they're heavy and—

"But I won't, unless it's okay with you." He clears his throat but doesn't take his eyes off my chest.

Biting my lips together, I drop my arms away, letting him look.

It feels so bold to do this, and my heart rate kicks up a notch as I pull my shoulders back and whisper, "You can touch me."

Holding my breath as he reaches for me, I keep that air locked in my lungs as he skims his finger down the line of my bra, then ever so slowly... ever so delicately... he pushes the strap off my shoulder and places a kiss in the groove on my skin.

I close my eyes again, running my fingers into his hair as he paints a line over my skin, kissing his way to the other strap while gently massaging my breasts.

Okay, now I want the bra gone.

The thought is as terrifying as it is tantalizing, so I quickly act before I can change my mind.

Reaching behind me, I unclasp my bra and stop breathing yet again.

Wily pulls back, giving me space to move. I don't know if he realizes he's doing it, but his head is bobbing. He's one eager beaver, and it's that sweet yearning on his face that finally gives me the courage to drop the bra at my feet.

His smile is instant, his eyes lighting as he stares at my breasts like they're an undiscovered wonder of the world.

He cups them in his hands, gently, with the utmost care, brushing his thumb over the sensitive skin before leaning toward me and trailing his tongue between them.

My breath catches yet again, my body electrifying as he explores my delicate skin with his lips and tongue. When he reaches my left nipple, I swear I have never felt anything so good. Ever. In my entire life. I have never felt this freaking good!

I moan, fisting the back of his hair while his tongue circles my nipple, then sucks it into his mouth.

Oh shit. This is incredible!

I'm whimpering before I can stop myself, and then he's trailing kisses over my stomach, dipping his nose into my belly button before brushing my lower abs with his short whiskers. They scratch and tickle. I bite my bottom lip, reeling at these new sensations. My heart is still thundering away, galloping through my chest and making me lightheaded.

Between my legs is tingling something fierce, and I want him to touch me there. I want to know what it's like to be with a man.

To be with Wily.

So I shift back on his bed, lifting my feet up and crab-crawling backward. The throw falls away from me, and I'm soon lying back on his pillows in nothing but my beige underwear.

He stands tall, gazing down at me.

I can't tell what he's thinking, and I shift uncomfortably, covering my chest with my arm and splaying a hand over the triangle between my legs.

"You don't have to hide yourself from me," he whispers, his gaze lingering slowly down my body. It's so obvious that he likes what he sees.

How is that possible?

I worry my lip, starting to tremble when he kneels on the end of the bed. I shift my feet so he can find a perch between my legs, and now stars are starting to scatter in front of my vision.

Am I really doing this?

Yes! You want this. You really want this.

His fingers skim lightly up my calf muscles, softly exploring my exposed curves until he's caressing the edge of my panty line again.

"Is this okay?" His voice is a husky rasp, his eyes darting to mine. "Do you want me to do this?"

"Yes." I breathe the word more than say it, then act on instinct and lift my hips.

He takes my cue and wriggles the underwear off my hips.

Oh my gosh, Wily Wilson is seeing me naked.

He keeps his eyes on me, his lips rising at the edges when he finally pulls the underwear off my feet and throws them on the floor.

I have no idea what he's thinking and I'm too afraid to look, so I quickly shut my eyes before I embarrass myself.

"It's okay, baby." His fingers skim over my thighs.

"I've never been naked around a guy before," I admit.

"I know." His voice is sweet with understanding, and I pop my eyes open, my breath whooshing out of me when he stands and pulls his sweats and boxer briefs off.

Sitting up on my elbows, I gape at his glorious, naked body. His penis is standing to attention, long and impressive, and I have no idea what to say.

"Now we're even. Both naked, and no one needs to be embarrassed." His boyish smirk is adorable, and my chest fills with affection as I gaze at him. His blue eyes turn serious with an intensity that makes my heart stop beating for a second. "I won't do anything you don't want me to, okay? You say stop and I will. If anything is too much... I'll back away. I promise. You can trust me."

I nod, my lips quivering as they rise into a smile. "I trust you."

His expression softens with affection as he crawls back onto the bed and nestles between my legs again.

"I don't know what I'm doing," I whisper, but it's already so freaking obvious I don't know why I said it.

He smiles, stretching out above me, then flopping to his side so we're next to each other. Totally naked.

We're naked.

His bare leg presses against mine, the tip of his penis skimming my thigh as he tucks his arm under his head and lightly presses a kiss to my cheek.

"Let's just take this slow," he whispers into my ear, his fingers trailing over my shoulder and down toward my breasts again.

His touch is featherlight, and I close my eyes, tipping my head back when he starts nibbling my neck and, inch by inch... working his way down my body.

CHAPTER 37
WILY

Satch is opening herself up to me, letting me in, and I don't want to take advantage of that by rushing this thing.

She's a nervous first timer.

She's not begging for it like that girl from last year. She's not horny and curious.

Well, maybe she is those things, but that's not glaringly obvious.

From what I can tell, she just wants to be with me. Be intimate with me. And I want to make this a lasting experience. Not one she cringes over when she relives it, but one she remembers with a smile for the rest of her life.

When she recalls losing her virginity, I want it to be this sweet, swoony thought in her mind, not some horror story about some selfish prick who hurt her, rushed her... and she immediately regretted it.

Sucking her nipple, I enjoy the catch of her breath, tuning into her every move and sound, trying to read her body as I skim my fingers over her belly button and lightly brush that sweet spot between her legs.

She flinches, letting out a soft gasp, and I gently cup her, checking her face to make sure she's okay.

"Still want this?" I whisper against the curve of her breast, not sure how I'm gonna stop if she says no but determined to be the man she needs.

"Yes."

My lips curl with relief as I go back to kissing her luscious tits, honored that I even get to do this.

For a girl who bolted after our first kiss, it hasn't taken her long to warm up to me... to us. Each make-out session has been hotter than the last, and now she's lying naked next to me, telling me she trusts me. And I have to honor that trust.

Drawing a circle around her nipple with my tongue, I enjoy her moan and get back to work, stroking her clit and feeling her tense and relax beneath my touch.

She's into it, I can tell. And slowly, her legs part a little wider, giving me easier access to her sweet oasis.

Holy shit, my dick is hard, straining to reach the one place it's going to have to wait for. It's not getting anywhere near her until she's wet and ready. And that's exactly what I'm gonna do—get her wet and ready.

Circling her clit with my finger, I keep rubbing, teasing, coaxing her into a new comfort zone until her breaths get ragged and she's grinding her hips into the mattress. I keep suckling her perfect tits, giving them each turns before darting up to her mouth and drinking deep, our tongues lashing together until she can't contain another moan or whimper.

My finger works her over, gently teasing her clit and loving the way she's falling under the wild spell of her first orgasm. Or at least the first time someone else has given her an orgasm.

Slipping my fingers between her folds, I tease her opening, loving how wet and glossy it feels.

"Oh," she pants, tipping her head back and gripping my shoulder. "What are you doing to me?"

"You like it?" I check.

"Yes," she squeaks, then lets out another groan. "Yes."

I smile, sitting up on my elbow to watch her for a second. She's getting close—it's obvious and beautiful—and I fucking love the way her tits are heaving, swaying across her chest while I take her to that high point and watch her tumble over the other side.

Gliding my finger back inside her, I tease her G-spot while stroking her clit with my thumb and sucking her nipples again.

"Oh my gosh." Her fingers dig in a little deeper, her nails starting to impale me, but like hell I'm asking her to stop. "Oh shit!"

She tenses, her body starting to shake, and then it happens.

She lets out this keening groan... and tumbles, her body convulsing with ecstasy as I work her clit a little faster and slip my finger in a little deeper.

"Oh! Oh. Ohhhh." Her eyes pop open, her mouth agape as she clamps her legs together, trapping my finger inside her and quivering from head to toe.

"You good?" I smile, pressing my nose into her cheek, then kissing her when she turns to answer me.

"Mm-hmm," she hums into my mouth, gripping the back of my neck and kissing me hard.

I slip my finger out of her, rolling her to her side and gathering her against me. Her leg swings up around mine, and my sensitive dick presses into her soft abdomen.

Oh man, my hips want to start jerking. It's taking everything in me not to roll her over, pin her to the mattress, and find a home between her legs.

But this has to come from her.

All I can do is keep kissing her and hope that she'll be ready. And if not, I can deal with that. I can—

She pulls away from me, her eyes studying my face. I work for neutral, not wanting to sway her decision. This can't just be about the hunger coursing through my body.

My jaw shakes just a little as I open my mouth to tell her that, but she speaks before I can.

"Do you want to..." She bites her lip, and I hold my breath, my entire body tensing as I wait for the rest of her question. "Do more?"

I can't help an instant grin.

She smiles back at my no doubt goofy-ass expression.

"Only if you want to," I manage to croak.

She starts to nod, and it takes everything in me not to punch the air with a whoop.

"You sure?" I check, tucking her hair behind her ear. "We don't have to if you're not ready. I know this is your first time, and—"

"I want to." She nods again. "I want to be with you... in this way." She swallows, brushing her teeth over her bottom lip. "I trust you, Wily. I lo..." Her words trail off and she shakes her head, blushing bright red as she dips her chin.

"I trust you, too, Satch." Tipping her face up to mine, I

lightly kiss her before reaching into my bedside drawer and pulling out a condom.

Ripping it open, I kneel beside her and roll it on.

She's watching me in fascination, lightly running her finger down my rigid dick.

"It's slimy." Her nose wrinkles.

"It's to help with…" I shake my head and reach back into my drawer for a tube of lube.

"What's that?" She sits up on her elbow, trying to read the side of it.

Her boobs jiggle when she moves, and I can't help taking a second to admire them before squirting the lube onto the tip of the condom.

"This is lube. It'll help reduce friction and make it more comfortable for you. The wetter you are, the easier it is." Shit, it feels so weird explaining this.

It's like I'm giving her a tutorial in sex.

Way to kill the romance.

But she doesn't seem to notice or mind, tipping her head to watch me rub the lube on.

Reaching forward again, she swipes her finger up my dick like she's conducting a scientific observation.

I gaze down at her, wondering what the hell she's thinking, then grinning when she gives me an impish look.

"Sorry, total newb and very curious."

"That's okay." I try to play it cool, sitting back on my heels. "Anything else you want to know before we do this?"

She actually thinks about it, her face scrunching in consideration before she shakes her head. "I don't think so. I feel like it's more a case of 'you learn as you go.'"

I nod, my chest thrumming at the cute expression on her face.

"I'm just glad you know what you're doing." Flopping back down, she starts biting her lip again, and I go in for a kiss before she can hurt herself.

My tongue glides across hers, a nice, slow movement... because everything about this has to be slow and soft and gentle.

Shit, I really don't want to hurt her.

Her fingers glide into my hair, lightly fisting the back as her body angles toward mine.

I shift, carefully climbing between her legs and trying not to touch her injured knee.

"You good?" I check between kisses. "Your knee okay for this?"

"What knee?" she murmurs, and I lean back, taking the weight on my elbows and making sure that she's not just using a joke to cover up her worries the way I sometimes do.

She gazes up at me, her eyes rich with affection, and holy shit... I could drown in that look. It's pure and... I don't know if any girl has ever looked at me this way before.

It makes something in my chest shift. It's this weird kind of pop, igniting a protective instinct that I already thought was pretty strong, but it's just amplified to epic proportions.

I want to keep this woman safe and close and care for her like no one else ever could.

I want to give her everything.

Brushing my fingers lightly through her hair, I gently smile at her and want to whisper something sweet.

Shit, the words *I love you* are dancing inside my head, but I can't go saying that.

What if it freaks her out? What if it's all too much?

No, I can't tell her I love her.

But I can show her.

Leaning down, I press my lips back to hers, sinking into a slow, languid kiss before pulling back and reaching between us.

Grabbing my dick, I skim the tip between her folds, drawing a line up and down until she starts to get used to the sensation.

Her eyes lock with mine and she swallows, giving me a little nod to keep going. So I gently push into her. Not all the way, just the head, until her pussy adjusts.

She sucks in a breath, her lips quivering into a wondrous smile. I use short, barely there thrusts, slipping in and out until I can dive a little deeper into this warm, wet oasis.

Holy fuck, she feels amazing.

She's so tight, and I swear my dick feels like an explorer right now, burrowing into new ground, uncovering the wonder of this new find.

Letting out a trembling breath, she squeezes my shoulders as I inch in a little further.

"Is this all right?"

"Yes," she squeaks. "Keep going."

And so I do, slowly pushing into her until we're both trembling, our panting breaths mingling in the air.

"Am I hurting you?"

She shakes her head.

"Are you sure?"

Her eyes flash with something, and I'm about ready to

rip out of her. "It's not pain, it's... it's just new. Like I'm being stretched or something. I've never felt anything like it."

"Do you want me to stay?" I double-check, scouring her face for any hint that she might be lying.

Cupping my cheek, she brushes her thumb across my chin and whispers, "I'm pretty sure I'll die if you leave me." Her lips rise into a stunning smile as she pulls my head down and takes me out with a deep, luscious kiss.

I can't even tell you when I start moving inside her.

At some point, I just became aware of my slow, soft thrusts. It's like walking through a park or floating along a river.

She starts to move with me, her hips swaying as I rock in and out, in and out, moving a touch deeper with each thrust.

Squeezing her thigh, I clench my butt, thrusting even farther as the heat builds within me. She responds, groaning into my neck, then pressing her lips to my shoulder, gripping it tightly and whimpering into my skin.

Fuck, I love her lips.

I love how soft and smooth they are.

Just like her insides. Everything about her is comfort and warmth and... shit, I'm gonna start coming soon. I can feel that rise inside me, my heart starting to take off as her whimpers increase in depth and power.

Her hips jerk beneath mine, moving a little faster, and I match her beat, our bodies shifting with a new energy that's hot and all-consuming.

"You feel good, baby," I groan against her cheek, leaning back to check her face.

Her eyes slide open, her hazel gaze taking me out. It's bright with wonder, beaming with this warmth that I can feel all the way to my core.

I grin back down at her, brushing the end of my nose against hers before trailing a line of kisses back down to her neck.

Holy shit, she's fucking amazing.

I don't know if I've ever been this intimate with a woman before, and it's driving me crazy—in all the right ways.

Rocking my hips, I push deep and slow, loving the way her body responds to me.

Her hands weave around my shoulders, traveling across my back, her fingers digging in. Her pants grow a little faster as I thrust and climb.

Yes, baby. Come with me.

With another long, steady thrust, I must hit her sweet spot, because she gasps, then presses her mouth into my shoulder, whimpering and keening.

I start to groan myself, picking up my pace when she spreads her legs a little wider, tipping back her head and wailing, "Ohhhhh."

Her pussy starts to spasm, clutching me tight, and I choke out this weird sound I swear I've never made before, the sensations riding through me beyond anything I've experienced in my life.

She's so fucking hot, and I can't hold out anymore.

Clenching my ass, I thrust deep and finally let go, burying myself in uncontrolled jerks and groaning into my pillow before pressing my lips against her soft neck and losing myself completely.

CHAPTER 38
ELIZABETH

So, sex is amazing.

Holy shit!

I'm struggling to get my breath back as Wily pants against my neck. He keeps giving me gentle kisses, and I can feel his heartbeat thundering against my chest. His weight on my body is delicious, and I want him to stay inside me forever.

Sure, I'm feeling stretched, and my body is definitely adjusting to this foreign invasion.

But it's not an invasion.

He's a welcome guest!

I've never felt anything like this before. He's inside me.

We're joined.

As one.

And the feelings rocketing through my body as he pushed into me, and then we did this sensual dance that was like...

And then it was so...

I mean, I can't even...

Finish a coherent sentence? my brain mocks me, and all I can do is giggle.

Wily's head pops off the pillow like he's suddenly coming to, waking up from a drunk-like trance. Blinking down at me, he quickly takes his weight on his elbows and shifts on top of me.

I clamp my thighs around his hips. "Don't move."

"Does it hurt?" He looks adorably worried, and I smile up at him, brushing my thumb over the lines creasing his forehead.

"It feels too good. I'm not ready for you to leave."

"You sure?"

I try to ease his concern by making my smile a little broader, and then I end up giggling again. "I am so freaking sure."

His expressions shifts, a sappy smile forming on his lips as he tilts his head to study me. "So, that was good for you, huh?"

"That was so good." I let out a giddy sigh, tipping my head back and melting all over again when he presses his lips to my throat.

"It was good for me, too, baby. So fucking good."

I bite my bottom lip, not sure how to respond to that.

I have no idea why he thinks *I* feel so good. I'm not some super-sexy, super-muscly sports person with a body to die for.

I'm just me with my lumpy curves and squishy edges.

But he seems to like being inside me, so...

Easing away, Wily slowly rises off me, naturally slipping out of me before reaching for the box of tissues next to his bed.

Pulling out a bunch, he hands them to me, and I suddenly feel self-conscious as I bunch them between my legs.

Everything feels very wet and squelchy down there, and I hope no humiliating sounds pop out of me when I go to move.

Checking the tissue, I blink at the blood and remind myself that this is all normal. I'm a first timer. My hymen would have been torn when he pushed into me. But he did it so slowly, so gently, that it didn't even hurt. Not really. It was just a stretching pressure, not any ripping kind of pain like it's sometimes described as.

Amazing.

Shaking my head in wonder, I press the tissues back against me, worrying about how I'm supposed to get to the bathroom. Will I bump into one of his football buddies on the way?

Eeep! That'd be so humiliating!

"What's wrong?" Wily's husky voices grabs my attention.

He's kneeling between my legs, pulling off the condom, which will definitely have blood on it as well.

Oh my gosh, is he going to be totally grossed out by me?

I wince, biting my lip for what feels like the thousandth time.

"Stop that," he softly reprimands, brushing his thumb over my lip. "Tell me what's up, Satch."

"It's nothing. I just..." Looking toward the door, I can feel my face scrunching.

He follows my line of sight, then looks back at me, his lips starting to twitch. "I've got an idea."

The look on his face isn't making me feel any better, but I still have to ask, "You do?"

"Come on." He jumps off the bed, and I watch his penis flop up and down as he balls the wad of tissue paper in his hand, then reaches out for mine.

"Oh. No." I shake my head. "This is gross, and you don't want to—"

"Satch." He laughs my name more than says it, reaching for my hand and pulling me off the bed.

Taking my disgusting tissues off me before I can protest again, he then wraps the throw around my body and takes my hand, opening his bedroom door—*what the hell!*—and marching us across the hallway to the bathroom.

He's still *totally* naked, his sensational ass cheeks smiling at me while I trail after him in a mild state of shock.

Closing the bathroom door behind us, he locks it, then proceeds to turn on the shower.

"Let's get cleaned up."

He winks at me, and I sink onto the lid of the toilet, gazing at this amazing man as he throws away our sex trash and starts to hum under his breath.

He's not embarrassed one bit by my virgin blood or the messy cleanup.

He's running me a hot shower and—

Pulling back the curtain over the bathtub, he tests the water and waggles his eyebrows at me. "Come on, sexy lady. Let me wash that body of yours."

How can I possibly say no to that?

Taking his hand, I let him pull me up and bravely let the throw blanket drop off my shoulders.

Stepping over the side of the tub, I find my grounding on the nonslip mat and close my eyes as the hot water hits my skin.

It's still feeling sensitive and tingly... and when the spray hits my grazed knee, I only then remember I was hurt just an hour or so ago.

And now I'm standing in a shower with the hottest guy I know soaping down my back and... I'm not a virgin anymore.

Because I just made myself his.

My lips twitch as Wily spins me around, nestling my back against his torso and taking his sweet time with my breasts.

I start to giggle as he lingers, teasing and lightly pinching my nipples.

I look up at him, squinting against the water hitting my face. He moves the showerhead, still massaging my breasts and giving me a *Is there a problem?* look.

Raising my eyebrows at him, I enjoy his boyish grin.

"What?" he protests. "I like 'em. Just let me make sure they're super, extra clean."

With a luscious groan, I tip my head back against his shoulder and let him keep soaping me down until I'm sure I'm the cleanest person in this house.

CHAPTER 39
WILY

So, we used up all the hot water, and I got a shouting lecture from Grady, who arrived home from a run and was anything but impressed to find nothing but stone-cold water in the bathroom.

And he knew it was me, too, because he saw me darting across the hallway, still dripping wet and chasing Satch through my bedroom door.

She was laughing, and shit, I love that sound. She's got this little giggle that's all things cute and addictive.

So, when Grady stole it away by thumping on my door and barking at me, I was not impressed.

She was just crawling into my bed, getting comfy between my sheets, totally clean... and totally naked. I was in for a good night.

Until he went and shat on it.

"You can't go using up all the hot water! Five-minute showers, man. That's the rule!"

"There were two people in there, so that allows me ten minutes."

"Bullshit! And you weren't just ten, you were like twenty!" He points at me, his dark eyes flashing. "If you were screwing her in there, I will—"

"Shut up," I stop him before he says something he'll regret.

Just because he's not loved-up anymore doesn't mean I'm not allowed to be.

With a short growl, I quickly put him in his place, and we have a scrappy little argument that is finally broken up by Tyrell, who walks up the stairs and stands right between us.

"Both of you chill." He gives me a pointed look. "You, get back to your woman." Then he turns to Grady. "You. Give it thirty minutes and there should be enough hot water for you to clean off."

We huff away from each other and I stalk back to my room, irritated that Grady is in such a rough place but also annoyed with myself that I let him get to me.

Shit. I'm usually the one breaking up arguments around here with funny jokes and quips to kill any tension, and I just threw myself into an argument because... I didn't want him saying anything against Satch.

Slipping back into my room, I find her curled up in bed, the covers clutched around her chest. She's wearing a worried frown, and I try to ease that look away with a smile.

"Is it still okay that I'm here?"

"Of course it is." I tug off the sweats I threw on to have my argument with Grady.

Her eyes shoot down my body, lingering on my cock,

her quirking lips making the guy want to stand at attention all over again.

I was hard in the shower. It was impossible not to be when she was right in front of me, her naked curves all soft and soapy like that.

Damn, I love her body.

Slipping into the bed beside her, I smooth the covers over us and wink at her.

Her smile is fleeting, lost behind a lip nibble. "Are you sure? Your roommate sounded kind of upset. I'm sorry we took too long in the shower."

"That was my fault. I couldn't take my hands off you." I give her a wolfish grin, lifting the covers so I can peek at those luscious tits again.

She blushes crimson, snatching the covers back and tucking them around her body. "He was mad, though. I don't want to annoy your roommates by being here."

"He's always mad at the moment," I counter, then sigh. "And I shouldn't have gotten shitty with him, but he was..." I sigh again. "He's hurting, and I should have been more patient with him. It just bummed me out that he was raining on my love parade."

"Your love parade?" Satch grins at me.

"Yeah." I tip my head, cupping her cheek. "This evening has been perfect."

She rests her hand over top of mine. "It really has. Thank you, Coyote."

My insides buzz with this warmth I could easily get used to before I lean forward and brush my lips over hers. "Believe me when I tell you that the pleasure is seriously all mine."

She laughs, nestling back against the pillows and asking what we're gonna do next.

"Well, I'm starving, so we're gonna eat those snacks over there." I point to them, jumping out of bed and gathering the food into a pile on the covers. "And then I thought we could watch a movie or... I could teach you how to play *Madden* or something."

"What's *Madden*?"

"Only the best video game ever invented."

She smiles and excitement buzzes through me as I grab the controllers and bring them over to the bed.

Satch starts opening chip packets and munching while I line up the game.

Digging out a huge mouthful of chips, I crunch through them while *Madden* loads, explaining the rules and how the controller works while I fill my stomach, spit crumbs all over the duvet, and make sure this girl knows how to play this NFL football simulation.

"You got it?"

She nods, checking the controller, then looking up at the screen and testing it out.

"And you know the best part?"

"What's that?" she murmurs, still looking at the screen.

"We get to do it naked."

Her cheeks blush a pretty pink as she turns to smile at me.

I waggle my eyebrows at her, mumbling, "Never played *Madden* naked with a girl before."

She giggles. "But you've played *Madden* naked by yourself before?"

"Abso-fucking-lutely."

Her snorting laughter makes me grin, and I pop a carrot stick into her mouth before starting the game.

CHAPTER 40
ELIZABETH

Playing *Madden* with Wily was so much fun.

I mean, I thought it might be, but I really got into it.

And I think Wily was stoked by how much I enjoyed playing "the best video game ever invented."

"You really are all about football, aren't you?" I hand him my controller and enjoy the view as he pads across his room, still totally naked, and dumps both of them onto the floor.

"It is the only game, Satch."

I grin when he turns to face me. "You do know there are other sports, right?"

"Really? I hadn't heard that. Are you totally sure?"

"Pretty sure," I play along with his teasing, fighting a laugh as he saunters back toward the bed.

It's impossible not to stare.

He really is the finest specimen I have ever seen.

Pausing at the end of the bed, he crosses his arms, showing off his biceps while I lose the ability to think coherently.

"You keep looking at me like that and I just might have to have you again," he warns.

"Oh really?" I smirk, then lick the side of my mouth and boldly drink him in like I'm parched.

With a playful growl, he pounces onto the bed, and I let out a squeal, laughing when he tugs me down and rolls over top of me. Peppering my face with kisses, he then stops to brush the tip of his nose across mine and check, "You sure? You're not too sore or anything?"

Oh my gosh, he's so sweet.

"I think I'll be okay," I murmur, not really sure if it'll hurt until he goes back down there again.

"Well..." He presses his lips to mine. "If it does, you just let me know and I'll kiss it better for you."

I snicker. "Down there?"

"Ye-ah." He draws out the word, his eyes starting to sparkle. "I'd love to kiss you down there."

"No, you wouldn't," I laugh, but the sound quickly disappears when I see that he's completely serious.

I swallow, wondering what that feels like.

I mean, I know people do that. I even know the scientific term for it—cunnilingus. And if I go down on him, that'd be fellatio.

Both words sound kind of gross to me, but... I wonder what it'd feel like.

Wily's lips twitch, his tongue darting out the corner of his mouth before he rolls off me, flicking the duvet away and silently asking me if I want to try.

"Ummm." My nose wrinkles. "I don't know if I'll like it."

Splaying his hand over my stomach, he rubs a slow

circle and kisses my shoulder. "It's okay if you don't, baby. I'll just stop."

Biting my lips together, I give him a tentative nod, rising up on my elbows to watch him settle between my legs. He kisses just above my pubic hair line before looking up at me with hooded eyes. His blue gaze sparkles with affection, and then his tongue darts out, licking my clit and making me gasp.

Okay, so that's new.

He watches me for a second and I nod, closing my eyes and losing myself in this new sensation.

"Mmmm." I can't stop myself from moaning when he flattens his tongue over my sensitive spot. Tipping my head back, I fist the sheet beneath me and fight for air as he keeps going, keeps licking, keeps tearing me apart with his delicate touch.

By the time his finger slips inside me, I'm crying out to the ceiling, unable to help myself as he sends me out to space with a rocketing orgasm that shakes my whole body.

"Good girl," he purrs as I buck my hips and whimper into the back of my hand. "You like that?"

"Uh-huh," I squeak, my chest heaving.

He crawls back up my body with a grin, sucking my nipples one at a time before nuzzling into my neck.

I pull him over me, relishing his weight as we sink into the mattress together.

This man.

Unbelievable!

He feels so good, and... I should really return the favor.

I swallow, not sure how I feel about that, but politeness dictates that I really should, right?

"Did you, um... want me to... kiss you? I mean, down there?"

He grins, I can feel his smile forming against my shoulder. "When you're ready, Satch. And not before then."

"But... what about you? I mean, don't you deserve an orgasm too? I want you to be happy."

His head pops up so he can look me in the eye. Brushing his finger down my cheek, he gives me another one of those affectionate smiles. "Watching you come makes me very happy."

"Really?"

"Yes. It's fucking sexy, and knowing I can do that to you makes me triumphant, baby. I don't need you to do anything else for me tonight but stay."

A warm buzz tingles through my chest. "You want me to stay all night?"

He kisses my lips—a delicate, tender peck—before whispering, "I want you to say all night."

So that's what I do.

It's really not a hard decision.

In fact, it was a no-brainer.

As soon as he rolled me to my side and nestled in behind me, I was in heaven. His big arm came around me, tucking under my right breast before he scooted forward and curled his body around mine.

Who knew spooning could be the most comfortable way to sleep?

But we did.

We totally drifted off, holding each other tight, and I

didn't wake until light filtered between the cracks in his curtains.

It was the craziest moment, coming to and realizing I was still lying beside Wily.

He's snoring behind me, just a soft rumble. The air spurting out of his nose hits my naked shoulder, and I smile against the pillow.

This is too incredible for words!

I just had the best night of my life. And it's all because of him.

Closing my eyes, I let out a sated breath, my insides tingling as I wonder how we'll spend our day. Wily doesn't have any football commitments, I don't think, and we might have to squish in some studying, but other than that... we can do what we like.

Me? I wouldn't mind staying naked, eating breakfast, lunch, and dinner in bed while playing *Madden*, watching movies, talking and—

My phone starts buzzing and I wince, my head popping off the pillow as I search for it.

Must be in my jacket pocket.

Still wincing, I lift Wily's deadweight arm from around my body, hoping not to disturb him. Rustling around in my coat pocket, I pull it out and see it's a video call from my parents.

I should just let it ring and call them back later, but what if they phone when I'm in the middle of...

My cheeks flare red, and I decide to quickly get the call out of the way now.

Snatching Wily's massive hoodie off the floor, I pull it on and slip out of the room.

Thankfully, he's really tall, so the hoodie comes down

mid-thigh and fits me just right around my butt. It's like wearing a dress, and I tug on the sides as I try to find a quiet space upstairs. I notice an open doorway and slip into what looks to be a guest room.

There's nothing personal on the walls, so I assume it's free and walk into the room, swinging the door shut behind me.

I end up missing the call and decide to play it safe and call them back with audio only. Putting it on speaker, I turn the volume down and hold the phone near my mouth.

"Hey, Mom." I try to sound as normal as I can, even though there's this giddy giggle bubbling in my stomach, threatening to burst out and give me away.

"Hello, my lovely," Dad calls. "How's my girl?"

Warm affection fills me as I respond, "Hey, Dad. I'm great. How are you?"

"I've been a busy boy. Working long hours at the diner, but we've finally found ourselves a new chef, so that's exciting."

"Oh, wow, that's great." I'm trying to keep my voice down, but it's hard when he's talking so loudly into the phone. I don't know what it is about my parents, but when it comes to technology, they think the volume with which you speak plays a key role in how well it'll work. "You must be relieved."

"I'm still sad to see Ralph go, but happy to find a replacement."

"This girl's a real firecracker," Mom tells me. "She'll have the kitchen running like a well-oiled machine."

"That's so good, you guys. I know it's been weighing on you, so I'm so glad it's worked out smoothly."

"How about you? What have you been up to?" Dad asks.

Oh, you know, just having sex for the first time. Multiple orgasms. Showers. Sleeping naked. My world's been blown wide open in all the best ways by a man you don't even know exists.

I bite my lip, wondering how I'm supposed to tell them any of this stuff.

I take the chicken's way out and settle for the safest option. "Working, studying. You know how it is."

"Oh, Bessie Boo, you work too hard," Dad tells me off in that soft way of his.

"You can talk." I laugh. "You work all the time."

"Now that's not true. I'm not working right this minute."

"And neither am I."

He laughs, and Mom talks over him. "Well, you won't be working next weekend either. You have to promise me that you won't be bringing any studying home with you. I want you to have your birthday off. Celebration time only."

"Birthday?" a deep voice says from the door. "It's your birthday next weekend? Why didn't you tell me?"

I spin around with a gasp, my eyes bulging as I take in Wily standing there in nothing but those low-slung sweats of his.

My lady parts start dancing without my say-so as he saunters into the room and asks, "Who are you talking to?"

At the same time, my parents ask, "Who's that?"

CHAPTER 41
WILY

"Um..." Satch bulges her eyes at me, and I give her a confused frown, then start to smirk when I realize she must be talking to her parents.

"Do they know about me?" I mouth, pointing at my chest.

She cringes and I nod, pressing my finger to my mouth and promising to stay quiet.

"Bess? Who's in the room with you, sweetheart?" Mom asks, and I watch my girl bite her lip and look to me for help.

"What do I call you?" she whispers.

"Do you want them to know about us?" I whisper back as softly as I can.

She nods but then shrugs and starts shaking her head. "But if you're not okay with that, I'll understand."

"What?" My head jerks back, and I give her a baleful look. I may not want *my* parents to know I'm falling for this girl, but letting hers know there's a man out there who's totally into her? Yeah, I'm okay with that.

Leaning down, I speak into the phone. "Hey, Mr. and Mrs. Satchwell. Wily Wilson here. I'm Elizabeth's boyfriend." Her mouth pops open, and I give her a funny look, leaning in and whispering, "After what we did last night, I'm not your boyfriend?"

"Well... I mean, I guess..." she sputters. "I just thought you didn't want to be tied down with a label."

"Boyfriend?" Her mom's voice perks up. "Bessie, you have a boyfriend?"

"Well, I..." She looks at the phone, then back to me.

I grin and shake my head at her before answering her mother. "She certainly does, ma'am."

"Oh, I see. Well, uh... this is a surprise. How long has this been going on?"

I take the phone from her hand before she drops it, holding it up to my mouth and telling them all about how Satch has been my tutor since the beginning of the year.

"She's been helping me pass my classes with excellent grades." I grin. "She's one smart lady. I'd be lost without her."

"She is," her dad agrees. "The smartest girl I know. She gets it from her mother."

I laugh, winking at my girl, who is blushing up a storm and covering those red cheeks with her hands.

"So, other than studying with my daughter, what else do you do?"

This opens up the door to an in-depth football conversation. Her dad never played but seems very impressed that I'm on my way to being drafted. Mrs. Satchwell gets all excited, asking what position I play, although I get the sense that she doesn't really know what any of it means.

Satch stands there shaking her head and looking pained as her parents get overly excited about me and the fact that I'm dating their daughter.

I lay it on thick, trying to impress them with my first-date antics and dancing in the snow.

Mrs. Satchwell starts giggling, the same way my girl always does, and I'm loving every second of this. No wonder Satch is so damn cool—her parents are sweet and funny, and shit, I really want to meet them. I want to shake the hand of the man who raised this angel of a girl. I want to hug the woman who no doubt nurtured and loved her through every phase of her childhood.

They both sound like they adore her, so they must be pretty cool.

"So, are you free next weekend?" Mrs. Satchwell asks.

"Mom, I don't... He's very busy," Satch tries to say, but I gently cover her mouth with my hand.

"I can be free next weekend."

"Well, we'd love to have you. We're putting together a special celebration for Bessie's birthday. It'd be wonderful to have you join us."

"That'd be great."

"Are you sure?" Satch mouths, looking totally confused by the fact that I'm saying yes to this invite.

What does she not get?

It's her birthday! Of course I'm going to be there.

Not only that, it's Valentine's Day, and like hell I'm missing out on celebrating it with her.

Satch's parents get all excited about meeting me while

my girl stands there blinking at her phone like she's trying to decipher a foreign language.

"Oh, we're so pleased. Our Bess has never brought a friend home from college before, and a boyfriend to boot. It's all so thrilling. We'll have the house all set up for you two. I can't wait to meet you, Wily."

"Thank you, ma'am. I'm looking forward to it too. And if you could do me a favor and send some gift ideas my way. Your girl here has been very secretive about when she was born, and I had no clue."

"Oh, that's so Bess." Mrs. Satchwell laughs. "Why don't you give me your number, and I'll send you some ideas."

I rattle it off while Satch waves her hands in the air. "You don't have to buy me anything. I really... It's not..."

Wrapping my arm around her, I pull her against me, trying to shut up her fussing. Like I'm not gonna buy her a gift.

"Thanks so much for your help, Mrs. Satchwell."

"Oh, please. Call me Darla."

"And you can call me Tommy!" Mr. Satchwell adds with a friendly chirp.

"Thank you, sir."

"This is so exciting." Darla's buzzing, and I squeeze Satch a little closer, kissing the top of her head.

"Can't wait."

They say the same thing, followed by a stream of affectionate goodbyes before hanging up.

I hold out the phone for Satch to take, but she doesn't move.

"Satch?" I shift, leaning down so I can check her face.

"What just happened?" She blinks at me.

"Oh shit, I'm sorry. Did I overstep?"

"You just made my parents fall in love with you." She takes the phone, shaking her head in obvious shock.

"Is that... bad?" I step back, running a hand through my hair. "I mean, do you not want me to come meet them?"

"Of course I do." Her voice pitches. "I just... It's all happened really fast. I didn't think you'd want to be my boyfriend and meet my parents. I mean, you're... you're..." She lets out a bewildered breath. "You're Wily Wilson."

I nod, looking at the ground and wondering what she's heard.

Probably too much.

I've all but told her I'm the guy who sleeps around and never commits. I'm the player who can't say no to a flirty lady.

But not anymore.

Shit, can a tiger change its stripes? I sure fucking hope so, because as I hold her shoulders and lean down, catching her eye, I mean every word that comes out of my mouth. "And you're different. You've... captured me, Satch. And I don't want this to be like anything else I've had before. I *want* to be your boyfriend. And I want the whole fucking world to know that you're mine."

Her lips part, her cheeks paling.

"Come on, you. Let's get you back to my bed." I take her hand, pulling her out of the spare room and grinning over my shoulder. "I've got plans for you today, my sweet. I have the best plans."

CHAPTER 42
ELIZABETH

Wily's plans involved a whole heap of everything I wanted to do that day... including two epic sexy sessions that will keep me floating for eternity.

On Sunday night, he dropped me back at my dorm room and ended up staying with me. I couldn't believe it. He stayed! Didn't even think it was that big of a deal just to slip into my twin XL and get cozy.

It was squishy, and I barely slept. He lightly snored behind me while I lay awake, staring across my darkened room and lightly pinching myself to remind me that yes, this is all real.

I finally drifted off at some point in the early hours of the morning, and I'm feeling a little worse for wear as I get ready for the day.

And I realize why when I go to the bathroom and see that I have my period. Rubbing my aching head, I stare at my stained underwear before talking myself off the toilet and into action mode.

I rinse my soiled clothes while I'm taking a shower,

then pop a few pain meds to get me through the day. I've learned to preempt these things, and it definitely eases the discomfort.

My knee is still a little tender, so I choose my softest dress and make sure I'm aiming for maximum comfort before heading out the door for my morning walk and coffee.

Wily left for his gym workout about an hour ago, and I'm not sure when I'll see him today... until I find him waiting for me outside Java Jeans.

"Hey, beautiful." He greets me with a grin, and my heart turns to putty.

How can it not?

He's smiling at me like I'm the best part of his day, and I still can't quite believe that he's my boyfriend.

Lining up beside him, we order our coffees to go and amble around the campus, sipping and laughing as he tells me about his intense workout and how the Scouting Combine is only two weeks away.

I can tell he's nervous-excited about it as he tries to lighten his anticipation with jokes about football.

Seeing right through them all, I give him a tender smile and tell him, "You're gonna be great. You can do anything, Wily."

"Thanks, baby," he murmurs, smiling down at me and leaning in for a kiss.

I'm a microsecond away from reaching up and kissing him back when I spot something out of the corner of my eye that makes me flinch and step away from him.

He frowns at me, then gives me a dry look, shaking his head. "Still not into the PDA, huh?"

I give him a tight smile and bob my head, because that's a great excuse. Yep. Let's go with that.

My heart kicks out of place, then starts thundering when I notice the cause of my angst walking toward us.

Shit, shit, shit!

"Man, I hope you get over that soon, Satchy babe, because I really want to kiss you right now in front of anyone who might be watching." He winks down at me. "You're my girl, and—"

"Hey, Wily." Jade's got her sweet voice on, and my skin immediately starts to itch and burn the second she's within range.

She smells like vanilla and lilacs, her intense perfume assaulting my senses as she steps between me and my boyfriend.

It's like I'm not even here the way she creates a quick barrier between us and smiles up at him.

I stare at the side of her face, wishing I could glare at her, tell her to fuck off and leave us the hell alone!

But my insides are frozen solid, and I can't utter a word, because I know she's livid with me. She's hiding it like the queen actress that she is, but I am going to pay big for going against her wishes and hanging out with Wily anyway.

Oh shit, did she see him leaning down to kiss me?

My insides flood with hot terror as I imagine what she'd say if she knew we'd slept together.

"How are you?" Jade runs her hand down Wily's arm.

He darts his gaze to me, then gives her his friendly smile. It's not his flirty one, just his standard friendly one that he uses with strangers. "I'm great."

"I haven't seen you around as much." She pouts. "I've been looking out for you, though."

Tipping her head, she runs her fingers through her hair and goes into full flirt mode.

I take another step away from them. I really don't need to see this, and I want nothing more than to get away from her.

"I've been a busy boy." Wily grins at her. "I've got myself a girlfriend now, and that's taking up all my spare time."

"Oh, really?" Jade laughs, slapping his arm playfully. "I can't believe you've been taken off the market. I missed my chance."

Wily forces out a laugh and inches around her. "Let me introduce you guys."

I stiffen. *No! No, no, no. I don't want—*

"This is my girl, Satch." He points at me, and I'm pretty sure I'm about to pass out.

Jade turns to face me, her eyes flashing me a warning before she puts on a sweet grin and holds out her hand. "Satch? Hi. I'm Jade."

I stare down at her open hand, the one that cracked me across the face. The memory burns bright, and it takes everything in me to reach out and wrap my short digits around her long ones. "Um... hi."

"Satch." She repeats the word, her fingers crunching mine together. "So nice to meet you."

Please let this stop.

"Uh, yeah, you too." I try to pull my hand away, hot ants crawling all over my body as she eyes me up, then looks at Wily.

"Isn't she a peach?" She giggles. "I'm really happy for you guys."

Oh man, those words must be acid in her mouth.

I am so dead.

Yep, she's definitely gonna kill me.

Giving me one last smirk, she makes a move to leave, then quickly swivels. Placing her hand on Wily's shoulder, she reaches up on her tiptoes and whispers something in his ear that I can't hear and... you know what? I don't even want to know.

His eyebrows rise, his cheeks turning a touch red, before he leans away from her and politely smiles again. "Thanks, but I'm good. I'll catch you around, Jane."

"Jade," she corrects him, lightly slapping his arm with a laugh. "I'll see you in class."

"Yep." Wily nods, hurrying after me because I'm already walking away. "Hey, wait up."

He reaches for my hand and tries to thread our fingers together, but I quickly shove my hand into my pocket before he can.

"Hey. Are you mad at me?"

"No." I shake my head, throwing him a tight smile that seems to hurt for some reason. "Just don't want to be late to class."

"Satch." He steps into my path, forcing me to stop. Leaning down, he waits until I'm looking at him, having to capture my chin and stop my head from moving. "You don't have to worry about that girl."

Yeah, right!

Part of me wonders if I should tell him. Maybe if he knew just how horrible she'd been to me over the years, he wouldn't be so nice to her.

But I don't want to.

How am I supposed to stand here and admit how shitty I've been treated? It's so humiliating. I don't want him to picture me like that. I just want him to look at me the way he did when I met him at Java Jeans this morning.

"I'd never cheat on you." He catches my eye when my gaze starts to wander. "You know that, right?"

"Yeah." I nod and force another smile—this one doesn't hurt as much. "I trust you."

And I do. Really. I know he'd never intentionally hurt me. He's too sweet. Too nice.

But what if he gets bored of me?

What if he gets drafted and leaves me? Which he totally will.

He'll be away, and I'll be out of sight, out of mind.

"Whatever is going on in that brain of yours, can you please just stop it?" he says, bringing my attention back to him. "I'm yours, baby. You've got to believe that."

"I just don't understand it," I mumble.

"What?" He leans closer, and I shake my head.

"Nothing." Desperate to get out of this hellishly awkward conversation, I lightly peck his lips.

He grins. "Did you just kiss me in public?"

"Maybe." I feel the heat rising in my cheeks and wrinkle my nose.

He laughs and grabs my face, kissing me soundly before pulling back and brushing his nose over mine. "Maybe we should skip our first class of the day and—"

"No." I lightly push him back. "We are not missing class just because you're horny. And besides, I..." Dropping my voice, I whisper, "I got my period this morning, so..." My cheeks flush red yet again. I no doubt look like a raspberry as I admit this to him, but he takes it with ease.

"Oh, bummer. How bad do you get them?" He stands tall, taking my hand and threading our fingers together.

"A little painful, but nothing a few Tylenol can't counter."

"That's good. My poor sister used to get the worst cramps. In fact, her periods were so bad she had to go on the pill."

I raise my eyebrows, wondering if his sister would want me to know that.

But Wily keeps going, telling me about Blake's heinous periods and how he learned to duck and cover through the worst of them.

"It was like navigating a minefield. She'd go from tantrums to tears to hysterical laughter within minutes. I swear, I had to mentally suit up once a month. She finally went on the pill when she was sixteen, and it gave us all a chance to breathe and not worry for our lives so much." His emphatic look makes me giggle, and I squeeze his hand. He's a good big brother, I can tell.

The way he talks about Blake makes me think they're close, and I can't help asking what it was like growing up with a sibling.

He continues to tell me stories as we amble slowly to my first class, and it distracts me from the Jade encounter this morning. When it's finally time to go our separate ways, I let him kiss me again and don't regret it until an hour later when I leave my class and bump into Jade and Kelsey, who have obviously been waiting for me.

Shit.

Jade's long nails dig into my arm when she grabs me,

getting in my face and hissing, "You're his girlfriend now?"

"I... I..." Fear chokes me out as she pulls me along the pathway, seething in my ear.

"You told me you were just his tutor, but now he's off the market."

"Because of you?" Kelsey scoffs. Her scorn is potent and burns the back of my throat. "What a joke. Are you paying him or something?"

"With what money?" Jade spits. "Seriously. Are you stupid?" She shakes my arm, her nails digging in that much deeper. I can feel her talons through my jacket.

I wince and try to wrangle out of her hold, but her grip is like a dog bite, cinching my arm.

"I told you to stay away from him."

"You can't tell me what to do," I reply so softly it's barely audible.

"There has got to be an ulterior motive here," Kelsey says to Jade. "There's no way he'd be into a girl like her. Something else is going on."

I frown at the pair of them as they discuss my love life like it's some big conspiracy.

With a soft growl, I try to take my arm back.

"Shut up," Jade barks at me. "Growling like a fucking bitch. Don't think this is over. We're gonna find out the truth about you two."

"There's no truth to find out," I quietly argue. "We're dating. Deal with it."

"You can't possibly expect us to believe he's into you." Kelsey scoffs again, then looks at her friend. "Jade's been crushing on him since she got here, and you need to back the hell off."

"He's not some property you can claim." Anger starts to bubble and flare within me. "He can date who he likes."

"Well, he's fucking delusional if he thinks that person is you." Jade's glare is hot and intimidating.

I dip my chin, unable to hold her eye. My insides are burning, and I want nothing more than to disappear, just melt right into the icy concrete beneath my feet.

"Don't think for a second that I'm backing down on this. I'll show Wily exactly what he's missing out on, and he'll see soon enough that you're a waste of his time."

"She must have hexed him or something," Kelsey mutters. "Wouldn't surprise me if this weirdo is a full-blown witch."

"I'm gonna break your little spell, hippo," Jade hisses, giving my arm one last, super-hard squeeze before finally letting me go and stalking away.

I stay where I am, staring at the concrete and feeling like total shit.

For a second, I wonder if I should save us all the brewing angst and just break up with Wily now.

No way! You're not doing that just because Jade told you to!

My insides rebel as I rub my aching arm and finally find the strength to shuffle forward.

I should probably warn Wily about her, tell him to watch his back because Jade will be coming on stronger than ever now.

But then I'll have to admit everything, and... and I can't!

I just have to trust what Wily said to me. He's no cheater.

He could still break up with you, though. Jade could win him over so easily. She's gorgeous and flirty and—

"A total bitch," I mutter to myself.

Wily's not stupid. He'll be able to pick up on that, right?

Doubts swirl through me as I shuffle off to my next class, wondering what the hell I'm supposed to do to keep this amazing, wonderful man who has burst into my life and stolen my heart without any kind of warning.

How am I supposed to compete with Jade Buchanan?

You can't.

All you can do is try to keep him as far away from her as you can.

Pulling out my phone, I send Wily a text to find out how his class went and ask if he wants to meet up for lunch.

Thankfully, he replies almost immediately, and I spend the next three hours praying Jade doesn't cross his path before I can hide him in my dorm room for a secret lunch away from prying eyes.

I'll probably need to come up with some better plays than that, but for now, I'll just have to keep him close and hope he doesn't get sick of me.

CHAPTER 43
WILY

Satch can't seem to get enough of me.

It makes me smile every time I think about it, but she's been borderline clingy, asking to meet up whenever I'm free.

Some people would tell me those are big red flags and I should stay the hell away, but I seriously don't want to.

I love spending time with her, and when she asks to meet up for lunch in her dorm room and I find myself half naked on her bed while she experiments with her first blow job, I'm not gonna complain about that.

It was fucking awesome, and I made sure she knew it. The shy smile she gave me as she watched in fascination while I jerked and came into a wad of tissues will be permanently burned in my brain.

"I get it," she whispered. "Making you come like that *is* triumphant."

I scooped her hair back over her shoulder, pulling her toward me and kissing that blushing grin.

Damn, she's so fucking sweet.

And I've spent my week hanging out with that sweetness any chance I can get. I've been a good boy and haven't skipped class or practice, but I've basically been MIA from everything else, skipping a night out with the guys and bailing on multiple lunch invitations so I can be with Satch instead.

It's not a great habit, and I'm gonna have to break it, but I get the feeling that Satch needs me right now, and I want to be there for her.

Grabbing the huge teddy bear that only just arrived last night, I tuck it under my arm and head out of my room. She doesn't know I'm showing up at her door this morning, but there's no way I'm not gonna be the first person to wish her happy birthday. It's also Valentine's Day, so I get to lavish her with extra gifts, and Mr. Teddy here is gonna be the first.

It's been fun shopping for Satch. Between Blake and Mrs. Satchwell, I've come up with a bunch of cool ideas. I've probably gone a little overboard. Satch will no doubt tell me I shouldn't have, but yes... yes, I should.

She deserves all the treats, and I want to be the one to give them to her.

Strolling into the kitchen, I open the fridge and grab out the ingredients for a protein smoothie. I'll quickly down it before heading over to see my girl.

"Seriously?" Grady walks in behind me, eyeing the teddy bear I just deposited on the kitchen chair so I could free my hands up.

"What?" I glance at his dry expression and grin. "It's awesome, right?"

"I guess." His frown turns skeptical, then kind of sad

as he pulls out the chair adjacent to the large stuffed animal and looks kind of glum.

Shit. He probably would have bought something this big and cheesy for Teah on a day like this.

"I'm sorry," I murmur, spinning around to lean against the counter. "Shit, man. I'm really sorry."

He gazes at me, his dark brown eyes darting over my face before returning to the table. "For what?"

"For getting shitty with you last weekend when I used up all the hot water. For not understanding what you're going through."

He shrugs.

"You ever gonna tell me what happened?"

With a heavy sigh, he rests his head in his hands and mutters, "She dumped me. Isn't it obvious?"

"Yeah." I nod. "But why did she dump you?"

His swallow is thick as he starts tracing the grooves on the table. "She said..." His expression crumples. "It's humiliating, bro."

Oh man. What the hell did she say to him?

"Come on," I gently coax him. "You can tell me anything. You know all of my embarrassing shit."

He gives me a side-eye before finally admitting, "She said our relationship was boring. That I was too serious and didn't know how to have fun anymore. We'd been together too long, and I was too comfortable, apparently. I wasn't putting in the effort anymore."

"Is that fair?" I ask, annoyed at her for being so harsh on the guy.

He shakes his head, but then his shoulder hitches. "Maybe. I don't know." Closing his eyes, he mutters, "I told her I'd try to do better, but she said it was too late. She doesn't love me anymore."

I hiss. "Dude, that's savage. She actually said that to you?"

"Her tone was sweet. She obviously felt bad saying it but wanted to be completely honest with me."

I nod, but I'm still not very happy with her. I'm all for honesty, but not when it's gonna slice someone in half. "Do you think there's someone else?"

He glances at me, his gaze tortured. "I thought maybe, but she promises me there's not. She just said she couldn't keep going like this. And then she asked me not to try winning her back. She wants space. End of story." Scrubbing a hand over his mouth, he then grips his chin. "Fuck. I wish I just could get over it. It's been nearly two months, and I'm still pining for her. It hurts, man." He taps his chest. "I just wish I could forget about her, but she was... she was my woman, you know?"

I look at the teddy bear sitting next to my buddy, and for the first time ever... I do actually know. If Satch said that shit to me, I'd be destroyed, and we've only been officially dating for around a month. Teah and Grady were together for almost a year.

"It sucks, man. I'm really sorry you're going through this."

"Yeah," he sighs. "Me too." Looking back at me, his expression buckles as he mumbles his own apology. "I'm sorry I've been such a shitty roommate lately. I don't want to drag everyone down with me. I'm just struggling to deal."

"It's okay." I step forward, giving his shoulder a reassuring squeeze. "We're here for you. Anything you need."

I scramble to think of ways to cheer him up and start firing off ideas. "I'm away this weekend, but maybe when I get back, we can take off for a hike or a camping weekend. That'd be fun. Or we could do it over spring break or something. That'll be here before we know it."

He turns to look at me, almost surprised by my suggestion. "You won't be too busy with your girl? You two are in that all-consumed-by-each-other phase. Sure you can break away for a day or two?"

I laugh. "I'll make sure I do. I'm not bailing on my friends." I cringe. "I know it's felt like that this week, but I promise I'm not turning into the douche who ditches." Stroking the top of the teddy bear's head, I try to explain. "It's Satch's birthday today, and I want to make it special. I'm going to meet her parents this weekend."

"Really?" His eyes bulge. "Wow, dude. This is serious."

"Yeah, man." I nod, looking him in the eye. "It is."

He raises his eyebrows, obviously surprised.

"She's different," I murmur, unable to fight my grin.

"Look at you," he teases me. "All loved-up and shit."

Cringing, I give him another apology. "That's probably the last thing you want to be around."

He sighs and gets to his feet. "That's okay. I need to get used to it. Between Zander, Carson, and you, I'm surrounded. You're dropping like flies."

I laugh, lightly slapping his arm. "You'll fall again someday, man. You're too much of a romantic not to."

"Yeah." Sliding his hands into his pockets, he gazes down at my Valentine's bear with a glum smile.

"Teah will fade," I try to encourage him, hoping I'm right.

She was cool. I liked her, and they seemed like an

awesome couple together. But something obviously wasn't right.

Damn, I hate that she hurt him, and I wish they were still together, but if she doesn't love him anymore, then I don't *want* them together. Grady deserves to be with someone who adores him, and that chick is out there somewhere. She'll cross his path soon enough, and I tell him that before he walks out of the kitchen.

"Thanks," he mumbles, obviously not believing me.

I watch him go, running a hand through my hair, glad we've cleared the air between us but still feeling bad for the guy.

I'll have to let Satch know that after the Scouting Combine, I'm gonna need a weekend to take Grady away for a hiking trip. The guy lives for the outdoors, comes to life in nature.

You know what? I'm gonna ask everyone in the house to set aside a weekend. Grady needs our support, and we can spare some time to do that.

Making a mental note to catch up with the rest of the guys, I start mapping out what we can do to snap Grady out of his funk.

He needs us, and I'm gonna be there for him.

Satch will understand that. Knowing her, she'll encourage me to make it happen.

Excitement sizzles through me as I think ahead to a weekend with the guys... then it shifts to a different buzz as I picture the look on Satch's face when she opens the door and finds me standing there with her first gift of the day.

CHAPTER 44
ELIZABETH

I'm just about to head out for my morning walk when there's a knock at my door.

Confused, I creep toward it, softly asking, "Who is it?"

"It's your boyfriend, birthday girl. Lemme in."

An instant smile lights my face, and I rush to unlock the door, pulling it open and laughing when I'm faced with the biggest teddy bear I have ever seen.

"Happy Valentine's Day!" Wily's voice is muffled by the bear as he talks behind it, moving its arms and stepping forward to wrap them around me.

I giggle into the soft fur, my heart melting into a mushy puddle at how incredibly sweet this man is.

He's the best boyfriend I've ever had.

He's the only *boyfriend you've ever had.*

He's still the best.

So sweet and attentive. I've been asking so much of him this week, desperately trying to keep him away from Jade, and he's accommodated me at every turn. I feel a little bad about it, like I'm stealing his life away, but he hasn't complained once and doesn't seem to mind showing up whenever I invite him.

In fact, I was making a concerted effort not to contact him this morning, knowing I was stealing him away for the entire weekend. If Jade happens to get her claws into him today, I can hopefully wipe away any damage in Fledgling.

At least I hope I can.

"You like it?" Wily's head pops around the bear, squishing it between us as he leans in to kiss me.

"I love it," I assure him, smiling against his lips and giving him one more kiss before pulling back to admire the bear. "This is the sweetest gift. It must have cost a fortune. I can't believe you went to all this trouble for me on my birthday."

He sets the bear down on my bed and pulls me into his arms. "This isn't your birthday present, baby."

"What?"

"It's your Valentine's Day gift."

I tense before wriggling out of his embrace and gaping up at him.

"I'll give you your birthday presents tonight, when we get to your parents' house."

"Presents? As in plural?"

"Yeah, it's your birthday." He shrugs, looking kind of mystified by why I would be so gobsmacked over that.

"Wily, it's... That's too much. You don't need to buy me anything." I wince. "I mean, I just wrote you a card for Valentine's Day. I didn't even get you anything else, and I'm so, so—"

He stops my apology with his lips, his tongue soon

claiming mine and making me forget everything but his addictive mouth.

Once I'm thoroughly drugged up, he pulls back and whispers against my cheek, "You're enough for me. I don't even need that card." He smiles. "Although I'll take it, because knowing you, you've squished it full of lovely words that are gonna make me feel like the most amazing guy on the planet."

"You are the most amazing guy on the planet," I clarify, reaching into my bag to pull out the red envelope.

"See, I didn't even get you a card, baby." He rips it open while I look at the huge teddy bear taking over my bed.

I grin and take a seat beside it, stroking its soft fur.

Wily's gone quiet, and I hold my breath, wondering what part he's up to.

He's right. That card is filled with ink. I wrote down everything I love about him, and his expression is telling me it was worth it.

I even found the courage to write, *With all my love*, at the bottom, which is the closest to *I love you* that I've managed to get.

I stared at those words until my vision blurred, wondering if I should have put them, but as Wily's lips twitch, then he looks up at me and lets that smile grow, I know I've done the right thing.

"Thanks for being the most amazing boyfriend," I whisper.

He drops to his knees in front of me, resting his large hands on my legs and giving them a gentle squeeze. "It's easy when you're the best girlfriend a guy could ask for."

Oh my gosh, he makes it so easy to love him.

Cupping his cheek, I give him a tender kiss, then ask if I can buy him a Valentine's Day coffee.

He's nice enough to let me, and we take our sweet time, walking to Java Jeans and back again.

I keep my eye out for Jade but don't spot her or Kelsey or Viper Girl. It helps me relax, and all I can hope is that they don't lavish my man with flirtatious invitations all day, using Valentine's as an excuse to try and lure him into whatever trap they no doubt have planned.

This week, I've only spotted them once but was far enough away to turn the corner and avoid them before they saw me.

I've subtly tried to ask Wily if he's seen Jade, but he only mentioned that she sat next to him in class on Wednesday and it was really annoying, because she kept passing him notes and he was trying to concentrate. In the end, he stopped reading them and made a concerted effort to ignore her.

"Think it pissed her off some, but I'm trying to grad-uate here."

That one little sentence made my week, but I'm still nervous about what she might try. I wouldn't put it past her to jump into his arms and start dry humping him. It'd be a desperate move on her part, but I'm sure she's scheming something, and I'm on edge waiting to find out what it is.

"So, I'll pick you up right after your last class. I've arranged with Coach to skip practice today so we can hit the road early."

My eyes bulge. Practices are sacred in Wily's world, and he's trying to get out of one? "Are you sure that's okay?"

He nods. "When I explained why, Coach said it was cool. My training and prep for the Scouting Combine is on track, so I can skip a practice."

I grin up at him. "That's so sweet that you'd do that for me. I know how important football is to you."

"You're important to me, too, baby." He winks and smiles down at me. "And when I told him it was your birthday, he caved in a heartbeat. The guy's a deep-down romantic, I swear."

"Lucky me."

His smile grows as he wraps his arm around my shoulders and pulls me close. Kissing the top of my head as we saunter along, he starts telling me how excited he is to meet my parents.

"Really?" I glance up, worry starting to niggle at me.

I've been so distracted by Jade this week that I haven't really had time to think about the fact that Wily is gonna be meeting my family. But now that the hour is nearly upon us, I'm starting to stress.

"They're your parents. Of course I'm excited."

"But..." I stop, tugging on his coat and guiding him to face me.

"But what, baby?" He brushes his knuckle down my face. "What are you worried about?"

"I'm just... They're probably very different to your parents."

He gives me an expectant nod, silently encouraging me to keep going.

"They're... older. Like, my dad turned sixty-six just after Christmas. I'm their miracle baby. The one they never thought they could have, so... I was a late arrival. I mean, Mom was forty-three when she had me."

"Okay."

"And... they're small-town and not very chic or... anything. They're very into their routine and—"

"I'm sure I'm gonna love them. If they're anything like you, I'll adore them."

I wrinkle my nose, not sure if I can really believe that. I saw a family portrait in his bedroom, and his family are so obviously wealthy and aware of what's cool and what's not.

My parents don't even have a cool radar.

They march to the beat of their own drum. They always have.

And I used to love it, until I got mercilessly teased about how weird my family is.

Those cutting comments slice me as I try to prep Wily for this experience, but he speaks before I can say anything else.

"Satch, you seriously need to stop worrying. I'm great with people. *All* kinds of people. Nothing can weird me out, okay?"

"Are you sure?"

He grins, tipping my chin up while assuring me, "Stop worrying. It's gonna be great. They're gonna love me, and I'm gonna love them."

Kissing the tip of my nose, he then pulls me into his arms and sings me a slightly off-key rendition of "Happy Birthday."

I giggle against his chest, my cheeks flaming when he raises the volume at the end, capturing the attention of everyone around us.

"Happy birthday!" someone shouts behind me, and I

groan, burrowing into Wily's jacket while he laughs and rubs my back.

"Thanks, man. Have a good one."

A few more people call out to us, and I raise my hand in thanks while Wily smiles and charms the lot of them.

Ugh. He's probably right. I have nothing to worry about.

My family is going to adore this guy, and Wily does seem pretty accepting of everybody. All I can hope is that they don't do anything so weird that they'll put him off for good.

CHAPTER 45
WILY

I have no idea why Satch was so worried. Her family is fucking awesome!

The second I walked through their front door, they were pulling me into hugs and telling me how amazing it was that I was there to celebrate with everyone.

They are seriously stoked that Satch has a boyfriend. It's like this epic news, and everyone is super curious about me, like they can't believe she scored a star football player.

But they've got it all wrong.

I've scored *her*.

That's the epic thing about all this. She's way too smart for me, but she puts up with my dumb ass anyway. She even laughs at my lame jokes and doesn't mind when I go on too much about football. She plays my favorite video game with me whenever she comes over and doesn't seem to mind my obsession with her sweet tits either.

I hide my smile behind my hand as I listen to her aunt

telling me all about her pottery exploits and how she's started making mugs and bowls to sell at the local market on Saturday mornings.

"Lizzy used to come and help me sell things when she was in middle school. She's got a real head for numbers, that one."

"Yeah, I know." I smile, glancing across the room at my girl while she plays with her young second-cousin. The little girl is teaching her a clapping game, and Satch is listening intently, making her feel like the only person in the room.

She's so fucking amazing.

"But then, of course, they made her feel bad about it, and ooooo, I could have slapped those girls that day."

"What?" I spin, trying to catch up on the conversation I zoned out of.

I've been doing that a lot tonight. There's so much chatter going on around me, it's hard to know which conversation to follow. At dinner they were all talking over one another, laughing and changing topics with a speed that was hard to keep up with. Satch sat beside me, quietly smiling at the frenzy of voices.

It's funny, at school she seems like the last person who'd want to be at a loud, chaotic dinner party, but she's comfortable here.

This home is her safe place, and I love seeing her smile appear so easily. Everybody in this room adores her, and I think she knows it, which is why she can relax and laugh and throw a few jokes across the table.

"What girls?" My stomach twists at the thought of anyone trying to make my woman feel bad. That viper still riles me whenever I stop to remember that day and her scathing taunts. Has this been happening to Satch for a while now?

The thought slays me.

I can't fucking deal with the idea of her spending middle school hiding away in the back corners of the library to avoid the bitchy girls. Judging by the pictures on the top of the piano, Satch has been a cutie from the day she was born. And her middle school photo is no exception, her round face all cute and pink, her camera smile forced yet adorable. The thought of her getting teased at that age sits ugly in my chest.

Shit. Is that what happened?

Clenching my jaw, I grit out as softly as I can, "What are you talking about?"

"Oh, she didn't tell you?" Her aunt looks flustered when I shake my head, glancing across the room at her niece before patting down her hair. "Well, maybe it's not my place to say."

"Please." I touch the woman's arm. "What girls?"

She sighs and tuts, watching Satch carefully while she rushes out a whispered explanation. "She had a bit of a hard time in middle school." Her expression crumples. "Even worse in high school. Became the target of a few bullies who were determined to verbally torture her. Some of their pranks were just... awful."

"What?" I practically growl.

The woman pats my hand. "Don't you worry. High school is over now."

Yeah, but she's facing the same thing in college. What the fuck gives?

If anyone tries to prank her, I'll—

"She got through." Her aunt keeps talking, unaware of

the internal thunderstorm raging in my belly. "It really kicked her confidence, though, which is why we're all so pleased she has a handsome, strong man like yourself to look after her now." She beams at me. "She deserves you, you know?"

I let out a soft snicker and gaze across the room, desperately trying to hide my angst and focus on the fact that right here, right now, she's completely safe. Secure. No one's gonna say shit to her in this place.

Satch laughs, pulling the little girl in for a hug and glancing my way. Her expression softens with affection, and she winks at me before kissing the top of her second-cousin's head and saying something that makes the girl smile.

"I'm the lucky one," I murmur to her aunt, then turn and look her right in the eye. "And I'll never let anyone hurt her."

"I know." She smiles, patting my hand again.

"Right, present time!" Tommy walks into the living room with a carefully wrapped box, and my insides skitter as I jump up and reach into my bag for the two presents I had to scramble to find. If Satch had given me warning, I would have done a better job, but knowing my girlfriend, I could be handing her a potato and she'd still be grateful for it.

This family doesn't have much compared to mine. Their three-bedroom, retro-style home with its one living area and single bathroom could probably fit into our rec room and garage. Maybe even just the garage. It's poky at best and looks to be at least seventy or eighty years old. Seriously, walking through the door was like stepping back in time. And it definitely explains a lot.

Her parents are obviously obsessed with the '50s and '60s, because their house is like a movie set from those old musicals Satch loves so much. Even the carpet has a swirling pattern that screams midcentury. I have no idea if it's ever been changed, and although they keep the place clean and tidy, you can tell it's tired.

My mother would not cope walking in here. It's cluttered, every surface covered in trinkets, knickknacks, and photographs that probably all have a story to go with them. It's a dusting nightmare, which is why I can spot layers of dust from the top of the old piano to the vinyl collection stacked on the floor. The old bookshelf under the window is crammed in a haphazard way—the exact opposite to Satch's immaculate collection that she's been curating as if it were a priceless art collection.

My lips twitch as I find a place beside her, resting my gifts on my lap while Satch grins at her family and opens the first one.

"Oh, I love it." She holds up the homemade pottery bowl, beaming at her aunt and going on about how talented the woman is.

I smile at her. Seriously. She's sweeter than that caramel fudge, my gramma used to make.

She has the same reaction to the homemade card her cousin's daughters give her and the box of brownies they baked from scratch.

"I hope you like them."

"I'm going to love them."

The older girl's chest pops out with pride. "I helped decorate your birthday cake too."

"Oh, she did," Satch's mom pipes up. "This girl is a whizz in the kitchen."

"Unlike her mother." Satch's cousin grins, giving his wife an affectionate smile.

She bats his arm for teasing her, but they end up sharing a kiss. I watch in fascination at this motley bunch, so unlike the sophisticated crew I'm used to being around. The only time a family function gets as bois- terous as this is when a football game is on.

Football Frat is different, of course, but it's fun seeing the way Satch's family interacts with one another.

"And this is from us." Her grandfather, who must surely be in his nineties, holds out a shaky hand while his wife sits beside him in her wheelchair, blinking at what look to be tears.

I wonder if she's all right, until I realize it's just emotion at the joy of seeing their granddaughter open the card.

"Fifty dollars?" Satch gapes as if she's just won the lottery. "Wow, you guys! That's so generous."

I have to bite my lips together.

Fifty bucks?

That's lunch money.

Getting up from her seat, Satch rushes over to them, gently kissing their cheeks and specially thanking them.

"You deserve it, sweet girl. We're proud of you, honey." Her grandma's comment is met with a room full of agree- ment, and I'm pretty sure I've never been in such a warm, loving space in my entire life.

This is a trip.

"Okay, Wily, you go next, sweetie. I want to save my gift for last." Darla bobs on her toes as she points to the box waiting at Satch's feet.

"Sure." I pass over my wrapped presents, and everyone leans in.

Shit. I hope they're okay. Are two presents that probably cost more than half the things in this room going to be able to compete with the meaningful, handmade stuff she's been getting all night?

"Oh, wow." Satch loses her breath the second she unwraps my first gift, then sucks in a gasp as she flips over the two books I bought, skimming the backs and then swooning over the covers. "This is amazing!" With a squeal, she throws her arms around me. "I've been wanting to complete this series! How did you know?"

I rub her back, stoked by her excitement. "I had a look at your bookshelf."

"Oh my gosh!" She plunks back into her seat, still giddy as she brushes her hand over the foiled covers. "These hardbacks are so expensive. I can't believe you bought me both! I've been saving up for these." She holds up the books and shows them to everyone in the room.

"Very pretty," her grandma muses while her mother nods, then winks at me.

Her thumbs-up means everything.

"And this one." I catch the smaller box that just slipped off her knee and hold it out for her.

For some reason, I'm even more nervous about this one, and I can't seem to breathe as she takes forever to carefully unwrap the paper, not wanting to rip it.

Her dad reaches forward, collecting the other wrapping and folding it, obviously set on reusing it.

"Thanks, Dad." Satch smiles at him before handing over the last of the wrapping, then opening the box with trembling fingers.

"You good?" I check, reaching forward to help her.

"Thanks," she squeaks, and then her lips part again, her eyes bulging at me. "It's a... You bought me a... It's..."

"A necklace. It's called a necklace." I wink at her, grinning at the way her cheeks splash pink. Leaning in, I softly whisper, "It's a coyote."

Her giggle is adorable, and I will forever remember her face as she gazes down at the silver emblem around the chain and whispers, "I love it."

"Phew," I joke, pulling it out of the box and asking if I can fasten it around her neck.

It takes me a minute because the clasp is so freaking small... and the entire time, her family is going on about how sweet and wonderful I am.

Seriously. They don't get that doing this shit for her is the easiest thing in the world.

"Coyote's my pet name for him," Satch admits with a shy giggle.

"That's so sweet."

"Now I'll always be with you." I brush my finger down the chain, and we share a look that makes the rest of the room disappear for a second.

There's so much implication in my soft statement, and we both know it.

I'm asking her to stick with me no matter what happens on drafting day.

I'm asking a lot, and her eyes are telling me she's here for it.

Holy shit.

This is happening.

"Thank you," she whispers, pressing a kiss to my lips while the room lets out oooohs and cheers.

We end up laughing against each other, and I'm forced to pull back and take on the teasing comments and blushing smiles from the females in the room.

Eyebrow wiggling continues until Satch reaches for the box at her feet, and the room seems to still with anticipation.

I have no idea what it could be, but Satch's hands don't shake as she lifts the lid, and then she loses her breath all over again.

"Mom, really?" She starts to blink at tears, pulling out a black-and-pink outfit that looks straight from the '50s.

I think it's a top with a scoop neck, and then there's this puffy pink—

"A poodle skirt!" Satch jumps to her feet, holding it against her body and swishing it back and forth. "This is amazing."

"It took her forever, but she was determined to make you the prettiest one she could." Tommy gives his wife a proud smile, wrapping his arm around her waist and kissing her cheek.

I eye the outfit, imagining my girl in a high ponytail with bobby socks and a little scarf around her neck, just like those chicks in that old movie *Grease*.

Shit, Satch would look adorable.

"I love it so much!" She bounces over to her parents, hugging them close, and I wonder when she's ever gonna get a chance to wear an outfit like that.

Will she walk around school like that?

Maybe.

She seems to like homemade clothes.

Man, I hope that viper bitch doesn't see her when she's wearing something like that. I'm gonna have to make sure I've got eyes on Satch when I can't be around to protect her. I'll rally the team, make sure they've got their ears to the ground.

Her aunt's comments from before are still eating at me.

The idea of anyone taunting her or hurting her makes me see red.

She deserves to walk with her head held high. She should be able to wear whatever the fuck she wants, go wherever she wants without worrying about being traumatized.

Sitting back, I watch her in the safety of her home and realize how much more alive and bubbly she is here.

She doesn't have to worry about any kind of criticism, and that's what I want for her in Nolan.

"Time for cake and karaoke!" the youngest member of the group yells, raising her hands with a whoop as she runs into the kitchen.

And that's how our night goes.

The cake is delicious, and I never knew "Happy Birthday" could be a beautifully harmonized choir piece.

This family is fucking amazing.

And they do not know how to do slightly drunken, off-key karaoke either. These guys can *sing*, and Satch is no exception.

As she stands by the screen, crooning out some old tune from... it's gotta be the '50s or something... she sounds like an angel. Her voice is rich and pure and—

"Beautiful, sweetheart. You sound just like Ella," her mother calls, then leans down to whisper in my ear. "Ella Fitzgerald is one of her favorite singers."

"Okay." I nod, having no idea who that woman is but guessing she's long gone.

Everything about this place seems to have a long-gone vibe. It's like stepping back in history—the artwork, the furniture, the patterned carpet.

This family is stuck in a past they didn't even grow up in. If my math is right, her parents were born in the '60s. Well, I guess that's not too far off, although, based on pictures I've seen on history websites, I'd say I was sitting firmly in the '50s.

And that's only confirmed when it's finally time for bed and I'm taken into a guest room with a light pink bedspread... and no Satch.

CHAPTER 46
ELIZABETH

I roll over in my single bed. It groans like it's too old and tired for me to be here.

It's smaller than the one I have at college, and my first night home is always an adjustment. This is the bed my parents bought me when I was seven. It was my birthday present that year—a brand-new bed. Well, it was second-hand but brand-new to me.

Mom had specially made a duvet cover for me. She'd found this cool retro fabric and then sewn badges from the 1950s and 60s all over it. There was a Coca Cola emblem and an old coffee shop logo, a burger bar sign, roller skates, vinyl records, and a bunch of other cool stuff.

I used to spend hours lying on this duvet and tracing the different symbols.

I was so happy in this safe little haven.

When it came time to move to college, Mom asked me if I wanted to take it, but I didn't want to mess up the look of my room. I knew I'd be home at least once a month, and I wanted to walk in and feel that sense of belonging every time I stepped in here.

But tonight... it feels different.

I'm not even sure why.

I've just had the best night. I should be drifting off to sleep in pure bliss, but I can't get comfy.

Shuffling around, I tuck the duvet around my neck, then start to play with the necklace Wily bought me. It's the sweetest gift ever. I'll never take it off.

"Now I'll always be with you."

His husky voice when he said that... and the look in his eyes... damn right he'll always be with me. That boy has a permanent place in my heart no matter what happens.

But did he really mean it?

He'll be gone after graduation, and I still have two years left at Nolan U. Is he honestly saying he'll wait for me?

The NFL is going to swallow him whole, take him on this amazing journey, and I don't know if there's room for me in that lifestyle.

But he'll always stay with me. I press the pendant to my lips, kissing it firmly before tucking it back inside my pajama top.

I wish he was with me right now.

If he was lying behind me with his strong arm wrapped around my body, I'd be asleep in minutes.

Staring through the darkness at my bedroom door, I toy with the idea of padding across the cold hallway and crawling into the guest bed with him, but...

My parents set us up in separate rooms, and I want to respect that.

They have no idea Wily and I are sleeping together, and I'm not sure how or when I'll tell them. I've been dating him for less than a month; they'll probably think it's way too fast. I could explain that I was falling for him well before our first date, but still...

It is fast.

Fast and amazing.

Fast and so natural that it feels like the most normal thing in the world.

My lips rise, my body tingling as I relive our last hot and heavy make-out session. I still had my period a few days ago. It's over now, but the other day... I got to give him my very first blow job, and it was so much better than I could have imagined. I was kind of nervous to do it, but I wanted to pleasure him, and the way he moaned and fisted my duvet cover told me everything. When his fingers plunged into my hair, his thighs going taut on either side of my body, I felt like the queen of the world. I was sending him over the edge, and it felt amazing.

My door handle turns, and I flinch at the sound, tensing in the dark as I listen to my door quietly creak open.

"Satch?" Wily whispers, and my heart springs into my throat.

"Wily? Are you okay?"

"Yeah." He creeps into the room, closing the door softly behind him.

With my eyes already adjusted to the dark, I enjoy the view as his shadowy body pads across to my bed and he lifts the covers.

"What are you doing?" I shuffle back to accommodate him, my butt hitting the wall.

There's no way we're both going to fit on this tiny bed.

"I missed you." He pecks my lips, nearly falling off the mattress as the bed groans again, its old frame complaining about the extra weight. "Here." Grabbing my hip, he pushes me around until I'm flat on my back, and then he finds a happy home between my legs. "Better?"

"Yes," I breathe, kissing his chin as I run my hands around his waist and up his back.

He's shirtless! And I love the feel of his skin beneath my fingertips. Tracing each muscle, I splay my hands over his broad back and enjoy the journey up to his shoulders.

I love it when he lies on top of me.

I love how close his lips are.

And I love the erection I can feel forming against my leg.

"You're already hard," I tease him.

"I told you." He kisses the side of my mouth. "I was missing my girl."

I bite my bottom lip, a broad smiling forming around my teeth.

"Had to come and give you a proper good night kiss," he whispers, nibbling his way across my jawline, then down my neck. "Your dad won't kill me, right?"

"I don't think so." My breath catches, and I can't help a contented sigh as his tongue skims the line of my new necklace, then starts to inch into my pajama top.

"You know, I think it's really unfair that you're still wearing this." His voice is laced with amusement. "If I'm half naked, you really should be too."

My hips rise of their own accord, and I grind into him as I boldly murmur, "Only half naked?"

"Oh, baby." He groans into my neck, quickly unbuttoning my pajama top and lavishing my breasts with kisses before inching down my body.

When he gets to my pajama pants, he sits back, lifting the duvet covers with him and letting a rush of cold air wash over me.

I shiver and he works fast, ridding me of my pants before yanking down his own. He leaves them around his ankles and quickly covers us back up. The bed groans again as he lies over top of me.

"You feel so good," I sigh with a smile as his warm body covers mine.

I love skin on skin with this man.

Kissing his shoulder, I draw patterns on his back, then giggle when he lightly nips my neck.

"Kiss me, baby," he whispers against my skin, and I turn to glide my tongue into his eager mouth.

We get lost in the simple act of kissing, the inferno inside my body the only thing to break me out of the heady spell.

My lady parts are yearning and needy, growing wet with desire. When he reaches between us and starts to massage my clit, I'm seconds away from orgasming. He barely has to touch me and I'm whimpering against his chest, gripping his shoulders and keening at the addictive fire racing through me.

There's a hot urgency between us and I relish it, whispering at him to hurry when he reaches under the pillow to grab out a condom.

"When did you put that there?" I grin as he unwraps it and rolls it over his gloriously hard cock.

"I slipped it under your pillow when I first came in. Wasn't trying to be presumptuous, just hopeful."

He lies back over me with the cutest grin. I can just make it out in the light through my window, and I seriously love this man.

I should tell him.

But he's at my entrance now, already nudging into me, and words are lost as I relish that mind-blowing sensation of our bodies connecting this way.

"You good?" He groans the words more than says them, obviously loving this as much as I am.

Hooking my foot around his very fine ass, I whisper into his ear, "I am so good."

"That's my girl." He starts to move, his long shaft owning me while the bed continues to groan and complain.

The poor thing has probably never experienced anything like this before, and the thought of the bed's grumpy expression as we grind on top of it has me biting back a grin.

"Baby, you're so fucking fine." Wily picks up his pace, leaning back on his elbow so he can squeeze my breast.

His thrusts continue at a heady pace, my body reveling in this glorious wonder.

Leaning forward, he sucks my nipple into his mouth. The angle is awkward and disrupts his rhythm, but I lean into his kisses, loving his tongue on such sensitive parts of my body.

His mouth makes a sweet pop when he pulls away, and then he picks up his pace again, sliding in and out of me with sexy moans that accelerate the heat already pulsing through my body.

Resting his hands on either side of my head, he pushes up on his arms, and I run my hands over his pecs and abs.

The bed keeps complaining, creaking in time with our rhythm, and I start to worry that my parents might hear us.

"Wily," I whisper, wondering if I should tell him to stop, even though I really don't want to.

"Yeah, baby." He leans down, dropping to his elbows with a thud before threading his hands under my shoulders and—

Crack!

The bed's groan shifts to an outright cry of surrender, and I let out a shocked yelp as the mattress beneath me lands with an embarrassingly loud thud on my bedroom floor.

"Oh shit!" Wily chokes out as we tip sideways, the duvet sliding off us as the bed settles on this weird angle and we cling to each other.

I gape up at him, my heart going nuts when the hallway lights come on and bustling feet can be heard rushing toward us.

"Bess?" Dad's voice is all worried concern until he pushes open my door, flicks on the light, and spots my naked boyfriend, his boxer shorts wrapped around his ankles, still inside me. "Oh... my... okay." Dad squeezes his eyes shut, and I think I'm about to die of humiliation.

I nearly tell Wily to get off me, but logic quickly reminds me that if he does that, he'll be exposing his dick to the entire room. The safest option is for him to stay exactly where he is.

Gripping his back, I stare up at his face, silently asking him what to do.

"Is everything okay in here?" Mom's voice wafts in from the hallway.

Shit!

I close my eyes, my entire body starting to heat with embarrassment when my mom gasps. "Oh! Wow. My goodness." She lets out a nervous laugh, and I pop my eyes open, begging her to please stop.

Dad is staring like he's going into shock, and my mom is...

Is she blushing right now?

She touches her curls, her lips twitching with a coy smile as she checks out my boyfriend!

Well, this is just great.

"Mom!" I bulge my eyes at her, and she has the decency to avert her gaze.

"Uh... hey, Darla. Tommy." Wily glances over his shoulder, then clears his throat and croaks, "I mean, Mr. and Mrs. Satchwell."

Mom brushes her hand through the air like he's still allowed to call her whatever he wants. Her eyes linger for a second, skimming over his perfect ass, and I have to glare at her once more.

"Seriously?"

"Sorry. Sorry!" She spins around, then grabs Dad's arm and forces him to turn. He mutely spins to face the wall. Yep, I'm pretty sure he's in shock.

Squeezing my eyes shut, I then have to listen to my parents whisper-barking at the wall.

"I told you we should have put them in the same room," Mom tuts.

"I didn't want to assume they were sleeping together."

"Of course they are. Look at them." Mom spins back, her smile all mushy. "They're in love, Tommy."

Dad glances over his shoulder, then winces and turns back around again.

Mom, on the other hand, is still gazing at my man, and now she's primping her hair.

"Mom!"

"Sorry." She laughs awkwardly, snapping her eyes shut. "We'll just let you, um... move to the guest room." Her eyes creep back open, running down the length of Wily's back before she glances at me with an excited smile. "Good job, Bessie Boo," she whispers way too loudly, giving me a double thumbs-up before grabbing my father's sleeve and tugging him out of the room.

Burying my face in Wily's chest, I let out a wail, and my boyfriend starts to laugh.

"Shit," he chuckles, dipping his head and kissing the side of my face. "Well, that was... interesting."

"Interesting? Really?" I deadpan, but that only makes him laugh harder.

Popping out of me, he sits back on his heels, taking in my body and nodding. "He didn't kill me."

"I'm pretty sure he was too busy going into catatonic shock."

"Right. So the death warrant might be issued tomorrow?"

I snort and shake my head. "Not if my mom has anything to say about it." I slap a hand over my eyes. "I am so sorry about her."

"Don't worry about it." Wily laughs, pulling my hand

away so I can see his wincing frown. "I'm really sorry about your bed."

I turn my head to check out the broken frame. "Not designed for two."

"My bed is." Wily's voice takes on a husky, sexy quality that sends a shiver coursing through my body.

I turn to give him a skeptical frown. Is he serious? After getting caught by my parents, he's happy to keep going?

"Should we take this to the guest room?"

"I'm not sure I can move." My face bunches. "I'm pretty sure I've just died from embarrassment."

He laughs and gets to his feet, kicking the pants off his ankles before reaching out a hand to help me up.

"Come on, you." Sweeping his arm under my legs, he hitches me against his chest and starts carrying me to the door.

Having never been carried like this before, I tense at the unexpected move and quietly tell him, "Stop. I'm too heavy. I can just walk."

Pausing at my doorframe, he gives me a stern frown and tells me, "Don't talk bullshit," before carrying me across the hallway and into the guest room.

Laying me down on top of the bed spread, he climbs up beside me, resting his hand on my belly and murmuring against my breast, "Now, where were we?"

CHAPTER 47
WILY

So yeah, Satch's parents saw my bare ass. They saw me actually inside their daughter, and I'm lucky not to be standing on the snowy street outside with my pants around my ankles.

Which is why I have to make this second chance count.

My gorgeous girl is lying beside me on this heinous pink duvet, and I can tell she's dubious about trying again. We were midway, my body heating with that electric fire, and it's not gonna take much for me to get back there.

But I won't force her into anything she doesn't want to do.

Her body is kind of stiff as I kiss my way from the curve of her breast to that beautiful pink nipple I love so much.

Sucking it into my mouth, I play with it for a selfish minute before glancing up at her face.

Shit.

My insides deflate as I sit back on my elbow and stare down at her. "We don't have to do this. We can just sleep if you want."

Her frown is uncertain, and I push the corners of her mouth up, trying to make her smile.

A breathy laugh makes her boobs jiggle, and I glance down at them. Yearning powers through me, but I force myself to say, "We can just snuggle up and fall asleep. I get it."

"I'm surprised you want to do anything after that embarrassment. I mean, my parents caught us having sex. Don't you want to curl into a ball and die?"

I laugh, unable to help myself.

Cupping her cheek, I guide her to look at me. "Satch, your parents saw me having sex with their daughter who I happen to..." My throat swells, my voice getting husky as I take a giant risk and just say it. "Love."

Her eyes dart to mine, wide and beautiful in the soft lamplight.

My insides turn to pliable putty, a smile teasing my lips as I say it with a little more conviction. "I love you, Satch. And I don't know if I've loved a girl before, because what I feel about you is off the charts. You know?"

"I know," she whispers, her eyes welling with tears as she stares up at me with a watery smile. "I love you." She sniffs. "And I'm not just saying that because you just said it. I really mean it. I've been feeling it for a while, but I thought it was too soon. I didn't want to freak you out, but... I love you. I do."

Brushing a tear off her cheek, I can't explain this sensation riding through me.

Holy shit.

I didn't realize how much I wanted to hear that from her.

I don't know what to say... and my throat's too thick to form any coherent words anyway.

Smiling up at me, she grabs my face and pulls me down to kiss her. Our tongues meet in the middle—so familiar and warm that it's easy to get sucked back into the vortex that is Satch's perfect mouth.

My hands start to roam before I can stop them, and she lets me feel her up.

I make her come with soft strokes between her legs, all the while kissing her lips until she can't hold out anymore.

Breaking away from me with sexy-ass whimpers and a groan that travels right through me, she falls apart in my arms and I roll between her thighs, slipping into her wet oasis with ease.

I'm still suited up, and although I should probably check the thing for breaks or tears, I can't leave her.

So I gently plunge and thrust until I'm forced to use some common sense.

Reluctantly slipping out of her, I rise to my knees, needing to check that my armor is still intact.

"Is everything okay?" she pants, disappointment marring her expression when I switch on the bedside lamp.

"Yeah, baby. I'm just checking that this thing is still bulletproof." I make sure we're good to go before winking at her, then flopping onto my back and asking if she wants to try something new.

Nervous anticipation lights her face as I guide her to sit on top of me.

Her breasts sway as she gets herself comfortable, and I cup them in my hands, holding them steady while she lines us up, then sinks onto me.

"Holy shit," I rasp, loving the way she encases me. Her weight on my thighs is delicious. Her body rocking over mine this way... holy shit.

She's all-consuming, and when she grips my wrists and starts to ride me with more confidence, I can't help telling her again.

"I love you. I love you so fucking much, Satch."

Her smile is nothing but beauty when she beams down at me, then takes my hands, threading our fingers together. I can't break eye contact with her as she rides me.

It's fucking intimate, and I can't make myself close my eyes or look away.

That gaze of hers is glassy with emotion and affection, and I want to bask in it for the rest of eternity.

I love you, I silently tell her, and she smiles, rising and falling over me until the heat spreading through my body is white-hot gold.

My breathing turns shallow, quick puffs of air punching out of me as my heart starts to pound. That heat continues to spread and glow until I'm the fucking Human Torch.

Squeezing her fingers, I lose myself, jerking beneath her as that fire takes me out, rocketing through me and blasting into her with an energy that is pure power— overwhelming, all-consuming electricity that binds us with a force I've never felt before.

She gasps and moans above me, her pussy clutching

my dick as she bounces and pumps, tipping her head back with an erotic moan.

Fuck, she's beautiful.

Squeezing her thighs on either side of me, she whimpers, resting her hands on my shoulders as she rides out her orgasm with a sexy-ass expression, then lets her body sag.

Pulling her down, I nestle her over my chest and squeeze her against me while we catch our breath.

I want to tell her that was fucking hot.

I want to ask her if we can please do that again.

But there is no space for words right now.

I just want to feel her body pressed against mine.

I want to listen to her soft breaths and revel in this moment.

I'm holding the woman I love.

And it can't get better than that.

CHAPTER 48
ELIZABETH

Holding my breath, I pad out to the kitchen, wondering what my parents are going to say about last night's escapades.

Dad's not around, and I sink onto the kitchen stool with a touch of relief.

That poor man.

He's probably gonna have nightmares for the rest of his life.

"Good morning," Mom greets me cheerfully.

I smile at her, grateful for the coffee she hands me. "Thanks." I blow on it and take a sip, testing the temperature.

"Where's your man?"

"He's in the shower," I mumble, heat flushing through me. We both needed cleaning after last night.

My insides tremor, my lips fighting a grin as I momentarily relive our lovemaking. It wasn't just once either. He nudged me awake with soft kisses sometime in the early hours of the morning, and we had each other all over again.

Will my body ever recover?

I'm not sure.

Do I ever want it to?

Not really.

Smirking into my mug, I take another sip and don't even notice my surroundings until Mom starts giggling at me. "You've got it bad, Bessie Boo."

I can't do anything but laugh along with her.

My cheeks must be fire-engine red right now, but I look up at her anyway. "He's so amazing, Mom."

"He certainly looked it." She waggles her eyebrows at me, then laughs off my baleful glare. "Oh, stop. He's gorgeous. There's no denying that."

"It's true." I give her a dreamy smile.

"But he's more than that." She tips her head, going back to stir the oatmeal on the stove. She's added nutmeg and cinnamon. I sniff the air, already looking forward to it. "He's kind, sweetie. And, unfortunately, that can be a rare quality in a man."

"Dad's kind."

"Oh, yes, he is." Mom grins.

And I can't help a wince. "Is he okay? After last night?"

She covers her mouth, laughing behind her fingers. "Not sure he ever wanted to see you that way, but he'll recover."

I groan, hiding my face behind my fingers.

"It's funny." Mom laughs.

"It's embarrassing!" My hands hit the counter when

my arms flop down. "Seriously, Mom. That's like a living nightmare."

"Oh stop. It's not. We caught our daughter getting frisky with a man she loves. A man who loves her back. That is a beautiful, natural thing, my darling girl."

"I do love him," I admit.

"I could tell the second you two walked through the front door." She beams at me. "And I'm so happy for you, sweetheart. You deserve a good man in your life."

I brush away her words and focus on my coffee, curling my fingers around the mug as I watch her move around the kitchen the way I have thousands of times before. She's my mom, and I couldn't love her more if I tried. She's the person I've always trusted most. Her and Dad. So, it's probably okay for me to say what's on my mind.

"It doesn't feel real sometimes, you know?" I purse my lips and force myself to say it. "Guys like him don't fall for girls like me."

"What?" Mom turns to face me. "You mean funny, talented, intelligent, sweet girls like you? Yes, they do. They fall for them all the time."

"No, Mom." I frown at her. "You know what I mean."

"No." Her voice gets firm, her expression hardening to match. "What I do understand is that my beautiful, amazing daughter has found herself a boyfriend who knows her well enough to buy the perfect birthday presents and thinks she's so sexy he can't even go one night without sharing a bed with her. That's what I know."

My lips twitch and I try to soak in her compliments, wondering how I'll ever explain this so she'll understand.

Wily is wonderful.

He's so incredibly wonderful.

And he's sexy as all get-out.

He could have any girl in the world.

Which makes me worry that this thing we've got going can't possibly last.

He told you he loves you. He gave you a coyote necklace so he'll always be with you.

My brain is begging me to believe it. But some small part of me is still struggling...

Because I'm me... and every time something amazing like this happens, something horrible comes along to screw it up.

CHAPTER 49
WILY

Feeling a little guilty about how things went down last night, I sought out Mr. Satchwell when my girl fell asleep in the guest room. I really tired her out last night, and I don't regret a second of it.

But I do regret all the embarrassment the broken bed caused everyone.

I find Darla in the kitchen, and she directs me to their family diner.

It takes me five minutes to walk there from the house, and the waitress who greets me bulges her eyes as soon as I tell her my name and then directs me to the kitchen.

Poor Mr. Satchwell is in there by himself, sweating up a storm and fighting tears as he slices onions, then turns to man the grill behind him.

"Hey." I raise my hand in greeting.

He glances up, gives me a noncommittal grunt, and starts flipping burger patties. "I'm not supposed to be working this weekend, but my part-time chef called in sick. And I don't want to hit up my new lady, because she worked like a Trojan last week."

"Looks like you're the Trojan now. Can I give you a hand?" I don't know shit about cooking, but I'm already reaching for an apron.

Hooking it over my head, I tie it behind me and walk toward him, wary of the hot spatula he's waving around.

The guy probably wants to slap that thing against my head and tell me to never touch his daughter again.

And I'd let him.

I've got a few inches on him and probably a hundred pounds of muscle, too, but he could take me in a second, because I love his daughter and I'd never do anything to hurt him.

"What can I do?" I ask.

He turns to face me, his tone skeptical. "You really want to help?"

"Yes, sir." I nod, braving a smile.

He gives me a deadpan glare, but then his lips start to twitch and a smile creeps across his face. "You're impossible not to like, you know that?"

I beam down at him. "Thank you, sir."

"And stop with the *sirs*. It's Tommy."

"Not sure you wanted me calling you anything after last night." I cringe.

Rolling his eyes with a huff, he hands me three tomatoes. "Slice those up for me, will ya?"

I place the tomatoes on the chopping board, then move to wash my hands.

He doesn't say anything, and I get to work, carefully cutting the tomatoes with as much precision as I can while also trying not to nip my fingers. This knife is lethally sharp.

"You love my girl?" The question comes out of nowhere, and I nearly slice my nail off when I whip around to face Satch's dad.

His gaze is piercing, unrelenting, and there's no space for lies in this moment.

So I nod and rasp, "Yes. I love her."

"That's pretty fast." His eyebrows dip.

"Yeah." I nod again. "Freaks me out a little, but..." I shrug.

"When you know, you know," he finishes for me, his smile growing wider. "I fell for Darla after only a week. Had to hold my tongue every time I was around her. Didn't want to scare her away."

"Oh yeah? How long did you last?"

He snickers. "Ten days."

I turn back to face him with a goofy laugh. "And what'd she say?"

Shaking his head, he gets a dopey smile on his face, moving the patties off the grill and turning back to the counter. "She said... 'What took you so long?'"

He starts to laugh, his shoulders shaking as he obviously relives the moment.

"Oh man." He wipes a finger under his eyes. "I'd do anything for that woman. She's had my heart since I was twenty-two."

Huh. That's my age.

"We waited a few years before getting married, though." He gives me a pointed look.

I nod, not exactly sure what he's expecting me to say

here. I wasn't about to drop to one knee. I only told Satch I love her last night.

With a soft swallow, I go back to slicing tomatoes until he grabs my wrist again and gruffly tells me, "Don't you go breaking her heart. She's a special one, and she needs a man who's gonna take care of her. Someone who's gonna love her just the way she is."

"I'd never hurt her." The words are easy to say because they're true. I'd never intentionally hurt Satch. I don't know why anyone would. "And I think she's awesome."

He waits a beat, watching me carefully before nodding, "Good. Because I don't want her to feel like she has to change for anybody. She might not be the fashion queen of Fledgling, and she might not keep up with all the latest and greatest trends, but my little girl is golden, through and through. I love that she's different to everybody else, and I don't want her changing to try and keep you happy."

I smile at him, appreciating his impassioned speech. "She doesn't need to change to keep me happy."

He clearly appreciates that, and I'm rewarded with a smile and a shoulder slap before he points at my chopping board. "Finish those up and I'll get you working on some onions for me."

"Yes, sir." I nod, returning to my slicing and dicing.

Tommy puts on music, and he's soon dancing around to a tune while filling orders like a seasoned pro. I doubt I contribute much, but he seems to appreciate the company, and I get an education in all things '50s.

He tells me all about the history of the diner and how

he fell in love with the place the second he walked into it. He wanted to stay true to its original design, and that's why every upgrade has simply been a shinier version of what once existed.

When there's a lull, he takes me for a quick tour of the place, resting his hand against the jukebox and staring down at it with affection.

"We've managed to keep this thing going. The maintenance costs way too much, but I just can't replace it. Our repair guy complains every time the thing breaks down," Tommy laughs. "But I can't let it go." He turns and points to the black-and-white checkered floor. "Bess used to be in here every day after school. She'd do her homework while sucking down a vanilla shake, and then she'd serve the various tables. People love our girl." He grins. "And every weekend, she'd come in early with me and help me open up for the later breakfast service. I'd let her choose songs from this jukebox and she'd dance and sing, spinning around in her own little world."

His smile is rich with fatherly tenderness.

"I take it that's where she got her love of all things retro, then?"

He chuckles. "Yep. You can blame Darla and me for that one. We met at a rock-n-roll dance club and never looked back. Our girl had no chance." He tips his head with a thoughtful pout. "I just wish she had more opportunities to really let that shine, you know?" Sadness sweeps across his expression then. "Darla spent hours at her sewing machine, perfecting that birthday present for our Bessie... and I'm not even sure when she'll get to wear it. I want the world to see that beautiful craftsmanship, but I worry that if she walks around Nolan U sporting a poodle skirt, she might get..." His expression buckles with obvious torment, and he blinks at a sudden rush of tears. "I just want her to have a good college experience." His voice wobbles.

"Tommy," I whisper, hating the distressed look on his face, "what happened to her in high school?"

He shakes his head, his shoulders sagging as he mumbles, "A lot of things that shouldn't have."

"Like what?"

He clenches his jaw, deep wrinkles forming across his forehead. "Name-calling, verbal abuse, ugly pranks set on embarrassing her. They were relentless, and I watched my little girl go from this happy ray of sunshine who used to skip and sing her way to school..." He shakes his head, his voice cracking. "To a loner who just wanted to hide in her room and read books all day."

He looks so wounded, my chest is starting to hurt.

"I just wanted her to be a normal kid and have friends like everybody else. But she couldn't catch a break." He sniffs, nodding like he's trying to pull himself together. "I understand why she hid herself away."

"She never told me any of this," I murmur, feeling like I've just been sprayed with a clip of bullets. Fuck, the truth hurts.

"She won't want me to tell you, so don't try forcing it out of her." He presses his lips together, then clears his throat and tries for a smile. "I'm just so grateful she's away from those bullies now. She's finally got a chance, you know?"

I stare at him, forcing myself to nod, because telling him the truth just might break his heart.

Grabbing my arm, he gives me a friendly squeeze, looking up at me with an expression I will never be able to say no to. "You take care of my girl, okay?"

"Of course I will." My voice is husky and raw, but it's an easy thing to agree to.

He gives me a closed-mouth smile. "I'd give anything to see her come out of that shell of hers, and I think you can help her do it. She seems... lighter since you've come into her life. You keep it up, son. I just want Bess to be happy."

I'm about to promise him that I'll do everything in my power to make her the happiest girl alive, but two new customers arrive before I can say it.

They're two of Tommy's regulars, meaning I'm dragged forward to meet this duo who've watched Satch grow from a young girl to the woman she is today.

They seem shocked that I'm her boyfriend, clearly thinking that Satch was destined to end up a lonely cat lady or something. And if she *was* lucky enough to find someone, it wasn't a strapping football player.

Dammit. I hate that.

What makes them think Satch doesn't deserve the best of everything? Like she'd be lucky to settle at all?

Well, fuck that!

My insides churn with irritation for the next hour as I move back into the kitchen, trying not to imagine what Satch had to face each day at school as I help Tommy put the orders together. I mentally swing from wanting to rant at him for not homeschooling his daughter— why didn't you protect her?!—to pleading with him to tell me every ugly detail so I can understand this thing in full.

But we work without speaking, me silently stewing while he hums along to the music.

It's not until I'm miserably coating chicken tenders with some secret breadcrumb concoction that an idea hits me.

And, oh shit, it's the best fucking idea I've ever had!

"Uh… can I take five?"

Tommy glances at me. "I'm not paying you, kid. Take whatever time you need."

I thank him, quickly washing my hands before darting out the back door and pulling my phone free. Pacing the cold parking lot, I walk to the dumpster and back, tucking my hand under my armpit and wishing I'd grabbed my coat.

"Hey, Wily. What's up?" I smile at the sound of Sienna's voice. "How's your weekend going?"

"What are her parents like?" Nylah calls.

"Whose parents?" another girl asks.

"Wywee!" Zoey yells, letting out a whine when Sienna won't hand the phone to her.

"Put me on speaker," I instruct with a laugh. "Hey, Zoey girl."

"Wywee!" She laughs my name, letting out an excited squeal.

"How's my favorite cowgirl?"

"Good. Me shopping."

"Are you now? Are you gonna buy me something pretty?"

"No." She laughs. "Buy me pity!"

Nylah and the other girl start to laugh.

"Who am I talking to right now?" I have to ask.

"Oh, it's me," Sienna says. "And Nylah and her room-mate, Jolie."

"Hi." Jolie's voice is sweet and kinda perky.

Have I met her before? I can't even remember.

"How's it going?" I ask as a way of introduction.

"Yeah, good, thanks." Her response is polite, and I figure it's about time I get to my point.

"So, guys. I've had an idea, and I need your help to pull it off."

"Ooo! Do tell." Sienna sounds excited already. Excellent.

"Okay, well... it was Satch's birthday yesterday, and I was wondering if we could throw a surprise party for her. She's never really had a big party with a bunch of friends, and I think she deserves it."

"I love that idea!" Nylah starts getting excited too. "So, what do you want us to do?"

"Should we go for a theme?" Sienna asks.

"Yes, definitely." I quickly tell them about Satch's love of all things '50s and how she was given this poodle skirt for her birthday. "She was stoked, and I want to give her the perfect event to wear it to."

"I love that so much," Jolie gushes, and the girls are soon all babbling together.

It's hard to keep up with their stream of ideas, but I catch little comments as they talk over top of one another.

"I've got a bunch of vinyls my grandparents used to own. You can borrow those."

"I have the soundtrack to *Grease*."

"What kinds of foods did they eat in the '50s?"

"Let me google it."

"Yes! I'm so pumped for this. I'm gonna make Carson dress like James Dean in *Rebel Without a Cause*." Nylah lets out a girlish *eeepp* sound. "He's gonna look so freaking hot. My gramma made me watch that movie a couple of years ago, and she'll flip if she knows Carson is gonna dress up as Jim Stark!"

"Who's Jim Stark?" Sienna asks.

"The guy in *Rebel Without a Cause*."

"I thought you said James Dean was that guy," Jolie questions.

Nylah groans. "Jim Stark is the character James Dean plays in that movie. You know what, we're watching it tonight. I don't care if you feel like it or not, you girls need a serious movie education."

"We should watch *Grease* too." Sienna gets into it. "We can use it as inspiration for this party."

"Yes! I love that idea." Nylah's voice is getting all high and excited again.

"Aw, now I want to come. Ben would make one hot Gary Cooper. He's the *High Noon* guy, right? My father loves old Westerns."

"You can come," Sienna quickly adds, then asks me, "She can come, right, Wily?"

I laugh. "Invite whoever you like, just make sure it's a bunch of cool people who are willing to dress up and really embrace the era. I want this to be a party that's all about Satch and what she loves."

"Okay, you are like the sweetest boyfriend e-ver." Nylah sings the last word, and the other two start gushing their agreement.

"Thanks, girls. I really appreciate your help."

"We are on it!" Sienna lets out an excited squeal,

which Zoey jumps all over. I can hear her cheering as I hold the phone away from ear and wince at the high-pitched noise.

Seriously, what have I unleashed?

"Thanks, guys." I raise my voice over their unrestrained enthusiasm. "I'll be back tomorrow and can help with the prep this week. It'd be great if we could have the party soon so it's not too far away from her birthday. Any chance we could hook this up for the coming weekend?"

"A week?" Sienna squawks. "You're giving us a week?"

"We can do it," Nylah assures her. "Don't worry about it, big guy. We'll rally everyone to pitch in and help. We can totally throw this thing together."

"And I want it to be a surprise," I remind them, "so you're gonna have to prep in stealth mode."

"Yay!" Jolie cheers. "Surprises are the best! Can I help? Please?"

"Of course you can," I laugh. "Now get to it, ladies. I'll see you tomorrow."

The girls are too busy talking to hear my goodbye and I end the call, a delayed wave of uncertainty running through me.

Is this a terrible idea?

I momentarily question my sanity until Satch appears around the corner.

"There you are." Her smile is bright with affection, and I tuck my phone away, holding my tongue against spilling my big surprise.

"Hey, baby." I pull her against me, leaning down to kiss those plump lips of hers. "How was your nap?"

She groans like it was orgasmic. "One hundred percent required." Looking up with a sleepy grin, she kisses me again. "But you can wear me out anytime, Coyote."

I waggle my eyebrows at her until she's giggling against my chest.

Wrapping my arms around her shoulders, I walk her back into the diner, determined to give her the best surprise party in the world.

I can't fucking wait!

CHAPTER 50
ELIZABETH

Wily's been evasive this week, and it's making me nervous. Ever since we got back to Nolan, he's been hiding something from me. I have no idea what it is, and okay... I'm more than nervous. It's freaking me out!

What did my dad say to him at the diner while I was napping?

Did he tell Wily to stay away from me?

No, that can't be right. They seemed to really like him. We had dinner together on Saturday night, and we taught Wily how to play Carcassonne. It's one of our favorite board games, and Wily did great. He built a huge city that got him a bunch of points, and he nearly beat my dad. And then we watched *The Sound of Music*, because Wily had never seen it before, and he didn't mind one bit that Mom and I sang along to every song, knowing every lyric. Wily had his arm around me, grinning and kissing the top of my head when I started singing "My Favorite Things."

It's so obvious he likes my parents, and he seemed to be having fun hanging out with us.

And Mom kept on gushing that I'd found myself a good man. She even gave him multiple hugs when we left, and Dad shook his hand just before Wily opened his truck door for me.

Oh, the way Mom swooned over that one.

"Such a gentleman." She beamed.

Yeah, well my *gentleman* has been lying to me, and I should definitely confront him about it, but what if he turns around, sighs a sad little sigh, and says something like "I don't want to hurt you, but..." or "I'm not sure how to say this, but..."?

Then he dumps me. And I'll never recover.

Sucking in a tremulous breath, I try to focus on my studies. I'm at the library, and Wily bailed on our tutoring session about twenty minutes ago. He said something came up and could I please meet him at Football Frat in an hour.

Ugh. This is the worst!

I don't know how the hell I'm supposed to concentrate on any of my work. My laptop screen keeps blurring as I stare at it, and the letters start to dance.

What's Wily going to say to me when I get to his place?

And why did he bail?

He's got an assignment due next week. He can't just slack off. I can't *let* him slack off.

Yes, I know the Scouting Combine is only a week away and it's been all-consuming as he prepares for it, but we've talked about this. He wants to graduate too! There has to be some compromise here, and I'm really going to have to have a word with him.

If we're still together.

If I'm still his tutor after tonight.

My throat thickens until it hurts to breathe, and I slap my laptop closed, checking the time yet again. Eight o'clock feels miles away.

It's thirty-six minutes. You can do this.

Sucking in a breath, I open my laptop back up, shuffle in my seat and try to at least write the next paragraph of my essay.

It's the hardest thing I've ever done, and by 7:41, I'm toast.

Grabbing up my stuff, I decide that arriving five minutes early will not be the end of the world. I order an Uber before walking down the library steps and go to wait outside in the cold.

Thankfully, it arrives quickly and I'm pulling up outside Football Frat at 7:52.

The place seems quiet, the lights shut off, but there are cars parked in the driveway. Wily's truck is here, but his bedroom light is off.

My stomach pinches as I thank the Uber driver and slip out of the car.

"Have a good night." She smiles at me before pulling away from the curb.

Yeah, right. I can't help my sarcasm.

This is potentially going to be the worst night of my life.

Shuffling up the path, I mount the steps and knock on the front door.

"It's open! Come on in!" someone shouts from inside.

I cringe. I hate letting myself into someone's house. Is it really that hard to answer your own door?

With a little huff, I turn the handle and ease the door open, wondering why it's so dark and quiet in here. I leave it open in case I need a quick escape and tentatively call out, "Hello?"

"SURPRISE!" The room erupts, the lights flicking on as a million people jump out of hiding.

I yelp and step back, banging into the half-open door as I take in the people crowding out the living room, popping out of the dining room archway, and filling up the hallway. They're all grinning and laughing and... I don't know these people.

My heart clutches in my chest until I start to notice what they're all wearing.

Everyone is dressed in garb from the 1950s, and when Wily walks toward me with a beaming smile, looking like a blond Danny Zuko from *Grease*, I don't even know what to say.

"Happy birthday, baby." He kisses my stunned mouth and then has to steady me when he pulls back. "Do you like it?"

I gape at him, then check out the sea of faces expectantly grinning at me. I don't know half these people, and all I can manage is, "What is this?"

They all laugh, and I tense, the sound making my stomach itch.

"It's a late birthday party!" Wily spreads his arms wide before pulling me into an all-encompassing hug and kissing the top of my head. "And it's '50s themed, just for you."

Leaning back, he grins down at me, and I can't believe this.

He threw me a surprise party?

I'm still blinking and trying to wrap my head around it all. This weird laugh kind of pops out of me, and then the music starts playing and Sienna skips over in a poodle skirt, her high ponytail swinging.

"Come on. Let's go get you ready!" Taking my hand, she pulls me upstairs with a laugh. We're soon in the guest room, and she's ordering me out of my clothes.

"What am I supposed to wear?" My hands are shaking as I unzip my skirt.

"This!" Sienna beams, pulling my birthday present from Mom out of the closet. "Wily grabbed it yesterday."

"When?"

She shrugs. "Maybe you were in the bathroom or something?"

I nod, struggling to... Oh yeah. I walked out after my shower, kind of bummed he hadn't wanted to join me, and he was sitting on my bed looking anything but innocent.

So that's why.

I can't help another weird-sounding, breathy laugh as I reach for the outfit. "I can't believe he's done this."

"He came up with the idea last weekend when you were in Fledgling, and he called for an assist. It's been a flurry of activity all week while we got ready for this thing."

"I'm so sorry," I murmur, pulling the skirt up over my hips.

"Why?" Sienna laughs and spins me around so she can zip me up. "It's been so much fun!"

"But so much work."

"Zoey and I loved it. We've been on a shopping spree with Wily's credit card. He told me to spare no expense, and I took him at his word." She spins me back, the grin on her face priceless. "Which is why I was able to arrange this." Reaching back into the closet, she pulls out a shiny black jacket with a pink collar and cuffs. Spinning it around, I take in the word *Satch* embroidered into the back in swirly pink letters. "You like it?"

"Wow." I reach for it, reverently stroking the jacket. "It looks just like something the Pink Ladies would wear."

"I know." Sienna dances on the spot excitedly. "I'm so stoked I managed to pull it together for you. And I hope you don't mind that I chose black with pink accents, but I just thought it'd match better with the poodle skirt."

"It's amazing," I whisper, still in awe of all the effort she's gone to for me.

Spinning me around, she helps me put the jacket on, then straightens everything, tweaking my shirt and collar until it's sitting just right.

"Now, I've got this scarf as well, but..." She tips her head, smiling as she checks out my necklace and brushes her thumb over the silver coyote emblem. "I don't think you need it."

Her smile is so kind. It reminds me of my Aunt Shayla, and I almost want to cry.

Shaking my head in wonder, I then flinch when there's a quick knock and the door opens. "Just me." Nylah bounces in wearing the cutest pair of jeans that are rolled up around her slim ankles. She's sporting a pair of black-and-white Oxfords and has a scarf around her neck. She's curled and coiffed her hair to look like a 1950s dame, and I swear she's the most beautiful girl I know.

"You look amazing." I drink her in, and she grins at me.

"And now it's my turn to do the same to you. Now, sit."

I do as I'm told, and I'm soon being worked on by both girls. Nylah's doing my makeup while Sienna deals with my hair, getting directions from Nylah about the best way to curl my fine locks.

It takes about twenty minutes, but I'm soon looking in the mirror and gasping.

I've been transformed into a poodle-skirt-wearing girl with my own pair of Oxfords.

The pink-and-black outfit hugs my body, made to fit me perfectly, and my hair has been curled and styled, draping around my shoulders with the front section swirled up and sitting on my head with enough hairspray and bobby pins that it's not moving an inch.

My eyes are made big and bold with eyeliner and mascara, and my lips are bright pink to match my outfit.

"Wow." It's all I can manage.

"You look amazing!" Sienna bobs on her feet, all giddy excitement. "This is gonna be the best night ever. Zoey is away with my parents for the weekend, and Zander looks hotter than the sun in his jeans and leather jacket. And the way you did his hair." She looks at Nylah with a grateful smile. "I feel like I'm dating Kenickie from *Grease.*"

"I knew you'd love that movie. So glad I made you watch it." Nylah laughs. "He totally looks like Kenickie. And my man looks like James Dean. Mmm." Her sound of appreciation makes me giggle. "He will definitely be getting some tonight." She winks at me. "Hopefully I can hold out until the end of the party."

Sienna laughs. "I'm not sure I can. I might just have to steal away for a quickie with Kenickie."

Both girls laugh and I can't help joining them, my cheeks flaming red before nerves start clattering through me.

"Thank you so much." I reach for their hands, and we stand in a little circle while I struggle not to be overcome with emotion. "This is so kind of you."

And no one other than my family has ever done anything this sweet and caring for me before.

"Hey." Nylah squeezes my hand with a tender smile. "It was really our pleasure. Wily's been so pumped getting this ready for you. And... you deserve this treat."

"Everyone deserves to be made to feel special on their birthday." Sienna grins.

I wince. "Mine was last week."

"This still counts." She gives me a peck on the cheek, then winks at me, and I'm pretty sure I'm getting my first girl crush.

Sienna and Nylah are amazing, and the thought of becoming friends with them makes my chest buzz, but... I'm not sure they'll ever like me enough to hang with me. They're just doing this for Wily, who they adore.

I have to accept and appreciate that.

And right now, it's time to leave this safe little room and head down to the party... and do what?

Talk to a bunch of people I don't know.

Is there dancing?

Oh shit, I hate dancing.

But it's so sweet that Wily's put this on for me, so I

paste on a smile and head downstairs, looking for *my* man. I just want his large hand to wrap around mine. Or maybe it can tuck around my waist, and he can hold me close and get me through this thing.

I'm halfway down the stairs when people start to notice me.

"You look amazing!" a girl I don't know calls up to me. She's standing next to a really tall guy who's dressed up like a cowboy and smiling at me. He raises his beer in my direction and shouts up, "Happy birthday!"

"Uh... thank you." I smile politely at the cute couple before walking down the rest of the stairs. "Do you know where Wily is?"

"I think I saw him heading down that way," the girl says.

"Try the kitchen." Tyrell raises his chin at me.

I smile my thanks, wanting to tell him he looks good, all dressed up like Ray Charles, but I can't find my voice.

This is overwhelming.

But at least the music's good. I bob my head to Little Richard's "Tutti Frutti" as I weave my way toward the kitchen.

I keep an eye out for Wily but can't see him immediately and have to stop and thank people for coming when they wish me happy birthday.

Seriously. Where are they all from?

Everyone at Football Frat must have invited their friends, and the house is humming.

And they all came for me.

Well, for Wily.

But Wily did this for me, and that really is so sweet. It almost makes me want to cry, and I can't wait to give him a solid thank-you kiss. I don't even care who's watching. He deserves it.

My lips twitch as I imagine myself boldly walking up to him, grabbing his face, and just going for it.

If I can find him.

Biting my bottom lip, I only just remember that I'm wearing lipstick and quickly rub my teeth, worried they'll be turning pink... when the last sound I ever want to hear sends a scratching shiver down my spine.

"Well, if it isn't the world's ugliest hippo, dressed up in a poodle skirt." Jade's voice is low and right in my ear. "Did you honestly think a little pink was going to make you look pretty?"

I spin around, my insides sinking when I notice all three of them lined up in front of me.

They're dressed as the Pink Ladies, and I can't *believe* they were invited.

Shit! I should have told Wily the truth. Does he even know they're here?

Why would he let Viper Girl in?

She's the one who insulted me right in front of him. He was livid.

"I don't think you three are supposed to be here," I try, looking around, desperate for my boyfriend to appear and get me out of this.

Jade steps a little closer and I back up, wary of the Solo cup she's holding and what might be in it. Flashes of moldy orange juice hit me, the remembered smell making my stomach turn.

I scratch my belly and shuffle back even farther. I'm in the kitchen now, and I look around, noticing a couple of hired kitchen hands and that's about it.

"Kitchen's off-limits, ladies." Someone walks in, kitted out in a chef's hat and looking like he's in charge.

"Sorry." I flush and make a beeline for the door, but the girls block my way, spitting little comments in my face as I try to push between them.

"You look ridiculous."

"This whole party is a joke."

"People are already mocking it."

"He's gonna dump your ass."

"You don't belong together."

"What are you even doing here, hippo?"

Their insults ring in my ears, making it impossible to hear the music or smile at anyone as I walk back through the house. People are touching my shoulders, my arms, laughing around me, shouting out words that I can't hear, and soon I'm not sure what's nice and what's not and...

And I can't do this!

The front door looms ahead of me and I make a break for it, flinging it open and rushing down the steps.

CHAPTER 51
WILY

"Satch!" I call her name the second I see her.

Why the hell is she bolting out the door so fast? Where's she going?

Damn, it's taken her forever to get ready. I wanted to wait outside her door like an eager puppy as the girls helped her, but then I got called away to deal with a toilet paper issue, and then someone smashed a bottle on the back lawn, so Zander and I quickly cleaned that up. Then I came back inside and rushed toward the living room, hoping to wait in the archway and see Satch coming down, but instead I see her running out the front door.

"Satch!" Chasing after her, I jump over the railing and land on the frosty grass, slipping in these stupid shoes before finally reaching her.

"Wait." I catch her wrist and pull her to a stop before she gets to the sidewalk. "Where are you going?"

Turning her toward me, I stare down at her pretty face and start to worry. Her plush pink lips are curving in the wrong direction, and as she shakes her head and pulls out of my hold, my stomach starts to sink.

She crosses her arms like she's putting on a suit of armor.

What the fuck is going on?

Trying to play it cool and hide my angst that she's not loving every second of the party, I keep my voice light and slide my hands into the pockets of my leather jacket.

"I've been looking all over for ya." I let my eyes travel the length of her body. She's all decked out, and with that jacket and that makeup... damn, she looks so fucking good.

I can't help a smile forming when I tell her, "You look amazing." Pulling my hands free, I unhook her arms and hold them wide so I can get the full effect of her outfit. My smile only gets bigger as I drink her in. "Seriously. You look so good. As soon as we get back inside, I'll have to take a picture. I promised your mom I'd..." My voice trails off.

She swallows, forcing a polite smile, and fuck, it hurts.

She hates the party.

Shit!

I thought she'd be into it, but I played this all wrong.

And now she wants to bail.

Fuck, I can't let that happen. Not when so many people have gone to so much effort.

But how do I coax her back inside?

"So... what are you doing out here?" I lean down, trying to catch her eye, but she looks past me at the house, her face scrunching into an even deeper frown before she dips her chin.

"Satch, baby, what's wrong? Do you not like the party?" It's impossible to hide my disappointment, and her head immediately pops up, her eyes wide with concern and maybe a touch of guilt.

"The party's amazing." She grabs my forearm, giving it a squeeze. "I can't believe you orchestrated all of this. I can't believe all of your friends went to so much effort for me."

My insides settle as I skim my knuckle down her cheek. "You deserve it."

She shakes her head, looking like she doesn't believe me. "It's a *lot* of effort. And money." She winces.

I want to tell her it's nothing. Seriously. It's no big deal. I've grown up around lavish parties my whole life, and this would be considered a cheap get-together in my mother's eyes.

But I don't want Satch to think she's not worth more than a cheap party, so I glance over my shoulder at the house and murmur, "It was worth it. For you." Turning back, I take her hands and give them a little swing. "But you're standing out here and not being part of it." My insides clench as I ask the question I don't really want to, because what if her answer means I have to take her away from this? Licking my bottom lip, I say it anyway. "Why aren't you in there having fun?"

Closing her eyes, she lets out a soft sigh. "I'm not very good in situations like this. Please don't get me wrong, I'm so touched that you would do this for me. I'm just not used to parties the way you are." She squirms and tries to let go of my hands, but I hold on, brushing my thumb across her knuckles.

"Satch."

"People are looking at me... and I know they think we shouldn't be together. You're too good for me, and—"

"What?" The sweet sentiment I was about to give her gets snatched away by a sharp irritation. "Why are you saying that?"

She sniffs and tugs her hands free with enough force that I have to let her go. Crossing her arms, she hunches her shoulders, and I fucking hate this.

Anger boils hot and fast as an ugly realization dawns. It sharpens my voice, and I end up snapping at her, "Did someone say that to you?"

She shakes her head, shrinking away from me.

Oh, fuck this...

Crouching down, I get in her face and whisper, "Satch, talk to me. Please."

"I don't want to make a big deal out it," she mumbles.

"This is *your* party, and if someone's saying nasty shit to you, then they can *fuck off!* I will go in there right now and I will drag them out of that house, because—"

"No!" Her head jolts up, her eyes bulging as she snatches my arm. "I don't want you to make a big scene or anything. They'll just cause trouble."

"They?" I spin to glare at the house. "Who?"

"It doesn't matter."

"It *does* matter." I turn to face her again. "Satch, no one should ever be saying mean shit to you, especially when it's your night. I'm not gonna let anyone screw with it. Now, you tell me who said it and they're *gone*."

Her face bunches into a pained frown. "I don't want you to do that. I don't want a big scene." Her voice catches, and she starts blinking like she's fighting tears. "Please, Wily, can we just forget this? I just..." She lets out a short breath. "I don't want everyone talking about it, and then I have to go to class on Monday and they'll—" Her voice catches, a panicked little sob ripping out of her.

"Okay." I rub her arm, desperate to ease her stress. "It's okay. Shhh, baby, it's okay."

Tucking her against my chest, I cup the back of her head and hold her close.

I wonder if she can hear how fast my heart is beating.

I'm furious with whoever told her we shouldn't be together. What the actual fuck!

She sniffs against my leather jacket, her breathing starting to slow. When I lean back, I gently take her arms and lean down so I can see her face again. "What do you want me to do?"

"Nothing." Her voice is barely more than a whisper.

Pursing my lips, I stand tall and study her. "I'm only gonna agree to that if you come back inside with me. People want to celebrate with you. This is your night."

She looks doubtful when she flicks her gaze up to mine.

My eyebrows crinkle with concern. Shit. Is she gonna ask me to take her back to her dorm? I really don't want to do that.

"Please tell me who they are so we can kick them out," I try again. "I don't even understand why they'd come if they don't like you. I mean, what the shit?"

She sighs and murmurs, "They like *you* and don't want me taking you off the market."

My jaw clenches, anger scorching me. It's an effort not to shout, *"That's not their decision!"* Thankfully, I manage to control my tone—because it's not her fault people are idiots—and grit out, "It's not up to them."

"But I don't belong here." She glances at the house, then back down to the ground. "I should just go."

"Don't talk bullshit," I rush out. "You belong with me."

"I don't."

"Yes, you do." I take her face in my hands, needing to stop this shit. Guiding her face up, I lean close. "You're mine, Satch."

Her eyes glass over, her lips trembling as she sucks in a ragged breath. "But I shouldn't be. I'm the wrong girl. You should be with someone pretty and sporty and cool—"

I cut her off with a kiss. I don't know what else to do, but I hate the words coming out of her mouth. How can she think that shit?

She *is* pretty, and sure, she's not the sportiest girl I know, but she's fucking cool! I love being with her. Why is she letting narrow-minded shit-stirrers mess with her head?

I cup the back of her curled hair, deepening the kiss so there can be no doubt on this. But she doesn't respond with her usual fervor. There's something hesitant about her kiss, like she's not sure she should be doing it.

Fuck those people. I wish she'd just tell me who they are so I can go in and deal with them... and then we can get on with our night together.

Pulling away, I hold her close, resting my chin on top of her head as I wrap my arms around her. "I want you. And I don't give a fuck what anyone else thinks. We're great together."

She steps out of my embrace and looks up at me, tears still glistening in her eyes.

"They don't know you." I brush my thumb under her eye. "But I do. I see you, Satch, and I love what I see."

Her lips tremble into a watery smile, and I lean forward and kiss her again. This time when I try to deepen the kiss, she meets me halfway, stroking her tongue against mine. This time, her arms wrap around my neck.

Lifting her off her feet, I keep the kiss going, hoping everyone in the fucking house can see us, because I'm claiming this woman for all to see.

She is mine, and whoever talked shit into her ear can fuck off.

Or have their faces rubbed in it.

Placing Satch back on her feet, I smirk down at her and waggle my eyebrows.

"What?" She lets out a breathy laugh. "What's that look for?"

Taking her hand, I thread our fingers together. "I have a challenge for you."

"Really?"

"Yeah." Glancing back at the house, I turn and put my arm around her shoulders so we're facing the party together. "Let's go back in there and show those doubters that we don't give a shit what they think."

Her breath catches, but she wraps her arm around my waist, gripping the side of my leather jacket.

"Let's kiss and laugh together. Let's spend the entire party showing everyone in there that you and I are made for each other." She glances up at me, and I grin down at her. "You up for it?"

Her smile is nervous, cut short when she sinks her teeth into her bottom lip.

I brush my thumb over it, then push my fingers on either side of her mouth, making her smile.

She giggles, and the grin turns genuine.

"Come on, let me take you inside and show everyone how much I love my girlfriend."

I kiss the top of her head and make a move toward the house.

It's safe to say my breath is on hold as I wait for her to resist me, but then she takes a step forward, then another.

"That's my girl." I smile down at her, pulling her up the stairs and walking back inside.

Fuck whoever said that to her.

I still wish she'd tell me so I could kick their asses, but if she doesn't want me to cause a scene, then fine.

But I'm gonna make sure this whole fucking party knows that she's mine—and that's exactly the way I want it to be.

CHAPTER 52
ELIZABETH

I'm doing this for Wily.

Because I couldn't handle that crushed puppy dog look on his face when he thought I didn't like his party.

Of course I love it!

I just wish there weren't so many people here, and I wish to God that he'd never invited Jade and her friends.

Picturing how that conversation went down is easy.

She would have put on her sweet "You're such a great boyfriend" routine, and he would have casually said, "You should come help us celebrate."

It wouldn't have occurred to him that they could ruin my night because I've never told him what Jade did to me. What she and her new crew *continue* to do to me.

And I can't go saying anything now.

I can tell he's scanning the crowd, trying to figure out who was hassling me, but I seriously don't want some big incident that will immediately land on the rumor mill, and then I'll have to spend the next few weeks fending off gossip as the story grows into something grotesque and overly dramatic.

Ugh!

I have lived through way too many years of whispers chasing me down hallways. I don't want or need that here.

I just have to keep my mouth shut and stay glued to Wily's side. They wouldn't dare say or do anything nasty in front of him. Not when Jade's still set on making him her man.

But he's mine.

That's what he keeps telling me, and so I cling to his fingers as he pulls me back through the door.

"Everything okay?" Zander's the first to approach us.

Wily gives him a stiff nod but then leans forward and whispers something in his ear. Zander's eyes dart to me, a fierce look crossing his face as he clenches his jaw and grits out, "Will do. I'll tell the guys."

"Tell the guys what?" I quietly ask, worry coursing through me in a sickening wave.

Wily smiles down at me, then kisses the top of my head. "Don't worry about it. Come on, let's go sing."

"Sing?" I squeak as he pulls me into the living room and finds Nylah and Carson messing around with a karaoke machine.

"Is it good to go?" Wily asks, and I start chewing my bottom lip.

Yes, I adore karaoke. It's one of my favorite things to do. But in front of all these people?

"Are you sure about this?" I softly ask, but he doesn't hear me. He's too busy leaning forward to whisper something in Carson's ear.

The guy's head jolts back, and he whips a quick look at me before his face goes just as hard as Zander's did.

"Who?" he seethes.

Wily shrugs. "Just keep an eye out, okay?"

"Of course, man." He raises his chin at his friend, then shoots me a stiff smile.

"Wily." I tug on my boyfriend's hand. "What are you saying?"

"Just asking them to look out for my girl." He winks, and I give him a pained frown. "Don't worry." He rests his hand on my neck. "They'll be subtle."

"But—"

"Okay, I think it's working now." Nylah stands up, brushing her hands on the back of her pants. "I'm no Grady Newman, but the plugs seem to all be in the right place."

"Where is Grady?" I look around, and now it's Wily's turn to look pained.

"He couldn't make it. I'm sorry."

"No, that's okay." I smile, trying to brighten my expression. "There are so many people here. You must have invited the whole school." I punch out a laugh, and he gives me a *"you're cute"* smile before turning back to grab the mic off Nylah.

"You should know this one." She winks at us, and before I know it, "You're the One That I Want" is playing, and I'm thrust into a duet with my boyfriend.

He's ridiculous, not knowing the lyrics and hamming up the song when he can't keep up. I can't help laughing out my lines, keeping my eyes trained on him and my back turned to the crowd that's cheering us on.

"Go, Sandy!" someone shouts from the back.

Wait, that's me. I'm Sandy in this duet. Are they... cheering me?

I glance over my shoulder, surprised by the sea of grinning faces.

And then it's my turn again, and I lift the mic to my lips and come in on the beat.

"Whoo!" Nylah cheers. "Girl, you can sing!" She looks so impressed that I sing a little louder and find the cheers crescendoing.

Is this really happening?

I eventually start to belt out the tune in earnest, getting into this song I love so much and trying to make up for Wily's terrible pitchiness.

He laughs at the hecklers, singing even louder until I can't help a wince.

When the song comes to an end, I grin up at him, and he kisses me soundly on the mouth while people applaud and whoop.

"Another one!" someone shouts.

"But take that mic off Wily!"

My boyfriend throws his head back with a laugh.

"Yeah, do us all a favor. We just want Satch!"

My eyes bulge and I turn, trying to figure out who just said that.

"Satch! Satch! Satch!"

"W-what are they doing?"

Wily leans down to grin at me. "They want to hear you sing, baby. You up for it?"

I blink, not really sure what to say. No one's ever chanted my name before. No one's ever wanted *me*.

"You sound amazing!" Nylah grabs my attention and

points to the screen. "Do you know this one?" I nod, and she laughs. "Yes! It's all you, girl."

Before I can protest, she presses Play on one of my favorite songs ever, and I just can't help myself. Closing my eyes, I let the beat kick in, bobbing my head as the music swells... and then words ease into the room smooth as honey.

"When the night... has come..."

The room seems to go still around me, but I keep singing anyway, swaying to "Stand by Me" and loving the sound rising through my body.

When I get to the chorus, Wily comes and stands right beside me, gazing down at me with an affectionate smile that makes my chest swell.

"So, darlin', darlin'..." I sing the chorus to him, and he threads our fingers together, kissing my knuckles and making the rest of the room disappear.

It's just us, swaying to this smooth beat while I ask him to stand beside me and know that he will.

How did I get so lucky?

When the song finishes, another cheer erupts throughout the room, breaking me out of my loved-up bubble.

Wily's arms come around me, and he lifts me off my feet. "That was incredible!" He kisses me again, then beams down at me like I'm the first prize he just won, and I can't help a soft giggle.

"One more! One more!" Sienna makes her way up to the front, stepping up beside Nylah and hunting down a new song.

I'm not sure I'm ready for another one, not with all of

these eyes on me, but then my mom's absolute favorite starts to play, and I have to do it for her.

So, I sing "Dream a Little Dream of Me," which apparently is also Zoey's favorite. Sienna pulls Zander into a slow dance, and Carson and Nylah follow suit. Soon the living room is swaying with dancing couples, and it makes me feel like a jazz singer in a bar.

Wily's recording me and I smile at his phone, knowing he's gonna be sending this to my parents. They'll love it.

When the tune comes to an end, I get lavished with a ton more praise, plus a big hug from Sienna, before finally handing the mic to someone else.

Two new people jump up. I have no idea who they are, but they're having fun massacring "La Bamba." I mean, their pronunciation is flawless, but neither of them can hold the tune. The tall cowboy and his girlfriend are whistling and laughing at them, hassling the... brother and sister maybe? They look pretty similar.

"You were so good." Wily catches my attention, leading me into the dining room and passing me a drink.

I sniff it, then take a little sip, grateful it's not beer. I really can't stand that stuff.

"It's Dr Pepper." He winks at me. "I know my girl."

Smiling up at him, I can feel myself finally starting to relax.

I have no idea where Team Evil 2.0 went while I was singing. I had my eyes closed most of the time so I wouldn't have to see them.

Maybe they've left.

Maybe they saw Wily kissing me in front of everybody and knew the battle was over.

I won.

You never win. Keep your guard up.

Sipping the drink, I sway to the beat beside Wily, who's leaning against the wall, smiling at people who keep greeting him, then glancing down to check on me.

"You feeling a little better?"

"Yeah." I let out a shaky laugh. "Singing was fun."

"You're so amazing at it." He grins. "We'll do some more soon, and then it's cake time."

"Cake? Really? You've gone all out."

"Of course I have. I want this night to be the best for you." He looks around, his eyes grazing the room as his expression gets a little tense. "Those people who were hassling you... they still here?"

I don't want to look and give away the culprits, but his expectant face forces me to do a quick sweep of the room. "I don't think so. Maybe your singing scared them off." I throw in a little joke to lighten the mood, and it works like a charm.

Grabbing me around the waist, he tickles me, and I nearly spill my drink all over him. He laughs, giving my neck a raspberry that makes me squawk.

"Stop," I laugh. "I take it back. Your singing is amazing."

"That's a bit of bullshit right there." He snickers against my neck, and I wrap my arms around him, wishing I had even an eighth of his confidence. He seems to have no problem owning his weaknesses.

My heart fills with affection for this incredible man, and I hold him a little tighter.

"Love you," I whisper, brushing my hands through the back of his hair.

He leans away from me, rubbing his nose against mine before our little moment is shattered by one of Wily's football buddies. He slaps my boyfriend on the back, pulling us apart so they can talk about the game for a minute. I hold Wily's hand, listening in and managing to keep up. Playing *Madden* has taught me so much about the game. Not to mention all of the conversations I've had with Wily about football.

As they continue talking, I start to relax even more, actually getting pumped to maybe do another singing session. That was pretty fun, and people cheering me on... that part felt pretty good too. I'm not used to being lavished with positive attention from people who aren't my family.

It felt weird.

But like a really cool weird.

The kind of weird I could get used to.

Maybe it *is* okay to have eyes on me sometimes.

"Good talking to you, man." Wily wraps up his chat while taking the cup from my hand and placing both our finished drinks on the sideboard. "I gotta go dance with my girl now."

"Cool." The guy smiles at me, then turns back to the table...and my insides start to spasm.

"Uh..." I wince, so not up for dancing in front of everybody. Wily will probably try to pull off some crazy rock-n-roll moves, and I don't want to embarrass him with my terrible lack of coordination. "I need to pee." I attempt to get out of it and start making a beeline for the bathroom. "Back in a sec."

"Cool." He follows me with his gaze, then starts

shifting through the crowd after me. He's watching me like he's my bodyguard, and I don't mind it so much.

He's so big and strong. He can protect me from anything.

That's the way he's making me feel as I slip past a couple making out, and then a group of girls who are preening their '50s costumes and hair.

They all look amazing, like they're about to attend that dance from *Back to the Future*.

Smiling at them when they tell me "Happy birthday," I give them a soft thanks before trying to open the bathroom door. It's occupied.

"Give us a minute," someone calls from inside.

I wince, stepping back from the door and checking over my shoulder to find Wily caught in a conversation with a couple who are dressed up like Archie and Betty.

His smile is so beautiful, and whatever he just said made them all laugh.

Aw, man, I don't want to disappoint him, but I so don't want to dance.

Maybe if I take my sweet time, he'll forget that option and just go straight to the singing.

Easing away from the bathroom door, I head down the corridor. I don't really need to pee; I just need a moment to myself.

Glancing around the corner, I spot a door that I think leads to a den or office or something. I haven't been in there before, and the sign says Do Not Enter, but it's probably okay for me to hide in there for just a second, right? I saw the stairwell had been roped off when I came back inside, so they've probably just closed off the bedrooms and office to protect their stuff. They know me. I'm not going to do anything.

Clearing my throat, I ease past another couple making out against the wall and am relieved when I try the door handle and it turns easily.

Slipping inside, I close it behind me, locking it for some privacy before resting my head against the wood... and immediately sensing that I've just made the biggest mistake.

CHAPTER 53
WILY

Leaning my shoulder against the wall, I wait near the bathroom, far enough away not to be a creeper, but close enough that I can be by Satch's side within seconds of her getting out.

I need to thank Sienna for arranging that jacket for her. I love that my pet name is plastered across my girl's back. I'm kind of tempted to get a Coyote one made, and we can be that couple who wears matching clothes.

So cheesy, but damn if that doesn't make me smile.

I can picture walking down the street with her in our matching jackets and can't help a soft snicker, my smile growing wide.

"Hey, Wiles." I slap a few hands and give out a few fist bumps while I wait for my girl.

She's taking her sweet time, but I think she's just nervous to dance with me.

I grin, shaking my head. She's always so unsure of herself, but she seriously has nothing to worry about. I'm the one with the clompy feet and no rhythm. All I want to do is wrap my arms around her and sway like we did on the football field while people sing bad karaoke.

Is that too much to ask?

I smile at the question and glance at the bathroom door again.

"It's going well, brah." Tyrell stops beside me. "And so far, people seem to be cool."

"Yeah." I nod. "Maybe those douche nuggets who were hassling her left. She said she didn't see them when I asked before."

"That's good. Now we can relax and just enjoy this thing."

A smile stretches across my face as I go to give him a light fist bump.

But shit.

We spoke too soon...

Something crashes at the end of the hallway, and I whip around in time to see Satch stumbling around a waiter who just dropped an entire tray of food.

He frowns down at the mess, obviously muttering something, and she blurts an apology over her shoulder as she bolts toward the kitchen like she's fleeing a crime scene.

I thought she was in the bathroom.

"What the fuck?" I race forward, jumping over the mess and glancing down the hallway. Three girls are huddled in the doorway of the den.

I take them in for a second, not even recognizing them until Jade turns face me properly. I glare at her, anger firing through me.

Was it her?

Was it fucking them hassling Satch before?

Jade's face flushes and she bites her lips together before putting on a pretty smirk.

Growling in my throat, I'm torn between storming toward them, demanding to know what they did, and chasing after my girl.

But, of course, I have to go for Satch, so I run into the kitchen and notice the back door gaping open.

"Did anyone come through here?" I bark at the kitchen helper who's just walked in.

She gives me a worried frown. "I'm not sure. Sorry."

Shit, Satch, where the fuck have you gone?

Groaning, I race out the back door.

"Satch?" I call but get zero reply. The lights from the kitchen are illuminating the rectangular patch of grass back here, and I can't see her on it. Turning right, I'm about to tear around the side of the house, hoping she hasn't taken off.

"What just happened?" Sienna appears in the kitchen doorway. "Did someone hurt Satch?"

"I don't know!" I fling my arms wide. "I can't find her!"

"Someone said they saw her crying." Sienna walks down the stairs looking just as worried as I feel.

Fuck, fuck, fuck!

I run a hand through my hair, trying to think of all the best hiding spots around here.

"Can you check around that side of the house?" I point to my right. "I'll go this way."

"Of course." Sienna veers to her left, and I turn for the driveway again.

Pausing at the edge of the house, I peer into the darkness, wondering if she's hiding behind a car... and that's when I hear a whimper behind me.

Spinning, I run for Zander and Sienna's sleepout and press my ear against the wood.

A muffled sob reaches me, and I wrench the door open, stepping into the darkness.

"Satch?" I whisper.

"No." She sobs. "Go away."

"Baby." I step forward, kicking my toe on something and grunting while I fumble for the light.

I don't know where any of the fucking switches are in this place!

Yanking out my phone, I turn on the flashlight and sweep the room until I illuminate my destroyed girlfriend who is sitting on the end of the double bed, her arms wrapped around her as she tries to hold her torn outfit in place.

What the actual FUCK!

Anger rips through me in a wave so toxic, I can barely see straight. Those girls are finished. I fucking swear!

"What happened?" I manage to grit out as I try to approach her slowly and not act like the raging bull I feel like.

Flicking on the lamp beside the bed, I crouch in front of her, taking in the tattered top. Sections of it have been torn apart, leaving her exposed and wounded. And there's a cut right through the black poodle that had been sewn onto her skirt. The pink fabric is torn right up to the waistband, exposing the layers of petticoat underneath.

"Where's your jacket?" I reach for her, but she flinches away from me. "What happened?"

She darts a look at me, and that vulnerable gaze is fucking slaying me right now.

She whimpers. "Mom spent hours on this outfit." Her

voice catches on a sobbing hiccup. It makes me want to fucking cry myself.

"She's not... she's..." I suck in a breath, trying to calm my raging emotions. "She's not gonna care about the skirt. She'll want to know that you're okay."

Satch shakes her head, covering her mouth with her hand.

She's trembling from head to foot, and this is fucking killing me. "Baby." I reach for her slowly, so she won't flinch, and very gently rest my hands on her arms. "Did they hurt you?"

She sniffs and shakes her head, but I don't believe her.

Rising a little higher, I check her neck and notice three red welts. Nail marks. They must have done that when they were tearing at her dress.

I brush my finger gently over them, and she leans away from me.

"I want to go."

"Yeah." I sigh, rubbing her arms. She's shaking so much that she must be cold, but her skin is all red, and when I brush over her exposed shoulder, she's hot to the touch.

She leans away from me, still grappling to keep her outfit in place. The shirt is totally torn down the front, exposing her bra. She must be so fucking humiliated right now.

I'm gonna end those bitches!

Jumping up, I pull off my leather jacket and drape it around her shoulders. She cinches it tight around herself, holding it together with fisted fingers.

I take a seat beside her and rub her back. "Why don't

you hide out here for just a minute, and I'm gonna go and—"

"No! I'm leaving now." She stands up, her voice trembling as she shuffles for the door. "I'm going back to my dorm."

"But I can take you. Let me just—"

"I can't do this." She stops, turning to face me. Her expression is hollow, her haunted eyes making my chest hurt. "You tried to convince me that it's possible for me to fit into your world, but you're wrong." Swiping a trembling finger under her nose, she sniffs and keeps going. "Throwing a party like this just proves it. I don't fit. I never *fit!*" She shouts the last word, and I blink at her sudden ferocity.

I've never seen her like this before.

Holding my hands up, I slowly stand and walk toward her. "You do fit. People are stoked to be here for you. They were cheering you on. They want to get to know you."

"No, they don't! They're just being nice to me because of you. Because they care about you. But I'm nothing to these people." She points toward the house.

"You're wrong." I reach for her, but she bats my hand away. It fucking hurts, but I get that she's going through shit right now, so I raise my hands again and tell her gently, "Look, I get it, okay? There are some really bitchy girls in there, but they won't be staying. I wish I'd known who they were because I would have told them to get the fuck out that first time. I shouldn't have been trying to make you prove anything. I should have protected you better. I'm sorry."

She doesn't say anything, and I stand my ground,

desperate to pull her against my chest and cocoon her within my arms.

Her chest rises and falls, her puffy red eyes glaring at the floor before she finally looks up at me.

"You get it?" she asks softly, then lets out a wispy scoff. "How can you possibly get it?" The words wobble and shake out of her as she flicks her hand at me. "Everybody loves you! You're gorgeous and friendly and popular. You have no idea what it's like to be me because you've never experienced open disgust or repulsion before. You don't know what it's like to do absolutely nothing wrong and get treated like an outcast." She sucks in a ragged breath. "So stop standing there acting like you understand! Because you *don't!*" She screams the last word at me before another sob pops out, and then she's running from the garage.

I'm frozen still by her wrath.

Or is it her agony?

The torment on her face. What she just screamed at me.

I can't move for a second.

All I can do is stand here, my chest heaving as I try to process this shit.

Fuck. She's right.

I don't get it.

I've never been treated like that before.

"Shit," I whisper under my breath and take off after her. "Satch!" I run onto the driveway just in time to see Zander's SUV pulling onto the street. "Satch!"

I chase after it, but Zander stops me when I reach the curb.

"Was she in there?" I shout, shoving him back when he rests a hand on my chest.

"Sienna's taking her back to her dorm," he calmly explains, as if it doesn't hurt like a bullet through the chest.

"Fuck!" I shout, kicking the freezing sidewalk.

"I'm sorry, man." Zander gives me a sad smile. "I don't know what went down, but—"

I growl, stalking away from him and back into the house.

My eyes rove the partygoers. Most of them are oblivious to what happened to my girl, but they are about to fucking find out.

Shoving my way between people, I soon see those three demons laughing around the drinks table. I can't believe they had the nerve to fucking stay. Even after I'd seen them huddled in that doorway snickering.

Approaching like a freight train, I stop just in front of them, and it's taking everything in me not to manhandle these bitches out of here.

"Oh." Jade turns around, feigning like she's only just noticed me. "Hey, Wily."

Her glossy smile is flirtatious, and a fresh wave of rage bubbles through me. And it only gets hotter when her friends turn to check me out and I spot the viper. The fucking *viper*!

My eyes flash at her and she swallows, quickly looking down at the glass in her hand.

Snatching it out of her grasp, I thump it onto the table behind her and snarl in a low, dangerous voice, "Get out."

"Excuse me?" She tries to look like the innocent victim, but I'm not putting up with this shit.

They terrorized my girlfriend. I don't know exactly what they did other than ripping her dress and scratching her, but... fuck.

Those nail marks flash through my mind, and it takes every ounce of control not to snatch their arms and haul them out of this party.

Instead, I have to settle for yelling in their faces.

"Get out!" I look across the three of them, and they actually have the fucking audacity to look surprised by my request. "Get the fuck out of my house!" I point to the door.

The people around us go still, every head turning in our direction as whispers travel throughout the party.

Jade blinks, swallowing and darting her eyes behind me.

Humiliation smothers her and she flicks her hair over her shoulder, trying and failing to look unaffected.

"Are you seriously going to make me tell you again?" I growl.

They jump sideways, scuttling into one another and clumping together at the end of the table.

"GET OUT!" I roar, and finally they get a fucking clue and yelp, scurrying out of the house like they're being chased by a swarm of bees.

People clear a pathway for them, and the sudden silence that follows my outburst is overpowering.

I can't take this shit.

There's no recovering from this point, so I thrust a finger at the door. "Party's over! Get out! Everybody just get out!"

People gape at me, no one moving an inch as I stand here glaring at them all.

"Time to go, people." Tyrell starts clearing the room, ushering partygoers calmly to the door while Zander heads into the living room to do the same thing.

Although the upstairs has been roped off, Carson jumps over the barrier and heads to the second floor, making sure the house is completely empty.

It takes fifteen minutes, but soon all we're left with is my football crew and Nylah. She stands beside Carson, shooting him a worried frown, and I pull out my phone, trying to call Satch.

It goes straight to voicemail, and I throw my phone onto the couch with a snarl before plunking onto the cushions and glaring at the karaoke machine.

So much for making my girl's night.

I was trying to do something special for her, and it went to complete shit.

The others start slowly cleaning up around me, and I know I should give them a hand, but I can't move.

All I can do is sit here stewing and waiting for Sienna to get back.

CHAPTER 54
ELIZABETH

We drive back to my dorm in silence.

Well, me sniffing and whimpering, clutching Wily's leather jacket as I vacillate from guilt at yelling at him to utter justification. He couldn't stand there saying he got it.

He doesn't get it.

Sienna probably doesn't get it either.

How could they possibly?

They don't know what it's like to be surrounded by people yet completely alone. There's no way they've been pointed at, laughed at, whispered about on a daily basis. They don't know what it's like to have everyone in your class conspiring against you to pull off a "hilarious" prank that's funny for everyone but you.

Pausing at the intersection, Sienna steals a look at me. I just happen to look up at the same time, and her sad smile makes me feel like shit.

I turn to stare out the window, a fresh wave of tears taking me out as I relive that horrible moment in the den when I locked the door and turned to find Team Evil 2.0 all standing in there.

It was like my personal nightmare come to life.

They spotted me at the same time, their surprise at my interruption turning to narrowed glares of triumph.

The way their eyes glinted as they approached me was terrifying, and I whipped around, scrambling to unbolt the door, but Kelsey's hand slapped against the wood while Viper Girl fisted my jacket and tried to wrench me around.

Jade got in on the action, tugging on my jacket until it was falling off my shoulders.

Kelsey cackled, leaning against the door and fisting the fabric so my hands were cuffed behind me.

"Please just let me go." I wish my voice had been stronger, but my heart was lodged in my throat, making it impossible to be. "Just let me go," I whimpered.

"Nice singing." Jade's eyes were glinting in a way that made my stomach drop down to my knees. "Everybody just *loves* you, don't they?"

I swallowed.

"If only they knew the truth." Her scathing glare traveled down my body then, her mocking snicker like a slap to the face. "That you're nothing more than a fat loser whose mommy has to make her pathetic clothes because she can't afford to buy any at a store."

Reaching for my neckline, she scratched my skin with her red-painted talons before fisting the fabric and yanking on it.

I gasped, relieved the precious outfit Mom had made didn't tear. It dug into my neck and really hurt, but it hadn't actually torn. "Please just let me go."

"Get some scissors." Jade smirked at Viper Girl, whose look of gleeful delight made my stomach pitch.

"No!" I tried to protest, wrestling against Kelsey's hold on me, but she used her shoulder to shove me back against the door.

Jade jumped in, pushing me hard while Viper Girl rummaged through the desk drawers and, much to my horror, found a pair of scissors.

"Yes!" Her triumphant gloating was as ugly as the expression on her face when I started crying and wrestling in vain.

They didn't relent, using their pointy knees and scratchy nails to pin me to the door so Viper Girl could snip the neckline, and Jade could finally have her satisfaction.

The tearing fabric was no doubt music to her ears.

As was the wail I released when I gazed down and saw my mother's hard work torn to shreds and my bra and pudgy waist exposed to the room.

"Ewww, gross." Kelsey looked me over like I was a blob of pus while Viper Girl started snickering and shaking her head.

Reaching for the bottom of my skirt, she cut and slashed with those little scissors until my poor poodle was sliced in half. The ripping of that pink fabric as she tore it apart decimated a piece of my soul.

I'm not sure I'd ever felt more broken than in that moment.

"Now he'll know the truth." Jade stepped away from me. "Now they'll all know." Smirking at me, she raised her chin at Kelsey, who finally let me go, but not before yanking the jacket off my wrists and shoving me away from the door.

The lock unbolted with a loud click and I stared at the handle, knowing I had to make my escape. But the idea of walking out there in my tatters was beyond humiliating. Pulling up the torn fabric with trembling hands, I tried to cover myself as best as I could.

The girls started to laugh at my lame attempts, and I had to get out of there before they did any more damage.

But how?

I couldn't even remember how I did it. I think my mind has already blanked out that harrowing escape through the house and into the shadows of the garage.

Zander and Sienna's special sleepout.

Shit.

"I'm sorry I invaded your space," I quickly murmur to Sienna, figuring I can at least get that out to the way.

"That's okay." Her voice is gentle. Kind. "I don't mind. I'm glad you could go in there to gather yourself for a second."

I can't help a humorless laugh.

Gather myself?

I've never felt more untethered in my life.

"I'm so sorry this happened to you at your birthday party."

A sigh rattles out of me. "This is why I never have them."

"What do you mean?" She glances at me, her voice surprised but sharp, her gaze intelligent. Alert.

I'm not gonna be able to pull the wool over her eyes.

And I don't even want to.

I honestly have nothing left right now. My humiliation is complete, so she may as well know the truth.

My face bunches, my voice starting to wobble all over again. "Ever since I was a kid, I've just... struggled with people my age." I sniff. "I don't know why Jade decided to make me her target, but—"

"Wait, was she one of those girls tonight?" Sienna's voice pitches in surprise.

I nod.

"You know them?"

It takes me a second to answer, but eventually I manage to confess. "We grew up together. Jade and me. Fledgling's a small town, and none of our parents moved away, so we were just in each other's lives. Everybody knows everybody in Fledgling." My voice is raw. Hollow.

Sienna pulls the car into a parking space outside Buckley Hall and leaves the engine running so the heater stays on. Turning to face me, she silently tells me to continue.

I have no idea why I do.

I never tell anyone this stuff, but my insides are shattered. Fragile. And I can't seem to stop myself.

"She and her friends were a year below me in school, but they had enough influence that they managed to turn most of the student body against me. Even the kids who probably would have been nice to me were too afraid to show it. I was their favorite sport, you know? They didn't want to come within firing range."

"Did you tell anybody?" Sienna softly asks.

I shrug. "I tried at first, but a little harmless name-calling? I was the one who needed to toughen up, you know? Grow a thicker skin. Sticks and stones and all that shit." My voice rings with a bitter edge, but I can't help it. "They knew how to put on their pretty smiles when they needed to and make me feel like I was blowing things way out of proportion."

"That sucks," Sienna mutters. "I can't believe... the adults in your life didn't do more." Her voice is softly cautious, like she's not trying to insult my parents, but she's pissed off that they didn't act more assertively on my behalf.

"I didn't tell them everything," I explain. "I didn't want my parents to worry. Me hurting hurt them, so I just tried to ignore it. Keep to myself, play the safe game, and on those days they got me... try to keep as much of my dignity intact as I could." I sniff, slashing a tear off my cheek as my insides recoil at the few times I did try to break free. Like when I took a risk and helped Peyton Feldman with his homework. What an epic backfire that was.

And now Wily's become another one.

Shit.

He means a million times more to me than Peyton ever will. Why couldn't they just let me have him?

Why does Jade always want what I have?

Why can't she just leave me alone!

Sienna's quiet sadness seems to permeate the car, and for some reason, I talk into it. Like, it's here already, so why not make it a few degrees colder, a couple of tons heavier.

"When I came here, I thought I'd be free of them. And last year, I had the chance to breathe for the first time in years. I didn't make any close friends or anything, but... I could walk this campus without looking over my shoulder all the time." My voice catches and my chin starts to bunch. "And then this year, I spotted Jade in my first week back, and she had these new friends... who are just like her old ones." I shake my head, my voice turning into a squeak. "I thought she was going to college in Denver." I start to cry in earnest. "And I haven't been able to tell anyone, because I don't want my parents freaking out. It was horrible for them watching me go through this in high school. They tried to protect me but didn't want me hiding away from the world, you know? So I just had to keep going. And I made it. I thought I'd made it." I whimper. "But Jade is always so strategic. She knows how to wait and pounce when the timing is just right. When her pranks can do the most damage. And she just has this way of convincing everyone to go along with her."

I cover my face, my shoulders shaking as I let out a couple of keening wails that turn into gut-wrenching sobs.

"Oh, sweetie," Sienna whispers, wrapping her arm around my shoulders and resting her cheek against the top of my head.

I let her hold me because I can't stop crying enough to pull away from her.

She doesn't say anything, just squeezes my shoulder and stays the course until my tears are under control.

With my stomach jerking, I sit up and reach for the door handle. "I should go."

"I can walk you up to your room." Sienna's already out her door, not taking no for an answer.

I really don't want her to, but when she helps me out of the passenger side and then wraps her arm around my shoulders again, I take it.

We shuffle up to my room together, taking the elevator in silence and not saying a word until I've unlocked my door.

I peer into my safe space, sadness sweeping through me as I picture Wily in here. His big body and bright smile used to fill this room so easily.

I don't know if it ever will again.

Will he honestly want me after I yelled in his face like that? I basically screamed at him.

Squeezing my eyes against the heavy dose of regret, I then have to counter the tidal wave of humiliation that follows.

How am I ever going to look him in the eye again?

I'm mortified.

Those girls destroyed me tonight.

And they know it.

And Wily knows it.

"Hey." Sienna rubs my back, getting my attention. "Can I get you anything? Do you want a shower or just to go straight to bed? What can I do for you?"

"Nothing," I croak. "I'll be okay." I let out a dry, wispy laugh. "I always am."

Sienna shifts to stand in front of me, gently holding my shoulders. "It's okay not to be."

Her eyes are so sweet and tender, her face the picture of sympathy.

I look away from it and shake my head.

"What those girls did to you tonight was completely unacceptable. That wasn't a prank, it was outright cruelty... and destruction of property, I might add." Her tone gets deep and sharp. "The way they tormented you all those years. That can't stand," she clips. "Wily will not put up with that shit. And neither will I."

I can't help a scoff. "There's nothing you can do. There's nothing anyone can do."

"Yes, there is."

"No, Sienna." I step out of her reach, crossing my arms. Wily's jacket is huge on me, and my hands disappear into the sleeves before I tuck them under my armpits. "Can you just go? Please."

She gives me a reluctant frown. "But—"

"Please." I'm begging now, and I don't even care. I just need to be left alone.

With an unhappy sigh, she moves for my door, pausing to ask me the worst question ever. "What should I tell Wily?"

I shrug, not even sure what to say.

"He's going to be worried about you."

My chest hurts, my belly jerking. "He shouldn't have to put up with it. He was trying to do something really nice for me, and it blew up. Things around me always blow up."

"Not because of you." Sienna's voice is strong with conviction. "It's because of *them*. Not you."

Dipping my chin, I can't respond.

I don't have the energy to disagree with her.

I'm not a fighter, and those girls proved it yet again tonight.

"I'll figure out something," Sienna softly murmurs. "Take care of yourself, okay?"

I glance up in time to see her kind, sad smile one more time before she disappears out the door.

It clicks and automatically locks behind her while I sag onto the edge of my bed. Covering my eyes with my hand, I suck in a few shaky breaths, then start crying all over again.

CHAPTER 55
WILY

Waiting for Sienna to get back was torture.

I ended up pacing because I didn't know what the fuck else to do, and then Zander got annoyed and shoved a broom in my hand.

"Make yourself useful before you drive us all batshit crazy," he growled, clearly out of patience with me.

So here I am, sweeping crumbs into piles in the dining room while the staff I hired finish up in the kitchen and the rest of the guys rearrange furniture and get the house back to what it looked like this morning.

"What would you like us to do about the cake?" A voice makes me spin, and I turn to glare at the man... shit, the boy. He's still got pimples on his face.

He gives me a nervous swallow, and I sigh, leaning the broom against the wall, about to tell him to just throw it out.

"Leave it on the counter." Tyrell steps into the room. "I'll deal with it."

I scowl at him, but he just shakes his head at me and trails the teenager into the kitchen.

Fuck. Satch would have loved that cake. Sienna and I picked out the design together, talking to the cake lady for nearly an hour while she came up with these cool ideas.

It's a tiered cake with a jukebox and an ice cream sundae, music notes going around the top tier and black-and-white tiles around the bottom. It's a fucking beautiful cake. I had to shell out extra for the rush job, but she stayed up through the night to get it done for me, and Satch didn't even get to see it.

Fuck!

Those girls are on my permanent shit list.

The fact that I only yelled them out of this house doesn't seem like enough. I want to go to the dean, tell him to kick them out of Nolan U! I want to see their asses on a bus, never to return.

I want—

"She's back," Zander calls to me from the living room, and I bolt into the entryway, opening the door for Sienna and battering her with questions before she can even step inside.

"Is she okay? What'd she say? How was she when you left her? Does she want to see me? Should I go?"

"Dude, give her some space," Zander growls, grabbing my arm and yanking me out of the way so his girlfriend can get into the house. "You okay?" He lightly touches her cheek, and she looks up with a sad smile.

It's obvious she's been crying, and I feel like shit as I watch Zander pull her into his arms and lead her into the living room.

She's such an empath, and her tears are making this raging inferno in my chest a million times worse.

It's an effort to keep my voice soft and calm when I grit out, "Is Satch okay?" My voice breaks, emotion slicing through my airways. "How was she when you left?"

"She asked me to leave." Sienna blinks, flashing a pained smile at Zander before looking back at me. "She was really upset, Wily. I felt so bad for her."

Nylah takes a seat on Carson's lap. He's in the armchair adjacent to the couch, and his knee was bobbing a mile a minute until she sat down.

The murderous look on his face reflects some of the emotion I'm feeling, and all I can manage is a feral-sounding "Fuck! I can't believe those bitches. They tore her clothes—they hurt her! I should have done more than just yell in their fucking faces! I should have told them if they even *look* at Satch again, they'll be sorry!"

Sienna's eyes are so glassy. Shit, is she gonna cry again?

I will myself to stop shouting, but I'm so fucking pissed!

Zander rubs the back of her neck when she sniffs. "She told me this girl Jade has been tormenting her for years."

"What?" My stomach drops out my ass, my legs buckling before I slump into the dining chair we have yet to put away. I hate myself for ever talking to that bitch, for ever letting her sit next to me in class. "What do you mean, *for years*?"

"She was talking about these girls she went to school with. I'm assuming the ringleader was the one who ruined this party for her. Apparently, she's made new friends this year and turned them against Satch as well." Sienna blinks at tears, her lips wobbling as she tries to keep going. "She said when she found out that Jade was attending Nolan U, she was gutted. She thought after she graduated and went to college, she'd finally be free of all the torment, but she only had one year of reprieve, and then Jade showed up with a new pair of bitches. She thought Jade was moving to Denver, but she ended up here. And she's been harassing her ever since school started."

"Why didn't she tell me?" It's a thunder punch to my chest, and I lean forward, cupping the back of my head and swearing at the floor. "She didn't say a word! I spoke to Jade a couple of weeks ago, fucking introduced her and Satch! They acted like they didn't know each other!"

And because I'm not feeling shitty enough, I'm suddenly hit with a memory from last weekend and my conversation with her dad. He'd told me about bullies that made Satch's life hell, and fuck! It was that girl! And her fucking friends!

I feel sick.

"Why didn't she tell me?" I whisper on repeat. "Why didn't she say anything?"

"This is such bullshit!" Nylah growls. "We're in college, for *fuck's sake*! This is such grade school behavior! I want to scratch those girls' eyes out," she snips, and it's like watching a chihuahua lose it.

Carson's lips are quirking with what looks like surprised amusement as he grips the back of her neck and murmurs something I can't hear.

She huffs and scowls at him. "I don't give a shit. They deserve to be punished. Satch has got to be one of the sweetest, most nonthreatening people I have ever met, and they made her their target!"

My voice is hollow as I back her up. "Her dad told me she'd had a hard time in school. Said she started hiding herself away because they wouldn't let up." I growl and shoot to my feet. "And they're still at it. Fuck, I want to punch something!" I fling my fist through the air and Tyrell quickly dodges me, leaning out of the way and giving me a pained frown.

I send him a silent apology, then accidentally catch Zander's eye. He's looking just as tortured as everyone else in this room.

They're not used to seeing me like this, but I can't fucking hide it from them.

I wear my heart on my sleeve. I don't keep secrets.

Unlike my girlfriend.

"This is not okay!" Nylah snips again.

"It's definitely not okay," Carson agrees, his head whipping toward the front door when it opens, then shuts with a creak.

"The party's over already?" Grady wanders in, looking confused. "I was making plans to sneak in the back door, but..." He looks around. "Everyone's gone."

"I kicked them out," I grumble.

"Why?" Grady's face buckles with confusion, and Zander quickly explains. I stand there fuming, watching Grady's expression change from surprise to an outright rage that matches the vibe in the room.

"What the fuck?" He scrubs a hand over his shaved head.

"I know, right?" Nylah bulges her eyes at him. "That's

what I'm saying. We need to do something to stand up for that poor girl."

"She doesn't want you to," Sienna interjects. "She just wants to drop it."

"Like she always does, I imagine." Zander rubs a hand over his mouth and lets out a heavy sigh. "She's probably been burying it for years. Taking it, escaping, and then just sweeping it under the rug."

"Which is a really shitty way of dealing with it."

"Hey!" I snap at Nylah, hating even the hint of insulting my girl.

Carson gives me a warning look, and I glare right back at him.

"Don't start turning on each other. It's not about the people in this room right now, it's about Satch and how we can help her." Tyrell throws a little calm into the brewing storm, and I look over my shoulder at him before huffing back to my seat.

Crossing my arms, I smack my back into the chair and shake my head. "If they'd been guys, I would have laid into them. Shit, I should have said more as it was. Told them never to speak to her, fucking *look* at her again. I just can't understand why she didn't tell me. If I'd known, I would have kicked them out the door as soon as I saw them!" I fling my arms wide in exasperation.

"How did they get in?" Grady asks.

We all shrug, and then I groan, scrubbing a hand down my face.

"Oh no. You didn't invite them, did you?" Nylah asks.

"No!" I look up, horrified by the idea. But then my shoulders slump. "I mean, I know Jade from school. We have a class together. I had no idea she was a first-class bitch, but I could have so easily invited her. I didn't, but if I'd happened to talk to her before the party, I probably would have thrown an invitation out there."

"But you didn't." Sienna smiles at me, obviously trying to make me feel better. "So who did?"

We all look around at one another, and Zander finally says, "We did tell people to bring a friend. Maybe those girls got wind of something going on and invited themselves."

"Fuck!" I close my eyes, hating myself for a second. "I shouldn't have gone so big. Satch probably would have been happier with just a few of us."

"You didn't know." Sienna reaches forward, lightly squeezing my knee.

"Why didn't she tell me?" The question pops out once again—all ragged, raw and tortured. "Shit. I saw one of those girls being mean to her weeks ago. I told that bitch to shut the fuck up and get lost... and Satch didn't say a thing about it." I'm so torn up my voice keeps wobbling. "I'm just so gutted that she's been going through this and I've been... *clueless*! I could have protected her. Why didn't she tell me?"

"She says she doesn't like to worry people." Sienna shrugs while everyone else in the room squirms uncomfortably. "I get the impression that she hid a lot from her parents as well."

"I don't think they know Jade's at Nolan U. Or that Satch is being bullied again. The way they were talking last weekend..." I shake my head. "They have no fucking idea."

"It kills me that she's been carrying this all by herself." Sienna's voice quakes. "I feel so bad for her."

Zander's expression buckles as he leans forward and kisses Sienna's cheek, no doubt trying to comfort her.

I want to comfort my girl.

Fuck, I want her in my arms.

But she doesn't want to be in mine right now.

Resting my head in my hands, I fight off another wave of nausea.

"Maybe she's battling some kind of shame?" Grady puts it out there, his voice low and gruff.

"For what?" My head snaps up. "She didn't do anything wrong!"

"Yeah, but sometimes victims try to hide stuff. They feel embarrassed that they can't fight their own battles or protect themselves."

"Yeah." Nylah nods. "I mean, maybe she's humiliated by everything that's been done to her, and she doesn't want you to know. She doesn't want you to see her like this tortured victim. I get that."

"But I could have helped her. Protected her," I whisper, my voice losing all its strength. "Tonight was supposed to be..." I trail off, and it's impossible to ignore the aching disappointment swirling around the room.

"I'm sorry that it wasn't." Sienna's crying now, tears trickling down her cheeks.

"Hey." Zander pulls her to his side, cupping her head when it comes to rest on his shoulder. "She's gonna be okay."

"How do you know that?" I shake my head.

Much to my annoyance, and heartache, he doesn't say anything. How can he? He doesn't fucking know, and the agonized frown he gives me tells me exactly that.

Standing up with a heavy sigh, I pad out of the room, climbing the stairs and calling Satch along the way.

Once again, it goes to voicemail. I don't bother leaving a message. Instead, I text her, telling her I'm sorry, that I didn't know about those girls, and that I'm livid with them. I ask her if she's okay and beg her to call me just so I can hear her voice.

I end the message with *x*'s and *o*'s and three little words that will hopefully make her feel better.

Because they're true.

I love her.

Maybe now more than I ever have.

CHAPTER 56
ELIZABETH

I'm woken from a restless sleep by my phone. I'm cursing the idiot who would call so early until I notice it's my mother and it's actually not that early.

It's nine thirty, and I normally would have been up for a few hours. Yes, even on the weekends, I'm an early bird. It doesn't seem to matter how late I stay up, my body clock wakes me right on time.

Except for last night, because I'd lain awake crying for so long, then had the worst headache and couldn't switch my tortured brain off. I think I'm running on about two hours' sleep, and I feel like shit.

My voice is raspy when I answer. I sound like a groggy drunk.

"Bessie? Sweetheart, are you okay?"

I shake my head, but she can't see me. All I can manage is a soft sniff as a fresh batch of tears rises up my throat. My eyes burn, and I don't even bother trying to fight them.

Tears trickle out of my aching, puffy eyes, running down either side of my nose.

"I was... calling to find out how the party went, but it sounds like I just woke you up or something. Sweetie, I'm sorry. I thought you'd definitely be awake by now. I can call you back later. You're probably in bed with that hunk of a man of yours and—"

"Mom." I wail her name, and she immediately stops talking.

Then she hangs up.

Two seconds later, my phone is ringing with a video call.

I close my eyes for a moment, sucking in a breath before answering it.

She takes one look at my face and her eyes glass with instant tears. "What happened? Did you two break up or something?"

I shake my head.

"Oh, thank God." Mom pats her chest. "He went to so much effort with your party. That boy is so in love with you. It's the sweetest thing in the world."

"You knew about the party?"

"Of course I did." She lets out a watery laugh. "I've been fielding text messages and calls from Wily all week. So... what went wrong?"

Biting my lips together, I stare down at her for a long beat, and I've got this feeling that she knows what I'm about to say before the words are out of my mouth.

"Jade," I croak. "Jade Buchanan."

My mother's eyebrows buckle. "She wasn't there, was she?"

I nod, my insides churning.

"How?" Mom bulges her wet eyes at me. "W-when? I mean, you haven't seen her and those horrible girls since high school! How would they even know? I made sure not to mention a word to any of their parents. You know me, I tend to avoid those couples like the plague. And I wasn't telling everyone at the diner what was happening. Just a few trusted friends. They—" Her voice cuts off when she takes in my pained, no doubt guilty expression.

And then her lips part and she looks about as heartbroken as I feel.

"What have you not been telling me, Elizabeth?" The words tremble out of her.

My chin shakes, my mouth curling into an ugly frown before I manage to confess, "She goes to Nolan U now."

Her skin pales to a near-translucent white. "What?"

"I saw her about a week after school started, and I couldn't believe it. She's made new friends, and they hate me as much as she does."

Tears line Mom's lashes, the buildup about to spill over and down her cheeks. "Have they been harassing you?"

I tip my head to the side but have to nod. "A little. When they see me. I'm perfecting the art of avoiding them, and Nolan U is a much bigger campus than high school, so it's easier. But then I got together with Wily, and he's so popular and everybody knows him and..." My voice trails off. I don't even know what else to say.

"Oh, my sweet Bessie girl." Mom presses two fingers against her lips, blinking rapidly and unable to speak for a moment.

I cry quietly, waiting her out.

"Why didn't you tell us?" she eventually asks.

With a little sniff, I shrug. "I didn't want you to worry. I know how much this kind of thing hurts you."

"Because we love you, sweetheart. We want you to be happy and safe." Mom's voice pitches and she lets out a short, desperate sob before asking, "What did they do to you at your party?"

Closing my eyes, I can't even face my mother as I blubber out the story, then profusely apologize. "I'm sorry," I whimper. "All your hard work and it got destroyed, and I couldn't stop them. I tried to fight, Mom, but they were so strong, and I'm so sorry."

"Oh, sweetie." Mom's crying full tears now, battling her own sobs as she quickly forgives me. "I don't care about the outfit. I can make you another one."

"But it took you months."

"I loved every moment of it." Her voice gets suddenly strong. "I was making it for you. Of course I loved doing it, and I will do it again without hesitation."

I swipe away my tears with the back of my hand.

"What's killing me most is that you got treated that way." She huffs in anger. "Those girls! Wily must have been livid. What did he do? Is he there now?"

I go still, a cold ache blooming in my chest until it's hurting every bone and muscle in my body.

I ache all over, my head pounding as I rub trembling fingers over my frown lines. "I'm at my dorm. Alone."

"Why?"

"I was so humiliated. I didn't want him to see me that way. He's so..." My expression crumples, my throat swelling, making it impossible to speak.

"He's so what?"

"So... perfect," I squeak. "And I'm just me, you know?

I'm just the fat, uncoordinated, socially awkward, completely uncool—"

"Okay, stop talking," Mom cuts me off, sniffing and swiping the tears off her face. "You are not sitting there telling me that you think he's better than you."

"But he is."

"No! Elizabeth Satchwell!" Her voice gets firm. "You do not talk about my daughter that way. She is incredible!"

"You have to say that. You're my mom," I grumble.

"I say it because it's true! And I'm not the only one who thinks that." Pulling a Kleenex out of the box, she dabs at her cheeks. "Do you honestly believe that Wily would have gone to so much effort for you if he didn't think you were worth it? He sees something in you that those... prissy, horrible, mean-spirited... *she-devils* will never see! And it's their loss, you know? They could have had a wonderful friend in you, and they missed out."

She's so firm, I don't bother arguing with her.

"Bess, sweetie, I love you more than anyone ever could, but one of your greatest weaknesses is that you've always thought of others as better than yourself... and they're really not. You are on an even playing field with the rest of the world."

"Mom, I'm not."

"Okay." She nods. "You're right. You are way above those scummy girls."

I cringe and start rubbing my forehead again. "Mom, come on."

"Please," she begs me. "Please stop comparing yourself to people you don't even want to be like."

"But—"

"No, no." Mom shakes her head. "Don't sit there and tell me that you want to be skinny and always wearing the latest fashions and worrying constantly about your looks. You would feel awful about yourself if you went around harassing people. Do you honestly believe those girls are happy?"

She's making so much sense that I can't argue with her, but the stubborn part of me can't admit it, so I just shrug.

"Wily doesn't want someone like them. He wants *you*."

"But he could do so much better." The words slip out before I can stop them, and I curse my vulnerable condition for pulling my guard down.

Mom sighs like the words hurt her, and I wince, scratching my stomach and biting my lips together.

"Sweetheart, you're the only one who's convinced you don't deserve good things. I have no idea why you do that." She gazes at me through the screen, her eyes bright with conviction. "But you are worthy of all good things. You are worthy of a loving relationship. You are worthy of joy and happiness."

I give her a weak smile.

"And Wily's not too good for you. You're equally good for each other. And you will regret it forever if you walk away from that man because of what those girls said. Because you're embarrassed or think you're undeserving." Her expression crumples with desperation. "He loves you."

"But why?" My voice catches. I'm trying so hard to believe all the nice things she's saying to me, but seriously... Wily and I look like such a mismatch. "I don't understand how someone as beautiful and amazing as him would want me when he could have *anybody* else."

Mom licks her lips, shaking her head like she's trying to summon some kind of calm. After a painful beat, she looks at me and smiles. "Why don't you go and ask him? Find out for yourself."

I frown. "He's too nice to tell me the truth. He'll just say something sweet, even if he doesn't mean it."

"And now you're projecting." Mom rolls her eyes, obviously losing patience with me. "Why do you let those nasty people get in your head? I think the fact that you walked away and left him hanging is probably breaking his heart. He's probably just had the worst night of his life, knowing how upset you are and not being able to do anything about it. It's cruel, Elizabeth. You can't just leave it like this."

I swallow, guilt hitting me like a battering ram.

Oh my gosh, I hadn't thought about it like that. He's been calling and texting, apologizing, begging me to get back to him, and I've been hiding myself away. Wallowing in self-pity and not even considering how he must be feeling.

How could I be so selfish?

I fist my pajama top, feeling sick.

"Love doesn't have to be complicated. When it's right, it's the simplest thing in the world. And I know, because I married the man I was meant to be with. We fell in love within weeks of meeting, and we knew it was right. We could feel it in our souls."

I love the way Mom's face softens when she talks about Dad.

"Do you love Wily? Does he light you up?"

I nod. "Yes."

"Then you go and do something about it. Don't you dare let those girls steal something beautiful away from you. You go and you *fight* for what you want. And don't call me again until you have."

"Mom—"

"I mean it." She points at the camera, and I've never seen her so stern before. "You go and you get your man right now, young lady."

All I can do is nod.

"Okay. I love you." She tinkles her fingers at me, blows a kiss, and then hangs up like we've just been having a chat about the weather.

I stare at my black phone screen, then rest my head back against the wall and gaze across the room until my vision goes blurry.

I'm so tired.

A big part of me just wants to lie back down and burrow under the covers.

But Mom's words won't leave me alone. They eat and fester until my entire body is itching. But this itch is different. It's not a hot, stingy burn. It's an antsy sensation that makes it impossible to sit still.

So, I get off the bed, battling a plethora of emotions as I grab my comfiest dress and softest cardigan from the closet. I brush my teeth, wincing at my blotchy reflection in the mirror, then head for my boots.

I have to go.

I can't keep Wily hanging like this, and a text isn't good enough.

I need to see him, look him in the eye.

Snatching my bag off the hook, I drop my phone

inside and pause by the door. My fingers are shaking as I get ready to leave the safety of my room.

But Mom's right.

Jade and her friends have been haunting me for years, stealing my high school experience, shitting all over this new opportunity in college.

Am I really going to let them take Wily too?

He might not want you after last night.

Hide. Just hide away. It's safer.

"But it's lonely," I argue. "And I deserve to be happy." My voice breaks when I repeat my mother's words.

Everybody deserves a little happiness, don't they?

Why should I be the exception?

Holding my breath, I fling the door open and march into the corridor, heading for the elevators at a fast clip and willing myself to keep moving forward, no matter what awaits me on the outside.

CHAPTER 57
ELIZABETH

I decide not to Uber and end up walking to Wily's place. It's dangerous—I could bump into anyone. But it gives me the chance to down a coffee, clear my head, and figure out what I want to say to him.

My mother told me what I needed to hear, and maybe there's a lot of truth to it, but she is my mother. And I guess I need to hear what Wily *really* thinks with no sweet sentiments or bullshit attached.

I need him to look me in the eye and tell it to me straight, even if it hurts.

Because I want to be able to trust him, and I can't do that if I think he's lying to me. Just being sweet to make me feel better but not actually meaning it.

Throwing the empty coffee cup away at the park closest to Wily's house, I turn down his street and feel my steps slow.

My body gets stiff and awkward as I keep forcing myself forward.

Somehow, I make it, climbing up those front steps and trying not to relive the torment of last night.

Sucking in a breath, I curl my fingers and lightly knock on the door. Thankfully, it doesn't take too long for someone to answer it, and I'm soon staring up at Carson's standard scowl and messy mop of hair.

The second he spots me, his expression lightens, but he doesn't get a chance to say anything, because Nylah ducks under his arm and pulls me into a hug.

"Oh, thank God!" She squeezes me tight. "I'm so glad you're here."

I pat her back, my cheeks heating to boiling as I try to step out of the embrace. She finally lets me go, her eyes shining with excitement. "He's upstairs."

Jumping out of my way, I walk between the couple, kicking off my boots in the entrance while they gaze at me. Nylah's still smiling while Carson's eyebrows wrinkle with worry.

"You okay?" His voice is gruff and has a morning croak to it.

Those two words are asking so much. After what happened here last night, they're asking *too* much.

So I quickly nod—my standard reply—before stashing my boots as a neat pair and darting for the staircase. I will myself not to turn back when I hear them whispering.

They're talking about me. I know they are.

That familiar itch starts to spread across my stomach until I make myself acknowledge that Nylah just bounded out of the house to hug me. She's excited that I'm here.

Happy.

To see me.

Reaching the landing, I stop for a second and really soak that in.

Nylah's happy that I'm here.

It's like I'm only just noticing it for the first time. The people in this house don't mind having me around. I'm not a plague or a menace. I'm not as annoying as a mosquito bite. They put on a party. For me. Went to all that effort. And they wouldn't have done that for someone who they wished didn't exist.

I force myself to really think about that as I inch toward Wily's room.

My lips twitch, this pleasant sensation cooling the itch on my skin, working like a balm as I gently knock on his door.

There's no response, so after a long, polite beat, I knock a little harder.

"I told you guys I'm fine. Can you please just fuck off already! I've had the shittiest night, and I need some fucking sleep!" Wily's roar makes me flinch, and I bulge my eyes at the wood, trying to decide what to do.

Don't leave! Don't you dare leave!

Forcing my body to stay put, I lean toward the crack in the door and say, "Wily. It's me."

There's an instant fumbling, a thud, and a scrambling of feet. I step back as the lock clicks, and then the door jerks open to reveal a wide-eyed Wily, his blond hair sticking up at all angles, his bare chest heaving as he grips the door and stares down at me.

"Are you okay?" His voice is so soft and tender, it's like a physical caress, and it makes my lips curl into a watery smile. The concern in his blue gaze is melting me.

"Yeah." I nod.

He gives me a pained frown, reaching for me, then thinking better of it and running a hand through his hair instead. "Shit, Satch. I'm so sorry that I—"

"No," I quickly interrupt him. "You didn't do anything wrong. It's me. It's me and my shit."

Wow. I've never said anything like that before, and it feels surprisingly good. Who knew honesty didn't have to be so terrifying?

I swallow, staring at his chest as I force myself to keep thinking, mulling, fighting for what I want. This morning is certainly full of revelations, and it's kind of overwhelming, to be honest. But I'll hate myself if I turn back now. And so I stand my ground and—

"Are you breaking up with me?" Wily's voice is strained, like saying those words is causing him physical pain.

My eyes dart to his pale expression, and I instantly shake my head. "I don't want to." I quickly look to the floor and mumble, "But I understand if you—"

"Are you fucking kidding me?" He grabs my wrist, pulling me into his room and flicking the door shut with his foot. "Of course I don't want to break up with you." Opening his arms wide, he comes in for a hug, but I take a quick step back, holding up my hand.

"Why?" I ask.

I have to know.

I have to hear him say it.

He gazes down at me like I'm weird, and I force myself to keep looking at him.

Tipping his head, he rests a hand over his heart and lightly pats his chest. "Because I love you."

Oh my gosh, his voice! It's so raw and rough. So sexy I can hardly stand it.

Swallowing down this swell of desire, I gnaw on my bottom lip and feel this tremor run through me.

"Wily," I squeak, then suck in a quick breath and force myself to say the rest. "I need you to tell me something. And it needs to be the absolute truth, okay? Please. You have to be totally honest with me. Even if you think it might hurt me."

His eyes narrow like he's trying to figure out where I'm going with this.

I keep looking at him, silently begging him to please just agree. To let me have this.

Finally, he nods. "Okay."

"You swear?"

"I swear."

"Okay." I take a ragged breath, nodding and pinching my bottom lip before shaking out my hands. "Okay. So... when you look at me... when you tell me you love me... I mean, why do you say that? What... what do you see? When you look at me..." My voice starts to shake, and I have to expel a breath before I can finish. "What do you see? And remember, you have to tell me the *truth*."

He seems surprised by the question, his eyebrows rising, his lips twitching until he starts to pick up just how serious I am.

His mouth bunches into a thoughtful pout and he nods, shifting to sit on the bed beside me. We're now at eye level, and I force myself to turn and face him.

"When I look at you..." He clears his throat, licking the edge of his mouth before gazing at my face with this soft affection that's going to undo me. "When I look at you, I see a girl—a woman—with a beautiful face and a smile that can knock me off my feet. I seriously love those plump lips of yours, baby. And the shape your mouth makes when you smile is..." He grins like he's picturing it and loving the view.

My heart starts to pound, and I squeeze my index finger.

Glancing down, he lightly takes my hand, threading our fingers together.

"You're shy. You don't have a lot of self-confidence, and you like to hide, which I don't always agree with. It kinda kills me when you say negative shit about yourself. I hate it when you put yourself down."

My stomach knots, but I keep listening. I asked for the truth, didn't I?

And I want both sides of it, the good and the bad; otherwise, it's meaningless.

Wily lets out a soft sigh, looking kind of sad. "And the fact that you didn't tell me you were going through a really hard time... didn't tell me about those girls and what they've been doing to you. It..." His shoulder hitches. "It hurt my feelings."

My lips part, and I can feel my forehead wrinkling in regret.

He leans forward, smoothing the lines away with his thumb. "I couldn't protect you the way I wanted to because you didn't tell me the truth. You didn't let me in."

"I'm sorry." My whisper is so soft, guilt squeezing my stomach into a tight, painful ball.

He forgives me with a smile and a wink, then asks, "Can I keep going? This is fun."

I give him a dubious frown, wondering if he knows what the word *fun* actually means.

He grins and kind of bounces on the bed, his voice picking up. "When I look at you, I see kindness. It just oozes out of you, you know? You've got a really sweet spirit." Cupping my face, he gazes into my eyes with a look that makes me want to swoon at his feet. "I see bright, intelligent eyes that look right into my soul. And I feel... *so good* whenever I'm around you. Like a better human or something. You never make me feel like a stupid idiot."

"Because you're not stupid. Or an idiot."

Leaning back, he keeps studying me, his smile shifting to a look of wonder. "When I talk to you, you listen. You really listen, and you hear me. You treat me like I'm the most important person in the room, and it makes me feel like a million bucks, every single time. You don't just want me because I'm good at football. You don't care about status or any of that bullshit."

My lips rise into an instant grin. "You are the most important person in my room. In this room. In any room I'm in."

His blue eyes light with appreciation, and I let him take my other hand. He gazes down at our connection, rubbing his thumb softly across my palm. "There are so many things I love about you, Satch. There are so many wonderful things I see."

I squirm in my fluffy socks, and he reaches for my hips, resting his hands on them.

"I get the sense that you're needing to hear this stuff so you can reassure yourself that I'm actually into you. That I really do love you. And it's true." He looks up, catching my eye. "I'm not saying this just to make you feel better. You asked for the truth, and I'm giving it to you straight."

I give him a weak smile. "You're just so nice that I was worried you'd say anything to make me feel better. And I really need the truth from you right now." My nose starts to tingle as I get to the last part. The hardest part. "And I believe that you love who I am as a person. And thank you." I try to smile but can't seem to form one. "But... what do you see when you look at my body?"

"What do you mean?" He tilts his head with a light frown.

"Come on, Wily. You're so incredibly hot." I point at his chest, indicating his entire body with a flick of my hand.

He glances down at himself, then up at me, his eyes rounding with a pointed look. "And you don't think you are?"

"Of course not." I laugh. "I'm... big!"

"No, you're not, Shorty."

I close my eyes, shaking my head at his teasing smile. "You know what I mean. I'm not skinny and pretty like all the other girls seem to be."

"Satch." He takes my hands again, giving them a little shake. "Open your eyes."

"I don't want to," I mumble.

"Open your eyes." His voice gets a little firmer.

Forcing my lids up, I take in his expression and don't know what to think.

He looks disappointed or upset or something, and I don't know why.

Should I apologize or—

"I hate that you just said that about yourself." He

sighs, completely gutted. "Didn't I say before how much this shit kills me?"

I swallow, then bite my bottom lip because I can't squeeze my finger or scratch my stomach right now. My hands are trapped within his, and he won't let go.

Leaning his head forward, he keeps chasing my gaze until I'm looking right at him. "When I first met you, I checked you out. You know I did."

My cheeks heat with color.

"And I saw this tutor who didn't dress like any other girl I knew."

I wince.

"And yeah, at first, I thought it was a little weird." He looks me over, his lips twitching as he tweaks my cardigan, pulling it up on my shoulder. "But I kinda love it now. Because it's who you are."

I let out a soft, wispy sound. It's supposed to be a laugh, but I seriously don't know what just popped out.

"You're hot, Satch. You have a great ass and these beautiful, *beautiful* boobs." He stares at them, his gaze softening as he trails his eyes down to my feet. Resting his hands back on my hips, he keeps admiring me. "I love the shape of your body. These luscious curves." His hands round over me, grabbing my fleshy butt cheeks and giving them a squeeze. "I love digging my fingers into your ass." He grins, then looks me right in the eye. "Your soft edges turn me on, baby. And that is the God's honest truth."

My lips part, and I'm pretty sure my heart stopped beating somewhere around the "great ass and beautiful boobs" part.

"C'mere." He stands up, taking my hands and walking me to his full-length mirror.

Turning me to face it, he stands behind me, bringing his hands around my body and cupping my breasts. Squeezing them, he lets out an appreciative moan before leaning down to whisper against my cheek. "You're so fucking sexy I can hardly stand it sometimes. You're no compromise, Satch. You're first prize."

CHAPTER 58
WILY

She shivers against me as I brush my lips across her cheek, then kiss a line down to her neck.

I hate her doubts and insecurities.

I hate that she doesn't see herself the way I do.

I have to make her believe how much she means to me. How fucking amazing she is.

"Satch?" I whisper, slowly pulling the cardigan off her shoulders.

"Yeah." Her voice is wispy, her vulnerable eyes tearing my heart out when I look at her reflection.

Smiling, I rest my chin on top of her head. "Tell me you're amazing."

She smiles. "You're amazing."

"No." I nip her waist, enjoying her yelp and giggle. "Say it."

Biting her lip, she gives me a pained wince. "Do I have to?"

"Yes." I start lifting her dress, pulling the soft fabric

up until she's forced to raise her arms and let me take it off.

She goes to cover her body so she doesn't have to look at herself, but I grab her wrists before she can, holding them lightly and caressing my thumb over her racing pulse.

"I need you to say it, baby." I kiss her bare shoulder. "Say 'I'm fucking amazing.'"

Her breath catches as I slip the strap of her bra down.

"Say it," I whisper against her skin.

"I'm... I'm a-amazing."

"Fucking amazing." My eyes dart to the mirror as I unclasp her bra.

She holds her breath when I slip it off her shoulders. It drops to the floor, landing by her feet, and I gaze at those luscious tits of hers.

Fuck. They are awesome.

"Tell me you're fucking amazing, baby." I cup her breasts, then lightly squeeze her nipples, enjoying the shudder racing down her spine.

She closes her eyes, tipping her head back with a soft whimper.

Kissing the tip of her nose, I grin and keep going. "Say it, baby. I gotta hear you say it."

"I'm fucking amazing." Her voice is dreamy, like she's not really hearing what she's saying, so I stop playing with her nipples and tip her head forward to face the mirror.

Wrapping my arms around her waist, I bend down and rest my chin on her shoulder. Giving her an expectant look, I keep staring until a pink blush rises over her skin. She's so sexy, all flushed and glowing like this.

"Say it," I mouth at our reflection, and her lips twitch.

"I'm fucking amazing."

"Good girl." I grin, kissing the side of her neck. "Now look yourself in the eye and say it."

Her breath catches, and she darts a look at her face before staring down at the floor.

"Satch," I gently warn her, dropping to my knees and nibbling her thighs, working my way up to her panty line.

"I'm fucking amazing." She rushes out the words, and I skim my hands up the backs of her legs, rounding her hips before turning her to face me.

Gazing up at her, I smile." And you have to believe that. Promise me you will."

Her smile is watery as she cups my cheeks. "I'll try."

"I'm not gonna stop telling you," I warn her. "And one day you'll believe it. One day, you might just see yourself the way I see you." I wink at her before inching her panties off her hips.

She lets out a short giggle, brushing her thumb across my cheeks and bending down to kiss me. "You're fucking amazing, too, you know?"

Pulling her mouth to mine again, I glide my tongue along hers, getting lost in the kiss for a moment before helping her step out of her panties.

She's now naked before me, and I can see her gorgeous ass in my mirror. Yeah, we're totally doing it right here.

Kissing her belly, I lick a path up between her boobs, then take my fill.

Her fingers scrape along my scalp before fisting the back of my hair. I grab her ass cheeks, holding them while sucking her nipples and loving every sound popping out of her mouth.

Those whimpers are driving me crazy, and my dick is soon standing at attention.

"I want you, baby," I murmur against the curve of her breast. "Let me take you right here on the floor."

She pulls back to look at me, nodding as she sinks to her knees.

I scramble for my nightstand, darting across the floor like a madman and yanking my drawer open.

I'm shoving down my boxers while trying to unwrap the condom and nearly end up stumbling, my knee catching with a sharp twang as my hip hits the bed.

"You okay?" Satch moves toward me, but I tell her to stay put.

"Baby, I am so fucking great right now." I roll the condom over my pulsing cock as I walk the last few steps toward her.

My knee stops hurting by the time I'm back in front of her, pulling her flush against me and kissing those plump lips.

They're fucking sensational, and I take my sweet time enjoying them before working my way back down her body.

She falls back on her ass, giggling when I spread her legs and lightly tug her across the carpet.

Oh shit, carpet burn.

"You okay?" I quickly check, and she nods with a grin, her fingers trailing a line up my cock. "The floor's okay?"

"Yeah." Her voice catches when I slip my finger inside her, loving how wet she already is.

Stroking the length of her warm oasis, I go back to

feasting on her tits, relishing the way her body shakes and shudders beneath me.

I need to get inside this woman.

"Can I come in, baby? Please."

"Yes," she moans. "Get in here."

She doesn't have to ask me twice. Stretching out over her, I love the way she grabs my dick, lining me up between her folds.

I ease in my tip, checking her face for final permission.

She nods, her smile sweet and adoring.

Resting my weight on my elbows, I fight the urge to plunge in and whisper, "Tell me you're fucking amazing."

Her nose wrinkles and I wait, my body starting to shake.

Biting her lip, she runs her hands up the length of my torso, curling her fingers around my quivering shoulders and whispering, "I'm fucking amazing."

I thrust into her, stealing her breath and reveling in that sweet moan of hers.

She clings to me, pressing her lips against my shoulder as we ride together, my fingers curling into her hair, her hands tracing my back and curving over my gyrating ass.

Fuck, I love her body. Her soul.

Seeking out her lips, I kiss her deeply, hoping she can feel how much I mean this.

CHAPTER 59
ELIZABETH

When Wily fills me like this, I'm lost to everything else around me.

He's it.

He's everything.

And he thinks I'm fucking amazing.

I still can't wrap my brain around it. When he undressed me in front of the mirror just now, I honestly wasn't sure I could handle it.

But I stayed. I fought, the internal battle raging as I clung to this man.

I said what he told me to, and it's getting easier each time the words slip out of my mouth.

He thinks I'm amazing.

He thinks I'm fucking amazing.

And now he's inside me, his body gliding over mine as his tongue sends me to some heavenly plane. I've been here before, every time I've kissed him, but this plane is brighter somehow. More intense.

Because he loves me, and I know it without a doubt.

He's not just saying it to make me feel better.

He *actually* means it.

Wily Wilson loves me!

All of me—my mind, my soul, my body.

The look on his face when he was telling me all those beautiful things...

I grip his back, desperate for him to know how much that all meant to me. My chest is full, swirling with this heady sensation that makes me feel like I could fly.

He plunges into me again, ripping his mouth off mine as he loses his breath, and the heat between us starts to burn like blue fire.

"Baby," he moans, curling his arms under my shoulders and pumping a little faster.

Yes! I love it when he goes deep like this. He's all I can feel, his impressive body covering me, owning me in ways I never thought possible.

Lifting my leg, I hook my foot around his back, and he grabs my thigh, his fingers digging in as he shifts angles and hits a sweet spot that makes me whimper.

It feels so good.

"Fuck, this is amazing," he pants, lying over me again, his breath hitting my ear.

I turn my face, kissing a trail across his bare shoulder, then catching our reflection in the mirror.

My body flushes with embarrassment, but I force myself to look. To watch his powerful thigh move when he bends his leg and keeps pumping into me.

His back muscles are beautiful, and I study the way they shift when he pulls back to rest on his elbows. I run my hands down his gorgeous bicep and forearm, still watching his body, then force myself to check out my profile beneath his.

My rounded, dimpled edges move and jiggle, nothing like his defined curves, but I somehow fit beneath him just fine.

He loves my soft edges.

I turn him on.

Lil' ol' me, who never felt good enough, is sending this Thor-like god to a full-blown orgasm. He *wants* to be inside me. He makes me feel like if he can't have me, it'll be the world's biggest travesty.

The thought makes my stomach quiver, and I turn back to face him just as his eyes pop open. Smiling up at his stunning face, I brush my teeth across my bottom lip. "I love you, Coyote."

He grins down at me, stealing my breath when he does a deep drive that I can feel all the way to my core.

Tipping my head back with a moan, I enjoy the heat spreading through me.

He drives into me again.

And again.

Another deep thrust has a gasp of pleasure popping out of my mouth. My eyes spring open and I snatch his taut forearms, my lips forming a perfect O as this sensation travels right through me. It's blinding and beautiful, and I'm coming! I'm... coming!

"Ah!" I wail with abandon, not even caring that people might be able to hear me. This feels too amazing. I can't stay quiet.

Releasing another guttural groan, I enjoy the triumphant look on Wily's face just before he starts to lose it himself.

"Oh, fuck. Baby," he rasps, slapping his hand on my hip and squeezing tight as he jerks and thrusts, his perfect ass cheeks clenching with a sexy shudder.

He groans some more, pumping a few more times until my arms flop to the floor in listless wonder.

Holy shit, that was incredible.

Dipping his head, Wily pants above me, his chest heaving.

I place my hand over his heart and smile at the thundering beat under my palm.

"It's official." He drops down over top of me. "You are the best sex I've ever had."

I giggle, patting his shoulder before running my hand down his back. "Really?"

"I'm serious, Satch. You do it for me, baby."

"You do it for me too." I kiss his shoulder. "You're absolutely the best sex I've ever had."

He leans up on his elbows, looking down at me with narrowed eyes. "I'm the only sex you've ever had."

"Even if you weren't, I'm guessing you'd still be the best." I rest my hands on his sides and revel in this giddy sensation bubbling inside me.

I could eternally bask in the affectionate look on his face right now. "It's an honor to be your first, you know?"

I bite my lip, then force myself to thank him and not tell him that I want him to be my last too. That feels like we're jumping the gun just a little, doesn't it?

But maybe I'm wrong.

Maybe the two of us will last the distance, just like my parents have.

After our bedroom floor sexcapades, we crawl into bed together and I finally get some sleep. Wily's head makes the best pillow, and I wake midafternoon, kind of groggy but definitely more refreshed. My eyes are still puffy from all of last night's crying, but I'm feeling so much better than I did when I first woke up.

I really don't feel like getting dressed again, but Wily lends me his ginormous bathrobe and coaxes me downstairs, assuring me that I'm fully covered.

Everyone is up and about. We catch Sienna and Zander making out in the kitchen, which is kind of funny. They've obviously been taking advantage of their child-free weekend and have only just stumbled out of bed themselves.

We eat birthday cake for lunch... or breakfast... and I gush over how stunning it is.

"You went to so much effort for me." I shake my head at Wily as he shoves another huge forkful of cake into his mouth.

"Because you're fucking amazing." Crumbs fly off his lips and I giggle, sharing a grateful look with Sienna, who winks at me before stealing the last bite off Zander's plate.

He gapes at her. "You did not just do that."

"What?" She laughs around her mouthful of cake, her cheeks poking out like a chipmunk's as she jumps out of her chair and dances out of Zander's reach. He gives chase and she screams, ducking out the back door.

Wily and I both rise from our chairs, grinning as he chases her around the backyard, then captures her and throws the girl over his shoulder. He marches back to the garage, and you only need one guess to figure out how they'll be spending the rest of their afternoon.

I'm about to suggest the same thing to Wily when Carson and Nylah stroll in, out of breath and gleaming with sweat.

"I'm telling you, the remake is not as good." Nylah frowns at her boyfriend as he grabs two glasses out of the kitchen cupboard.

"And I'm agreeing with you, kitten!" He hands her a water, obviously exasperated. "Stop bitching to me about it and write a letter to the fucking production company if it's such a problem."

She huffs, crossing her arms and glaring at him. "I just hate it when they screw up like that. They had gold, and they turned it into a pile of steaming cow turd."

I quietly giggle, too scared to ask what movie they're talking about. It's obvious they've just been out running together, and they must have gotten into this discussion partway through.

Carson sighs, wrapping his arms around her and pulling her close. Rubbing her sweaty back, he rolls his eyes at Wily, and you can almost hear him thinking, *"Women!"*

I cross my arms, boldly giving him a pointed look. He's got an amazing woman in his arms, and I hope those red cheeks he's sporting are to do with him getting my silent reprimand and not the fact that he's recovering from a run.

"This is why we should just stick with the oldies," he murmurs, his lips twitching as he pulls back and cups her cheeks. "So, why don't we head upstairs, take a quick shower together, and then put a little *Terminator* on my laptop." He waggles his eyebrows.

Nylah smirks. "You trying to get me hot with a sci-fi, alien, robot movie?"

"You bet I am, kitty cat."

She fights a grin. "I should really hate that it's working."

"Should you?" He swings his arm around her shoulders and starts guiding her out of the kitchen. "Now I'm trying to decide if I should be worried that the thought of a movie about a killer robot from the future turns you on more than the idea of showering with me."

She giggles, reaching up to peck his cheek. "They both do, caveman. They both do."

"Yeah, right," he murmurs. "Maybe we should start with the movie, and I'll get you all hot and bothered. Then I can do you in the shower."

My nose wrinkles as their voices start to fade away up the stairs.

Turning back to my man, I find him grinning down at me and can't help a soft giggle. "Your friends are funny."

"Yeah, they'll grow on you pretty damn fast."

"Most definitely," I agree. "You live with very cool people."

"I do." He kisses the tip of my nose, then looks just a touch sad. "I'm gonna miss them when I leave."

And the air around me suddenly weighs three thousand pounds. It's impossible to keep my smile in place.

Wrapping my arms around his waist, I nestle my head against his chest and murmur, "I'm gonna miss you when you leave. We all will."

Kissing the top of my head, he rubs my arms before

holding me close. "What are we gonna do when I'm drafted?"

I squeeze his back. "You're gonna go and play football, and I'm gonna watch every one of your games."

"Will you fly out to see me play?" His voice rises hopefully.

I lean back to take in his expression. I wish I could tell him yes, but I can't afford that. Instead, I smile and promise him, "No matter what happens or where you end up, I will always support you. I know how much you love football, and I'm excited that you're gonna follow your dreams."

"But I love you too." He looks pained as he cups my cheeks.

"You playing football doesn't need to change that." I rest my hand over his, knowing the answer is not that easy and not wanting to spoil what has turned into the most incredible day. "Let's not worry about it now. We still have a few months before you graduate." Stepping back up against him, I will myself not to cry when I think about him leaving me and how horrible that's going to be. "Right now, we just need to focus on getting you ready for the Scouting Combine thing, and then the drafting in April. Who knows, maybe you'll get picked up by the Broncos."

I say it so hopefully and squeeze my eyes shut, wishing it with all my heart.

I don't want this man to leave me!

But I love him enough to let him go when the time comes.

I can't do anything else.

Because football is his dream, and I can't stand in the way of it.

CHAPTER 60
WILY

Something has shifted between Satch and me. Our relationship has been evolving ever since our first tutoring session, but spending the weekend with her, hours of talking and being with each other... It's changed something between us.

She ended up telling me everything that happened to her in high school. It was brutal, but I clenched my jaw, and I didn't say a fucking word. I kept my anger in check while she softly shared how horrible it all was.

I made love to her after that—slow and easy, reminding her how amazing she is and how much I love her. How much my friends already care about her.

She's gonna find a home here at Football Frat. For the first time in her life, she's gonna belong.

She belongs with me, so it's inevitable, right?

This girl's the one.

I can feel it in my bones.

And if we can somehow survive whatever is coming

with my future career and living apart until she gradu-ates, then I honestly think we can make it.

Which means I have to tell my parents about her.

The thought is like a rock in my stomach.

You'd think they'd be open to me falling in love. They're happily married (I think), so why wouldn't they be all over me finding a girl?

But I just know the second I drop that news, they're gonna start stressing.

"She'll distract you."

"You have to focus on football right now."

"Great, now he's not going to want to leave her."

"This is a disaster."

"We told you not to get serious with anyone."

"You don't have space in your life for love right now."

Their voices bombard me as I head to football train-ing, and I just know that I can't breathe a word about Satch until after the Scouting Combine. If I kick ass there —and I will—then I can prove to them that having a girl-friend and handling football is completely doable. They'll have no argument because I will have already shown them it's possible.

That way I can protect Satch. The last thing she needs is to take on any animosity from my parents and their warped view on how I should be living my life.

I guess I used to agree with them.

Until I met her.

And now it's all different.

Because *she's* different.

My lips twitch as I relive moments from our weekend. She's so sexy and beautiful. Most of Saturday, she was naked in my bed, and damn if I couldn't get used to a life-time of that.

I love her giggle. I love that I can make her laugh.

The way she looks at me.

Her sweet voice.

The expression on her face when I'm talking to her.

She sees me, and I fucking love it.

And she wants me to follow my dreams. I know me leaving Nolan is going to be hard on her, but she's still telling me that she'll be cheering me on at the Scouting Combine. She made me promise to send her updates when I have a chance. She wants to support me on this, and I know she and Sienna were texting this morning about throwing a massive draft party for us in April.

I can't help a grin as I take the spot next to Zander's SUV in the stadium parking lot.

Satch is amazing.

She's fucking amazing.

I chuckle, shouldering the door open and picturing her in her room. She said she's got an assignment looming and is going to spend the afternoon working on it so we can have dinner together later.

I've been really good and left her alone like she asked me to.

I spent the morning texting her and making sure she was avoiding Team Evil 2.0, but she got through the day without seeing them, and now that I know she's tucked safely away in her room, I can breathe easy.

I tried to convince her to press charges—property damage or some shit. They scratched her, so that's physical abuse, right? Surely the police will pay attention to that.

535

But she doesn't want to.

She just wants to keep her head down and forget it happened.

I'm gonna have to keep working on her, because fuck, what am I going to do when I leave and I'm not here to keep her safe anymore?

Maybe I can convince her to transfer to a college in whatever city I end up playing in.

Would she go for it?

That's not asking too much, is it?

I just can't stand the thought of her being here without me nearby. I want to protect her from any more bullies. Sure, Grady and Carson will be around to keep an eye on her, but is that gonna be enough? I can't expect them to play bodyguard every day.

Shit. I really need to come up with a plan around this thing.

"Wywee!" A sweet voice grabs my attention, and I turn to see Zoey running toward me. She's carrying a football, her little legs eating up the space between us.

"Hey, Cowgirl." I crouch low, capturing her in my arms and standing tall. "How was your weekend?"

"Fun! Fissing!"

"You went fishing?"

She nods. "Ganpa show me."

"Wow, that is awesome. Did you catch anything?"

She nods again, her smile priceless as she holds her arms out wide, dropping the football in the process.

"You caught a fish that big?"

"Uh-huh." Her big eyes are so convinced while her father strolls up behind her, shaking his head and winking at me.

I grin. "That's impressive, kid." I give her stomach a light poke.

She giggles, slapping a hand over her cute little belly. She's wearing her "I'm a princess. Deal with it" sweater today. It's bright pink with sparkly writing, and it fits her perfectly.

Crouching down, I pop her on her feet and grab the football. "Are you sticking around for practice today?"

"Sienna's got her here just while everyone gets ready." Zander brushes his hands through Zoey's curls. "Couldn't go another hour without seeing my lil' love bug."

Zoey grins up at her father like he's the sun in her universe.

Scooping her up, he gives her a raspberry, and I walk away from the squeals echoing down the tunnel.

"See you guys in a minute." Shaking out my leg, I pick up my pace and head to the locker room, changing fast enough to beat half the guys still in there and running out to the grass.

Zoey is giggling, running away from Carson and Tyrell, who are chasing her. She's got the ball in her hand and is screaming, "Daddy!" with this huge grin on her face.

"Throw the ball, Zo!" Zander holds up his hands, and she chucks it at him. He gathers it up off the grass, dodging right when Tyrell comes in with a tackle and jumping around Carson.

Zoey cheers and starts running for her father again.

He slows his pace, backing up a step when she starts to fall. Snatching the back of her coat, he holds her like a briefcase and starts running down the field. She's laughing and squealing, then stretches her arms wide and enjoys the flight.

Sienna's on the sidelines, chatting with Grady. Her smile is broad as she watches her man and daughter, having fun together.

Even Grady's lips are twitching.

Poor guy still seems to be walking around with a cloud over his head, but this past week he's been a little less glum, so that's something. It takes time to recover from heartbreak, I guess. I think I'd be pretty damn shattered if Satch broke up with me, that's for sure.

Tightening up my laces, I then jog into the action, helping Zander out and making Zoey giggle some more. But the shenanigans don't last long. Coach Jones is soon blowing his whistle and getting us into a warm-up drill.

"I'll see you after practice." Zander passes Zoey back to Sienna, kissing his woman before pecking Zoey's cheek.

"Bye, Daddeeeeeee!"

"Love you, lil' bug." He blows her a kiss, then shares an affectionate smile with Sienna before running to catch up with the drill.

I watch Sienna walk away and nearly fall on my face when an image hits me hard. I see it so clearly—Satch on the sidelines, rounding up our brood of children. There are four, maybe even five, and they've come down to watch Daddy play.

She'll have a baby on her hip and be smiling as the older children race around with me; then she'll gather them up and find a perch in the stands.

Catching my balance, I keep running, touching the ground, then spinning back to do the next length.

I see them in the stands, cheering me on. The older kids will be doing their homework while they wait for me. The two youngest will be on Satch's knee, and she'll be reading them a story, glancing up to watch me, sending me smiles and blowing kisses.

Holy shit, I want that.

I mean, I always knew I wanted a big family, and I've imagined myself being a dad, but I could never picture how that could happen and who it might happen with. But I can see it now.

It's crystal clear.

And I really need to tell my parents that I've found the one.

After the Scouting Combine. That makes the most sense.

I nod, settling on that decision and forcing future Mrs. Wilson and our brood out of my mind so I can focus on practice.

Coach pulls us in, giving us a pep talk about how the team can help any of the players who declared their intention to enter the draft best prepare for next week. He talks through some of the drills Zander, a few other players, and I will be doing at the Scouting Combine, and we run those first.

It's fun and busy—there's an awesome energy buzzing through the team.

Practice goes by in a rush, and when Coach Perkins suggests that we finish with a friendly game, everyone's on board.

"Only if you play too!" Zander goads the coaches into joining in, and soon everyone is on the field, scrapping for the ball and having a blast.

Shouts and laughter ring across the stadium, and it's fucking epic.

It takes me back to my childhood when football was just the game. We lived for this shit, and I'd play any chance I got, because this is what I love so much. The game without all the pressure of the crowds and the media. Just a bunch of friends having fun playing the best sport in the world.

Changing up positions, we all take turns doing something a little different, and I set for the play, pushing Fleischer out of the way and spinning to chase after the ball.

It pings off my fingers, and I scramble after it. Aware of the player coming at me on my right, I pivot to my left, go for a quick dodge... and my knee twists as I hit the ground.

Pop!

"Ah! Fuck!" I land with a thud, reaching for my knee as a pain like nothing I've ever experienced takes me out.

The agony is blinding, and I roll onto my back, swearing up a storm as players race toward me.

"Wily." Carson drops to one knee beside me.

Grady takes the other side, resting his hand on my stomach. "Where does it hurt, man?"

"My knee." I choke out the words, writhing at the searing burn shooting through me when I try to move it. "Shit! Ahhh!"

"Out of the way!" a voice directs from behind Carson, and I open my eyes in time to see the head trainer crouching down for a look. "Your knee?" he asks.

"Yeah," Grady answers for me when all I can do is cover my face with my arm and whimper.

"I heard a pop," Carson tells him.

"Okay." The trainer's tone is gravely serious, and it only amplifies my terror.

Shit. My knee. I've just fucked up my knee.

Shit, shit, shit!

"How's it looking?" Coach Jones says from somewhere above me.

There's a pregnant pause, and I hold my breath, willing the guy to say I'm being a baby and it's really not so bad. But the pain ricocheting through me at his lightest touch is like a warning alarm.

It's blaring so loud and deafening that I almost don't hear his prognosis.

"I think it might be an ACL tear."

"Oh fuck," Grady whispers just as the words register in my brain.

An ACL tear.

And there goes my world. My fucking life.

CHAPTER 61
ELIZABETH

It's taken maximum effort and some decent classical music, but I've finally managed to stop thinking about my weekend and focus on school.

I'm minutes away from finishing my conclusion, and then I can let this essay percolate for a day or two. After that, I'll do my next round of edits, and I'll be one step closer to acing this assignment.

With a little grin, I add my final sentence, happy with the wording because I've been playing around with it for a few days now. It feels so good to finally type it out.

Yes!

I love this sense of completion.

Sitting back with a happy grin, I look at the calendar on my wall and quickly calculate that I'm well ahead of schedule.

"Edits on Wednesday," I murmur to myself, adding the task to my to-do list before checking what's next on today's list.

I'm about to pull up my notes for my Literary Theory class, which I am *loving*, when my phone starts buzzing.

I don't recognize the number and nearly let it go to voicemail, but something stops me.

Swiping my thumb across the screen, I give the person a tentative "Hello?"

"Satch?"

"Um..." I frown, slightly confused because this is not Wily's voice.

"It's Zander." His tone is so serious, I go on immediate alert. "Wily's on his way to the hospital."

My stomach bottoms out as I lurch from my seat and gape at the wall. "What happened?"

"A suspected ACL tear."

"What does that mean?" I plunk back down in my chair, putting the phone on speaker and pulling up a fresh Google search window.

Zander sighs. "Nothing good. Depending on how bad the ligament is damaged, he may need surgery, and then it's months of recovery."

A cold chill sweeps through me, my hands freezing over the keys.

"The Scouting Combine," I rasp. "The draft."

"I know." Zander's voice is so deep, so cut up, it makes me want to cry.

Covering my mouth, I fight that onslaught of emotion.

No. This can't be happening. It's Wily's dream!

He's going to be destroyed by this. Football means everything to him. He's been working so hard. He's—

"Is there any way you can get to the hospital? I think he could really use your support."

"Yes, of course." I sniff, willing myself not to break down as I throw on a coat and shove my feet into my boots.

Zander signs off while I finish getting ready, and I'm soon running out of the building, ordering an Uber, and waiting impatiently for it to arrive.

I try calling Wily, but it goes straight to voicemail.

"I'm so sorry this is happening." My voice quakes as I leave a garbled message. "I'm so sorry, baby. I'm on my way, okay? I'm coming."

He probably won't get it.

Shit!

How's he getting to the hospital?

Is he in an ambulance right now?

What state will I find him in when I arrive?

Worry eats me alive, and by the time the Uber arrives, my stomach feels like it's settled in my knees. I slip into the back and give the driver a shaky greeting, not even sure how I'm going to converse with him.

Thankfully, the man seems happy to drive in silence, and I scour my phone, looking for every piece of information on ACL tears I can find. It's not good. It's *really* not good. I chew on my bottom lip as we weave through town and get caught in a little traffic around Main Street.

The hospital is on the other side of Nolan, and even though it's considered a small town, I feel like it takes forever to get there.

Finally, we're pulling up outside, and I thank the Uber driver in a rush before racing into the emergency room.

I scan everyone and don't see Wily, so I run up to the counter, all out of breath and flustered.

"I need to see Wily Wilson!" I practically yell at the poor receptionist.

She gives me an unimpressed scowl before the lady behind her steps forward with an efficient air. "Are you his girlfriend?"

"Yes." I nod.

She flashes me a smile. "His friend told me you'd be coming. This way." She flicks her finger, and I follow her through the NO ENTRY doors and into a large treatment room separated by curtained-off sections, a bed in each one.

"The last one on your left." She gives me a wince. "I would walk you down there, but we're under the pump, so if you could just..." She points, and I nod my thanks.

Gripping my beanie, I creep across the shiny linoleum floor, shuffling past two closed curtains. One of them has a child wailing behind it. The curtain after that is open, revealing a lady lying on her back with an oxygen mask over her face. She has a bandage on her head, and she's so pale, I can see the veins in her neck. Her eyes are closed, and I glance away, wanting to respect her privacy.

This place is really full. I don't think there's a spare bed in the treatment room.

Glancing over my shoulder, I take in the hustle and bustle going on behind those sliding glass doors I just walked through. There's a frenetic energy about this place that's unsettling.

I slow to a stop just before the last curtain on the left, my heart rate spiking as I catch the murmured conversation behind it. The voices are low and rumbly, and the second I peek my head around the pale blue fabric, the conversation stops.

Zander and Grady, who are standing on either side of a shellshocked Wily, give me equally sad smiles. But all I can see is my boyfriend.

He's lying on the bed, looking hollow, like he can't believe this is happening.

His leg is propped up on a stack of pillows, and he has an ice pack over his left knee.

I gaze at the injury, my face crumpling to show just a touch of the heartache I'm feeling.

Wily's broken. The look on his face right now has me fighting tears.

"Thanks for coming." Zander lightly squeezes my shoulder, then looks at Grady. "I'm gonna go call the house, give them an update."

"Yeah." Grady nods, then looks from me to Wily before murmuring, "I'll come with you, see if Coach Jones has managed to speak with a doctor yet."

And so it becomes just Wily and me.

I'm at the end of the bed, staring at his ashen face and wondering how to approach this heinous situation.

Wily won't look at me. He's staring at his knee, caught in a dazed stupor as he no doubt tries to wrap his brain around this thing.

"Wily," I whisper, inching around the bed. His eyes dart to mine, and it's like he's noticing me for the first time. "Hey." I give him a weak smile, then reach for his hand. "I'm here."

"Satch." He sucks in a breath, sudden tears filling his eyes as he grips my hand. "What am I gonna do?"

"It's gonna be okay." I perch on the bed beside him.

"It's not." He shakes his head. "I can't play like this."

"I know." I look down at his knee, about to tell him that he'll heal and this is not the end, just a delay.

"I'm nothing without football." The words wobble out of him. "I'm nothing without the game."

"That's not true." I stand, taking his face in my hands and forcing those glassy eyes to look at me. "You don't *need* this game. You can be *anything*."

He shakes his head, not believing me.

"I know it's what you *want*, and because of that, you're gonna play again. I know you will." I try to give him an encouraging smile. "Just not yet."

His lips dip into a heart-wrenching frown, and then it happens. My big, strong, tough boyfriend shatters. It starts with a breathy sob that scrunches his entire face, and then he pulls me close, clinging to me as he rests his head on my shoulder and weeps.

It's impossible not to cry along with him.

Cupping the back of his head, I kiss the side of his face and close my eyes. Tears trickle down my cheeks as I listen to his keening sobs, my heart breaking right along with his.

Stroking my fingers through his hair, I do my best to comfort him. But there are no words.

I just have to hold him and let him know I'm not going anywhere.

I have no idea how long it takes.

My back is aching by the time he finally pulls away from me.

I want to ask him if he's okay, but that's the stupidest thing I can say. Of course he's not okay. He's completely wrecked.

Brushing the tears off his face, I then take his hand and press it to my lips, letting him know that I'm here in whatever capacity he needs me to be.

He's still not talking, and I have to admit it's unnerving. Wily's usually the chatterbox of the two of us, and I don't know how to fill this space.

But maybe I don't have to.

Maybe just holding his hand and being with him through this is exactly what he needs right now.

The doctor finally comes to check on him, Coach Jones hot on his heels. They both look flustered, like maybe they've been arguing. Wily's coach is glaring at the floor, his jaw clenched while the doctor apologizes for the delay.

"Your timing couldn't be worse," he explains. "We've just had a minivan collide with two other cars on the highway going out of town. Those surgeries take priority, so you're going to have to wait, I'm afraid."

"You haven't even examined him. Is he going to need surgery?" Coach Jones growls in his throat, and the doctor gives him a look of forced patience.

"One of my residents checked him when we first brought him through, and according to her assessment, Mr. Wilson is going to need surgery. We just can't perform it as soon as we'd like." The doctor turns to Wily again. "I'm sorry. I know that's not what you want to hear, but we only have so many surgeons in this hospital, and they'll be working throughout the night trying to save lives." He points to Wily's knee. "We'll manage the swelling as best we can and keep the pain meds coming. But for now, that's all I can offer."

I stare at Coach Jones, holding my breath as I wait for his reaction. After a painful beat, he runs a hand over his head and lets out an irritated huff while the doctor checks Wily's chart.

My boyfriend hasn't said a word yet. He's just lying there like a desolate statue.

"How are your pain levels?" the doctor asks. "I can get you something stronger if you need it."

Wily shakes his head, and I want to question his decision. He doesn't have to be in agony.

"Okay, well, just press the buzzer if you change your mind. The nurses will continue with their regular rounds, although please be aware, the staff is under enormous pressure right now. We'll get to you as soon as we can."

Wily nods, and I watch the doctor clip away, his steps hurried.

Turning back, I check Wily's expression. His eyes are closed, his head tipped back against the pillows. I've never seen him so pale. So sad.

This is horrible. Devastating.

"Are you okay?" Coach Jones asks.

I assume he's talking to Wily, but when I glance up, his eyes are trained on me. I flush, my head bobbing. "Yes. I'm going to stay here."

He didn't ask me that, but I tell him anyway so there's no confusion. I'm not leaving Wily, no matter what.

Coach Jones nods, giving Wily one more pained frown before softly murmuring, "I'm gonna go make some calls. But if you need anything..." He digs a business card out of his jacket pocket. "You let me know, and I'll come right back, okay? I've already been in touch with his parents. They're on their way."

"Thank you," I whisper, my fingers trembling as I take the card off him.

He walks away and I run my hand down Wily's arm, curling my fingers around his listless hand and silently begging him to look at me.

But he won't open his eyes.

My phone buzzes, and I enter into a lengthy text conversation with Sienna, and then I have one with Nylah, who's worried as well.

Nylah: Carson won't stop pacing. He's so stressed!

I try to send reassuring messages while my insides are in utter chaos.

Poor Wily.

I check his face again. His eyes are still closed, and I wonder if he's sleeping. That's good. He needs a reprieve from this nightmare.

I'm so gutted for him and worried that I won't know how to help him through this. I'm desperate to make it all better. Desperate for this setback not to kill his soul.

His dream has just been squashed.

But hopefully not shattered.

I have to remind him that this isn't over. It's just delayed.

From the stuff I've googled, this doesn't need to end his career. He may not get drafted this year... or he may just get drafted lower down on the list. I think that's how drafting works.

Whatever. He might still get picked up by a pro team.

And if he doesn't, I'm sure there are still other options.

He can come back from this injury. If anyone's strong enough, it's my coyote.

Although... I seriously have to make sure that he knows he *is* something without football. He's everything. He's so incredibly amazing, and football is lucky to have *him*, not the other way around.

A bustling and a rush of voices behind the curtain have me glancing up from my phone.

Two worried-looking people walk in, and I immediately know who they are.

Wily's parents.

I haven't met them yet, but it's so obvious. He looks just like his father but has his mother's coloring.

She's a blue-eyed blonde, stunningly beautiful and slender. His father is shorter than Wily but just as imposing, a broad man with a square face and strong jaw.

He doesn't even notice me as I move away from the side of the bed, my skin starting to itch as I fight the urge to step behind the curtain so they can't see me.

"Wily." His mom's voice trembles as she approaches the bed. "My darling boy." Her fingers skim over his leg, stopping just above the knee. "This is terrible."

Wily's eyes are open now, and he's gazing at his parents. He suddenly looks small and incredibly vulnerable. I see flashes of a little boy on the verge of being told off, and confusion tightens my stomach.

"Well, this is..." His dad shakes his head, his expression buckling. "I don't even know what to say."

"Dad..." Wily tries to talk, but his voice quakes and disappears.

"Why aren't you in surgery yet?" Mr. Wilson barks.

"David," Wily's mom softly warns. "Coach already gave us the update. You know why."

He runs a hand through his hair, so obviously stressed. "Maybe we should be transferring him to a different hospital."

My chest hitches. No! I need him to stay here so I can be close by. They can't just take off with him!

It's not about you. It's about what's best for Wily!

I swallow my protests as Mr. Wilson's phone starts ringing. He snatches it out of his pocket and checks the screen.

"Austin," he murmurs to his wife before taking the call. "Hey, buddy... Yeah, I'm with him now." His eyes dart to his son, and he looks agonized. "Not great. There's been a delay on his surgery..." He winces but then starts nodding. "Yeah. Yeah, I know." Closing his eyes, he pinches the bridge of his nose. "It's not over. We just need to figure out a new game plan..." He nods again. "Do you want to speak to him?"

Wily shakes his head, holding up his hand and refusing the phone when Mr. Wilson holds it out to him.

"Come on, son."

"No." Wily's voice is weak, but the expression on his face leaves no room for argument.

After a short sigh, Mr. Wilson wraps up the conversation, promising to call back with updates and their next move forward.

I wonder who he was talking to. Mrs. Wilson seems unfazed by the call. She hasn't taken her eyes off Wily since she stepped in here. She's now stroking his arm and looking just as devastated as his father.

Maybe that man was Wily's agent. I'm sure he'd have something to say about all this.

Wily told me the guy is really close to his father.

I hold my breath, watching Mr. Wilson as he starts talking. His voice is deep, more serious, gruffer than Wily's, and I can't help another instinctual step back.

"It'll be all right, son. We've still got options. You won't be a Top Ten pick for the draft anymore. Austin's guess is that you've dropped down to around the forty to fifty mark." He sighs, resting his hands on the bar at the end of hospital bed. "Team's still take on injured athletes if they've shown great potential, which you most definitely have. This isn't the end of the world, although you're worth more than a shitty contract." Mr. Wilson shakes his head, his mind clearly racing as he tries to problem-solve his way out of this disaster. "Let's not entertain the free agent option until we know for sure what your recovery time is going to be." Pinging straight, he starts looking around, and I shift to hide myself behind Mrs. Wilson. "Is there a doctor around anywhere? I need to speak with one. If we can get a time frame, we'll be able to sort out a plan moving forward."

With a delicate sniff, Mrs. Wilson ignores her husband, brushing her hand over Wily's cheek, her disappointment raw and overpowering.

Wily shakes his head, still not able to say anything, and I want to tell them all that it's going to be okay.

Why are they bombarding him with stupid game plans?

Why aren't they telling him they love him?

Why aren't they hugging him? Supporting him?

"When did you see the doctor?" his father asks.

Wily replies in a croaky voice, telling him what he knows, which doesn't feel like much, to be honest.

There's so much worry swirling around them, like this torn ACL is the most devastating thing that could happen to their son. But I want to shout that he's still alive! That it's a knee injury, not cancer!

"It's going to be okay." Mr. Wilson nods, still running a hand over the back of his head like he's trying to comfort himself. Stress is emanating from him in waves. It's impossible not to feel it. "I'll get in touch with the Scouting Combine people. Explain the situation. We'll find a way around this."

"It's not gonna happen this year, Dad." Wily's voice is cold. Stony.

"No, don't talk like that. We'll get you back on your feet. I'm gonna get you the best medical care. We'll talk to any experts we have to. There are options. Austin's already told me about a private training camp we can get you into. It means—"

"Dad, just..." Wily raises his hand to slow the guy down.

"This can't be over, son." His father's voice cracks. "You've worked too hard. I won't let you give up on your dream."

Wily sighs, shaking his head.

Wow. He really thinks he's done. Is that just shock talking? Where's my *"I can conquer the world"* man gone?

I step forward, ready to reach for his hand and assure him that he's not even close to being done. We can work through this. He's got his whole life ahead of him, and I'll help him become whatever he wants to be.

"Excuse me," his mother snaps when she senses my movements. Her blue eyes land on mine, surprise quickly morphing to sharp annoyance. "This is a private family matter. Who are you?"

"Oh, I..." Forcing a smile, I reach out a hand to introduce myself. "I'm Elizabeth. I'm Wily's—"

"Tutor," he interjects. "This is the girl who's been helping me. She's the reason I'll be able to graduate."

I glance at him, but he won't look at me. His jaw clenches, and he keeps his eyes trained on his knee.

Wow. Okay.

So, he's in love with me, but his parents don't know I exist, and he's calling me his tutor, not his girlfriend.

Ouch.

No, more than ouch.

This is brutal.

It hurts.

Like deep in my gut, I'm writhing in pain right now.

Trying to keep my expression neutral is so freaking hard, but I'm not about to start crying in front of these people.

Why isn't Wily claiming me?

Why—?

"Okay." His mother nods, still looking confused. "And why are you here?"

It's hard to talk past the lump in my throat.

My chest is tight, and it's taking everything in me to keep my voice even as I carry on this lie for my boyfriend.

Wait. Is he still my boyfriend or...?

My stomach clenches and I have to clear my throat, my voice coming out soft and raspy. "I just wanted to stop by and let him know that I'm going to speak to each of his professors and tell them about the injury." I have to clear my throat again before I can continue. "I'll let them know that I'll still be helping him so he can get the credits he needs to graduate."

His father frowns at me. "I hardly think that's important right now. In fact, it's probably best that you run along and let Wily focus on healing his body. The last thing he needs to be worrying about is school and graduation."

I nod, inching away from the bed.

My resolve to stay by Wily's side no matter what has completely vanished, snatched away by his parents' forceful voices... and the fact that Wily just called me his tutor and nothing more.

Flipping my coat over my arm, I lift my bag off the floor and murmur, "Bye, Wily."

"See ya, Satch," he croaks.

Just before disappearing behind the curtain, I glance over my shoulder and catch his eye. He looks about ready to cry all over again, and my heart starts burning as I walk out of the emergency treatment room and try to figure out what the hell just happened.

CHAPTER 62
WILY

Fuck.

The look on Satch's face as she left.

I feel even worse now than I did before.

I need to explain it to her, but I couldn't do that with my parents right there. I should have told her weeks ago, but whenever we've talked about my family, I've always steered conversation toward football and their love of the game. I've told her surface-level stuff and not once brought up the fact that if they know she's my girlfriend, they'll somehow find a way to blame her for my injury.

It sounds insane, but they're so obsessed with my football career and devastated over what's happened to me.

Introducing her as my girl right then would have put her directly in their line of fire, and I don't have the head-space to cope with that right now.

My knee is busted.

I have to have surgery.

I'll probably be out for months.

No Scouting Combine. I'll be lucky to get drafted at all, because who the fuck wants to take on an injured rookie?

My dad's comments are all bravado and bullshit.

The truth is... I'm fucking screwed!

My parents' grand plans for me and my bright pro future are going up in smoke.

Glaring down at my injured leg, I clench my jaw and berate myself for not mentioning the twinges I've been having. They were only little spikes of pain occasionally. I thought they were no big deal. It's not like I limped off the field. Every little tweak could be shaken off, so I left it.

I fucking left it, and now I'm laid up in a hospital bed waiting for surgery and freaking the fuck out.

I want Satch back.

I need her.

She held me and let me cry on her shoulder. She told me everything was going to be okay.

She's wrong, but just hearing her say it soothed something inside me.

And now she's walked away, no doubt gutted that I introduced her as my tutor and nothing more.

Fuck, fuck, fuck!

My parents are talking to me, but I don't know what they're saying.

I keep staring down at my knee, my heart thumping a dull beat, my head pounding right along with it.

"It's Blake." Mom holds her phone out to me.

I didn't even hear it ring.

Or did Mom call her?

"Wily?" My sister's voice is tinny through the speaker. I take the phone, pressing it against my ear and grunting so she knows I'm listening. "Holy shit, dude! This can't be happening! I'm so sorry."

I remain quiet, unable to speak past the boulder in my throat.

"I'm coming down, okay? I'm already on my way to the airport."

But what about school? You can't just fly across the country for me? I want to ask her those questions, but my voice is shot.

"What did she just say?" Mom tips her head, pulling the phone out of my hand. "You're coming here? You have class tomorrow." She blinks, then looks at Dad, obviously confused. "But we've got this. You need to stay in Chicago." After a listening beat, she scoffs. "I hardly think your professors said that."

"Gimme the phone." Dad takes it from Mom's hand. "What's going on, bean?" He listens intently, nodding, his mouth curling at the corners. "Well, I'm sure your brother will appreciate the support. And you can catch up on the classes later."

"David," Mom interjects.

He raises his hand to silence her.

She tuts, then huffs, her gold bracelets clinking as she flicks her hands wide and gives him an exasperated look.

"Love you, honey." Dad hangs up and passes Mom's phone back to her.

"Why did you say that?" she snips. "Blake has studying to do. We've got this. She doesn't need to be flying down here to sit by Wily's bedside. I can do that."

"She's worried about her brother," Dad tries to soothe her. "And she's ahead of schedule on her assignments and has already arranged with a friend to record any classes she's missing. She'll catch up on the work. You know Blake."

Mom rolls her eyes but has to concede.

Blake is smart and will no doubt breeze through this year with minimal effort, although knowing her, she'll put in maximum effort.

That girl will end up studying on the plane, hang out with me, and then spend her nights catching up on the classes she missed.

We really should be backing Mom up on this one and telling Blake to stay put.

But selfishly, I want her here.

We've always had each other's backs, and she'll support me when I tell my parents about Satch.

Shit, I should probably do it now.

Or maybe I can wait until Blake arrives.

Fuck! I want Satch to come back.

Dad lets out a heavy sigh, his expression glum when I glance at him. "I'm so sorry this has happened, Wily."

His genuine sadness makes my chest hurt in new ways. Shit. I feel like I'm letting him down.

"But everything's going to be okay." Perching on the side of my bed, he's careful to avoid jostling my body and softly rests his hand over mine. "Your career isn't over." He starts to smile—just a soft, closed-mouth look that's no doubt supposed to comfort me, but my stomach is still writhing. "When I first heard, I was absolutely devastated, but Austin reassured me on our drive up here that there are plenty of great options to get you back on track."

"Can't we just get through the surgery before talking about all this?" Mom complains. "Look at his face, David. He needs to rest."

"I'm trying to give him hope," Dad bites back. "And if we're going to pursue this private training camp idea, then we need to get on it now." He looks at me. "Austin said he can easily get you into one."

I nod, silently asking for more information.

"You'll do your rehab at the camp, be surrounded by expert care, and they'll prep you for the season ahead, make sure you're on track to be playing as soon as humanly possible. If the draft knows you're going to these efforts, it'll no doubt put you higher up on the list, and you might still get picked by a really great team and be offered a decent contract."

Hope starts to stir just a little, but my stomach is still twisted into a tight knot. I don't understand why. I should be jumping all over this thing. I think my brain just heard that pop, felt that searing pain in my knee, and immediately thought my career was over. Everyone keeps telling me it's not, but it fritzed out and went to worst-case scenario.

I try to blink past my pounding headache and focus on what Dad's saying.

It's not over.

There's still hope.

So what the fuck is my problem?

"It would mean dropping out of school now. There'd be no graduation, but you hate school anyway, right?"

My eyes dart to Dad's face as he keeps running through this epic solution... and now my chest is caving in.

Leave immediately?

Drop out?

A few months ago, I probably would have accepted that idea without a problem.

But now...

Satch.

Her face floats through my head, the look of sad acceptance she'll no doubt give me when I tell her the news. She'll be disappointed that I won't be graduating. I know it won't sit right with her.

And I don't even know if it sits right with me.

"Austin and I think that's your best move." Dad pats my hand, his eyes lighting as he gives me a genuine smile. "We're going to see our football dreams come true, son. You just hang in there and get better as fast as you can. It's all about mindset. I want you to start filling your head with positive thoughts, telling your body that it wants to heal and is capable of coming out even stronger than before."

Mom sniffs and starts nodding, her eyes glassy as she takes my other hand. "It's all going to work out, darling. Austin and Dad will take care of the details, and you can just sit back and enjoy this new adventure, okay? I know it's not the way we originally planned, but we've got your back. We'll do everything we can to help you through this."

I glance between my parents' hopeful faces and know I should be cracking a smile right now.

They're giving me solutions that I should *want* to hear. But all I can feel is a deep disappointment, because I don't love either scenario. If I drop out of school for this training camp thing, I'll be kissing my degree goodbye... and Satch. I'll have to leave her sooner than I want.

If I stay, I could fuck up my chances of getting drafted with the best team possible.

I don't know what the hell to do.

This should be a no-brainer, but it's not.

I've never felt more uncertain before in my life. My course has always been so narrow and singularly focused, but I have a woman who I love now...

A woman who has opened my eyes to more than just the game.

A woman who my parents will never accept if they think she'll sway my decision away from football.

CHAPTER 63
ELIZABETH

I admit it—I left the hospital, tucked myself around the corner of the building, and had a decent cry. The cold air made my tears feel like icicles, but I just stood there in the glacial breeze and let them fall.

I didn't sob.

There was no jerking stomach or hiccups popping out of my mouth.

These were silent tears that swelled my throat and made it ache.

I wasn't crying just because of Wily not introducing me as his girlfriend. It was everything. It all caught up to me in a rush, and I wept for Wily's heartbreak, for the pain he was going through, and all that he'd still suffer on his road to recovery.

I wept for the fact that his parents didn't seem to be lavishing him with the care and understanding I felt he needed.

And yeah, I cried because he didn't claim me.

I'm not sure why he didn't.

The pained look on his face when he caught my eye before I left the room told me there was more to it.

I need to let logic win on this, keep calm and force those ugly emotions away.

They're battling to break down the bridge we built over the weekend.

They're mocking me and whispering in my ear, *"He never really wanted you. You're not worth his time. He was just being nice when he said he loved you."*

But each nasty taunt is countered by the look on Wily's face when he told me I'm amazing and made me promise to believe him.

He meant it, right?

He wasn't lying. And he wasn't just being nice.

He really does think I'm amazing.

So why wouldn't he tell his parents that?

There has to be a decent reason. Wily's too kind to just throw me off a cliff. Something was holding him back, and I need to find out what it is.

Curling my fingers into fists, I start walking back to my dorm. It's too far to go the whole way on foot, but the cold, crisp air stings my cheeks, and I welcome it.

I walk for a good fifteen minutes before stopping at a diner for a bite to eat.

Craving comfort, I order fries, a slice of chocolate pie, and a Coke.

All the fat and sugar tastes delicious, and I down the meal in record time, momentarily relieved. Although, as I pay, the sad emotion I tried to bury under all that food quickly resurfaces, and by the time my Uber arrives and is dropping me off outside Buckley Hall, I'm back in the war zone again.

Shit.

Why didn't Wily tell his parents the truth?

Is he ashamed of me?

I don't want that to be right, but he must be embarrassed because—

"There she is."

I hear that familiar female voice and immediately tense.

No, no, no!

Not tonight.

My entire body convulses, my skin instantly breaking out in an itchy burn as Team Evil 2.0 clip toward me. They've obviously been waiting to pounce, and I so can't face this right now.

Hunching my shoulders, I grip my bag strap and mumble, "Not tonight, you guys. Please."

"Oh, this is happening, Fatty Satchwell." Jade grabs my coat sleeve and pulls me to a stop. "We were humiliated at the party!"

I can't help a scathing scoff as I spin to face them. "Oh no. Did someone embarrass you?"

My words are drenched in such a thick layer of sarcasm that all they can do is scowl at me, like how dare I have the audacity to mock them.

Are they seriously not getting the irony here?

They have been humiliating me for most of my life!

Anger fires through me so hot and fast it takes everything in me not to lash out with my fists. I want to grab their perfect shiny hair and rip chunks of it out of their scalps. I want to kick and maim and unleash a little hellfire in retaliation for all they've done to me.

I have no idea where this rage is suddenly coming

from. Maybe it's because of the harrowing afternoon I've just had trying to process my boyfriend's devastation. But it's like the lid just flew off my boiling pot of water, and I'm so beyond pissed off that fear has taken a back seat for once.

Damn, it actually feels quite good.

I'm not stupid enough to act on any of this anger coursing through me, but it does give me the strength to turn and try to walk away.

"Rumor has it your boyfriend's in the hospital." Viper Girl spits out the words. "What happened? Did you try to ride him, and you broke his poor body?"

Oh. That. Is. It!

They can insult me, but they are not saying a word about Wily. He's going through hell right now, and they're mocking it?

"Shut the fuck up," I seethe.

"What did you just say?" Jade's indignant surprise makes me spin, just so I can get a glimpse of her horrified expression.

It's with a sick sense of smug satisfaction that I walk back toward her and yell right in their faces. "I said 'Shut the FUCK up!'"

Jade leans back, her eyebrow arching as she crosses her arms and sneers, "Oh, you must be on crack if you think you can speak to me that way."

"Yet you're allowed to speak to me any way you want?" I argue. "What makes *you* so special?"

Jade gives me a pointed look, like *"Isn't it obvious?"*

But it's not.

It's seriously not.

These girls may be beautiful on the outside, but

they're horrible people, and they've made a sport of trying to ruin me.

Well, fuck that.

I'm not letting them make my night any worse than it already has been.

Staring at them, Mom's words filter back to me, and even though she probably had the same message through my high school years, for the first time in my life, I feel like I'm actually getting it.

Jade is unhappy.

And her little minions are too lost to think for themselves... so they're unhappy too.

Their treatment of me has nothing to do with who I am as a person and everything to do with them.

Expelling a pitying laugh, I shake my head. "You know... you have been tormenting me since I was ten years old. And I never did anything to deserve it." I scan Jade's expression for even just an inkling of remorse or guilt, but all I catch is a slight squirm from Kelsey, who hides it by crossing her arms the way Jade is doing. "You made me feel so small."

"Small?" Viper Girl lets out a mocking laugh.

I ignore it and keep going, fueled by a courage I've never felt before. "Small and insignificant and like I was less than you." I point to myself. "But that's all bullshit! None of this is my problem—it's yours!" I point at them, my voice rising. "So whatever hole you need to fill by putting people down all the time, you have to fix that shit and stop making me part of your problems."

Jade's face contorts into a comical frown. "What the fuck?"

"I'm a good person!" I slap a hand against my chest,

and it finally starts to dawn on me like the sun rising over a lake. Staring past them, I let the words soak into me and whisper, "I'm a really good person. I'm... I'm fucking amazing." I smile, the look on Wily's face coming back to me in a rush.

"You have to believe that. Promise me you will."

My eyes snap back to the girls, and I look each one in the eye, something I'm not used to doing. I think it unnerves them a little, and it gives my voice the strength it needs to be unequivocally clear. "I'm not going to let you do this to me again."

"What?" Viper Girl looks at her friends, pointing at me like I'm weird.

So I spell it out for them. "You're not my problem anymore. Your opinion means nothing to me."

Jade's eyes narrow into a dark glare.

"And you can try to taunt me or hurt me, but it's not gonna work. I have people in my life whose opinions actually count, and they think I'm beautiful. And they love me just the way I am. They don't have to mock me or rip my clothes or ruin my birthday party to feel better about themselves. They care about me, and they treat me like I'm important. And they're the people who deserve my time and attention."

My mind flicks immediately to Wily lying in a hospital bed, tortured and vulnerable.

Shit, I shouldn't have let his father kick me out of that room.

I don't know why Wily didn't claim me, but I should have claimed *him*... no matter what the consequences were.

Because I love him.

And I need to stop letting my doubts and insecurities take away the things I want most, like being there for my boyfriend when he's hurting and stressed.

Shit, I need to go to him.

Right now.

I step sideways, ready to walk around the girls and order another Uber, but they move into my path, pushing me back

I stumble but find my ground before I can fall over.

Fear pinches me, begging me to run, hide, get away before they tear up my clothes and scratch me again.

But fuck that.

Fuck them!

I'm not going to let these stupid, petty, immature girls keep robbing me of my dignity!

Standing as tall as I can, I pull my coat straight and glare at them. "I never should have let you hurt me for so long." My voice is hard. Steely. I've never heard it like this before... and neither have they.

Viper Girl's forehead wrinkles, while Kelsey glances at Jade for guidance.

Their leader is glaring daggers at me, but this time I face them head-on.

"Say whatever you want to me... it's vapor now."

She scoffs.

And I smile, pointing between them. "We're done here."

I've never spoken with such firm authority in my life, and I fucking love it!

Pride bursts through me as I pull my shoulders back and move around them.

This time, no one tries to grab for my coat, although Jade does throw one more proverbial knife my way.

"You'll always be a fat harpy, and you'll never deserve him!"

Spinning back around, I thunder toward her, getting right up in her face and hissing, "Enough! This is over."

She goes to touch me, but I shove her back before she can.

With a yelp, she stumbles against Kelsey, who only just catches her. They wobble on their feet, trying not to fall over, and I glare at all three of them, giving them one last warning.

"It's over!" I shout before spinning around and going back to the curb.

"Psycho bitch." I don't know which girl says it, but for some reason, it makes me laugh as I stalk away, pulling out my phone and ordering an Uber as I go.

I need to get back to Wily. It's all I can think about as I walk down the street with my head held high.

I'm not running.

I'm not hiding.

I'm heading to see my boyfriend, and whatever awaits me, I'm gonna somehow handle it.

Because I just put my lifelong tormentor in her place... and I'm still standing.

Fuck yeah!

I am still standing!

CHAPTER 64
WILY

I'm still waiting for surgery. The hours ticked by as my parents got more and more agitated. I couldn't give my father a firm yes on the training camp situation, and it was pissing him off.

He's pushing hard for it, and logically, I know it's the right thing to do, but I just can't bring myself to agree for some reason.

You know the reason.

Shit, if I tell them it's because I'm not ready to leave my girl, they will never get over it.

But is that all it is?

What is this niggle inside me?

Why can't I jump all over this idea?

A nurse came through about an hour ago to check my chart and ask if I needed more meds. I took them because my head was splitting, and my knee was killing me.

Dad peppered her with questions as she sorted me out, and when she told him it was most likely that my surgery wouldn't happen until the morning, he lost it.

Mom had to calm him down, but she was just as gutted as he was. I could tell because she went really, *really* quiet, and she only does that when shit is bad.

And it was so fucking quiet.

I couldn't talk. Dad sat there staring at nothing while Mom perched on a chair, her knee bobbing as she messed around on her phone, obviously trying to distract herself.

Thank fuck, the nurse came back and told my parents visiting hours were nearly over. They could come back and see me tomorrow, and probably after the surgery would be best.

Before my parents finally left, they moved me up to a room for the night—my parents insisting that I have one to myself. It was fucking embarrassing, but thankfully it worked out that there was a single room available, so they parked me in there and told me to try and get some sleep. I'd be prepped for surgery first thing in the morning.

They didn't give me a specific time, and it will no doubt feel like an age, stuck in this bed with a dead phone and a little TV that doesn't work.

I can't watch anything anyway.

I'm aching and can't get comfortable.

I have no way of contacting my friends or my girl.

Shit.

I have no idea what she's going through right now, but I should have fucking told my parents she was my girlfriend!

After her disaster of a birthday party and how hard I had to work convincing her she was everything I wanted, I then went and blew it!

And I can't contact her to apologize because my fucking phone is out of juice and—

The door creaks open and I glance up, hoping it's a kind nurse who might find me a charger.

But the second my visitor walks through the door, the air leaves my lungs in a whoosh. "Thank God." I choke out the words, relief swamping me as I hold my arms wide and silently ask for a hug.

I might not get one.

I probably don't deserve it without some kind of explanation, but then I spot Satch's smile as she walks toward me, nestling against my side and laying her head on my shoulder.

I can't describe the emotion welling up inside me.

Cupping the back of her soft hair, I hold her close and whisper on repeat, "I'm sorry. I'm so fucking sorry."

She stops me after my third time, sitting back to look at me with a gentle smile. "It's okay."

"It's not okay." I tuck the hair behind her ear, running my knuckles down her smooth cheek. "I hurt you."

Resting her hand on my chest, I cover her short fingers with my large ones as she softly says, "You confused me. At first, yes, I guess I was hurt, but the more I thought about it, the more I realized that you must have done it for a reason. Because... I'm fucking amazing, right? You made me promise to believe that."

My lips twitch, then rise into a slow smile, which I press against her fingers the second I raise them to my mouth.

"You are fucking amazing," I whisper.

She watches me, her gaze burning with that silent question: *"Why?"*

Releasing a heavy sigh, I ignore the pain in my knee and lean forward anyway, wrapping my hand around her hip and pulling her closer to me.

She tucks her legs up beneath her, careful to avoid my injury, and rests her head against my shoulder.

"My parents don't know about you," I admit.

"Yeah, I got that part." Her tone is rueful, and I take it as forgiveness.

Kissing the top of her head, I thread our fingers together and continue, "The reason I didn't tell them is because they have this idea in their heads that girls are a distraction. They don't seem to mind me messing around and having fun, but anything serious is gonna hinder my career. They've been so set on me getting established in the football world and really making a name for myself. In their minds, falling in love will only stop that from happening. They're convinced I'll be distracted. It'll be a split-focus situation, and that'll affect my game and my training."

"Do you think that's true?" Her voice is small.

After a long pause, I finally admit the truth with a sigh. "To some degree." I kiss her head again, assuring her that this isn't a breakup speech. "I guess when they got here and asked who you were, I was worried that if it all came out, they might accuse you of getting in the way. I was just trying to protect you, but I wasn't able to explain it, and my phone's died, and I've been lying here hating myself and worried sick that you were thinking I don't want you. Because I do." I squeeze her against me. "You're my woman, and I just... I need you here with me. And I fucking hate that I let my dad dismiss you. I should have said something. I should have—"

"Shhh." She calms me, rubbing a hand over my stomach, then up to rest on my chest. "It's nice that you wanted to protect me." She kisses my pec before nestling her head back down again. "But you can't always do that. I need to be strong enough to stand up for myself. And we could have faced your parents together." She lets out a soft sigh. "I probably should have said something when you introduced me as your tutor."

I grunt, resting my cheek against her head and refusing to let her take any of the blame for this. "It was my fault, Satch. I played it all wrong."

Wrapping her arm around my waist, she holds me a little tighter, then lets out a soft giggle.

"What?" I shift my head at the same time she does, leaning back so I can look at the cute smile on her face.

She looks... proud as she licks her lips, then tells me, "I played something right tonight."

"What do you mean?"

"Well... I think you're gonna be really proud of me."

"Oh yeah?"

Her smile grows, and then she proceeds to tell me exactly what went down outside Buckley Hall.

At first, I tense up, my muscles coiling with fury at the thought of those girls ambushing her outside her fucking dorm! A place she's supposed to feel safe. A place to rest and study and—

But then she tells me what she said to them.

"Really?" I interrupt her to clarify a few details, and she's right.

I am *so* fucking proud.

She stood up to those girls. She put them in their place, and she—

"I don't know if they'll come at me again, but at least I know how to handle them next time. I'll just keep up that 'your words are vapor' mantra, and if they try to step things up a notch, then I'll—"

"There won't be a next time," I growl.

"Wily." She sits up to look at me. "There might be. And you can't always be there to stop them."

Shit. I hate that she's right, especially if I go to this private training camp. I won't be around to protect her, and it's weighing on me big-time.

My expression must be giving this all away, because she gifts me a sweet smile before pecking my lips.

"I love that you want to stop them, but that's not always possible. The point is, *I* handled it. Me. And you know how I did that?"

"How?" I grumble, still riled by the idea that they might try again.

"I believed my boyfriend when he told me I'm fucking amazing." She grins, and I swear she's never looked more beautiful than in this moment right here.

Weaving my hand around the back of her neck, I pull her forward to kiss me, taking my time to strength the connection between us.

I love this woman.

She *is* fucking amazing, and I never want her to doubt it.

Tipping my head, I deepen the kiss and dance a slow, sweet tongue tango with her, then softly ask her to stay with me. Because the thought of watching her walk out of here again is too devastating. I need her tonight. I need to hold her tight and draw from the strength she's offering.

I need to talk to her about the decision that's looming in front of me, but right now, I just want to hold her.

My heart is bruised and metaphorically bleeding as I face this unexpected injury.

But I'll survive.

I'll heal.

And having her beside me is only going to speed up that process.

CHAPTER 65
ELIZABETH

Sleeping against Wily, as good as it might feel, is not an easy feat in a hospital bed. My arm goes numb, and I need to shift, but I don't want to disturb him. And then around two in the morning, he starts getting pain as the meds have worn off, and I rush out to get the night nurse, who then scolds me for being there.

I try to tell her that Wily needs me, but she isn't having it.

In the end, Wily loses his shit and yells at her that I'm not leaving, and I back him up, saying if I'm not allowed on the bed, then I'll park myself on the floor for the night.

She looks about ready to call security, but she must have seen the desperate, pleading look on Wily's face and ends up relenting with a sigh.

"Don't let anyone see you in here," she whispers at me, pulling the curtain around so no one can see us through the glass in the door before leaving to get Wily his meds.

He's sad and restless, so I take his hand, brushing my

thumb over his knuckles. "What should we talk about?" I smile, trying to distract him. "I've got some great diner stories I can tell you, or we could—"

"Satch." He sighs my name, squeezing my fingers, the look on his face making me instantly nervous.

"What is it?" I coax him when his eyes finally track up to my face... and he doesn't say anything.

His blue gaze is glassy... tortured.

"Baby?" I touch his face.

"I might have to leave you," he whispers, his voice raw and wounded.

"What do you mean?" I keep my tone gentle, stuffing down the bloom of panic that wants to expand and blow up in my chest.

"I—" His explanation is cut short by the nurse, who returns with the meds and is clearly appeased to see my butt in the chair and not Wily's bed.

She waits until he's swallowed the pills and sipped some more water before checking on his knee and making a small adjustment. He hisses, and I flinch at the pain on his face.

"I know," she murmurs softly, her smile compassionate when she takes the empty cup from him and glances at me. "Make sure he rests."

I nod, waiting for the door to click shut behind her before looking back at my boyfriend, who is so obviously weighed down. And totally exhausted.

I have to know why he might have to leave me, but I also need him to rest.

Worrying my lip, I gnaw on it until Wily softly reprimands me, "Stop that."

He reaches out, brushing his thumb over my bottom

lip, and I'm losing my battle with this whole *hiding my panic* thing.

Sucking in a shaky breath, I know I shouldn't ask, but I have to. I selfishly have to know now or that panic is going to get the better of me.

"Why do you have to leave?"

His sigh is so heavy, I feel the weight off it smother me, pushing on my shoulders. They sink, curling in as I start gnawing on my lip again.

"There's this... training camp I can probably get into."

"Okay." I nod.

"Dad's really pushing for it." Wily swallows. I watch his Adam's apple bob, too afraid to look him in the eye in case I give something away. Something that might stop him from making the best choice for him. "It would mean dropping out of school and going straight to the camp. I'd do all of my recovery there, get myself fit for the next season. It's probably my best shot at scoring a decent contract. Getting drafted with a good team."

I nod, willing myself not to cry as I play with his fingers.

"I don't know what to do," he softly whispers, and my head jolts up.

My eyebrows dip in confusion; I can feel them furrowing as I give him a questioning frown. "What do you mean?"

Working his jaw to the side, he scratches his short whiskers. "I don't want to leave you."

Aw. My heart folds, turning to putty as I fight the urge to do the wrong thing.

"But Wily, you..." *Say it. Don't be a selfish bitch. Just say it!* "You have to. This is your dream. Your goal. If it's going to help you get there, then..." My nose wrinkles, and I can't help a short huff. "Sucks that you won't be able to graduate, though. You deserve that too."

He stares at me, and I will my gaze to cross over his. His eyes are so blue, so vibrant. "You know, before I met you, this would have been a no-brainer. But now..." His expression crumples. "Now, I'm torn."

As much as I don't want to say it, I force myself to be the bigger person. This isn't about me and my needy self. I want him to pursue his dreams. I love him enough to encourage him in whatever he wants to do.

"It's okay to leave me." I reach for the necklace that I haven't taken off since he clipped it around my neck. Holding up the coyote pendant, I force myself to smile. "You'll always be with me. And I will only ever be a phone call away. If you want us to stay together, then we will."

"Of course I want us to." He lifts my hand, pressing it against his cheek and holding it there. "It would suck to live away from you, but I know you're still my girl."

"Yes, I am." I smile, tears filling my eyes.

He swallows, pressing his lips against my wrist before running circles over my soft skin. His thumb is warm and comforting and... Why is he trying to comfort me? Shouldn't I be the one doing all the soothing right now?

"Coyote," I whisper. "It's okay. It's—"

"It's not the only reason I'm torn," he mumbles, cutting me off without even noticing. He's staring at his knee now, looking sweetly confused when he turns back to face me. "I'm hating the idea of dropping out of school." He shrugs. "I want to graduate."

"Then you should do that." It's so easy for me to jump

in with that encouragement. Of course I want him to graduate! Dropping out this close to the finish line is insane.

But I'm aware that I'm coming at this from a very different perspective than a football-obsessed offensive lineman.

He sighs, shaking his head. "Dad will hate that."

I wince, my voice soft and breathy as I argue back. "It's your life. The choice has to be yours."

"I know." He nods. "I just want both, you know? I want my original plan back." His voice wobbles, then breaks as he glares at his knee. "Stupid fucking ACL."

I stand up, resting my hand on his cheek and guiding him to face me. "It's not a decision you have to make right this second, okay? You have time. Let's just get you through this surgery, and then we can hash it out and you can settle on whatever feels best."

His frown is pained and heartbreaking. "Both are gonna hurt."

There's nothing I can do but nod and give him a sad smile.

His expression crumples all over again, and I pull him close, kissing the side of his head and softly stroking his hair.

He slowly starts to relax, the pain relief obviously kicking in. I think it might be making him sleepy, too, because his head gets heavy. I rest it back against the pillow as his eyes slip shut and he drifts off to sleep.

I hold his hand and watch him for as long as I can keep my eyes open, then finally shut down and end up falling asleep with my butt in the chair and my head on the mattress.

CHAPTER 66
ELIZABETH

Okay, so my back is pretty annoyed with me right now.

Waking up with an ache in my spine, I wipe the drool from my mouth, do a slow, painful stretch, then turn to find Wily giving me a sleepy smile. It's edged with pain, and I stand up, kissing his lips before pulling back to check on him.

"How bad?"

"I'm gonna be okay, Satch."

I'm not sure I believe him. I've never seen him so pale, and his eyes are glassy again.

He rests his hands on my arms, and we share a silent conversation until the curtain swishes back and the nurse comes in to help Wily use the bathroom and freshen up.

I wander down the hall to find the public restroom and relieve myself.

Catching my reflection in the mirror, I grimace at my raccoon eyes and attempt to tidy up my ponytail before heading back to Wily's room.

He's just sitting back down, wincing in pain as the nurse lifts his leg, then checks the compression bandage.

"There's a bit of swelling, but they should still be able to operate." The nurse smiles at him. "Morning shift is just going through the debrief, and then it'll be your turn. As soon as the changeover has gone through, a new nurse will be back to prep you. Should be about an hour, okay?" She pats his shoulder, then glances at me. "You two take care."

"Thank you for all you've done." I smile at her. "And for letting me stay."

She winks, grinning at me before walking out of the room.

I take a seat in the chair and thread my fingers back through Wily's.

He's staring at his knee, his troubled expression doing my heart in.

"Coyote," I whisper to get his attention, and he looks at me with a sad smile.

"You should get going," he croaks. "I don't want you to be late to class, and I'm guessing you want to grab yourself a coffee and some breakfast first, so..."

"I'm not going today." I leave no room for argument, but he doesn't even try to convince me otherwise. Yeah, he's really feeling vulnerable.

For such a tall, strong, positive man, it's hard to see.

But I'm also honored that he wants me here with him.

I've never felt so needed in my life.

The minutes tick by, and we fill them with bursts of conversation. I'm getting hungry, and not having my usual caffeine kick is starting to give me a headache, but if Wily's not allowed anything, then I can last too.

I'll eat while he's in surgery.

A nurse, a doctor, and an anesthetist filter in one after the other, filling out forms, scribbling notes, asking questions, reassuring us with friendly smiles and calm voices. There's been one more delay, adding an extra hour to Wily's wait, and I feel so bad for him, but he remains stoic.

In fact, his lips barely twitch, and then they dip into an outright frown when his parents and a girl with long blonde curls walks in.

"They said we could see you before you go in for surgery." His mom beams at him, having obviously put on her *positive* face this morning.

But that smile can't hide the strain in her eyes. The makeup she's wearing is no doubt covering dark circles. She probably got zero sleep last night, and I get it. She's worried about her son.

His dad doesn't look much better. I steal a quick glance at him, wondering how long it will take him to notice me this time.

I'll no doubt be asked to leave in five, four, three, two—

"Oh, shithead, what have you done to yourself?" The young woman takes one look at him and shakes her head, while her mother gasps and promptly tells her off for talking to her brother that way.

This must be Wily's sister, Blake.

I glance at my boyfriend, watching him share a secret smile with his sibling.

Squeezing his fingers under the blanket, I try to catch his eye. I want to share a smile with him, too, but he's staring at his father, and it's only then that I realize Mr. Wilson is glaring at me.

I turn to face him, my insides jittering when he crosses his arms and narrows his eyes. "Why are you back here? Wily shouldn't be thinking about school right now. He's got enough on his plate!"

"Oh, I'm..."

"She's not here for school," Wily clarifies.

"Oh yeah?" His dad frowns. "Why is she here, then?"

"Because I'm his girlfriend." The words are out of me before I could even think, and I nearly gape in surprise at my boldness but manage to bite my lips together instead, stealing a quick glance at Wily.

Whoops. He probably didn't want me to just blurt it like that, but... Oh hey, he's smiling at me. He looks... grateful.

I grin back at him, lost in our silent conversation, until his mother tears us apart.

"His girlfriend? I don't think so. Wily doesn't have time for women. He's focused on his football career right now. He needs to pour all of his energy into getting better, so you, little miss, can just be on your way. This is a family affair."

Blake winces at her mother's rudeness, pulling a face behind the woman's back, which makes my lips twitch.

Her dad snaps his head to look at her and she puts on a sweet smile for him, her entire demeanor changing to that of a perfect angel.

Reaching for her hand, Mr. Wilson pulls his daughter close, wrapping an arm around her shoulders before looking at me.

Shit. Is he about to back up his wife?

"It's time to go." He tips his head toward the door, and my legs are honestly itching to just get up and flee, but Wily's fingers tighten around mine, and I force myself to stay.

"She's not going anywhere," Wily softly informs them. "I need her here."

"Son—" his dad starts, but he doesn't get a chance to finish.

"She's my girlfriend, okay? And she's been that for a while now."

"No, she hasn't." Mrs. Wilson laughs. "You haven't said anything about having a girlfriend."

Wily shuts his eyes with a sigh. "Because I knew if I did, you'd tell me to end it and get all stressed that she'd be distracting me when I was on the field."

"Well, girls *are* a distraction," Mr. Wilson says. "College is not the time to be getting into a serious relationship. You need to focus right now, son." He points to Wily's leg. "Look what happens when you don't stay the course."

"His injury has nothing to do with our relationship," I pipe up, once again shocking myself by being so bold.

I glance at Wily, and he nods. "It's true. She wasn't even at my practice. In fact, she hasn't come to any of my practices or my games. Satch is not distracting me."

"Satch?" Mrs. Wilson's nose wrinkles. "Your name is Satch? I thought you said it was Elizabeth."

"Nickname," I clarify, standing up to smooth down my skirt and extend my hand. "I'm Elizabeth Satchwell."

No one shakes my hand, but Blake slaps me a little skin, giving me a subtle wink before blinking up at her father. "What, Daddy?"

He growls in his throat, frowning at Wily before throwing that look at me.

"Don't look at her like that." Wily's voice comes out firm and cutting. "Don't look at her like she's not welcome. Or that she's some problem that has to be solved."

I swallow, grateful for Wily's fierce protection of me.

"This is so disappointing," Mrs. Wilson whispers.

"Mom." Wily frowns, whipping his head to scowl at her.

"I was talking about your knee. Just this whole situation." She flicks her hand through the air. "I just really hope you're telling the truth when you say she hasn't been distracting you, because you guys lost the final, and now you're injured. Nothing like this has ever happened to you before, and I can only come back to what your father was saying about focus. We're talking about your life here, Wily! You've worked so hard to throw it all away now." Her eyes glass over.

"I'm not throwing anything away," Wily croaks, and I can't stand this.

All I can hope is that they're just clueless and not intentionally trying to make him feel bad.

"Mr. and Mrs. Wilson." I grab their attention, swallowing when their laser glares land on me. "I know how important football is to your family. I know Wily's your superstar." I glance at him and smile before turning back to face the firing squad. "But I also know that he's worth more than the game. His life isn't over. He's smart and creative and has the most amazing people skills. He's going to do wonderful things, and if that's football, then awesome. I will be right there beside him, cheering him on. But if this doesn't work out the way you all planned, then I'm not worried about his future." I look at him, hoping he doesn't mind me saying this. "Whatever happens, he's going to find something else that will inspire him, and he's going to be really good at it."

He's staring up at me like he can't believe what I just said.

But it's true.

Smiling at him, I throw in a little wink before turning back to his parents and ignoring the itch across my stomach.

Keep going. Wily's worth itching for.

"This injury won't stop him, I know that. But I hope it's also making you all realize that football isn't the only option. This is an opportunity to see what else might be out there. What other future plans he could make."

"He will be playing football," his dad argues. "I'm already working to secure him a spot at a private training camp. You need to stay out of this, young lady."

"If Wily wants to drop out of college and go to the training camp, then of course I will support that." My chest spasms at the idea of him leaving so soon, but I keep going, my voice only shaking a little. "I know how much he wants to play for the NFL. I'm not standing in the way of that, but I'm also aware that he's more than capable of graduating. There's nothing wrong with giving himself a chance to think about what he might want to do *after* football. This is a window of opportunity, and you need to stop treating it like a fatal disaster. Wily's not dying. He's not locked in. He's not running out of time. He has his whole life ahead of him, and it's going to be an *amazing* one."

They both gape at me, like how dare I be so bold, but then I notice Blake fighting a grin, and Wily's fingers brush over mine before wrapping around them.

I turn to check that he's okay with what I said and am rewarded with a silent "I love you."

Reading his lips, I mouth back, "You're fucking amazing." And then I say aloud, "I love you too."

His mother gasps, touching her chest, and I glance over to catch his father's intense stare.

He's not smiling, but he's not glaring at me either.

Blake runs her hand down her mother's arm and gives her wrist a little squeeze. "It's gonna be okay, Mom. I like this one."

She winks at me, her smile playful and encouraging.

Oh, thank God.

It's not the immediately warm reception my parents gave Wily, but with Blake's help, I might just have a chance at finding a place in this family. Especially if I can make them understand that Wily's life is not a one-way street but a multilayered pathway.

And we're going to walk those roads together.

CHAPTER 67
WILY

The surgery went as well as could be expected, and four days later, I'm carefully hobbling up the front steps of Football Frat. Sienna has set up a bed for me in the living room, which is a pain in the ass for everyone, but none of them seem to mind.

Everyone's been so fucking nice and accommodating.

When I woke up from surgery, Satch was the first face I saw, after the nurses, and I clung to her hand like my life depended on it. For the first couple of days, she didn't leave my side unless absolutely necessary, doing her homework in a chair by my bed when my parents visited with me, then snuggling against my side as soon as they left.

They're not loving the idea of her, but they're quickly warming to her as a person. It's impossible not to; she's sweet and so obviously in love with me. I think my parents are appreciating the fact that she has my best interests at heart while also being completely compassionate about how unsettling this injury has been for all of us.

Each time they popped in, their reaction to Satch was a little less frosty, so there's hope.

My teammates have come to see me a few times, the coaches too. Coach Jones gave me a few hours of his time on Wednesday, talking through my options. It was nice to talk to a neutral party, and I opened up about the training camp and how torn I was over the whole not graduating thing.

He gave me some things to think about, reminding me—just the way Satch had—that there's more to life than football. It was surprising to hear, coming from a guy who has lived and breathed the game most of his life.

"I think I want to graduate," I finally told him, just before he had to leave.

He paused after rising from the chair, giving me a proud smile. "I don't think you'll regret that decision. You'll get drafted—I have no doubts in my mind about that. You're too good. And you might not be Top Ten anymore, but these selectors aren't stupid. They know talent, and they've been watching you for a while now."

Damn, I wished my parents had been there to hear that. Telling them my decision after Coach left was brutal. They didn't get it. Dad was livid, calling Austin, who he wanted to win me over, and when that didn't work, he tried to sell me on all the reasons why his way was better than mine.

"Would you stop," I barked. "I want to get my degree, okay? I've spent nearly four years here battling through, and I won't quit this close to the finish line. I'm good enough to heal and play professional football. But I also deserve to graduate, so I'm taking my damn chances on that draft and believing in myself. It'd be nice if you could do the same!"

My parents gaped at me after that, clearly shocked by my outburst, and when Satch arrived after her classes to see me, the poor girl walked into a minefield.

"Uh... is everything okay?" Her eyes darted around the three of us, landing on me with a worried frown.

Letting out a heavy sigh, I glanced at my parents before mumbling, "I've decided to graduate and take my chances with the draft."

Satch's face instantly bloomed with a smile, which she tried to clamp down but couldn't.

Dad cleared his throat, glaring at her, and she shrank away from his gaze until I barked, "Stop! Stop looking at her like that."

"Well, tell her to stop smiling." He flicked a hand in her direction.

"I'm sorry, Mr. Wilson." She squeezed her index finger, which she only ever did when she was nervous. I reached for her hand. "I'm just proud of him. For believing in himself. I don't think he'll regret this decision. And I know... I mean *know*"—she tapped her finger against her heart—"that he's going to play professional football. He's too good not to. But then he'll also have a degree backing him up. We can't predict the future or if he might get injured again."

Mom gasped, covering her mouth, and Satch scrambled to finish.

"He probably won't. I'm just saying that... options aren't a bad thing."

Dad huffed, crossing his arms and still looking kind of dark over my decision.

"Come on, you guys," I murmured. "You know she's right. Just believe in me. Please. I need you to do that."

"Of course we believe in you." Mom turned to me, her eyes getting misty. "I guess we've just had this plan for so long, and we're struggling to adjust to this spanner in the works." Her expression softened as she smiled at me. "But we will adjust. And we'll support you. This is your decision." Glancing at my father, she gave him a pointed look, and after a painful beat, he finally nodded.

"I just want what's best for you." His voice was gruff and rigid.

"This feels right, Dad. Please, I really need you behind me on this." Reaching out my hand, I waited for my father to take it... and much to my relief, he didn't make me wait long.

Grasping my fingers, he gave them a reassuring squeeze before calling Austin and updating my agent on the plan.

It'll take them time to process their disappointment, but the longer we all sit on my choice, the easier it is for them to accept.

I'll still have my moments. I'm sure we all will. But I'm thinking long-term here, and I won't be playing football forever. It's good to have a backup plan, and with Satch's help, I'm gonna secure a really good one.

If I'm honest, right now... with the amount of pain I've been in, the thought of running onto a field is too much.

I just want to sit the fuck down and get better.

Carson and Tyrell are on either side of me, helping me up the front steps and into the living room. Easing onto the couch with a wince, I stare across the space to my bed in the corner and can't help an unhappy sigh. This is gonna suck.

"Wywee picta." Zoey runs in, holding up drawings for me.

I take them with the best smile I can give her, although I'm sure it's not as sunny as it would usually be.

"Careful of his leg, Zo," Carson warns, steering her away from my busted knee.

She gapes at the bandage before giving me a serious look and running back out of the room again.

I gaze down at the scribbly colors. She's gone for circles in orange and lines of blue and red. *For Wily* is written in neat handwriting at the bottom corner with a heart next to it. That must be Sienna's writing. I brush my thumb over it and look at the next picture while Tyrell goes back to my truck to unload the rest of my stuff.

Satch will be here soon.

She really wanted to ride home with me, but I made her go to class. She's missed so much school already and is getting too far behind now. I don't want her working until three in the morning to catch up.

I wouldn't let it go, and she huffed off to her classes this morning.

She'll forgive me, and I already can't wait to see her this afternoon.

"Okay, I think that's everything." Tyrell dumps my bag on top of my temporary bed, and I give him a closed-mouth smile. He sighs, resting his hands on his hips. "You'll be back in your own room in no time, man. You gotta believe it."

"Yeah, thanks." I nod. "I'll work hard, do everything I can to speed up the recovery."

"I know you will." He grins, walking out of the room as my sister bustles in with her stuff.

"Am I sleeping in your room or Zander's old room?"

"Blake," I whine, tipping my head back. "You should be heading back to Chicago."

She rolls her eyes. "Are we seriously having this discussion again?"

I glare at her. She's frustratingly stubborn, and no one can talk her out of sticking around in Nolan to help with my recovery. I didn't ask her to, but she won't fucking let up!

Between her, Sienna, and Satch, I'm gonna be fucking henpecked, not to mention the visits my parents will no doubt make. It's safe to say, I'll be well looked after. I shouldn't complain, but I'm pissed off that people are gonna have to sacrifice and rearrange their schedules for me.

"We do it because we love you," Satch reminded me. That thought helped a little.

Still, looking at my sister, I try one last time. "It's your freshman year. You should be—"

"Exactly. My freshman year. Ridiculously easy, and the perfect one to make compromises on. I've already told you I've contacted each of my professors to explain the situation, and they're happy for my friends to record every lecture. It's like doing online school for a few weeks, and I don't understand why you're so against it. It's a fucking brilliant plan, shithead!"

Her cute face scrunches into a scowl, and I can't help a snicker. "You're a pain in my ass, butt face."

"Yeah, well, I love you too." Her sneer is adorable, and I grin at her, hoping to break the tension. She huffs, snatching her bag and stomping up the stairs, grumbling about ungrateful brothers.

Shit. Staring down at my bandaged leg, I will my body to heal as fast as it can. The doctor told me it'd be months of recovery before I'd be fit to play again. Whichever team drafts me is taking on a risk, but I'll work my ass off to prove it's the best decision they could make.

I won't get much game time, if any, in the coming season, but I'll become part of whatever team takes me and make it count.

Although... Satch is making me realize that football doesn't have to be my *only* career. Shit, that speech she gave my parents—hell, *everything* she's said to my parents—I can't stop thinking about it. She's so convinced of my capabilities, and maybe I'm starting to believe it too. I have no idea what else might inspire me other than football, but for the first time in my life, I'm kind of open to exploring it.

"Doter Zoey here!" Zoey runs back into the room with her plastic medical kit, and it's impossible not to smile at her.

She's put on her doctor's coat but buttoned it wrong, so it's all out of alignment. Brushing a curl off her face, she sets the kit down on the floor and proceeds to go through all the toys, taking my temperature and blood pressure.

She seems to know not to go near my leg, and even though she stares at the bandage a few times, she resists the urge to investigate it.

I get my knuckles tapped by the little hammer instead

and am sure to make my fingers shoot out in response. She giggles and does it again. Her sweet amusement continues to fill the room until she tires of my antics... and to be honest, I'm tiring fast too.

Getting over surgery fucking sucks.

I feel depleted, and I'm gonna need more painkillers soon. I try to hold out for as long as I can each time, but the pain is already starting to creep in, my knee throbbing.

Shifting gently, I reposition my butt on the couch just as Sienna walks in.

"Just heard from Zander's dad." She eyes me cautiously, and I nod, telling her it's okay. As much as it kills me that I'm not there, I really want to know how Zander's getting on at the Scouting Combine. "He's doing great." Her eyes start to sparkle. "In this latest update, his dad couldn't talk fast enough. I think Zander's really showing them how amazing and committed he is."

I nod, pleased with the news. "He's gonna get drafted by the best. It's a guarantee."

"Yeah." Sienna nods, glancing down at Zoey, then back up at me. "I think you're right." Her smile is nervous as she clutches the phone to her chest. "I wonder where we'll end up."

I shrug and smile, hoping to ease her uncertainty. "At least you'll be together."

"True." Her shoulders relax as her smile starts to grow. "That's very true."

"And you'll make new friends and set up a really great life for yourselves." She nods, and I throw in one last nugget. "And we're only ever a phone call away."

Walking across the room, she bends down and

presses a kiss to my cheek. "You're the best, Wily. Thank you."

"Tank you," Zoey adds, collecting the last of her toy medical kit and grinning at me. "Better soon, Wywee."

"I'll definitely get better now that Doctor Zoey's patched me up."

She giggles, taking her mom's hand and walking out of the room.

Blake pops back down the stairs a few minutes later, asking if I need anything.

I boss her around, figuring I might as well take advantage since her stubborn ass isn't leaving me.

I still don't get it.

I'm not sure I'd drop everything and give up my life to nurse her. Shit, that makes me sound like an ass. Maybe I would.

But I have other people who can help me, and we can afford to hire a nurse or something. She doesn't need to be doing this.

Which I tell her for the thousandth time when she pops the pills in my hand and holds out a glass of water.

"Would you seriously shut up about this? I've made my decision! And this is going to be so painful if you keep going on about it."

"I just don't understand your decision," I grumble.

"You're my brother, I love you, and you need my help right now. What's not to get?" She flicks her hands wide with exasperation before plunking down on the couch beside me.

I give her a once-over, my eyes narrowing as I try to read her.

She huffs and shuffles around to face me, bulging her eyes with a pointed look. "What?"

"I'm just trying to figure out if that's the full story."

"What's that supposed to mean?"

"Why are you really here?"

"I've told you!" Her face bunches with irritation. "Seriously, dude. I thought you'd be grateful for my help."

"I am." I grab her forearm and give it a soft squeeze. "It's really nice of you, and I'm sorry to keep pushing this, but I'm just trying to make sure you're okay."

Her delicate features stiffen, and I don't miss the tic in her jaw before she turns to smile at me. "I'm great. Seriously. If I was super stressed about school, I wouldn't be doing this, but I'm breezing through the year, and it's a good time to be able to help you out. I'll stick around until at least spring break, and then we can reassess from there. And I promise I'll make myself scarce when Satch comes over."

"It's not that—"

"I will," she cuts me off with another one of her pointed looks. "And when she can't be here and Sienna's busy with Zoey, I'll be the one to drive you to appointments and stuff. This is gonna work, bro."

I shoot her a side-eye, my lips quirking up at the sides. "I'm already recovering from a serious injury, and you're expecting me to get in a car with you? I thought you cared about me."

She fights a laugh, lightly punching my arm. "Suck it up, shithead. And we'll be taking your truck."

I whip my head to look at her, feigning horror. "Not my baby."

Her laughter grows, and she goes to punch me again.

We have a little laughing tussle on the couch until my knee catches and I let out an involuntary hiss.

"Would you behave yourself?" Blake tells me off, spinning back to face the TV on the wall.

Nudging me with her elbow, we both fight silly grins when she reaches for the remote and turns on the TV, scrolling through the channels until she lands on a rerun of *Trollhunters*.

"Remember this?" Blake giggles, tucking her legs beneath her and nestling on the couch beside me.

I stare at the TV, drawn back in time as I sit with my sister and lose myself in the adventurous cartoon. She rests her head on my shoulder, just the way she used to, and I swear I try my best not to worry about her, but something is eating at my gut, warning me that Blake staying here is not just about me.

Something has happened in Chicago, and I need to find out what.

CHAPTER 68
ELIZABETH

As soon as my last class finished, I rushed to Wily's house, just like I did the day before. I'm so glad it's the weekend tomorrow and we can spend some decent time together. This week has been hectic and stressful, trying to fit in classes and hospital visits, dealing with his parents, and then watching him try and adjust to this new, short-term living situation. I have to keep reminding him of that.

It's short-term. Everything about this injury is short-term.

He's been on my mind constantly. I know how hard it must have been getting updates about Zander doing the thing he was supposed to be doing.

He couldn't even go along and support his friend from the stands, which is so sad, because they were so excited about going together. When Zander called last night to check in on Wily, you could tell he was gutted that his friend wasn't there with him. At first, he tried to downplay how great it was, obviously worried about

Wily's feelings, but my boyfriend quickly told him off for that one, and Zander opened up.

Wily is so amazing. The way he celebrated Zander's success just made me love him more.

And the sad look on his face after he hung up, the glassy-eyed, heartbreaking smile he gave me once the call was over... yeah, that made me fall even harder.

I stayed with him last night, sleeping on the couch in the living room. He wanted me on the bed beside him, but that's not helping his knee heal, and he gets super uncomfortable throughout the night. I could hear the bed crinkling every time he shifted.

I can't do too many nights on that couch myself, and it kills me that I'll have to go back to my dorm again, but I have to get some decent sleep.

Not before seeing my man, though.

I'm out of breath and flushed by the time I reach Football Frat, but I don't care how I must look as I rush up the stairs and push the door open.

"Hey, Coyote," I call, wandering into the living room.

He's on the couch, obviously waiting for me, his face lighting with a huge grin as I approach.

"Hey, baby." Tugging on my coat, he pulls me down, his hungry kisses melting my brain.

I sink against his mouth, practically swooning over the arm of the couch when his tongue glides against mine and tells me everything I need to know.

He missed me today.

He loves it when I show up.

He loves me.

Because I'm fucking amazing.

I internally grin. Wily's made me promise to look in

the mirror every day and tell myself how great I am. It's a really weird exercise, but I'm sure it'll get easier as time goes by. And this morning when I looked at my reflection and said, "I really love what you're wearing today. You look good," I actually believed myself.

Mom's package arrived in the mail yesterday, and I squealed when I collected it this morning. It's a brand-new dress. This one was bought, not homemade, so it wasn't quite as special, but I was so stoked. It's blue with white polka dots and has a V-neck that really suits my body shape. It accentuates my waist and makes my boobs look pretty good too. I can't wait for Wily to see it.

Reluctantly pulling out of the kiss, I straighten up and start unbuttoning my coat. "I want to show you something."

"Oh yeah?" Wily's eyes are bright with interest. The poor man is probably so bored, stuck in this house for the first week of recovery. He's not allowed to really get out and about doing stuff until Monday, and he's counting the days.

Slipping the coat off my shoulders, I then shed my wool cardigan before spinning to face him.

"What do you think?" I do a twirl in my new dress, loving the way the skirt flares out around my legs. "Mom sent it to me."

I glance at his face, my insides tingling at the look of pure desire in his eyes.

"You are fire, baby," he whispers, beckoning me with his fingers.

Skipping forward, I take his hand, then giggle when he pulls me onto his lap.

He grunts, and I quickly lurch up in his arms. "Your knee."

I try to scramble off his lap, but he holds me tight, shifting my body and rearranging my legs until I'm straddling his lap. He pulls me forward so I'm not putting any pressure on his legs, all of my weight tucked against his hips and pelvis.

"Is this okay?" I carefully drape my arms over his shoulders. "It doesn't hurt?"

"I'm good, baby." Trailing his hands up my legs, he finds a perch on my hips and gives them a gentle squeeze. "The things I want to do to you right now." He tips his hips, and I can't help grinding against him before I come to my senses.

"Not this week."

"I could just sit here, and you could do all the work." He gives me a hopeful smile.

I laugh. "We're not doing anything to aggravate your injury. You'll just have to wait."

He groans, tipping his head back.

I smile, leaning down to press my lips against his Adam's apple. "It's okay, Coyote. You can have me again soon."

His hands run up my back, curving over my shoulders before he nudges me back so he can cup my breasts.

Damn, he feels so good.

His hooded gaze is turning my insides to liquid fire, and it's taking maximum effort not to ignore all the doctor's instructions and just ride him anyway.

"You know what I want to do with this body right now?" His eyes travel over me as he runs a finger down the line of my V-neck.

"I think you're about to tell me." I grin, biting my lip in excited anticipation.

His mouth twitches, and then he goes on to describe it in great detail. "I want to unbutton this dress." He touches each of the white buttons down my front. "Then kiss this luscious neck." He skims his fingers lightly around my throat before running his knuckle down past my collarbone and in between my breasts.

My insides thrum. This is a sweet kind of torture, knowing we can't go there just yet, but oh man, when we can...

He keeps going, telling me how he'll unclasp my bra and suck my nipples.

"I love your tits, baby. You have the best tits in the world." He squeezes them again before detailing how he'll explore every inch of my skin with his tongue. By the time he gets to the bottom half of my body, I'm horny as anything, and I practically come when he tells me how deep he wants to plunge inside me.

His words are liquid honey, coating my quivering heart and trembling soul.

Leaning forward, he whispers in my ear, "And I'm gonna keep thrusting and plunging and taking you to the edge, baby."

I grip the back of his neck, closing my eyes and pressing my hips against the hard length in his pants.

Holy shit, I'm so hot right now, there's a chance I'm gonna *actually* come.

"You'll be whimpering beneath me, and it'll feel so good having your warm pussy wrapped around my cock. I'm gonna lose my mind." His breath is soft against my ear, and I let out a shaky whimper.

"And then I'm gonna come inside you until I'm completely spent, and that pussy of yours is gonna be singing my name."

"It already is." I close my eyes, gripping the back of his neck and letting out another uncontrolled whimper.

Grabbing my ass, he shunts me forward, rocking his hips against mine in slow, erotic thrusts until I'm starting to shake from head to toe.

"Baby," I whimper in his ear, barely able to control this energy firing through me.

"Come for me, Satch. I want you to come on my lap."

Pressing a kiss to my jaw, he trails his lips down to my neck, tenderly sucking my skin. I'm so close, I'm basically weeping against him, and when his fingers inch around my thigh and he wriggles them under my dress, my insides start to flail.

The pads of his fingers take a smooth, delicate ride up my thighs, sending spikes of pleasure coursing through me. When his thumb brushes my clit through my underwear, I'm gone.

Two soft circles of pressure and I fall apart in his arms, crying out as my body jerks above him. I clutch the back of his neck, riding the erotic wave with little pants against his cheek.

"That's my girl," he croons, shifting his hand and pulling me flush against him so I can grind on the shaft in his pants and finish out the rest of my orgasm.

Holy shit, this man blows my mind.

I cling to him, shaking from head to toe, loving his hard length pressed against my delicate center and the way his large hands travel up my back before holding me tight.

I want to immediately return the orgasm favor and am about to tell him that. But my chance gets stolen when the front door flicks open, then shuts with a loud bang.

Gasping, I bulge my eyes at Wily, but he just grins back at me, obviously finding the fact that we're about to get caught hilarious.

I clutch his shoulders. I should really get off him, but then whoever just walked in will see his erection and—

"Okay." Grady's dry tone fills the room. "Really, guys?"

"What?" Wily laughs when I groan and hide my face behind his neck. He cups the back of my head, gently stroking my hair. "This room doesn't have a door. What am I supposed to do here?"

"We're hanging a curtain," Grady grumbles, thumping up the stairs. "We're hanging a fucking curtain!"

Wily snickers and I lean back, giving him a guilty wince.

"Stop." He kisses me before I can say anything. "That was hot, baby."

"It was," I have to admit, my skin scorching pink. My cheeks must be neon right now.

Wily tucks my hair back behind my ear. "Damn, you're beautiful."

I glance up, drinking in his expression and knowing he means it. I smile back at him, hopefully reflecting the same admiration. "I love you, Wily Wilson."

Emotion rockets through me when that smile I love so freaking much lights his entire face.

"Life's gonna be awesome with you," he whispers. "No matter what I end up doing, where I end up playing football and whatever comes next after that... if you're there, I'm gonna be happy. I just know I am."

My heart melts, stealing my voice and making me want to cry those happy tears you see in emotional rom-com movies.

Who would have thought that a nerd like me could fall for a big, strong jock?

But I did.

I fell fast and hard, and I'm pretty sure I'm gonna keep falling for a long while yet.

Cupping the back of his head, I lean forward and press my lips to his. This isn't a hungry, *"I want to rip your clothes off"* kiss. This one is gentle, filled with unspoken promises I have no intention of breaking.

His arms curl around my back again, and he fuses our bodies together.

This is how it's gonna be.

Me and Wily... together forever.

I just know it.

CHAPTER 69
GRADY

Romantic saps. I just can't fucking get away from them.

Stomping up the stairs, I growl in my throat, anger firing through me.

Well, anger and a bunch of other stuff I don't want to deal with.

Shit!

Fuck!

Gripping my door handle, I shove it open. It takes everything in me not to slam it closed with maximum force.

I'm so pissed off right now I can't even see straight.

You're not pissed off, you're... wounded.

I don't want to be.

I'd rather be pissed and raging.

This feeling is so much worse.

As I plunk onto the end of my bed and rest my head in my hands, I hate myself for having any emotion left over this relationship that ended two months ago!

But I'd be stupid to deny the truth.

I know what I just saw, and it hurts like a knife through the abdomen.

Teah's found herself another guy.

And not just any guy.

She was making out with Finn Macalister. He has a rep. Enough for me to know about him, anyway. He's a basketball player with skin so white he looks like a fucking vampire. Girls always go on about how hot he is, but I seriously don't see the appeal. He's got piercings in who knows how many places, raven-black hair, and these pale blue eyes. Fucking demon eyes.

But that's not why I know him.

He's wild.

I've heard the rumors. Stories are rife about the guy and the trouble he constantly gets into.

And Teah's dating him?

What the actual shit?

He's everything I'm not.

Maybe that's why she's into him.

I sigh, groaning into my hands and hating myself for even obsessing over this. We've been broken up since New Year's, and the last couple of weeks, I've started to feel more like myself again, like I'm moving on. And then I have to round the corner and find them practically dry humping against the building wall.

Teah's eyes were closed, her head tipped back, this sexy-ass look on her face while Macalister ate at her neck like...

"Like a fucking vampire," I seethe.

How the fuck did he get her under his spell?

The guy's a complete asshole, and I'm—

Growling, I shoot to my feet and start pacing the room.

I'm good. I'm sensible. I'm the guy everyone can rely on. Mr. Fix-It. The tech-man.

Mr. Fucking Boring!

Punching the air with another growl, I pace around like a caged tiger until I can't handle it anymore.

I need to go for a run.

I've been doing that a lot lately, burning off my energy with sprints through the snow-lined streets. I blast my music and get lost in the rhythm of my breathing.

It helps.

At least I think it does.

As the sky turns dark, I pound the pavement, dodging visions of Teah and Mac doing the dirty in every position imaginable. I'm about to lose my fucking mind when I dart out onto the road, lights flashing over me just before the squeal of brakes and a loud horn blast.

I jump out of the way, raising my hand in apology, my heart pounding.

Shit. I nearly got hit by a fucking car.

Slowing to a walk, I try to rein in my reckless emotions and use some common sense.

I can't let a girl control me this way anymore. Teah's lived rent-free in my head for too long, and although I can't imagine her shifting out anytime soon, the least I can do is move her into a back corner.

It's what I'd been naturally doing until I saw her this afternoon.

Sucking in a few deep breaths, I rest my hands on my hips and walk back to Football Frat. By the time I reach the front door, my heart rate has dropped back to normal, and I climb the stairs, determined not to let my night be ruined by one woman.

The woman I'd wondered if I might marry.

The one who'd stolen my heart with zero effort.

Shit, I was a romantic sap. I can't let myself get snared again so easily.

"Never," I grit out as I pull out my earbuds and kick off my running shoes.

Whipping off my shirt and socks, I dump them in the hamper, then peel off my running shorts and underwear, wrapping a towel around my waist before heading to the bathroom. I'm so busy lathering myself in self-talk and reprimands that I don't even notice the bar of light under the doorway.

The bathroom isn't locked, and I burst in, flicking the door closed behind me.

I'm not even aware of anybody else in here until I notice the steamy mirror, then glance right to spot a completely naked woman shaving her legs. Her foot is resting against the bathtub, and I bulge my eyes at her.

Oh fuck. It's Blake.

I just stand there in stunned silence for a second.

Turn the fuck around, man. What are you doing? Apologize and get out!

But my eyes are locked on her stunning body for a second, and I'm waiting for her to yelp or turn, grab a towel, and cover herself. But she does none of those things.

Instead, she stands tall, the razor still in her hand as she smirks at me and asks, "Can I help you with something?"

Her boobs are on full display, and I blink at their

perfect shape. They're perky and sweet with a puckered pink nipple on each.

Holy shit.

For reasons beyond my belief, I'm suddenly picturing myself sucking them, massaging those pert tits, and—

Look the fuck away!

I snap my eyes closed and stammer, "I... I'm... uh..."

She giggles, and I'm so surprised by the sound, my eyes pop straight back open. She's now facing me fully, and I can see everything. From the top of her wild curls to her delicate nose, then those perfect breasts and slender stomach...

And my rebellious eyes just keep traveling...

Checking out that neatly maintained triangle of dark brown hair covering her pussy to a pair of slender, perfectly shaped legs.

I can't stop my gaze from trailing down those luscious legs, skipping over the shaving cream and landing on ten cute little toes that are painted black.

"Enjoying the view?" Her voice is laced with amusement, and I step back, crashing into the door and wrestling with the handle behind me.

"I'm so sorry," I manage.

She grins at me. Flicking her hair over her shoulder, she raises her right eyebrow, her eyes traveling down my body now. She's gazing at my torso, her lips twitching before she brushes her teeth over her bottom lip and shocks the hell out of me.

"I've shown you mine. Maybe you can show me yours." The tip of her pink tongue pokes out the side of her mouth, and...

Holy fuck.

Her bold flirting is beyond sexy, but I would be out of my damn mind to entertain something like that with her.

One little flick of my towel and we'd both be naked.

And Wily would kill my ass.

Then he'd revive me just so he could finish me off again.

There is no fucking way I'm going there with his baby sister.

The thought of Wily's outrage jolts me into action, and I manage to turn the handle and pull the door open. Squeezing through the gap, I quickly shut it behind me and lean my head against the wood.

My heart's pounding again, but for a whole different reason.

Adjusting myself, I then have to cover my tented towel as I rush back to my room and shut the door, beyond relieved that Wily can't be upstairs right now.

Fuck, I am one shitty friend.

Slumping onto my bed, I bury my face beneath my arm and groan.

I am in so much fucking trouble.

Blake is *living* at Football Frat for who knows how long, and I've just seen her butt naked.

And damn, did I like what I saw.

My insides churn with a desire I haven't felt since losing Teah and—

"Nope!" I jerk up, squeezing the bridge of my nose and giving myself the loudest warning I fucking can. "Do *not* go there, man. Just don't."

But we all know he's going to, right?
Because Blake can't get enough of this game, and she's

*determined to make herself impossible to resist... until Grady
starts to see right through her and she's forced to trust him
with her secrets.*
*Can these two save each other before Wily finds out and all
hell breaks loose?*

*Find out in THE ILLICIT PLAY, due for release September
30, 2025.*

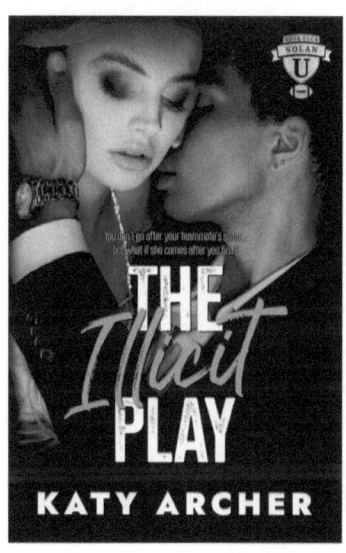

NOTE FROM KATY

Dear reader,

Thanks for reading Wily and Satch's romance. Writing it was just the best. It's so sweet and swoony. I found Elizabeth so relatable and Wily was just... 😵 🤍 He definitely stole my heart and I hope he stole yours too.

It'll be interesting to see how he goes with his recovery... and his little sister living at Football Frat. The poor guy is gonna get the shock of his life when he finds out what "sweet" lil Blakey's been up to in Chicago.

Yep, this girl has got herself some secrets and her big brother is not gonna be the first to find out what they are. I thought it'd be way more fun to throw Grady into the deep end. Whether he wants to or not, he'll get caught up in Blake's drama. But I think he's exactly what she needs to get her out of trouble... And I think this blonde spitfire is the woman Grady needs to spark a fire inside him and help him move on realize that Teah wasn't his one and only.

Are you excited?
Oh man, I hope so. Writing this story is going to be a blast. I've already mapped it all out and he's gonna be rescuing Blake in all the protective ways I love in a good book boyfriend. And in the process, she's gonna save his heart from drowning. These two together are sizzling, fiery dynamite and I'm so pumped for you to read *The Illicit Play* in September. 🐷

If you enjoyed *The Surprise Play*, I would so appreciate you leaving an honest review on Amazon and/or Goodreads. Even just a star rating is helpful. You don't have to write anything if you don't want to. But star ratings and even short reviews really help validate the book, letting readers know it's worth a shot. It also tells Amazon and Goodreads that this book is worth shining a spotlight on. I know there are a bunch of readers out there who love college sports romance just as much as we do. If you can help me reach them, then that would be freaking fantastic.
Thanks for the assist!

I'd also like to thank a few key people who have been instrumental in helping me get this book off the ground —Megan, Kristin, Beth and Rachael. You are such a great team to work with and I appreciate all your time and effort. You never complain and are always there for whatever I need. Amazing!

Maggie and Trudi—my writing buddies who keep me on track, cheering me on and giving me the best advice. Thanks for always being only a DM away.

My review team—what would I do without you? I love and appreciate you so much. Thank you for being the best cheer squad around.

My readers—I love you too! Seriously, you are fucking amazing! Thanks for taking the time to read these Nolan U novels. And thank you for all the love.

My husband—you made me laugh, you gave me the confidence to catch a ball and you pulled me into your world...where I finally found a place to belong. Thank you for always making me feel worth it 🩶

My creator—it's taken me way too long to realize that I am, in fact, a masterpiece, one of your adored creations. Thank you for loving me through every doubt. And thank you for making me who I am 🩶

xoxo
Katy

BOOKS BY KATY ARCHER

NOLAN U HOCKEY
Hockey House V-cards (prequel)
The Forbidden Freshman
The Heart Stealer
The Game Changer
The Love Penalty
The Only Goal
The Forever Game

NOLAN U FOOTBALL
Releasing in 2025
The First Play (prequel)
The Forever Play
The Off-Limits Play
The Surprise Play
The Illicit Play
The Perfect Play
The Christmas Play

NOLAN U BASKETBALL

Releasing in 2026

NOLAN U - GEN 2

Starting in 2027

CONTACT KATY

I love to hear from my readers, so feel free to email me anytime. You can also find out more on my website.

EMAIL: katy@katyarcher.com

WEBSITE: www.katyarcher.com

And if you want to connect with me on social media, you can find me Addicted to College Sports Romance on...

INSTAGRAM:
www.instagram.com/addictedtocollegesportsromance/

FACEBOOK:
www.facebook.com/people/College-Sports-Romance-Books/61553919569131/

TIKTOK:
www.tiktok.com/@katyarcherbooks